WAYN

FALLEN HUNTER

A JESSE MCDERMITT NOVEL

◆◆◆

Caribbean Adventure Series
Volume 3

2013

Published by DOWN ISLAND PRESS, 2013
Travelers Rest, SC

Copyright © 2013 by Wayne Stinnett

All rights reserved. No part of this book may be reproduced, scanned, or distributed in any printed, or electronic form without express written permission.

Please do not participate in, or encourage piracy of copyrighted materials in violation of the author's rights. Purchase only authorized editions.

Library of Congress cataloging-in-publication Data
Stinnett, Wayne
Fallen Hunter/Wayne Stinnett
p. cm. - (A Jesse McDermitt novel)
ISBN-13: 978-1493671595
ISBN-10: 1493671956

FOREWORD

This is a work of fiction. Names, characters, and incidents either are the product of the author's imagination or are used fictitiously, and any resemblance to actual persons, living or dead, businesses, companies, events, or locales is entirely coincidental.

Most of the locations herein are fictional, or used fictitiously. However, I took great pains to depict the location and description of the many islands, locales, beaches, reefs, bars, and restaurants in the Keys and the Caribbean, to the best of my memory and ability. The *Rusty Anchor* is not a real place, but if I were to open a bar in the Florida Keys, it would probably be a lot like I depict here. Its location is actually a vacant piece of land on the south side of A-1-A. I've spent a lot of time in El Caribe, fishing, diving, sailing, boating, and of course, drinking and have tried my best to convey the island attitude in this work.

I'd like to thank the many people who encouraged me to write a second novel, especially my wife, Greta. Her love, encouragement, motivation, support, dreams for the future, and the many ideas she keeps coming up with have been a great blessing. At times, I swear she was a Key West Wrecker in another life. Or maybe a Galley Wench, I'm not always sure. A special thanks to my youngest daughter Jordy for her many contributions and sometimes truly outlandish ideas.

While only a twelve-year-old mind can conceive some of the wacky ideas she has, many of them planted a seed in my own mind. Also, I need to thank our other kids for their support, but mostly for not laughing at a tired old truck driver thinking he could write a book during down time in the sleeper of the truck. A special thanks to Tim Ebaugh Photography and Design, for the beautiful photo and cover design. You can see more of his work at www.timebaughdesigns.com.

DEDICATION

Dedicated to Laura.

Remember our dream when you were little?
To sail around the world and visit exotic places?
Although that dream never came to fruition,
it's a dream I've always cherished in my heart.
Maybe this work can take us there in our minds.
Although not as far, nor for very long.

"Humanity has a limited biological capacity for change but an unlimited capacity for spiritual change. The only human institution incapable of evolving spiritually is a cemetery."
S.M. Tomlinson
One Fathom Above Sea Level

If you'd like to receive my newsletter,
please sign up on my website:

WWW.WAYNESTINNETT.COM

Every two weeks, I'll bring you insights into my private life and writing habits, with updates on what I'm working on, special deals I hear about, and new books by other authors that I'm reading.

The Charity Styles Caribbean Thriller Series

Merciless Charity
Ruthless Charity
Reckless Charity
Enduring Charity
Vigilant Charity

The Jesse McDermitt Caribbean Adventure Series

Fallen Out	*Fallen Angel*
Fallen Palm	*Fallen Hero*
Fallen Hunter	*Rising Storm*
Fallen Pride	*Rising Fury*
Fallen Mangrove	*Rising Force*
Fallen King	*Rising Charity*
Fallen Honor	*Rising Water*
Fallen Tide	

The Gaspar's Revenge Ship's Store is open. There, you can purchase all kinds of swag related to my books. You can find it at:

WWW.GASPARS-REVENGE.COM

FALLEN HUNTER

MAPS

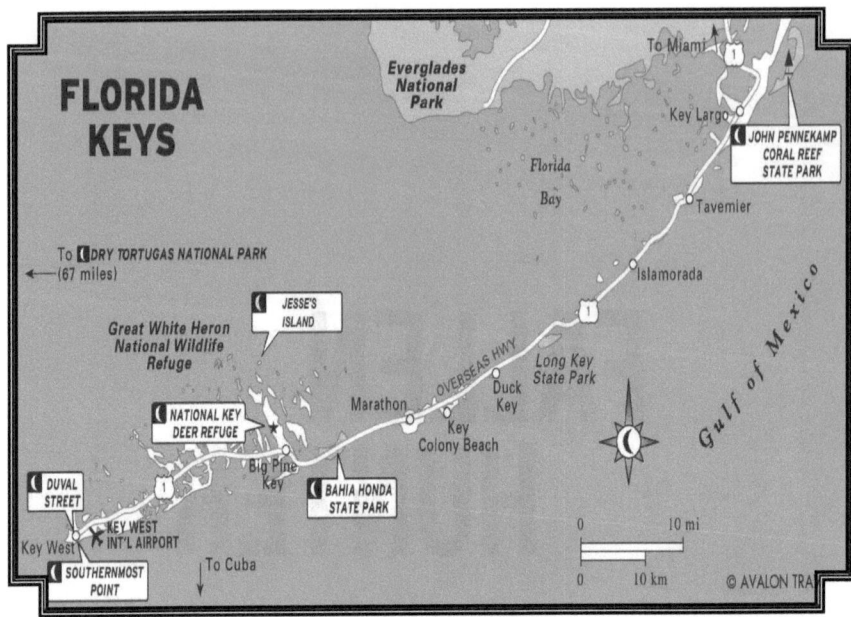

The Florida Keys

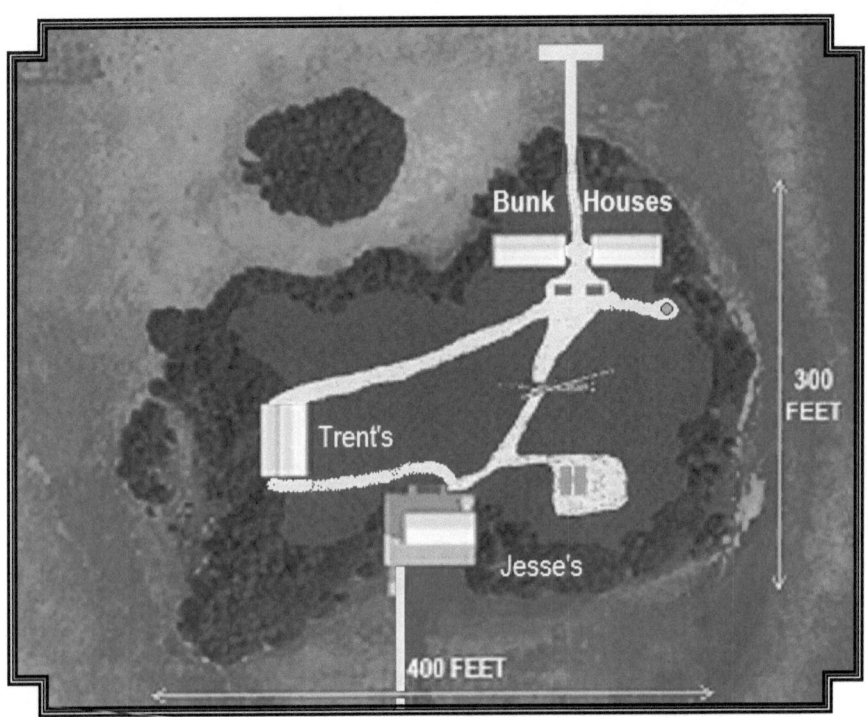

Jesse's Island

CHAPTER ONE:
Mission Ready

The two men sat across from one another at a table outside a Cuban restaurant. It was on Calle Ocho, at the end of SW Sixteenth Avenue, in the Little Havana part of Miami. The older man was about average height and weight, neither tanned nor pale. His dark hair was graying a little at the temples. He wore a light blue guayabera shirt, white slacks, and expensive-looking dress shoes. He looked at home in his surroundings, which is what he strived to do. The younger man was taller and heavier, but without an ounce of fat. He had fair hair, cut short, and tanned skin, with piercing blue eyes. He wore faded jeans, a black tee shirt, a fisherman's hat, and topsider shoes. Unlike the older man, he stood out in the Cuban exile community, which is what he strived for, also. As people walked by the little sidewalk cafe and looked over, they noticed the younger man, but the older man was nearly invisible.

"Do you think he's ready?" asked the younger man, in a serious tone.

The older man thought about the question, taking a sip of Cuban espresso from a tiny porcelain cup before answering. "I hope so. We need him on this. It's been four months, the man can't sit around on that little island forever. You intimated yourself that the message he gave me for you meant that he was ready."

"Yeah, but that was just a week after his wife died. Most likely, he was still in shock."

The older man took another sip of the strong drink and looked at the people moving up and down the sidewalk. It was sunny, but cooler, near sixty degrees. A warm day in DC, where the older man had flown down from just hours earlier. Here in Miami, that's nearly freezing and the people on the sidewalk were dressed accordingly. "Go down and visit him, Deuce. Tell him what's coming up. Use your own judgment as to whether or not he's ready. I'm sure you'd like to see your young lady again, too."

"Yes sir, Mister Smith," Deuce said. "He's a tough old salt, so maybe he'll bounce back quicker than most."

"Let's hope so," Smith said. "This mission is tailor-made for his unique skill set."

"How long do we have?"

"Your team needs to be mission-ready in two weeks, no later."

Deuce stood up and walked east on Calle Ocho for eleven blocks to the parking garage where he'd left his car. He never parked near where he was going to meet someone. He'd been trained that a tail is easier to spot if you're on foot. Besides, he liked to walk. He had an office about twelve miles away at the United States Southern Command headquarters in Doral, just northwest of the city. However, he and his men stayed and trained at Homestead Air Force Base.

As he walked along Calle Ocho, he thought about the events of four months ago. He'd gone down to Marathon to find his dad's old Marine buddy, to have him help spread his dad's ashes on a reef that only the two of them had known about. Together, they'd survived a hurricane and then either caught or killed the men who had been responsible for his dad's death. Those same men happened to be the targets of a terrorist investigation his newly formed team had been conducting. During the course of the investigation, he'd tried to recruit his dad's friend, but only succeeded in getting the man's wife kidnapped on their wedding day by the subject of the investigation. She'd been brutally raped and murdered. That's a lot for a guy to get over in just four months, he thought. Even a warrior who was reputed to be one of the best Marine Recon snipers in the Corps.

While in Marathon, he'd met a woman that he enjoyed being with, that much was true. He still had his doubts if they could make it work, though. He was Team Leader for a Caribbean terrorist interdiction team with the Department of Homeland Security. Being a former SEAL, he was used to sudden deployments, but would she be able to handle it? Not many women could.

Instead of returning to his office, Lieutenant Commander Russell "Deuce" Livingston Junior drove to Homestead. When he got there, he went straight to the barracks where his team stayed. He met Tony Jacobs and Art Newman, two of his former SEAL team operatives, just as he was parking his sedan.

"How'd it go with the Director?" Tony asked.

"He's insistent on McDermitt being part of the mission. Says it's 'tailor-made for his unique skill set.' I'm flying down there to meet with him."

"Don't suppose you'll have time to visit a certain waitress while you're there, will ya?" Art asked.

Deuce rolled his eyes at the jab. "I might, but it's doubtful. Need to get back here ASAP."

"Well, tell Jesse we said hi," Tony said and the two men walked on toward the training building next to the barracks.

Deuce walked the opposite direction, toward a small hangar where a white helicopter with US Customs and Border Protection markings on the side was warming up. He'd called the pilot on the drive down and told him to be ready. He boarded the chopper and handed a slip of paper to the pilot, who punched the numbers on it into the aircraft's GPS.

"You sure about this destination, sir?" the pilot asked. "It's just a tiny island in the middle of nowhere. No place to set down."

"There'll be an LZ there," he answered. The pilot nodded, being used to some of the places he was assigned to fly to for these DHS spooks. Most weren't even on a map.

The flight took less than forty-five minutes in the Eurocopter AS350 Squirrel. Within seconds of takeoff, they were enveloped in a primordial world of water and grass, with the occasional cypress stand and palm tree. They flew southwest out of Homestead and climbed to five hundred feet. There were no landmarks for the first several minutes, then they flew over the small fishing village of Flamingo, then Cape Sable and out over the

sparkling turquoise water of the Gulf of Mexico. Twenty minutes later they neared the island marked on the GPS and the pilot came in low from the northeast. He saw two flags flying above a small house, one an American flag and the other the unmistakable red Marine Corps flag. Noting the wind direction, he flew over the island, turned and approached from the west. From this angle he could see two smaller buildings on the north side of the large clearing in the middle of the island. He brought the chopper down in the center of the clearing, expecting someone to come out of one of the buildings.

"Shut her down," Deuce said. "I'll be here a while."

Deuce got out of the chopper and looked around. The two buildings to the north were new. He didn't recall seeing them when he'd been here four months ago. He walked toward the house, which sat high above the ground on stilts. He also noticed that the underside of the house, which had been open, with boat dockage underneath, was now fully enclosed. *McDermitt's been busy*, he thought. He walked up the steps to the rear deck and called out, "Jesse! It's me, Deuce."

The only sound he heard was the ticking of the chopper's engine as it cooled. He tried the door and found it locked. From the vantage point of the elevated deck, he looked all around, but aside from some pelicans diving on bait fish in the channel, he saw no movement. He walked back down the steps and crossed the clearing toward the new buildings. Both were low structures, built of wood, no more than fifty feet by twenty feet. Approaching the first one, he looked in through a window. Nothing inside except two rows of bunk beds along the back. He walked over to the second building and looked

inside. It was a mirror image of the first. They both had a door at each end, one door facing the other at one end, and another in the back, between the rows of bunks.

Barracks, was his first thought. Next to the buildings was a huge stone grill, with a large pile of driftwood beside it. Walking between the buildings took him through a new cut in the brush and trees surrounding the island, to a long floating dock extending over two hundred feet to deeper water.

He walked back over to the chopper and the pilot asked, "Nobody home?"

"Doesn't appear to be. Take me to Marathon Airport."

Minutes later, they were airborne again. The pilot called the airport to request permission to land and in ten minutes, they set down on the tarmac by the General Aviation terminal. Deuce told the pilot to go inside and get lunch as he might be a few hours and that he'd call when he was ready to leave. This was another thing the pilot was used to.

Deuce entered the terminal and flashed his credentials at the TSA agent at the arrival desk, then walked on through the building and out to the taxi stand. There was only one taxi waiting there, and the driver stood up from the bench he was sitting on, opening the front door for him.

"You know the *Rusty Anchor*?" Deuce asked the long-haired old man.

"Sure, man," the driver replied. "Five dollars."

Deuce handed the man a ten and asked for his card. The old man handed him one and they drove off. Five minutes later they turned down the familiar crushed-shell driveway and through the overhanging casuarinas and gumbo limbo trees. He got out and walked into the bar.

"Russell!" the auburn-haired woman behind the bar exclaimed. "Why didn't you call to say you were coming?"

"Hi, Julie," he said. "Didn't know I was coming until a few minutes ago." She ran out from behind the bar and hugged him tightly. She then looked up and kissed him deeply, right in front of all two customers. Neither of them even noticed.

"How long can you stay?"

Deuce looked down into her hypnotic brown eyes. She was a sight to behold. She took his hand and led him over to the bar. "Beer?"

"Tea would be nice," he replied. Her eyes lost a bit of the sparkle when he said that, the significance being that he couldn't stay long. She'd grown used to his unannounced arrivals and sudden departures over the last four months they'd been seeing each other.

"Sorry," he said. "I flew down to meet with Jesse, but he wasn't at his house. Any idea where he might be?"

"I don't suppose you can tell me anything about it," she said and he shook his head. "He hasn't been here since the week after... what happened."

The memory of those three days was still fresh in her mind. It wasn't something a young woman could throw off very quickly. She had been maid of honor at their friends' wedding. The bride, Alex, had been kidnapped and brutally murdered the night of the wedding. It was the groom, Jesse McDermitt, that Deuce had come to see. He'd been sort of recruited by DHS to ferry their teams to and from places they needed to go. He owned a big charter fishing boat that was the perfect cover. *Not a good*

way to start a recruitment, losing your wife on your wedding day, Deuce thought.

Just then, a short, very round man with a bald head and thick red beard walked through the back door. He was talking with an older black man. The two of them stopped when they saw Deuce.

"Julie!" the fat man said. "What'd I tell you about letting Squids in my bar?" Then he walked up to Deuce and put him in a big bear hug.

"How ya been, Deuce?" he said. "Hope you can stay for supper. Rufus here just bought some fresh hogfish from one of the local spear fishermen."

"Welcome bak, Mistah Livinston, sar," said the old black man, extending his hand.

Deuce shook his hand and turned to the fat man and said, "Thanks for the invite, Rusty. I was looking for Jesse. Any idea where he's at?"

"Up at his house, I'd guess," Rusty replied.

"No, I was just up there."

"Wah I heah," Rufus said, "he be hepin Carl Trent wit a trouble he be havin."

"Trent?" Rusty asked. "Where'd you hear that?"

"Jimmy was tellin mi bout it," he replied.

"Who's Carl Trent?" Deuce asked.

"Owns a shrimp boat down to Key Weird," Rusty said.

"Is Jimmy around?"

"He just left a few minutes before you got here," Julie said. "Probably at Angie's houseboat. Carl is Angie's dad."

"Can I steal your daughter for an hour, Rusty?" Deuce asked.

"Sure, y'all run along. Me and Rufus can mind the store for a while. Just be back here by sixteen hundred,

or that hogfish will disappear. Oh, and if ya find Jesse, there's been a lawyer fella coming around looking for him. Let him know, okay?"

"Sure will, Rusty," Deuce said.

Julie removed her apron and took Deuce's hand as they walked out of the bar. They crossed the shell parking lot, then walked around the end of the small marina toward a path that led through the woods.

"Rusty's fixed up the canal," Deuce said.

"Yeah, we have three liveaboards staying here now," Julie said. "Plenty of room for one more," she added, elbowing Deuce in the ribs.

"I stay on enough boats as it is, babe," he said. "Why would you want to live on one?" They'd been talking about getting a place together, but he was leaning more toward an apartment.

"Living on a boat would be so romantic," she said.

"Yeah, for about a week."

They walked on through the woods and came out onto Sombrero Beach Road, which wasn't on any beach that Deuce could tell. Another hundred yards further and they turned onto Sombrero Beach Boulevard. They walked hand in hand past Dockside Lounge and out onto the docks. They saw Jimmy and Angie on the sundeck of her houseboat and Jimmy quickly smushed out a joint they were smoking.

"Hey, Deuce," he called down. "Hey, Julie. Y'all come aboard."

They chatted for several minutes, Jimmy looking anxious because he knew that Deuce was a federal agent.

Finally, Deuce said, "I need to find Jesse, Jimmy. Rufus said y'all might know where he is."

"Yeah," Angie said. "He's down in Key West, trying to help my dad out of a jam."

She went on to tell them how her dad had been having trouble making ends meet by pulling shrimp and had been approached by one of his deckhands on the subject of picking up pot and bringing it in for a friend of his. This made Jimmy even more nervous. She said that her dad had done a few runs and then decided he wanted out and didn't want to do it anymore. The deckhand's so-called friend turned out to be a Cuban smuggler and had threatened her dad and family. Jesse had gone down there to take over running the shrimp boat and get the smuggler out of their hair.

"Honest, man," Jimmy said, "Carl ain't the smuggling type. He just got in a little over his head, man."

"Don't worry, Jimmy," Deuce said. "I'm not here to pop anyone for dope. I just need to see Jesse. I don't begrudge a man doing what he has to do to take care of his family. Shrimping's a hard business."

Turning to Julie he said, "Can you take me down there? I came in on a company chopper. Might blow Jesse's cover, me arriving down there in it."

CHAPTER TWO:
Two Days Earlier

I'd been working hard for over four months. Working with my hands allows my mind to drift. The first week after my wife was murdered, I blamed myself. So, for the last eight weeks, while working to enlarge my channel and turning basin, I'd been thinking and rethinking the steps I'd taken. I finally came to the realization that sometimes shit just happens. You hear all the time about good things happening to bad people and bad things happening to good people. Alex was just in the wrong place at the wrong time. That settled things in my head, but not my heart. In the first week it took me to come to grips with that, I'd finished the channel and basin and then started on my island. Hurricane Wilma had sure made a mess of it. There was a lot of flotsam blown up onto the southern and western shores and quite a few trees knocked down by the high wind. I bagged all the small stuff that wouldn't burn and dragged the bigger pieces to the barge my friend Rusty had loaned me.

It was his barge and backhoe that I'd used to dig the channel. My dog, Pescador, helped by carrying and dragging assorted debris to me from the water. He's a Portuguese water dog and really big. Equally adept in the water and on shore, it was nothing for him to drag a large tree branch hundreds of yards through the water. Most of what he brought ashore, I piled on the fire in the center of the island.

Alex and I had found Pescador the day after the hurricane. He was stranded on a little island, no more than a sandbar really, just east of my tiny island. He's very intelligent and we were sure that he belonged to someone, but after we'd had him scanned for a microchip, placed ads in all the south Florida papers and entered his picture and description on a Hurricane Wilma lost and found website, nobody had claimed him.

When the work on the channel and island was nearly complete, I'd contacted a lumberyard and arranged to have a floating dock built and barged out to me, along with nearly three tons of building material. My first chore was cutting down a tall coconut palm that stood in the middle of a clearing I'd created a couple of years ago in the hopes of planting a small vegetable garden. The soil had proven to be too sandy and the groundwater too salty to grow much of anything. But, I still had hopes of maybe bringing in good topsoil and growing my own food one day. Lately, I'd been thinking of growing enough food for more than just myself.

The clearing was now a landing zone for a single helicopter. At least for one flown by a good pilot, since the LZ was small. A friend who helped me take down the men who murdered my wife worked for the Department of

Homeland Security and they'd offered me a job, of sorts. It involved moving men and materials to places around the Caribbean, aboard my forty-five foot Rampage fishing boat, *Gaspar's Revenge*. He was the Team Leader of a new unit within the DHS that would be working to eradicate terrorist threats in the Caribbean Basin. Eradicate, by any means necessary.

I figured that since I had an LZ, they might also need a dock and living quarters. Using Rusty's backhoe, I'd attached the auger that was laying on the deck of the barge and run two deep holes about two hundred feet out from the northern shoreline in eight feet of water. I ran the holes down a good twelve feet through limestone and ancient coral rock, until only five feet of the twenty-five-foot-long telephone poles stuck out above the high tide. When the floating dock and lumber arrived, I'd only needed to attach the dock to the pilings and anchor it on shore. I'd helped the men on the barge carry the lumber ashore and stack it at the northern edge of the clearing.

The first thing I did was enclose the underside of my house with hardwood siding. The siding came from my friend Rusty Thurman, who owns a bar in Marathon. He had a huge lignum vitae tree come down in the storm and we'd sent it all up to a sawmill in Homestead. I now had four boats docked under the house, and the siding would keep prying eyes from seeing them. Along with my forty-five-foot Rampage, I had both mine and Alex's eighteen-foot Maverick Mirage flats skiffs, and a twenty-foot Grady-White center console that my friend Deuce Livingston had given me. It had belonged to his dad, who I'd served with in the Marines. His dad was murdered by the same men who killed my wife.

Deuce had given me the boat and all his dad's dive gear to sell for him. Rather than sell it, I'd made him an offer on it myself, intending to expand my charter business. He'd said he'd think it over, but then given it to Alex and me as a wedding gift. Alex and Julie, Rusty's daughter, were launching it when Alex was abducted. I'd planned to just sink the thing, because of what it represented. However, after the weeks of working and thinking, I'd come to realize that it was just an inanimate object and it too was just in the wrong place at the wrong time. So, I kept her and thought about having the name *Alex's Revenge* painted on the stern.

I didn't really need plans or a building permit for the work I was doing. The purchase of my island six years ago had come with the stipulation that it be improved and maintained as a fishing camp within ten years. So, building two bunkhouses would satisfy that stipulation. I'd known in my mind how they should be built and I'd simply turned the picture in my head into reality. They were simple structures, built on a three-foot-high pier system. The piers were anchored on concrete footings, which extended five feet down into the limestone. Each building was identical, only twenty feet wide and fifty feet long, but flip-flopped and facing one another. Each one had six bunk beds and could house up to twelve people. Deuce had said his team consisted of about thirty people, but only half were field operatives. I figured my island might be able to be used as a remote training facility. I'd even put up a flagpole with a concrete-and-shell base, centered between the two bunkhouses, and a large stone grill with a chimney for cooking.

I'd just finished the flagpole and was fishing for lunch off the pier. Truth is, it would have been easier to let Pescador do the fishing. I'd seen him catch fish by diving into the water many times. But, the weather was nice for January and I wanted to feel that yank on the end of the line. I'd put two nice snapper in the cooler when I heard the sound of an outboard approaching from the south. I trotted across the island, which isn't hard since it only covers a little over two acres. I climbed the steps to the deck and got my binoculars from the hook just inside the door. Looking out across the mangroves, I could see two people, a man and a woman, approaching in what looked like my friend Rusty's skiff.

I went down to the new dock I'd built on top of the spoils from the dredging. It ran alongside the channel from the house out about fifty feet, nearly to the main channel, and rising only a foot above high water. My First Mate, Jimmy, and his girlfriend Angie, were tying the skiff to the dock.

"Wow, dude," Jimmy said. "You've done a lot of work out here."

Jimmy was a good First Mate, but also a stoner and he was obviously stoned now. So was Angie by the look of her eyes. Or, she'd been crying. I helped her up from the skiff and turned to Jimmy, saying, "What are you guys doing way out here?"

"Ang needs to talk to you, man."

"Well, come on up to the deck, then," I said.

The two of them followed me up. Jimmy had been here a few times, most recently when he'd helped bring the boats out and shown me how to run the backhoe. "You completely closed in the docks?" he asked.

"Yeah, had to," I said. "A house way out here, with four boats parked beneath it, would just invite scrutiny." I suddenly realized that this was the first time I'd talked to anyone other than Pescador in almost four months. Since the barge came that delivered the lumber.

"Have a seat," I said, pointing toward the built-in wooden table that served as both an outdoor dining table and a workbench. I opened a cooler sitting next to the bench and got out two cold Jamaican Red Stripe beers and a bottle of water. The water was for Jimmy, who rarely drank alcohol. "What's on your mind, Angie?" I asked.

They both were looking out across the clearing, to the two new bunkhouses. "You planning on opening a fish camp or something, Jesse?" Jimmy asked.

"Yeah, something like that. Now, what's the problem, Angie?"

She turned back to look at me and her eyes were moist. No, she wasn't high, I thought. Something was weighing heavy on her mind.

"It's my dad," she said. "He's a shrimper, out of Key West."

"Yeah," I said. "I've met Carl a couple of times."

"The thing is, Jesse, about a month ago he got into smuggling weed. He didn't want to, but he just wasn't making ends meet with his boat, what with all the new taxes and regulations. One of his crew suggested it. Said he knew a guy that would pay him good to just hide a few bales in his boat, while he's out trawling. He decided he'd try it once. You know, just to see what he could make. Well, one thing led to another and he wound up making several runs for the guy. Now, he wants to get out of it, says he can't justify the risk for the money. The

guy threatened him, Jesse. Not just him, mind you. Dad's a pretty rough guy and can handle himself okay. The guy threatened our family, though. I'm the oldest and I been helping him as much as I can. He and my stepmom have two little kids, my half-brother and half-sister. They're just little kids, and the guy said that if he didn't keep running the weed, he might come home from a trawl and find that they all died in a fire."

I listened to her politely, not seeing where I fit in. A lot of commercial fishermen have done the same thing. Hell, if it weren't for my inheritance seven years ago from my grandpa, I might have been tempted.

"So, why are you telling me all this?" I asked.

Jimmy answered, "Carl needs help, man. He doesn't have any family left here, besides Angie and the little kids. He respects you, man. I think you might be able to help him out somehow."

"He respects me?" I asked. "We've barely nodded to one another over a beer at the *Anchor*. He doesn't even know me."

"Jesse," Angie said, "you could probably count the number of close friends you have on your fingers, but everyone knows you and knows you're a stand-up guy. Can you at least talk to him?" Her eyes started to well with tears.

"Does he know you came out here to see me?" I asked.

Jimmy started to fidget on the bench, a sure sign that he was nervous about something. "Not exactly, man," he said. "Truth is, Carl's a proud dude and will probably try to handle this himself. I'm, er, that is, we're worried he might get himself hurt, or worse."

"Okay," I said. "I'll go talk to him. Maybe we can come up with a way to get him off the hook with this guy without anyone getting hurt." The fact is, I'd been able to do a lot of thinking. It's amazing how you can just let your mind wander while doing hard, physical labor from before sunrise until after sunset. I probably went through the whole grief cycle in the four months since Alex's death. I was ready to move on and getting off this rock would be a good first step.

Angie hugged me around the neck and said, "Oh, thank you, Jesse. You have no idea what this means to me."

"I can't promise anything, Angie. He might not even cop to what he's doing. And if he does, we might not be able to come up with an answer. But I'll go talk to him. Where's he live?"

She got a piece of paper and a pen from her purse and wrote down an address on Stock Island, the last island before Key West. I knew that most of the people that lived there were working stiffs. A lot of trailer parks. She said he'd be home for a couple days before going back out. I agreed that I'd go down there tomorrow and asked Angie if there was a dock near where he lived. She gave me the name of a marina just a couple blocks from his house. We talked about other things for a few more minutes, then Jimmy said they had to get back because Angie had to work. Once they left, I walked back and sat down on the bench. Pescador looked up at me expectantly.

"What do you think, Pescador?" I said. He looked across the clearing, toward the bunkhouses and the dock beyond, and barked once, then looked back up at me. "I agree. Let's go catch some more."

CHAPTER THREE:
Civil War History

I woke up the next morning well before sunrise. As usual, Pescador was awake and laying on his old poncho liner when I walked into the living room. He followed me to the door and I opened it. He waited until I nodded at him, then he was off like a shot, bounding down the steps at the back of the house to relieve himself on a banyan tree. I did likewise over the side of the deck. I went back inside and put on a pair of cargo shorts, a denim shirt and topsiders, then grabbed my 'go bag' from the closet by the door. It's a small duffle full of all kinds of things that a boater might need if stranded, including a small case that held my Sig Sauer P226 nine millimeter semiautomatic pistols and three loaded magazines.

I wanted to stop by Big Pine Key Fishing Lodge to get a breakfast sandwich and catch up on the Coconut Telegraph with some fishing guides that were always there early in the morning. I'd been away from civilization long enough. After that, I planned to run on the outside, following the reef line down to Stock Island in the Grady-White.

I locked up the house and carried the bag down to the docks, along with a cooler full of ice, bottled water, and beer. I put them on the boat and untied her, then opened the door behind the Grady-White and the skiffs. It was a tight squeeze getting all four boats under the house. The *Revenge* was nestled in the west side, with her own door. Alex's skiff was docked crossways in the back of the east side, with my skiff and the Grady in front of it. I whistled loudly and stepped aboard the Grady, starting the big Mercury 300-horse engine. The engine used to be on Alex's skiff. She'd wanted more power for tournament fishing. It was way more than I would ever think of having on a flats skiff. It was only slightly bigger than recommended for the Grady. The engine raced for a second, then settled into a nice quiet burble.

Pescador bounded down the steps and leaped aboard as I put the boat in gear. I slowly idled out from under the house and once I was clear, I used the key fob that started the electric motor that pulled the door closed. Everything in my house is run off of ten deep-cycle marine batteries, kept charged by a solar panel and wind turbine. Another button on the fob released the catch, and the door opened on large tension spring hinges. As we idled through the tunnel created by the mangroves, I looked back at the house, as I always do. I'd built the place myself over two years ago with Alex in mind, even though she was three thousand miles away at the time. We'd only been friends, and occasional workout and swimming partners the first time she was here. That had changed really fast when she came back. We were

married within a week. I guess the turmoil of Hurricane Wilma speeded things along. Looking back at the house, I suddenly felt very lonely.

I'd been alone before, many times. In fact, I'd been alone most of my life. Deployments to the Middle East, Grenada, Panama, Japan, and several other places had cost me two prior marriages. I'd never really felt lonely, though. Not like this. There was still a huge hole in my heart that would probably never heal. The big dog up on the bow was now my constant companion. The man who'd killed my wife nearly killed me with a switchblade hidden in his shirt sleeve. He missed my heart by less than an inch, the doctor said. Pescador had leaped past me and torn the man's throat right out of his neck. The dog had saved my life and, best of all, he loved to fish as much as I did. Good thing, too. Because we ate fish for just about every meal. Right now, I wanted a ham-and-egg sandwich.

Once I cleared my channel, I headed east toward Big Spanish Key, then into Big Spanish Channel and south into Bogie Channel. That would take me along the eastern side of Big Pine Key all the way down to the lodge. I knew the water really well and wasn't worried about anything, except an early morning boater. The channels are well marked, and I'd mounted a powerful spotlight to the bow to light the way. I'm pretty sure that Pescador would alert me to anything before I could see it, anyway. The first sign of civilization was the bridge from Big Pine to No Name Key. We crossed under it and never saw a car on it. Of course, it was still well before sunrise and most of the folks on No Name live according to the sun, not the clock. Ten minutes later, we slowed as we neared

the Old Seven Mile Bridge. The channel into Big Pine Key Fishing Lodge runs west between the old bridge and the new one, then turns south right where the bridges make landfall, then west again into the canal.

I tied up at the gas dock and went ahead and topped off the tanks before walking up to the ship's store to eat and get my big Marine Recon coffee mug filled. I told Pescador to wait by the door while I went inside to get us both a breakfast sandwich and fill my mug. I also bought a boaters' guidebook for the Florida Keys that had GPS coordinates for lots of marinas. I walked outside and around the corner, where the store had a couple of large picnic tables under an awning. Sitting down with a couple fishermen I'd seen around, I unwrapped both sandwiches, putting one on the boards of the dock, where Pescador wolfed it down in two bites as I enjoyed mine.

"You're McDermitt, right?" one of the men asked.

"Yeah, how ya doing? Don't recall your name."

"Not surprised," he said, "we never really met. You own that big ole Rampage, right? She here?"

"Yeah, *Gaspar's Revenge*," I replied. "But no, just out and about in my Grady today. How's the fishing been?"

"About the same as always," the other man replied. "Name's Jackson and this here's Willy T. We heard about what happened to you up in Miami. Damn shame. Really sorry for your loss."

"Thanks," I said, but really hoped he'd change the subject. He did. We talked about fishing for a few minutes while I enjoyed my sandwich and coffee. Willy T. was a flats guide and Jackson was First Mate on a charter dive boat. The discussion turned to diving, which I was familiar with, then, of course, turned to treasure.

"Either of you ever hear about a wreck up in Fort Pierce called the *Lynx*?" I asked, just being conversational.

"Sure have," said Jackson. "She was supposed to have a French passenger aboard when the Yankees sunk her. Man by the name of Douzaine Lingots Dior. Story is he was negotiating with a Light Colonel by the name of Abner McCormick to provide funds for the Southern cause. His body was never found. Ya know, you're the second person to ask me about that wreck in the last six months."

"Douzaine Lingots Dior?" I said. *My French really sucks*, I thought. Too bad Deuce wasn't here. I was pretty sure Dior meant gold, though. I didn't think it was actually a name at all.

"Yeah," Jackson said. "The other fellow that asked me about it, I heard on the news a couple weeks later, he drowned up there."

Drowned? No way. What were the odds that he was talking about my old friend Russ?

"In fact," Jackson continued, pointing at my left forearm, "he had a tattoo just like the one you got there."

I glanced down at the winged skull with a scuba regulator in its teeth and crossed oars behind it. It's the logo for Force Recon. Both Russ and I were Recon Marines. In fact, he was my Platoon Sergeant for a time. "Just like this?" I asked.

"Yeah," Jackson said, "Maybe you heard about it on the news."

"No," I lied. "I live up in the Content Keys. No phone, no lights, no motor cars."

"Not a single luxury," Willy T. added, laughing. "Man, I loved that show when I was a kid."

"Yeah," I laughed. "Me too." Then turning to Jackson, I said, "You seem to know a lot about an obscure Civil War wreck."

"Didn't tell ya my last name," Jackson said.

"Oh," I said. "I thought Jackson was your last name."

"Nope, Jackson McCormick's the name. Colonel McCormick was my great-great-grandpa."

"Ahhh," I said. "That explains it."

"This other guy that was looking, he'd heard I was the Colonel's direct descendent and came down here to talk to me. Showed him some letters from Gramps to Granny where he mentioned this French fella. Seems kinda funny, him and you both askin' me about that wreck and both of ya having the same ink."

"Lot of guys were in Force Recon," I said. "If we served at the same time, I might know him. What was his name?"

Jackson looked up toward the awning, obviously thinking. "Don't recall the first name, but his last name was Livingston. I remember, 'cause that was my first wife's maiden name."

"Russell Livingston?" I asked, even though I knew the answer.

Jackson snapped his fingers and pointed at me, saying, "Yeah, that's it. You knew him?"

"Yeah, we served together in the eighties. I haven't seen him since about 1988," I lied.

Jackson seemed to buy it. I don't know why I wanted to keep it secret from the man, but I always tend to withhold information that's not directly needed.

"So, anyway," Jackson continued, "your friend seemed to be a decent fella. Sorry to be the one to tell ya. He was interested in Civil War history and said he was doing re-

search on the Second Florida Cavalry. Not a lot of people know about those guys. Gramps was their commanding officer and he wrote to Granny in one letter, saying that he was taking this Douzaine Dior fella to Colonel Harrison of the First Florida Battalion, intending to fund the Southern cause."

"Why would the French do that?" I asked. "Sorry, I don't know much about the Civil War, except what I learned in high school. And I was more intent on girls and cars, anyway,"

"Yeah," Willy T. said, "weren't we all."

"It's simple," Jackson continued. "With a fractured country, the French would have not one, but two trading partners."

"Makes sense, I guess." My mind was already wandering elsewhere. I'd have to give Deuce a call and find out if my hunch was right about 'Douzaine Lingots Dior'.

"Well guys," I said, as I stood up, "I gotta get. Heading down to Key West for a few days." I shook hands with both men and headed back to the dock, with Pescador trotting along beside me.

I stepped aboard the Grady, started the engine and cast off. Pescador took his usual spot in the bow, sitting on the starboard-side bench seat. There're shallow shoals just off the campground, directly south of the canal, so I took the channel between the bridges to Spanish Harbor Channel, then turned and went under the new Seven Mile Bridge. I turned southwest until I was almost to G Marker, just inside the reef line in fifteen feet of water, and turned west by southwest. Next stop, Stock Island.

The more I used it, the more I really liked this boat. The Grady-White is a real bulldog of a small offshore

boat. Its deep vee slices through the water with ease and being heavier than other boats its size, it takes the rough stuff much better. Comes up a little too high in the bow before it gets up on plane, but with a little trim tab adjustment, that's no big deal. The head below the center console was a plus, too. Not many center cockpit, open fisherman-type boats have a head.

I'd reinstalled the GPS that I'd found over three months ago when I came across Russ's killer, stranded on a nearby island. He was nearly dead from dehydration and didn't seem to need it anymore. I switched it on and scrolled through the recent saves. One was dated the same day he was killed and looked to be a spot about two miles out from Fort Pierce inlet. Pretty much where the Marine Patrol had said they found his boat and body.

I took out the book I'd bought, looked up the marina Angie had told me about, and punched in the numbers. It was about thirty miles, so it'd be about an hour before we got there. The sun had risen while I was talking to Jackson and Willy T. and I could feel its warmth on the back of my neck. There was a light wind out of the south and the ocean was calm, with only small rollers that offered nothing more than a slight side to side rolling motion as they went by under the hull. I love being on the water early in the morning. A small pod of dolphins surfaced just twenty feet off the port bow. Probably moving along the reef, looking for breakfast.

I rode on, while thinking. I really didn't have any idea what I'd say to Trent when I got there. "Hey, Trent, I hear you been hauling dope." Guess I'd just have to wing it, kind of feel the guy out. I knew he was a Conch, born and raised in the Keys. His folks were, too. The people who

managed to eke out a living on these islands for generations are a hard bunch. They've endured hurricanes, pirates and the drug trade, just to name a few of the many things they've overcome. Though I embraced the island lifestyle, I was still considered an outsider. Someone not to be trusted.

I was nearing Stock Island so I got my book out, to find out how to get to Oceanside Marina. The book said the channel was a due north approach toward the center of Stock Island, then another channel would cut off to the northeast before turning due north. The name of the marina was on the roof, easily visible from a mile away. I slowed the boat and looked shoreward while checking the GPS. It said I was due south of the marina, so I probably needed to go just a little further west. I began a slow turn to the north and pulled my binoculars out of the storage bin. I could easily see the marina and turned toward it. I picked up the channel markers easy enough and the side channel was well marked. A few minutes later, I idled up to the gas dock at Oceanside Marina. After tying off and filling the tank, I paid the attendant and asked where I could dock for an hour or two to visit a friend.

"You can just tie off up the dock a ways," he said. "Away from the pumps, here. It's five dollars an hour." I gave the kid a twenty and asked if he could tell me how to get to the address Angie had given me.

"Just go out to the road out front and turn left. It's probably the trailer park just around the bend, on the left."

"Thanks," I said. "Keep an eye on my boat for me, will ya?"

"Sure, mister," he said. "No problem."

"Oh, one other thing. You know of a hotel that allows pets?"

"Probably a few across the bridge, in Key West," he said. "None here on Stock Island. Closest would probably be the Double Tree by the airport. I know they allow pets, for certain."

I thanked him and walked toward the front of the marina, with Pescador trotting along, sniffing at everything along the way. I went around the bend in the road and just like the kid said, there was a trailer park on the left. One on the right too, and more just up the road. There was a fence around this one, and the trailers looked a bit more upscale. I came to a gate, where a road had once been. It had a sign hung slightly crooked that said it was for residents and guests only. There was an old lady sitting on her porch, just the other side of it.

"Excuse me, ma'am," I said. "Is this Harbor Boulevard?"

"Yep," she replied. "Who ya lookin' for?"

"Carl Trent," I said.

"Friend a' his?"

"Yes ma'am," I replied. "From Big Pine."

"Third trailer down past mine," she said. "You can lift that latch there and come through the gate, if ya want."

I guess she was the neighborhood watch captain. "Thanks, ma'am," I said, lifting the latch.

CHAPTER FOUR:
Trouble on the Water

I walked through the gate, closed it behind me and walked down the road until I found the address. It was a large double-wide trailer, with an enclosed porch that ran around both sides and the front. I walked up the sidewalk and pushed the button beside the door. Hearing nothing, I tapped on the aluminum frame of the door. A woman in her mid-thirties opened the inner door and a blast of cold air came out the opening. Country music was playing low inside the house and a little boy was hiding behind her leg.

"Is Carl home?" I asked.

She eyed me up and down and said, "Who are you?"

"Name's Jesse McDermitt. I'm a friend of Angie's."

She turned away from the door and I could hear her say something, but couldn't make out what it was. Then Carl came to the door. I could see in his eyes that he recognized me.

"Hey, Carl," I said. "Angie asked me to stop by. She said maybe I could give you a hand with something."

"I know who you are, Jesse. Come on in. Fool girl called last night and said you might be down here."

He opened the door and I turned to Pescador and said, "Find some shade." He walked over to a bougainvillea and sat down under it, facing the road.

"He'll run off, if he ain't tied," Trent said.

"Never has before. We could drink this whole six-pack," I said, lifting the Hatueys, "and he'll be sitting just like that, two hours from now."

"Takes you two hours to drink three beers?" he said with a chuckle.

I walked inside and the woman turned and headed into the kitchen. She came back with two glasses, took the six-pack from my hands and poured the glasses full, then went back into the kitchen with the rest of the beer.

"Have a seat, Jesse," Trent said. "What's on your mind?"

I sat down on an overstuffed couch and he sat in an equally overstuffed recliner. The place was nice, lots of comfortable-looking furniture, clean and orderly.

"Angie and Jimmy came up to my house yesterday. They told me about the trouble you're in." I figured that the straight-ahead approach would be the best route and just let him think on it. He did, his eyes never wavering from mine. He wasn't a big man, maybe five feet nine or ten and 180 pounds. He looked hard as granite, with a dark, lined face and hands and his hair bleached from the sun. I'd guess him to be close to my own age, but he looked older.

"Wasn't her call to involve you, or Jimmy for that matter."

I kept my eyes on his and said, "A man's gotta do what has to be done to take care of his family. Whatever it is."

"Yeah, you're right about that," he said with a sigh. "But what I did was too risky and now I can't undo it or get out of it."

"That sort, you just can't reason with," I said. "They've lost their souls."

He sighed again and looked down at the floor, at his feet. I could almost feel his dejection. After a minute, he looked up and said, "Truth is, I just don't know what to do, or where to turn. Been a shrimper all my life, my dad before me. His dad was a long-liner. Business took a downturn a couple years back and I been losing money since."

"Who's the one making the threats?" I asked.

"Man name of Carlos Santiago. He's from up in Miami, one of the Mariel people. Was just a kid when he came over, I guess. About thirty-five years old now and goes back down to Cuba on a regular basis. At least, this is what I hear. I also hear his dad was one of the ones Castro turned loose from the prisons. Bad people, man. Real bad. But I didn't know that the first couple times I ran for him."

"I know, Carl. People up in Marathon speak highly of you."

"Thanks, I hear the same about you." He took a long pull from his beer and set it down on the table between us. "I just don't know how you can help, man."

I thought about it for a minute. Usually I break things down by just following a course in my mind and predicting the outcome. When one course breaks down, I back up and try another. Putting my thoughts into words this way is something I've never been good at.

"Okay," I said, "let's just run it down. What'd he say when you told him you wanted out?"

"Said that if I didn't keep hauling for him, I'd come home one day and find my house burned down and my family dead."

"Well, that's not an option," I said. "What do you think he'd say if your boat broke down, or you sold it?"

"Not an option, either, man," Trent said. "I'm a shrimper, nothing else. Can't sell it and if it breaks down, I gotta fix it. This whole thing's making me sick."

"There's an idea," I said. "What would he do if you got sick? Like, real sick?"

"One of my crew's in his pocket," he said. "They'd go out anyway."

"Not without a licensed Captain," I said. "Any of your crew got papers?"

"No," he said. "Santiago'd put his own Skipper on board."

"Not if you hired one," I said. "What do you think he'd do about that?"

"Not sure. What you getting at?"

"Hire me, Carl. Let me run your boat and I'll find an angle. Take your wife and kids up to my island for a week or two. Let's see what happens."

"You have papers?" he asked.

"One-hundred-ton Master's," I said. "I've never actually skippered a shrimp boat, but I run my own offshore fishing charter. The crewman that's in Santiago's pocket? It's not your Mate, is it?"

"No, my Mate's a solid young man. He wants out of this too. Said he was gonna quit me if I couldn't find a way out."

"Perfect," I said. "A good Mate can run the boat by himself. Only the Skipper needs to be licensed, right?"

"Right. Bob, my Mate, does have a First Mate's license, though."

"I'd like to meet him," I said.

"He lives just around the corner, I can call him. Why do you want to get involved in my mess, Jesse?"

"Guess I just don't like it when an honest guy gets bullied," I replied. "Yeah, give Bob a call. See if he's got a few minutes."

Trent made the call. While he talked I asked myself the same question. Why was I getting involved? Angie was a friend, but I barely knew her. Jimmy was a good friend, but Trent was two steps away from me there. I really don't like bullies—was that all it was? Or was it just to occupy myself, to keep from thinking about Alex, since I'd finished the work on the island?

Trent finished his call and said, "He'll be over in a few minutes. That's it, then? You don't like seeing people bullied?"

"That's not just it," I said. "To be honest, I'm not sure. Four months ago, my wife was murdered by some bad people." I just blurted it out, like that must be the reason.

"I'd heard about that," he said. "Couldn't imagine what it musta been like for you."

The front door opened and a young man walked in. He was almost my height, but slimmer than my two-thirty. He had sandy-colored hair down past his ears and a deep tan except around his eyes, where he obviously wore sunglasses. He was dressed like a waterman, jeans, tee shirt and worn topsiders.

Trent and I both stood up. "Jesse, this is my First Mate, Bob Talbot. Bob, Jesse McDermitt, from up in Marathon." I shook his hand and noticed the tattoo on his forearm. A winged staff, called a caduceus, entwined with two snakes, the emblem of the Navy Corpsman. He had a firm, dry grip and clear green eyes that held mine steady.

"Good to meet you, Jesse," he said.

"You too, Doc," I responded.

He started to say something to Trent, then stopped and looked back at me, more appraisingly. Then his eyes found the Recon tattoo and he looked up and smiled. "Force Recon, huh?"

I nodded and he added, "Served with some Jarheads, both artillery and infantry, Four-Ten my first year, then One-Nine1/9." First Battalion, Ninth Marines had a long, storied history in the Corps. They earned the nickname Walking Dead in Vietnam, but he was way too young for that. I knew that Tenth Marines was an artillery regiment, based at Camp Lejeune, also.

"Walking Dead?" I asked.

"Yeah, they were reactivated a few years back. Afghanistan."

Trent looked from one of us to the other and said, "You guys know each other?"

"No," I said laughing. "But we definitely chewed some of the same sand."

"So," Doc said, "what's this about you wanting to help us out?"

So, I told both men a little about my background for starters, both in the Corps and since then. We discussed a lot of options, finishing off the rest of the Hatueys I'd brought. Although Trent didn't like the idea of hiding out, Doc and I convinced him that for the safety of his family, it would be the best thing to do. I told him about my island and said that they'd have plenty of room and the use of my skiff and the Grady. He decided that maybe his family could use a short fishing vacation, away from the rat race.

They were due to go back out in two days and Santiago had a pickup arranged in the Gulf, on their second day out, before returning with their catch. That gave us plenty of time for Trent to get things together. Then I'd ferry them out to my island.

After two more hours, we had a pretty good working plan. Everything would go as usual, until I showed up at the docks instead of Trent. Bob would act surprised and concerned when I told him that Trent had hired me to Skipper while he was undergoing hyperbaric treatment at the hospital in Key Largo, suffering from an embolism and decompression sickness caused by a scuba diving accident.

"What if Santiago has someone check the hospital?" Bob said as the three of us walked outside.

"I'll call in a favor," I said. "If anyone checks, there will be a patient there by the name of Carl Trent. In the chamber, with no access to a phone."

"That's some favor," Trent said. Then, seeing Pescador still sitting in the same spot, although no longer in the shade, he said, "I'll be damned. Your dog hasn't even moved."

Pescador looked back at me expectantly. I nodded at him and he stood, walked over to the bougainvillea and relieved himself, then came over and sat down at my feet.

"You did a hell of a job training that dog," Trent said. "Must be a hundred cats roaming around here. I thought sure he woulda took off chasing one and got lost. What kinda dog is he?"

"He's a Portuguese water dog, or so I'm told. I didn't train him, though. Found him on a deserted island near my house, the day after Hurricane Wilma blew through. Tried to find his owner for a month, with no luck. So, he's just sort of adopted me."

We shook hands all around and agreed that I'd pick Trent and his family up at noon tomorrow. On the return, I was going to bring the *Revenge* down in case I needed a place to stay. Since it didn't make sense to go home and come back again, I asked Doc if he could give me a lift to the Double Tree, just across the bridge in Key West.

"Pretty expensive place," he said.

"Yeah, but they allow pets."

"Sure," he said. "I'll give you a ride."

We left Trent and walked around the block to Doc's house. As we walked, I asked Doc more about the crewman that was in the drug smugglers' pocket.

"His name's John Lupori," he said. "He's from New York. I think he was connected up there."

"Connected?"

"He's dropped hints from time to time that he was a bag man and ran numbers for the mob."

"Have you met Santiago?"

"Once," he replied. "Cold dude. Dead-looking eyes, like a shark. Either him or one of his men shows up at the dock, just before we sail, to give the Skipper the GPS coordinates and the name of the boat for the pickup."

"Don't let the crew know anything about me taking over for Trent. I'll show up at the boat an hour before we sail. You'll be pissed because Trent's late. Act surprised and concerned when I tell you about the accident. We'll make out like he was just sent up to Key Largo that morning and called me while he was on the way. And remember, semper Gumby."

"Always flexible, got it," he said. "Haven't heard that phrase in a while. This is my place. Let me tell my girlfriend I'm giving you a lift. Wanna come in? She's a Jarhead, too."

"Sure," I said. "Wait here, Pescador."

"Is that Spanish?" he asked.

"Yeah, it means fisherman. When I found him, he'd just caught a three-pound snapper."

"No shit?" he said as he opened the door to the trailer. "Hey, babe, I'm back," he called into the kitchen. A woman walked into the living room and he said, "This is Jesse, I'm gonna give him a lift over to Key West. He's a Marine, like you."

"Pleased to meet you, Jesse," she said. "I'm Nicole Godsey, my friends call me Nikki."

"Nice to meet you, too," I said as I shook her hand. She was a pretty girl. Nearly as tall as Doc, with shoulder-length black hair, tattoos, dark eyes and eyeglasses.

"So, you're a Marine, huh?" she asked.

"Retired in 1999," I said. "Force Recon."

"Bob and I met in the Corps. I was in the Regimental S-4 office, Ninth Marines and he was the Corpsman for Weapons Company, One-Nine."

"Was Matt Andrews still the Regimental Sergeant Major when you were there?" I asked.

"Yes! You knew him?"

"We tipped a few beers together."

"He retired just a couple of months after I arrived there. Good Marine."

"We better get going, Jesse," Doc said.

"Can we swing by Oceanside Marina first?" I asked. "I want to reserve dock space for the Rampage and move the Grady to it until tomorrow. Nice meeting you, Nikki."

"Good to meet you too, Jesse," she said. Then as we started out the door she added, "Don't be long, Bob. Remember you promised to take me shopping."

"You own a Rampage?" he asked as we walked across the yard to his car. "How big?"

"Forty-five-foot convertible. When I take Trent and his family up to the Content Keys tomorrow, I'm going to bring it down here, so I don't have to stay in a hotel. Hoping we can solve this problem in a week, but you just never know. Besides, I might want to hang out in Key Weird for a while."

We drove over to the dock and I made arrangements for a slip on the private dock and moved the Grady over there. The private dock had a gate that used one of those key cards to open it, like hotels use. After moving the Grady, Doc took me over to the hotel. The Double Tree is just off South Roosevelt, before the airport. Doc dropped me off and after checking in, Pescador and I went up to our room. I dropped my go bag on the table, then took a shower to get the day's salt off of me.

CHAPTER FIVE:
Paradise Lost

After showering, I called down to the desk and asked for a cab, then got dressed. It'd been a while since I'd been in Key West and my mouth was watering for Frankie's cooking. I pulled Pescador's poncho liner out of the bag and spread it in a corner.

"I'll be back in a couple of hours. You want the TV on?" I asked him. He cocked his head at that. "Yeah, didn't think so." I switched on the bedside radio and tuned it to a jazz station. He went over to the poncho liner and, after turning around a couple of times, lay down on it.

I took the stairs down to the lobby. The girl at the desk smiled and said, "Your taxi's waiting outside, Mister McDermitt. Will you be out all evening?"

I smiled back and said, "Thanks, it's Jesse. No, just going to Blue Heaven for something to eat." People that worked in hospitality in Key West were really good at remembering guests' names, I was thinking. When I glanced back, as I went through the door, she was still smiling at me. I wondered for a minute why she wanted to know if I'd be out all night.

I got in the taxi, and told the driver where to go. He was an island man, judging from his accent. A little older than me, I'd guess. Clean cut and friendly.

"Yuh guh be der long time?" he asked, handing me a card.

"No, just for supper," I replied, wondering again what was it with everyone wanting to know my itinerary?

"Yuh call mi at dat numbuh, sar. I bring yuh bahk, too."

"I don't have a cell phone," I lied. I had one, but it was on the Grady and I rarely turned it on.

"No problem, mon," he said. "Yuh tell Miss Tina La Mons, behind di bar, when yuh ready ta go, she call me. Yuh won take di scenic way, or straight head?"

I looked at the name on the card, Lawrence Lovett, and stuck it in the pocket of my guayabera. "You can take South Roosevelt, Lawrence. I'm not in any hurry."

He took South Roosevelt along the water, all the way to First Street, then north to Truman and west all the way to Thomas and the Blue Heaven. I looked out at the water, noting its turquoise and green color. The wind was out of the south, but there was hardly any wave activity. The sun was nearing the water to the west and I knew that Mallory Square would be winding up to a fever pitch about now. That's where the daily sunset celebration took place. I'd been there a few times and marveled at how the tourists would crowd the square, ogling the street performers, while the pickpockets moved through the crowd. Most of them were very good and the tourists didn't notice their missing wallets and watches until the pickpockets were already gone.

We pulled up to Blue Heaven and I got out of the cab. "Thanks for the ride, Lawrence," I said as I handed him a ten.

"No problem, mon. Yuh enjoy yuh dinnuh."

I walked through the palm-and-hibiscus-covered arch into the side yard of Blue Heaven. It was a funky little Key West place, with all the trappings of your typical Key West dive, but the food was awesome. Mostly because of the chef, Frankie. Tables were set right on the sand all around the yard, with umbrellas over them. A waitress was going around lighting the jar candles at each table, getting ready for the dinner crowd. Cats, chickens, and parrots lazed in the late evening sun. It was still early, but a couple of tables were already occupied, mostly by tourists, I noted. I took a seat at the far end of the open-air bar, next to the wall, and immediately had a coaster placed in front of me by a pretty woman about thirty, with long dark hair and dark eyes. Her name tag said 'Christina', so I assumed she was the Tina La Mons the cab driver had mentioned.

"What can I get for you, Captain?" she asked.

"Red Stripe, please," I responded, wondering if it was that easy for her to tell I wasn't one of the cruise ship tourists. But, in her line of work, dealing with people day in and day out, she'd probably become good at it. She reached into an icebox under the bar and placed a dripping, cold bottle on a coaster in front of me, no glass. *Yep,* I thought, *she's good at reading people.*

"Would you like to see a menu, or do you already know what you'd like?" she asked, smiling brightly.

I smiled back and said, "Does Frankie have any hogfish?"

She nodded and said, "A local spear fisherman just brought some in. They were swimming only an hour ago. Blackened?"

"Yeah," I replied. She was very good, I'd give her that much.

"Frankie's in back," Tina said. "Want me to tell her you're here?"

"Yeah, haven't seen her in a long time, name's Jesse."

She went on to tell me what came with my order and I told her that'd be just fine. "But, double the fish order and put half in a go box, would you?"

"Think you'll get hungry later?" she asked.

"Probably," I said, "but it's for my dog."

She turned and slid the order across a counter at a little window and leaned in to say something I couldn't hear. A second later, Frankie Poe came running out of the kitchen.

"Jesse McDermitt!" she yelled loud enough for the revelers on Mallory Square to hear. She hugged me tight and got flour all over my guayabera.

"Sorry about that," she said, brushing it off. "How've you been? I heard about what happened up there, I'm real sorry."

"Doing okay, Frankie, thanks. How've you been?"

"Just great, thanks. Why didn't you call to say you were coming down? Bob talks about that fishing trip you took him and his friends on all the time."

"Yeah, that was a lot of fun," I said, laughing at the memory. "Bimini will never be the same after those guys."

"You in town long?" she asked.

"Don't really know. In and out, probably for the next few days, helping out a friend.

"Well, I gotta get back to the kitchen. So good to see you again, I'll tell Bob you're in town."

"I'll probably see y'all around," I said.

"You better," she said and headed back into the kitchen. I turned around on my stool and surveyed the clientele a little closer. It was an old habit. Move quickly into a room and to a far corner, then check out the people and exits. It was a yard, so I pretty much had a lot of options for a hasty exit, if need be. Only three tables were occupied. The nearest one was a young tourist couple, slightly sunburned. In the far-right corner of the yard, another table had three obvious tourist couples, fresh off a cruise ship. The third table was occupied by two men, who were probably locals, or tourists very adept at island camouflage. They sat across the table from one another, leaning in close, talking low.

Just as I took the last pull from my beer, Tina set another one on the bar and said, "Stay away from those two, Captain."

I turned back to the bar and said, "Why's that?"

"I can tell you're not a tourist," she said. "Dive boat captain? The guy in the jacket, he's a drug dealer."

"Fishing boat, actually. Up in Marathon. And you're right, not interested in buying drugs. How do you know he's a drug dealer?"

"Didn't think you were," she said, smiling warmly at me. "Besides being the best bartender in Key West, I'm also a Monroe County Reserve Deputy. What's a Marathon charter Captain doing in Key West on a Friday night? Known Frankie long?"

"Boat's getting some work done," I lied. "Yeah, I've known her and her husband for a few years. Slow night?"

"For now," she said. "Should get a little friskier later on."

A bell rang behind her and she went to the window, coming back with a plate loaded with two huge fillets, a big mound of Spanish rice, broccoli and a baked potato. She placed it in front of me and I suddenly realized how hungry I was and dug right in. Since there wasn't anyone else at the bar, she lingered while chatting about the weather and the water. I nodded at the right times, added a comment between bites and polished off the meal in short order. Another habit, formed from many years of eating what you can, when you can, not knowing when the next meal might be.

Tina took my plate when I was finished, put it on the counter at the window and set another cold beer in front of me. "So, you're in town for a while?" she asked. "Couldn't help overhearing."

I looked at her closer. She was about a foot shorter than my six three, with a head full of thick, dark brown hair framing a pretty face with no makeup that I could tell. She had a natural radiant beauty. She wore a cutoff tee shirt with 'Blue Heaven' written across the front. It showed her tan, flat belly. Everywhere else I looked was all curves.

"Not sure," I said. "At least a few days, maybe longer. A friend's sick and I'm skippering his boat until he's better." Enough of a truth, I thought.

"So," she said, dragging out the word, "I'll probably see more of you?"

"You might," I said, smiling. I handed her the card the taxi driver had given me and asked if she'd call him for me. She glanced at the card, slid it back to me, and picked her cell phone up from the shelf behind the bar.

She only punched one number and after a second she said into the phone, "Lawrence, it's Tina. I have a fare for you." Then she looked at me and smiled, before continuing. "Yeah, a tall, handsome guy at the bar, disappointing me."

A few minutes later, the taxi driver walked through the gate and came over to the bar, where I still sat talking to Tina. He noticed my half-full beer and took a seat next to me and ordered a bottle of Coke. "Be no hurry, mon," he said. "Is still a slow night."

Tina brought his Coke, as I drained the last of my beer and laid two twenties on the bar, saying, "I'm all set, Lawrence."

We walked through the yard, chickens scattering out of our way. As we went through the gate, I looked back and Tina smiled and winked at me. I smiled and waved back to her, then got in the front seat of the cab.

When Lawrence got behind the wheel, he said, "Dat gull be sweet on yuh, mon. Yuh sure yuh wanna leave?"

"Yeah," I said. "Got an early day tomorrow."

He took the same route back to the hotel. I've learned over the years that some of the best sources of local intel were bartenders and taxi drivers. Once we passed Smathers Beach, I looked at Lawrence and asked, "You ever hear of a man by the name of Carlos Santiago?"

"Dot be a bod mon," he said. "Why yuh wanna know bout him, mon?"

"Might need to know more about him is all," I said. "What can you tell me about him?"

"Ah grew up on Andros," he said. "Yuh know Andros?"

"Sure," I replied, letting him tell me at his own pace. "I've been there many times. Great fishing."

"Ah come heah bout two yeah go," he said. "Buy dis taxi cab, den. Santiago, he try ta get mi to bring druggies to him, when I did. Say he pay fuh bringin um. Tole da mon to go fock hisself, I did. I not be needin money dat bod, mon. Yuh stay way from dot mon, if yuh smart."

"He make any threats against you, when you told him no?" I asked.

"Ya, mon," he said. "Say he gwon hurt mi family. I jes laugh, I got no famly."

I thought on that for a minute, as Lawrence drove. Santiago seems to be the kind that makes a lot of threats to get people to do his bidding.

"Anything come of his threats?" I asked.

"No, mon. Like I say, got no famly and I don live pon dis island. He be a big time smug drugglah, mon. I and I jes small fry."

"Good for you, Lawrence," I said. "Keep it that way."

He pulled up to the front of the hotel and I got out, handing him a twenty. "You up and about early?" I asked. "Need a ride over to Stock Island, about eight."

"No problem, mon. I be sittin right heah, at eight shop."

I walked into the lobby and the girl that was at the desk earlier was still there. She smiled warmly and motioned me over.

"A letter came for you while you were out, Mister McDermitt. Nikki Godsey dropped it off an hour ago." She handed me a sealed envelope. I opened it and saw that it was from Trent, telling me that he'd be ready at nine.

I glanced at the girl's name tag, which said 'Susan Marrs', and said, "Thanks, Susan."

I started to turn and she said, "You know Nikki well?"

"Only met her today," I said. "Her and Doc, er, Bob, I mean. We were stationed together a few years back."

"I noticed your dog when you checked in," she said, seeming to want to make small talk. She was a tiny blonde girl, no more than five feet tall and probably a hundred and ten soaking wet. I guessed her to be late twenties at best. "I get off in a few minutes. If you'd like I can bring some dog food up."

"Thanks," I said, smiling. "I brought him some leftover fish."

"He likes fish?" she asked. "Never heard of a dog that likes fish before."

"Well, he usually prefers his fish raw," I said.

"You mean like sushi?"

"No, more like swimming in the ocean."

She smiled again and said, "Well, like I said, I get off in a few minutes. If I can bring you anything, just name it."

Was she coming on to me, too? Two women in the last two hours? I looked her over and though she was pretty, as was Tina, neither held a candle to my late wife. I kind of tapped my left ring finger to the box I held, drawing her attention to the ring I still wore and said, "Thanks, Susan. Good night."

She actually pouted just a bit and said, "Good night, Mister McDermitt."

I headed up the stairs, wondering about the two women I'd just met. Both were very attractive and I'm pretty sure both were hitting on me. But, why? One was a good ten years younger than me and one not much older than my oldest daughter. I'm not an overly good-looking man, I knew that. A lot of water under the keel. I stay in shape and still have all my hair, but either woman could have her pick of much better-looking and younger guys. Here on Key West, they arrive and depart at regular intervals. Maybe that was it. Women looking for something more than just a weekend or one-night stand.

I got to the room and used the key card to open the door. As is my habit, I pushed it open just a crack and listened. Hearing nothing, I pushed it the rest of the way open and walked in. Pescador was sitting where I'd left him, his big tail pounding a beat on the wall.

"Supper's on, boy," I said and he walked over, sniffing the air. I opened the box and set it on the floor, in front of him. He looked down at the two hogfish fillets and then looked back up at me, expectantly.

"You know," I said, "you don't have to wait for permission every time." He simply stood there, looking at me, licking his lips.

"Go ahead," I said and he tore into the fish.

"Unbelievable," I muttered.

CHAPTER SIX:
Escape to Content Keys

Waking before sunrise, I took Pescador outside for a walk along the breakwater, across Roosevelt from the hotel. When he'd taken care of his business, we went back to the room and I gathered up my gear. Not that there was much to gather, just my dirty clothes from the day before, which I put into a plastic trash bag and stuffed in my go bag. I told Pescador to wait and I'd bring breakfast back, then headed down to the hotel restaurant. I ordered a big breakfast and asked the waitress if she could put some scrambled eggs in a box with some bacon and sausage for my dog.

"How big's your dog?" she asked.

"Big dog, about a hundred pounds."

"Got it," she said and headed off to the kitchen.

I was nearly finished with my breakfast when she brought the box to me. I opened it and looked inside. Pescador was going to be happy.

"Think that'll be enough for him?" she asked.

"Perfect, thanks."

She left the bill on the table and I left a generous tip, went to the counter and paid the bill. I took Pescador's food up to him and he acted like he was starving.

"I might have to get you checked for tape worms," I told him. "You eat like a horse."

We took another walk along the breakwater and sat on the rocks to watch the sun come up. Though it was January, it looked like it was going to be a pretty warm day, already in the upper sixties. Once the sun was up, we went back to the room, grabbed my go bag, and then went back down to the lobby to check out. I was surprised to see Susan behind the desk.

"Pulling a double?" I asked.

She smiled. "Yeah, the lady that works the day shift called to say her husband wasn't feeling well and she was taking him to a doctor. The manager called and asked if I could fill in."

She took my card, closed out my room account and handed me the receipt, saying, "I hope you enjoyed your stay, Mister McDermitt. And I'm sorry if I was too forward last night."

"Forward?" I asked. "I didn't notice."

"It's just there aren't a lot of decent men on this island," she said. "And the tourists are always trying to get with the local women, if you know what I mean."

"Don't worry about it, kid," I said.

"I hope you'll come back and stay with us again."

"I'll see you around, Susan," I said, which caused her to smile all the more.

I glanced up at the clock on the wall, noting it was a few minutes before eight. I looked out through the front door and saw Lawrence's taxi pull up, right on time, just like he'd said. I picked up my bag, headed out the door and climbed into the front seat, after letting Pescador in the back.

"Hope you don't mind my dog, Lawrence. Forgot to tell you I wasn't traveling alone."

"No problem, mon. He prolly cleaner dan a lot a di tourists I carry roun. Where yuh goin on Stock Island, sar?"

"Oceanside Marina," I replied.

"Yuh know, I picked up a coupla fares lass night at Blue Heaven. Miss Tina ask bout yuh."

"She did?" I asked. "What's with all these local women? The desk clerk here at the hotel was hitting on me last night."

"Don know bout her," he said. "But, I know Miss Tina is a fine lady. Married once, but he was a drunk and run off. I guess a lot a di local ladies be lonely. Not a lotta good mons on dis island. Dem dat is, get snatched up quick like. I can tell yuh a good mon, why I was wondrin bout yuh asking bout dat no good Santiago."

I've always been a good read on people and I sized Lawrence up to be a decent man, someone that could be not only trusted, but relied upon. "Lawrence," I said as we crossed the short bridge to Stock Island, "I'm down here to help a friend. He's in the same sort of trouble with Santiago that he tried with you, only about a hundred times worse. He does have a family, though, and lives here on Stock Island."

"Yuh must be talkin bout Cap'n Trent," he said, and noting the surprise on my face, he added, "Is a small island, sar."

Without a second thought, I knew this man could be trusted and said, "Yeah, I'm taking him and his family up the Keys a way. Then I'm coming back down here to skipper his boat and see if there's some way to get him out of this mess."

"Well," he said, "yuh watch yuh back, mon. Dat Santiago be a bad mon. Yuh bettah watch yuh front too, mon," he added, laughing, "Dem ladies be trollin fah a mon jest like yuh."

We pulled up on the backside of the marina and I got out, handing him a twenty.

"No sar, dis ride be on me," he protested.

"No way, Lawrence. You take this and keep your ears open for me, okay." I took another of his cards and wrote my cell phone number on the back. "If you hear anything on the Coconut Telegraph that you think I might be interested in, call me and leave a message."

"I do dat, mon," he said, taking the twenty and the card. I opened the back door, and Pescador bounded out and went directly to a banyan tree and hiked his leg as Lawrence drove away. We walked over to the marina office and I told the manager that I was leaving, but would be back later today in the Rampage and to hold my slip for me.

We went to the private dock, unlocked the gate and walked out to the Grady. I started the engine and untied her, as Pescador jumped aboard and found his spot on the bow. I turned the key and the big Mercury outboard revved to life, then settled to a low idle. Casting off the stern line, I put the engine in gear and idled over to the gas dock. I tied off, just past the pumps, shut the engine off and climbed up to the dock.

Trent and his family came around the corner of the building, carrying two large duffle bags. His wife was carrying a small case, which I assumed held all the family's toiletries and such.

"Right on time," I said. "Did anyone see you walking over here?"

"Just Miss Churray," the wife said. "She lives at the end of our road, at the gate. Donna sees everything."

It dawned on me that I didn't know her or the kids' names and here I was about to take them to my house to stay without me, for who knows how long.

I gave her a hand, as she stepped aboard, saying, "I'm Jesse, Mrs. Trent."

She stepped down lightly, turned and said, "It's Charlotte, but my friends call me Charlie."

"Welcome aboard, Charlie," I said as I helped the little boy down to the deck.

Trent said, "The boy there, he's Carl Junior. The girl's name is Patty."

Helping the scared-looking little girl to the deck, I said, "Welcome aboard, Patty and Carl. My dog's up in the bow, if you want to go see him?"

Trent handed me the bags and climbed down to the deck as the kids tentatively moved toward the bow. Pescador lifted his big head from where he'd been laying it and I said, "Pescador, we have visitors. Say hi to the kids and make room up there."

The kids looked at me as I said it, then looked back to the big shaggy dog. Pescador barked once and wagged his thick tail, thumping against the hull, before stepping down off the seat and standing between the two front benches in the bow. Both kids looked at each other and smiled, then moved further up into the bow and started petting him and talking to him.

"Fisherman, huh?" Trent said. "How'd you come up with that name?"

"It just came to me," I said. "You'll find out soon enough. He's going to stay at the house with you. I think you'll find he's a pretty useful guide."

"What I heard was," Trent said, "the guy that killed your wife had his throat torn open by a dog. Same dog?"

"One and the same, Trent," I replied. "He'll likely do the same to anyone that threatens those kids."

As I started up the engine, we both looked forward, where the kids were hugging and petting Pescador, whose tail was beating against both fish coolers. I cast off the bowline and shoved the Grady out away from the dock, then put it into gear and started slowly idling away from the marina and into the channel.

It was a nice easy ride back to my island home, calm seas and blue skies all the way. Trent and I both half stood at the helm, one leg cocked on the wide bench seat. The two kids finally got tired of petting Pescador and sat on the starboard bow seat, with their mother on the port bow seat and Pescador standing between them with his front paws up on the bow and his ears blowing in the wind. Several times, I glanced at Trent and could see myself in his face. It was obvious he was a man who loved the sea.

As we approached the house, through the tunnel of mangroves, I pushed the release buttons on both key fobs and the spring-loaded doors slowly eased open.

"You can use this boat and the white skiff, Trent," I said, "I'd appreciate you not using Alex's red skiff."

"Wow," he said. "You really got quite a place out here. That Rampage is beautiful."

"There's only one bed in the main house," I said.

"There's more than one house?" Trent exclaimed.

"Yeah, on the north end of the island are two bunkhouses, if the main house isn't enough room. No kitchens in those, though. There's a huge grill I built between the two that you can cook on with driftwood. Only one of the bunkhouses is completely finished. I still have to paint the other and put the mattresses on the bunks. You'll be plenty comfortable anywhere. There's a long dock on the north side, too. Great place for the kids to play in the water."

"I really appreciate all this, Jesse," he said. "Still don't understand why you'd want to help a near stranger, though."

I turned the Grady in the basin and backed in next to my skiff. Trent helped me make her fast, while Pescador took the kids on a tour of the island. I handed the two duffle bags up to Trent on the dock and he took his wife's hand and helped her up. She hadn't talked much on the trip, but as I stepped up onto the dock with them, she suddenly hugged me, sobbing softly into my shoulder. After a few seconds, she composed herself and stepped away.

"Whatever your reason, Jesse," she said, "I'm very grateful." Then she turned and went up the steps to the deck. I showed Trent the back-up hand cranks for the doors and how the fobs worked, then showed him where all the fishing and snorkeling gear was stored and everything else he might need in the many storage closets around the dock area.

"If you continue up the channel we just came out of, about a hundred yards, there's a hole on the northwest side of the channel that's good for grouper and lobster. About a half mile further, there's several cuts through the banks at Upper Harbor Key. There's snook there on a falling tide. I've speared some nice-sized hogfish all over the flats up there. Jimmy and Angie will be up here in the morning with enough vegetables to fill the fridge, and there's a whole pantry full of canned stuff down at the bunkhouse."

He took everything in stride, checking some of the fishing gear, obviously familiar with everything. "A man could hole up here forever, it looks like."

"Yeah," I laughed. "If the man likes fish."

"We do," Trent said. "You built all this yourself?"

"Over several years, yeah," I said.

Looking up, he said, "Now, that's hard to come by. Holy wood?"

"Yeah, good eye," I said. "A friend had a lignum vitae fall a few years ago and gave me the wood. Had to hire two damn semis to haul it up to a lumberyard in Homestead, then back again. It was enough to do all the floors. Walls are mostly mahogany."

"Mahogany? You're shittin' me," he said as we started up the steps. I unlocked the door and handed him the key, then we continued to the back deck, where Charlie was sitting on the bench, watching the kids play with Pescador.

When we walked up, she looked at me and asked, "Is it true what Carl said? Your dog killed a man?"

"You don't have anything to worry about. The man had just stuck a switchblade in my chest. Pescador's an extremely loyal and protective friend. He's taken to those two kids and will make a great babysitter."

We heard a squeal from down below and looked to see both kids piling on top of the big dog, laughing and squirming. Pescador just laid there and let them have fun. Truth is, it was probably going to be a lot of fun for him to have someone to play with.

Pointing to the key in Trent's hand, I said, "That opens both bunkhouses, too. Come on, I'll show you the house."

The three of us walked inside. Trent dropped the two duffles on the floor next to the door, and Charlie walked into the head with the little case she was carrying. Trent looked all around the small house and nodded approvingly.

"The lights are twelve volt, powered by six deep-cycle marine batteries. They're charged by a wind turbine and solar panels. Out back is a cold-water shower and in the head is a hot-water shower, there's a two-thousand-gallon cistern on the roof in back, and a propane water heater in a closet in the bedroom."

"Hasn't been a lot of rain, since Wilma came through," he said.

"I pumped it full from the *Revenge* two days ago. She has a desalinization unit on board. You can bring a couple mattresses from the unfinished bunkhouse up here and lay them out on the floor in the bedroom. There's plenty of room in there. I already cleared the dresser out and put all my clothes aboard the *Revenge*."

"When you going back down?" he asked.

"Now, unless you have any questions, or anything else you can tell me about Santiago."

"Either him or one of his men will be at the dock before you shove off," he said. "To give you the coordinates for the pickup. What're you gonna do then?"

"Tell him to piss up a rope," I said.

Trent laughed hard and long at that. Finally, he got control and said, "He's not the kinda guy that takes no for an answer real well."

"Well, no is all he's gonna get," I said. "Once I see how he reacts to being bullied, that'll tell me which way to tack."

Charlie came out of the head. I guess she was arranging everything to her liking. "God," she said, "I had to go so bad."

"You should have said something," I said. "The Grady has a small head, under the center console."

We all laughed at that, then I said, "Speaking of which, the head, as you just found out, is a marine head. It discharges into a septic system that flows into a deep well, off on the west side of the island." Turning to Trent I said, "Like I said, it's only a two-thousand-gallon cistern, so with four of you, I'd recommend a jump off the dock to clean up now and then."

"We'll be fine, Jesse," Charlie said. "Are you leaving soon?"

"Now's as good a time as any," I said. "Cell service is sketchy up here, best spot I've found was right at the top of the front steps. If you need anything, it'd probably be better if you call Angie to bring it up."

We walked out onto the deck and I whistled once. Pescador came running up the deck and sat in front of me. "Pescador," I said. "I'm leaving. You stay here and have fun with those kids." I nodded toward the kids waiting at the bottom of the steps, then pointed to Trent and said, "He's in charge."

He turned his big head toward Trent expectantly, and I told him, "Tell him to do something."

"Go play," he said and Pescador bounded back down the steps to the squealing kids.

"One last thing about him," I said. "When you put food in front of him, he won't eat until you tell him to."

"Unbelievable," Trent said.

"Yep, that's what I keep saying."

We walked back down to the dock and Trent helped me untie the *Revenge*. I climbed up to the bridge and started the engines. I waved down to them as I put both engines in forward.

"Be careful, my friend," Trent said.

"Thanks for everything, Jesse," Charlie said.

"Y'all just enjoy the time off," I said back. "With luck, I'll even catch a shrimp or two."

Idling out, I turned northeast into Harbor Channel. A quick look at the flats on either side told me the tide was falling. Though it was a longer route, I decided I didn't want to run the shallower channels to the south. Too slow. I followed Harbor Channel until it turned north, just past the light at Harbor Key Bank, into the Gulf of Mexico. Then I headed northwest and turned on the sonar. I had fifteen feet under the keel now, so I nudged the throttles and brought the big boat up onto plane.

Gaspar's Revenge is my primary fishing boat. She's a forty-five-foot Rampage Convertible, custom built for the drug trade, with twin 1015-horsepower engines. She came up at a Coast Guard auction, just after I retired from the Corps and moved down here a little over six years ago. So, I bought her and lived aboard at Dockside Marina, in Boot Key Harbor, for a few years, before I bought the island and built the house. She's the perfect boat for charter fishing and with the big engines, she can really move out.

Turning southwest, I followed the twenty-fathom line, then turned on the GPS and radar. I punched in the numbers for Oceanside Marina and the GPS showed a line on the chart plotter that would take me to Northwest Passage, just past Key West, then south to the Atlantic side and east to the channel up to the marina. I checked the radar and saw that the only vessel anywhere in front of me was a tanker twenty miles away. I nudged the throttles a bit more, to thirty knots, and turned on the autopilot. It would keep me on the line the chart plotter showed. Then I climbed down to the cockpit and unlocked the door to the salon.

Beyond the salon was the crew quarters on the port side and the master stateroom beyond that. I went in and kneeled down at the foot of the bunk. Pushing the covers back, I punched in a code into a keypad. The green light came on and I pulled the lever next to it, raising the bunk. I store a lot of gear under the bunk, but what I was after was in a large chest in the forward part of the storage area. I unlocked it and removed a long fly rod case and two smaller boxes.

I carried all three to the big settee in the salon and opened the first of the smaller boxes. I opened my sea bag, which I'd already packed my clothes into, and reached into the box and pulled out a smaller case. Opening it, I pulled out my nine millimeter Sig Sauer semiautomatic. I jacked the slide and inspected it, even though I knew it was unloaded and clean. I released the slide and put it back in the case. I then took out three magazines and, opening the second box, I took out a box of cartridges and loaded all three mags. I inserted one of the magazines in the pistol, then placed it and the two other magazines back in the case and put the case in the sea bag.

The second case in the box held a Beretta nine millimeter and three mags. I did the same thing with it, then put it and the two spare mags back in the case and also stored it in the sea bag.

I put the empty box on the bench seat and opened the fly rod case. Inside was an M40A3 sniper rifle, with a mounted U.S. Optics MST-100 scope, designed by John Unertl. It's a modernized version of the M40A1 rifle that I used very effectively in the Corps. I bought it a few years back and fell in love with it. I inspected the rifle, then loaded the two magazines with Lapua .308 moly-coated boat tails from the box. I placed the rifle and magazines back in the fly rod case, closed the sea bag and strapped the case to it.

Odds were that I wouldn't need any of the firearms. However, I always thought it was crazy to go out on the water without protection. Call me paranoid.

I took the two boxes back to the stateroom and put them back inside the large chest. As an afterthought, I pulled out two other small boxes and carried them to the salon. Opening the first, I removed a small case and opened it. Inside was a Night Spirit XT-3 night vision monocular. I replaced the batteries and put it back in the box, opened the sea bag and stored it inside. The second box contained six grenades, two white smoke, two black smoke and two high explosive. *No need to inspect those,*

I thought, and stuck the whole box in the sea bag and closed it. I took the other box back and put it in the chest, closed it and lowered the bunk.

Returning to the bridge, I switched off the autopilot and sat back, enjoying the feel of the big boat gently skimming the flat water. The tanker was within sight now, moving to the north and well out of my way. The radar showed only a couple of small craft, heading out of Northwest Passage. Shrimp boats, most likely, judging by the size and speed of the images on the radar.

I kicked back and just enjoyed the ride while chasing the sun westward. I glanced down to the foredeck, half expecting to see Pescador down there. When I looked at the hatch to the stateroom, I thought of Alex. I suddenly realized that it was the first time I'd thought about her all day. In fact, since yesterday. Maybe getting back in the game, helping someone, was just what I needed. Just how long is the grief process? We'd been friends for a year, then she left for a year. When she came back, we took the friendship much further and were actually married within a week. I knew it was right, at the time. I lost her on our wedding day. Worst part was, I wasn't even with her when she passed, being laid up and unconscious in the same hospital, with a hole in my lung. That was nearly four months ago, but it seemed like a lifetime already.

An hour later, I was tying up in Oceanside Marina. After getting all the lines secure, I connected the water line and shore power and turned on the water heater. A long, hot shower was in order. Then I was going to go over to Key West for supper and a few beers.

CHAPTER SEVEN:
Saturday Night, Rock and Roll

After my shower I powered up my laptop to see what I could find out about Santiago. My First Mate, Jimmy Saunders, is some kind of computer whiz and set up a secure satellite Internet link on the boat. I ran a few searches for Carlos Santiago, but didn't find much. He owned a successful chain of laundromats in Miami, which was about it.

My cell phone was in a cupboard when I finally found it. Hell, I didn't even remember how long ago I'd put it there. The battery was dead, so I plugged the charging cord in and turned it on. I had sixteen missed calls, four text messages, and two voicemail messages.

I checked the text messages first. One was from Deuce. He's a DHS agent and former Navy SEAL. The men who killed my wife had also murdered his dad, Russ. Two of those men died in Miami, when we found Alex. The one that killed Russ is nothing but a pile of bones on an island about two miles from my house. Deuce's message was short and to the point, as he usually is. It said, 'Call me. Mission on the near horizon.' The other three text messages were from Julie, my friend Rusty Thurman's daughter. All three said pretty much the same thing. A lawyer was trying to reach me and to call her or Rusty as soon as possible. A lawyer? What was that about?

I pushed the button to listen to the voicemails. The first one was from Julie, restating that a lawyer wanted to see me and urging me to come down to Marathon to visit her and Rusty. The second voicemail caught my attention. It was from the taxi driver, Lawrence. He said that Santiago was in town and staying at the Casablanca, an expensive hotel on Duval Street, just four blocks from Blue Heaven. I smiled. Then I called Lawrence. He picked up on the first ring and I told him who I was, and could he pick me up at the marina in half an hour?

"Ya sar," he said. "Miss Tina been askin bout yuh," he added with a chuckle.

I closed the phone and set it on the table, then went to the head to shave and shower. Wearing black jeans and a dark blue guayabera shirt, I went up to the bridge and looked out over the marina, toward Trent's house, wondering what these next few days were going to bring. I had tonight and tomorrow to find out all I could about Santiago and his operation, not a lot of time. I debated calling Deuce, but decided against it. If he had a mission coming up, he'd be busy. Sooner or later, if he really needed my help on it, he'd show up here. Ten minutes later, I saw Lawrence's big black sedan turn into the parking lot. I climbed down and went to the dock. He spotted me and pulled the car up to the gate and got out.

"Dat yuh boat dere, Cap'n?" he asked.

"Yeah, the Rampage at the end," I replied.

"Ver nice," he said.

"Thanks. You had dinner yet, Lawrence?"

"No sar, was guh get a bite, aftuh I drop yuh off."

"Join me at the Blue Heaven. My treat. But, drop the sir. Call me Jesse."

"Well, thank yuh, Jesse. I will."

We climbed into his taxi and he took the short route to Blue Heaven, on North Roosevelt. I noticed he didn't turn the meter on.

"Thanks for the message about Santiago. Got any idea why he's in town?" I asked.

"Nah, he heah bout ever udder week," Lawrence said.

Minutes later, we pulled to the curb about half a block from Blue Heaven. Finding a parking spot anywhere in Key West is problematic. You take whatever's available. Lawrence and I walked to the archway into the yard and then across the yard to the bar. Tina was on duty and smiled when she saw us. It was still early, but there were already quite a few people at the tables around the yard. Inside, I could hear live acoustical music. Sounded like a solo act, a guy singing about being lucky to live by blue water. It sure sounded good to me.

"Hi, Jesse," Tina said, setting two cold Red Stripes in front of us as we sat down at the bar.

"Thanks, Tina. How's the best bartending deputy in Key West doing on this beautiful evening?"

"Fine, thank you," she said. Then leaning in closer, she said, "I want to apologize for last night. I had no idea you recently lost your wife. Frankie told me after you left."

"Don't worry about it," I said. "I'd like to talk to you, later. When you get off work."

"Sure!" she said, smiling warmly. "But, that won't be for a couple of hours. You hungry?"

"I tink we both be hungry," Lawrence said.

We each gave her our orders and she slid the slips through the window. There was a corner table that was just opening up and I nodded toward it, to Lawrence.

We walked over and waited while the busboy wiped it down, then took a seat, me against one wall and Lawrence against another. I told him the whole story about why I was here in Key West, the trouble that Trent was having and my plans to try to get him out of it.

"Yuh tink yuh can do all dat?" he asked.

"With a little help from friends," I replied.

Our food came, brought by one of the waitresses. She was friendly, but professional. Tina was busy with several tourists that had just come into the yard. The singer inside was now singing about a small island. I listened for a minute, as did Lawrence. I liked the easy sound and thought I might go inside later and hear more. The waitress delivered our check and glancing at it, I laid three twenties on it.

"Good music, good beer, ahn good fellowship," Lawrence said. "But I and I got to get bock to di streets, mon."

"Be careful, Lawrence. Call me if you hear anything that might help me and Trent out."

"Ya sar, I will," he said as he stood up and headed toward the gate.

I drank my beer and watched the people in the yard. The guys at the bar were starting to get a little loud and obnoxious. I got up from the table and walked to the corner of the bar. Tina had another cold one sitting there before I even got on my stool.

"You and Lawrence seem to be getting along pretty well," she said.

"He's a nice man," I said. "Reminds me of an old Jamaican man I know in Marathon."

"He is," she said. Then she headed back to the tourist bunch, who seemed to be drinking pretty fast. In fact, at the pace they were tossing down shots it didn't look like they were going to make it through the night.

I looked around the yard at the other people, mostly tourist couples from a cruise ship, I guessed. The singer inside said he was going to do a Jimmy Buffett song and when he started into a slow ballad, the crowd inside about went nuts. I caught part of it, where he sang about a Blue Heaven rendezvous. No wonder the crowd ratcheted it up a notch. Just then, I heard a loud smacking sound and turned to see one of the drunks trying to climb across the bar, grabbing for Tina while holding one hand to the side of his face.

Without thinking, I launched myself off the stool and pushed through the guy's buddies, grabbing him by the collar of his shirt. I yanked him backwards and he landed solidly on his butt in the sand. I felt someone grab my right shoulder and instinctively swiveled my body toward him, loosening the guy's grip, while I brought my right elbow around and took him in the side of the head. He landed in a heap next to the first guy.

Stepping backwards along the bar, I put all of them in front of me. Two were still on the ground, but their three friends were arranged in front of me and they didn't look happy. Two were medium height and a little overweight, but the guy in the middle was at least six one and over two hundred pounds of mostly muscle.

I said, "If you boys help your friends up and walk out now, nobody else will get hurt."

The guy that I elbowed wasn't going to be moving under his own power anytime soon, but the one Tina smacked was struggling to get to his feet. He said, "You're the one gonna get hurt, old man."

He was on his feet then, reaching into his pocket. He came up with a Buck knife, flipping it open dramatically. Guys with knives are usually very overconfident and this guy was about as typical as they come. He lunged with the knife in his right hand. I took his knife hand with my left, brought it high and landed a hard right to his solar plexus. A rush of air escaped his lungs as I took the back of his neck in my right hand, still holding his knife hand high. I stepped back toward the bar and as he came off balance, I shoved down hard on the back of his neck. His face hit the hard wooden armrest on the bar and he collapsed in the sand like a suddenly deflated parachute.

When faced with multiple opponents, you have to take out any with a weapon first, then go after the biggest. Usually the others will retreat once the big man is down. I stepped over the two men in the sand and with both arms raised wide, at shoulder level, I said, "Come on, guys. It doesn't have to be this way."

With my arms still stretched out wide, I took a long stride forward and head butted the big guy in the face. I heard a satisfying crunch as his nose broke, and felt something warm on my forehead. The forehead is a marvel of genetic evolutionary engineering. To protect the brain, it's harder than even the toughest bare-knuckle brawler's fists. Few fighters expect a head butt.

The big man crumpled to his knees, both hands over his ruined face. I turned to the last two men and growled, "Do you guys want to walk out, or be carried out?"

They were both ass over teakettle, trying to get the big guy up so they could drag the other two out. A bouncer appeared through the door just as the five guys got through the gate and several people at the nearby tables started clapping. The bouncer walked toward me in a menacing way, but Tina stepped in front of him and put a hand on his chest.

"It's alright, Jared," she said. "He's a friend. One of those guys grabbed my boob and I slapped him. Then he tried to come across the bar. Jesse stopped them."

Then she turned to me and grabbing a clean bar rag, said, "Oh my God, Jesse. You're bleeding."

As she started wiping the blood from my forehead and face, I said, "It's not my blood. It's that big dude's."

She wiped the rest of the blood from my face, and finding no injury she looked up at me and said, "Thanks, but you didn't have to do that."

"Yeah," Jared said. "That's my job."

"Sorry," I said. "You weren't here."

He gave me a hard look, but then softened a little and said to Tina, "Are you okay?"

"I'm fine," she replied. "Jared, meet Captain Jesse McDermitt, from Marathon. Jesse, this is Jared Williams."

I extended my hand and the man hesitated, then stepped forward and took it. Young guys, especially the big ones, will try to crush your hand. I guess it's an alpha male thing. I was expecting it and took his hand firmly, with a deep grip, so that he didn't have my fingers in his grip. He tried to squeeze, but he wasn't in an advantageous position.

After a second he released his grip, then surprised me with a smile and said, "Any friend of Miss La Mons. Thanks, man."

He turned and went back inside. I took a closer look at his retreating form. His shoulders were wide enough that he nearly had to turn to get through the door. If he had any training, and he likely did, he'd be a tough one to handle.

"Jared's our mother hen," Tina said. "He watches over the waitresses like we were his sisters."

"Big guy," I said, nodding my head. "I'd sure hate to have to tangle with him."

"Thanks again," she said. "I gotta get back behind the bar. Why don't you go listen to Scott play? I'll be off in a few minutes, then I'll join you."

I nodded and headed through the door Jared had just gone through, the music getting much louder on the other side. It was still early, by Key West standards, but the place was more than half full. I found a seat against the back wall, away from the crowd, and sat down. Jared was standing in the back corner on the other side and noticed me take a seat. He stepped forward as a waitress walked by, took her elbow, and whispered in her ear. She looked my way and then walked over, placing a napkin on the table in front of me.

"Red Stripe," I said quite loudly, just as the music stopped.

We both laughed for a second and she said, "Be right back, Captain."

Okay, I thought, *either I'm wearing a Captain's hat, and I'm not, or the communication between workers here is very good*. Minutes later, she brought my beer and a glass. *Well*, I thought, *maybe not perfect communication*.

I sat for the next forty-five minutes listening to the singer and watching the crowd of people. I decided the mixture was probably half and half, tourists and locals. When Tina walked over, I stood and pulled out a chair for her.

"Thank you, Jesse," she said smiling. She'd changed out of her Blue Heaven tee shirt and was wearing a short pleated skirt, with a floral design, mostly red and blue, and a skin-tight dark blue tank top under a sheer white long-sleeve blouse.

The waitress came over and smiled at Tina. She ordered a diet Coke and I asked for another Red Stripe. When the waitress left, she said, "So, how long have you been charter fishing?"

"Not long," I said. "Started about six years ago, but I don't take out a lot of charters."

"Hard to make a boat payment if you don't charter," she said.

"I don't need much. My boats and house are paid for. My only bills are fuel and my cell phone, which I rarely even turn on."

"I'd love to see it," she said. "I've never been on a boat before."

"You live on an island over a hundred miles from the mainland and you've never been on a boat?"

"I just moved here from Nebraska last winter. Guess I'd just had enough of snow and sub-freezing temperatures."

"That's quite a move," I said.

"I'd just gotten out of a bad relationship. I bought a map of the whole country and studied it to find the furthest place from Lincoln. It was either here or Caribou, Maine, which was a little further away."

"Caribou's loss is Key West's gain," I said.

We talked for a while, but when the waitress came and asked if I wanted another beer, I told her no. Then I asked Tina if she'd like to go for a walk. I left a twenty on the table under the empty bottle, and we got up and went out into the cooling night. The smell of jasmine and frangipani filled the air as we walked away from Blue Heaven. We wound our way through the quieter streets going south on Thomas, then east on Olivia, toward Old Town. She took my arm as we walked across Duval Street and asked me what I was really doing in Key West.

I looked down into her eyes and decided I could trust her. So, I told her all about Trent's problem with Santiago and how I was trying to get him out of it.

"He was at the bar last night," she said. "The drug dealer I told you about. That was Santiago. Be careful, I hear he's pretty ruthless."

We walked in silence for a few minutes. There was still a bit of foot traffic on this part of the island, but not so many cars. "Would you keep your eyes open for me and call me if you see him, or hear anything about him?" I asked.

"Are you asking in my capacity as a bartender, or a Reserve Deputy?" she asked.

"I've learned that bartenders, waitresses, waiters and taxi drivers know more about what's going on around town than any of the cops," I said.

"I'll do what I can, but I've only seen him a few times." She continued to tell me all she knew about him, but said that most of it was just gossip.

We'd walked quite a way, zigzagging through the narrow streets of Old Town, and I had no idea where we were going, if anywhere. I was just enjoying walking down the quiet lanes, lined with old-style Conch houses. Large oak and gumbo limbo trees lined the streets.

She stopped at a gate in a white picket fence and said, "This is where I live. Would you like to come in for a while?"

I had to admit, I was tempted. Instead I said, "I'd like to, but I don't think I should." Her smile turned into a frown and without thinking I added, "Why don't you come by the marina tomorrow and we'll go for a boat ride."

She smiled brightly and asked, "You have your boat down here?"

"Yeah," I said. "Not really much of a choice. *The Beast*, that's my car, probably wouldn't survive the trip."

"I'd love to," she said. "What time? I'm off all day tomorrow."

"I usually get up before sunrise, so any time is fine. Do you know where Oceanside Marina is, on Stock Island?"

She nodded and I said, "They have a private, gated dock there. Just come to the gate and push the little button for slip number fourteen and I'll come down and let you through."

"It's a date, then," she said. "See you in the morning." Then she stood up on her toes to kiss me on the cheek before opening the little gate and walking up to the door of her little house.

When she got up to the porch she called back, "What should I wear?"

"Supposed to be warm, a little over eighty," I said. "Shorts-and-tee-shirt weather. Bathing suit if you want to swim, or get some sun. The water will be a little cold, though. About seventy degrees."

"Good night," she said. "See you in the morning."

"Night," I called back.

I suddenly realized I had no idea where I was. I knew I was somewhere on the east side of Duval Street, in Old Town. A quick glance up at the nearly full moon gave me a direction, so I started walking toward Duval Street. If anywhere, that's where I could find a cab. Turns out, I was almost a mile off of Duval.

Joining the throngs of people on the most famous street in Florida, I walked north toward the busier end, near the docks. I stopped at Irish Kevin's Bar for a cold Guinness and to call Lawrence. It was very crowded inside. I made my way to the bar and ordered my ale, then handed Lawrence's card to the bartender and asked if he could call me a cab.

"What's ye name, mate?" he asked in a decidedly Irish accent.

"Jesse McDermitt," I replied.

"An Irishman, eh? Guinness on the house, mate. Me name's Paul, Paul McGahee. Of the Gregor Highlands clan."

I reached across the bar, took the offered hand and said, "Pleased to meet you, Paul. Looks like Irish Kevin has a gold mine here."

"Thank ye, lad. 'Tis doing okay, I reckon. Ye don't look like na tourist. From up the Keys?" he asked, dialing the phone.

"Yeah, out of Marathon," I replied, wondering yet again what my tell was.

He turned away for a minute, covering an ear to talk into the phone, then hung up and turned back, saying, "Lawrence'll be here in a wee bit."

I thanked him and even though he'd offered the free beer, I laid a five on the bar and walked over by the door, so I could see outside. Minutes later, Lawrence pulled up. I finished the beer, went out and got in the front seat.

"Evenin' sar," he said. "Callin' it a early night?"

"Yeah," I replied. "Taking Tina for a boat ride at first light."

"Knew it, mon!" he exclaimed while weaving down Duval, dodging and braking for pedestrians and scooters. He turned left on Eaton Street, taking a shortcut through Old Town.

"Nothing like that," I said. "She mentioned she'd never been on a boat before. That's all."

"Ya, mon," he said with a huge grin.

We rode on, crossing the Palm Avenue Causeway, then south on First and east on Truman. Crossing the bridge to Stock Island, Lawrence said, "I ask roun bout Santiago, mon. Mostly gossip, but a frien say dat di mon stood an watch as his goons near beat his brudder to deat. He a bod mon, fuh shore."

We got to the marina a minute later and I gave Lawrence a ten and told him if he learned anything more, like where the man liked to eat, or any habits he had, to call me. Then I got out, walked to the private dock, opened it and climbed aboard my boat.

The lights in the harbor were low, but the moon was bright. Instead of going below I climbed up to the bridge, sat down and looked out over the low island toward home, wondering how Trent, his family and Pescador were doing.

Turning on my phone, I saw that Deuce had called again, but left no message. I called the number Trent had given me and he picked up on the first ring.

"Jesse," he said. "I was just debating calling you. A chopper landed here earlier this afternoon."

"Who was it?" I asked.

"No idea, we were anchored on Raccoon Key so the kids could swim," he replied, then added with a laugh, "Hey, I figured out why you named that mutt Pescador. We had his catch for supper."

I laughed with him, then asked, "That chopper have any markings?"

"Couldn't make it out real well. We were a couple miles off. Looked like it mighta been Customs. It only stayed a minute, then flew off toward the southeast."

"Don't worry about it. It was a friend of mine. How are you guys doing up there?"

"Couldn't be better," he said. "The kids love the dock and the dog. We're camping out. Built a nice fire in the clearing with some of the deadfalls you piled up."

"Okay, well, call me if you need anything. I'm going out to the Tortugas tomorrow morning with a friend. Then calling Doc tomorrow evening."

"Sunday evening?" he asked. "You'll probably catch him and Nikki at the Harley dealer, or over at Hog's

Breath, depending on the time. Nikki works there and Bob turns wrenches there on the weekend. A bunch of local bikers get together at Hog's Breath on Sunday afternoon."

"Thanks," I said. "Want me to tell him anything?"

"Just tell him I hope he'll stick this out. He's a good Mate and replacing him will be a tough task."

"I'll do that," I said. "Don't worry, Carl. I'll come up with something to get this turd fondler off your back. Y'all just enjoy yourselves."

I ended the call, then decided to call Deuce. It rang four times and I hung up. As I started to get up, it chimed, Deuce calling me back.

"Hey, Deuce," I said.

"You're still a hard man to find, Jarhead."

"Well, if it was easy, a Squid could do it," I replied, laughing. Rivalries between services is common, but between Marines and Sailors, it reaches epic legendary status.

"Where the hell are you?" he asked.

"I'm in Key West for a little while. I heard you landed at my house earlier. What can I do for you?"

"How'd you know I'd been there?" he asked.

"A friend spotted you in a Customs chopper. Not very good spycraft, buddy."

"I'm not even going to ask where your friend was when he spotted me. Probably laying right under the chopper in a freaking ghillie suit."

"Close, but not that close," I said. "What's up?"

"Need to talk to you," he said. "Face to face. We've been asking all over Key West, but you islanders are a tight-lipped bunch."

"You're here? Who's we?"

"Me and Julie," he replied. "We just checked in at the Double Tree and were about to go back out and look some more."

"You have wheels?"

"Yeah, where are you?"

"See Susan at the desk," I said playing with him a little. "She'll have written directions even a Swab could follow."

I ended the call and pulled up the number to the Double Tree and called. Susan was on duty, as I expected. I said, "Hi, Susan. This is Jesse McDermitt."

"Hi, Captain," she said. I could almost hear her smile over the phone.

"Hey, could you do me a favor?" I asked. "Do you know where Oceanside Marina is?"

She did, so I told her what I wanted her to do. She wrote it down and I asked her to read it back.

"Go back the way you came," she said, "until you pass where you feel most at home. Then keep going until you see what was on my shoulder, but not on yours. Turn windward and make your course ninety degrees for half a click. Then make your course one hundred and thirty-five degrees for one click. Then look for where seals and dogs mingle. Go to the private dock and punch the button for fourteen."

"Perfect," I said. "A man and woman will come down and ask you for directions to where I am. Give them that, okay."

"Well, sure, Jesse," she said. "But it makes no sense."

"It will to him," I said.

I ended the call, went down to the galley and put a six-pack in a cooler, then carried it back up to the bridge. A few minutes later, I could see headlights moving slowly toward the marina gate, then accelerate into the parking lot. It was Alex's Jeep. Since I didn't have much use for it, I'd given it to Julie. I felt a pang of pain for a moment, then pushed it aside with the knowledge that it's just a tool to move people, nothing more.

Opening the gate as they walked up, Julie gave me a big hug. "Very funny, mister."

"Thought you'd get a kick out of it," I said, shaking Deuce's big hand. "How've you been?"

"Good," he said. "Almost had me at the end, until I saw the sign for Oceanside."

"I didn't get that part at all," Julie said. "Until Russell explained that Oceanside, California, was a little town between a Marine base and the SEAL base. How are you doing, Jesse?"

"Just fine," I said. "Y'all come aboard. I have some cold ones up on the bridge."

We climbed up to the bridge and I passed a cold Hatuey to each of them. "So, what's on your mind, Deuce?"

Deuce looked at Julie, then said, "Right now, all I can say is we have a mission and the Director thinks you're the man to take us in. Ever been to Cuba?"

"Americans aren't allowed to go to Cuba," I reminded him.

"We have special dispensation, you might say. All you have to do is get us to within two miles of shore."

"That's still ten miles inside of Cuban waters," I said. "What's the target?"

Deuce looked at Julie, who rolled her eyes and said, "Do you have any wine down there, Jesse?"

"Sure, there's several bottles in the wine cooler, down in the galley. Help yourself."

Once she climbed down and went through the hatch to the salon, Deuce said, "Man, I hate this. How the hell did you do it with your first two wives?"

"Pretty much like we just did with Julie. It's not healthy, man. Better to just not talk about it at all. Who's the target?"

"A drug smuggler, also suspected of arms smuggling. He's moving a great deal of marijuana, coke, and meth into the States through Key West and Miami. A legit businessman in Miami, by the name of Carlos Santiago."

"You're shitting me," I said. "Man, we gotta quit working like this."

"What do you mean?" he asked.

"Did Jimmy and Angie tell you why I was down here?" I asked.

"Yeah, something to do with helping Angie's dad. She said he'd been roped into smuggling marijuana on his shrimp boat. Wait. You don't mean..."

"Yeah, the guy who's forcing Trent to keep smuggling is your guy, Santiago."

"You're kidding," Deuce said.

Four months ago, when Deuce and I met, he had come to me only to ask that I take him to a reef to spread his dad's ashes. At the time, he had an upcoming mission to take down a terrorist smuggling operation, but it turned out that the people involved were also the ones that killed both his dad and my wife.

"So," I said, "If you and your guys take him down, Trent's off the hook."

"Our intel says he's in Cuba this weekend," he said, "And he makes a trip there about every month."

"Your intel is wrong," I said. "He's right here in Key West."

"Not possible," he said. "Where'd you hear this?"

"I have my own intel community," I said. "Apparently more reliable than Uncle Sam's."

Just then my cell phone chimed. I looked and saw that it was Lawrence. "Hang on, I gotta get this."

I opened the phone and said, "Hey, Lawrence, got something?" I listened for a minute, then said, "Thanks, I owe you."

I ended the call and grinned at Deuce. "Santiago is partying at the Green Parrot, right now. Lines of coke on the table, with hot and cold running women. You could ride over there, pop him and put him under the jail. Problem solved."

Deuce shook his head. "We want him on arms smuggling. Who's this Lawrence guy?" he asked.

Julie called up from the cockpit, "Are y'all done talking? Can I come back up?"

"Yeah," I called down. Then to Deuce, I said, "Lawrence is my cab driver. Never underestimate cabbies and bartenders as good intel sources. They're invisible, but see and hear everything."

Julie climbed back up and took a seat on the bench next to Deuce. "You have a nice selection down there," she said.

"So?" Deuce asked, "Are you in?"

I thought it over for a minute and asked, "When?"

"A week to ten days," he said. "How are you playing it with Trent?"

"He and his family are at my house. That's who spotted you. I'm skippering his shrimp boat, starting Monday morning."

Deuce thought about it for a few minutes while he took a long pull on his beer and looked out over the marina. "Think you might be able to cozy up to him?"

"Well, my initial plan was to just blow him off and say no. What's on your mind?"

"I'll have to get back to you on that," he said. "Keep your damn phone turned on. I'll call you tomorrow, after I talk to the boss."

"I'll be incommunicado tomorrow until later in the evening," I said. "Taking a friend out to Fort Jefferson. Send me an email if you can't reach me by phone. I'll plug the laptop into the stereo speaker to hear the chime."

We talked about things in Marathon and the changes I'd made on the island for another twenty minutes. Then Julie said they had to go, it was getting late. I walked them down to the gate and shook hands with Deuce, and Julie gave me another big hug.

"You better get down to the *Anchor* soon and see Dad. Oh, that reminds me, there's a lawyer looking for you. Here's his card," she said, handing me a business card.

"Y'all run along," I said. "I'll give the guy a call tomorrow."

They were halfway to the gate when I remembered and called out, "Hey, Deuce. Does the name Douzaine Lingots Dior mean anything to you?"

Deuce turned around and said, "It's not a name, Jesse. Douzaine lingots d'or is French for dozen gold bars. Why?"

CHAPTER EIGHT:
Fun in the Sun

I woke up about an hour before dawn to the sound of the coffeemaker gurgling in the galley. Padding barefoot across the salon deck in my boxers, I poured coffee into a heavy mug with the Marine Recon logo on it and went outside. I've always been an early riser, even as a kid. The hour or two before dawn is a very calm and peaceful time of day. I took my coffee up to the bridge and sat down at the helm. Looking across the bridge and out at the western sky I could see the constellation of Orion the Hunter, on his side as though fallen, slowly sinking toward the horizon.

Since it was still way too early for any lawyer to be in his office, I called the number on the card Julie had given me last night, curious about what a lawyer wanted to talk to me about. As I figured, I got the voicemail and left a message, telling him that I'd be unavailable by phone most of the day and asking him to email me what it was he wanted to talk to me about. Then I left my email address and repeated it a second time.

I was almost done with my first cup of coffee and was climbing down to get a second cup when the bell on the dock rang, signaling someone was at the gate for me. I hadn't seen any cars pull into the lot, though. Looking down the dock, I could barely make out a woman on a bicycle at the gate. *Damn*, I thought, *she's early*. I dropped quickly to the deck, almost leaped through the salon and grabbed a pair of cargo pants and a tee shirt from the dresser in the stateroom. Struggling to put the shorts and shirt on, I banged my toe on the steps, going back up to the salon. I finally limped down the dock to the gate and opened it for her.

"I didn't expect you this early," I said.

"I'm sorry. I didn't wake you, did I?"

"No, no," I replied. "I was on the bridge, having coffee, but I wasn't even dressed yet."

"You drink coffee in your birthday suit?"

"Well, sometimes, yeah," I said. "But I had my skivvies on, just now."

"Your skivvies?"

"Marine slang for boxer shorts," I said. Then to change the subject, I asked, "Would you like some coffee?"

"What should I do about my bike? I didn't even think about that when I left. Guess I should have taken a cab."

"Bring it over to the dock. Nobody will bother it inside the gate. You don't have a car?"

I walked her bike to the storage box at the foot of my slip, then helped her step over the transom.

"No," she said. "I sold it when I moved down here. Seemed wasteful to have a car on an island that's less than six square miles. Your boat is beautiful."

We went into the galley and I poured us both a cup of coffee. I showed her around the galley and salon area, then we went up to the bridge. She asked all kinds of questions about my boat, which I was happy to answer. Then she asked about my time in the Corps, which I'm a little reluctant to talk about. She sensed that and steered the conversation back to my boat, asking, "So, where are you going to take me?"

"I thought that since you've never been on a boat, you might like to see Fort Jefferson."

"Where's that?" she asked. "I've never heard of it."

"It's an old fort, built to protect the shipping lanes to the Caribbean right after we bought Florida from Spain. It's about eighty miles west of here."

"Eighty miles? I thought Key West was the last island in the Keys."

"Last one you can get to by car," I said. "There's quite a few others between here and the Dry Tortugas."

"How long will it take to get there?"

"Not long," I said. "Unless we get caught by a lot of traffic lights."

She looked at me for a second, then punched me on the shoulder. "I almost fell for that."

I rubbed the place where she'd punched me and said, "You ready to go?"

She nodded enthusiastically, so I turned around and started the engines, which settled into a throaty rumble. "I'll be right back. Gotta cast off the lines."

Climbing down to the cockpit, I vaulted over the transom to the dock and untied the mooring lines. A minute later, I was back on the bridge. The sun was just starting to purple the eastern sky, so I switched the bridge lights from white to red to allow my eyesight to adjust. I turned on the radar, sonar, VHF radio, and running lights. I turned on the GPS and selected the coordinates for Fort Jefferson, which I'd saved before going to bed last night.

Bumping the engines into gear momentarily, then shifting both to neutral again, the boat eased forward. When the stern was near the end of the dock, I reversed the starboard engine to allow the big boat to turn tightly between the two docks. Once we were clear and headed south toward the channel I switched on the big spotlight on the roof of the bridge. It was already facing forward, barely illuminating the pulpit on the bow, but casting a long beam of light out on the water. It easily picked up the markers going all the way out to the main channel. A few minutes later, we were past the last marker and in the open ocean, with barely a swell rolling under the keel.

"Hold on," I said and pushed both throttles about halfway. The bow came up as the *Revenge* gathered speed, finally coming back down as she got up on plane. It's a great feeling, when a boat goes from cutting through the water to skimming over its surface. I never get tired of it.

I started a long, slow turn to the west and looked over at Tina in the second seat. She was grinning like the Cheshire cat. "How fast are we going?" she asked.

Looking at the knot meter and running the calculation in my head, I said, "About twenty-five miles per hour." Not wanting to frighten her, I added, "I can slow down if you want."

She looked over at me and said, "Can you go faster?"

I checked the radar and there was absolutely nothing ahead of us. Both temperature gauges indicated the engines were both warmed up, so I pushed the throttles further, but not all the way to the stops. The *Revenge* was built for the drug trade and her big eighteen-liter engines pushed the boat well beyond her cruising speed of twenty-six knots and I settled her to about forty knots. Faster than I liked to run to save fuel, but the lady wanted speed.

"Is forty-five fast enough?" I asked.

"Really? We're going that fast? It doesn't seem like it."

"Because we're sitting about as high as the roof of a house," I said. "I could use another cup of coffee. Take the helm for me. Would you like some more?"

"You want me to drive? I might hit someone."

I stood up and looked all around. "There's nobody to hit. I could turn on the auto pilot, if you'd rather not."

She slid over into the first seat and said, "What do I do?"

I pointed to the GPS and said, "See the line, here? If you stray too far away from it, an arrow will point you back. Or, just check the compass now and then and keep us on a course of about two hundred and sixty-five degrees. Third option, and my favorite, just pick a cloud up in front of us and head toward it. I'll be back in a minute."

I left her at the helm and climbed down to the galley to pour us both another cup. I took my time getting back up topside, to let her get a feel for it. When I did, I took the second seat, checked the compass and handed Tina the mug.

"This is great!" she exclaimed. "Nothing like my friends have told me."

"Your friends don't like boats?"

"Well," she said, "I don't think any of them have been in a boat like this. It's a frigging yacht."

"No, just a work boat. Even a small yacht would cost ten times what this one did."

I sat back and watched her enjoying the feel of the big boat under her control. She had her raven hair pulled back in a ponytail and was wearing a loose-fitting red blouse, cutoff blue jeans and flip-flops.

"There's a little more there," I said, pointing at the throttles, "if you want it."

Tina looked over at me, smiling, and then shoved the throttles to the stops. The big boat surged forward momentarily, reaching her top speed of forty-five knots in seconds. Tina slowly turned the wheel to the right, then back to the left.

"How fast is this?" she asked.

I pointed to the digital knot meter on the GPS and said, "Multiply by one point one five. About fifty-two miles per hour. You're really enjoying yourself, aren't you?"

"Yes, absolutely," she said. "And you do this for a living?"

Pulling back on the throttles, I dropped our speed to about twenty-eight knots, just slightly above the best cruising speed, and said, "Not often, lately. Truth is, this week was the first time the *Revenge* has been out in four months. We can't run wide open like that for long. Even at this speed, we're burning about seventy-five gallons an hour."

"Wow! That's a lot of gas. You don't work much?"

"We live on an island. No bills at all, except fuel and my cell phone, and I've thought about throwing it overboard quite a few times. My dog and I eat fish and lobster, mostly. Crab, on occasion. We have enough canned vegetables to last a year. I work when I need to and when I don't, I don't."

"You have a dog? And he likes fish?"

"He's a better fisherman than me," I said, grinning. "His name's Pescador. Right now, he's entertaining friends at our house for the week."

"Pescador? Is that Spanish?"

"It means fisherman. We better change seats, the approach to Fort Jefferson is coming up."

As we switched seats, Tina wriggling between me and the helm, she brushed against me and I could smell her hair. It didn't smell like perfume, just that kind of clean girl smell I like. The close proximity caused a stirring in me.

Settling back behind the helm, with Fort Jefferson just coming into view, to distract myself, I said, "It's the biggest brick structure in the western hemisphere, or so I've been told."

As we approached the ancient fort, I slowed, the stern lifted and the *Revenge* came down off plane. Tina stood up for a better view, placing one hand on my right shoulder and the other on the corner of the helm for balance, as we were now wallowing in the small rollers, gently rocking side to side as they went by under the keel.

"It's huge," she said. "What was it built for, way out here in the ocean?"

"I don't know all the history," I said. "But I heard that it was a place for the Navy to station one or two ships of the line, to protect the shipping lanes. If bad weather came up, the inner harbor could provide a safe haven for four or five ships. Later, the Union used it to keep Confederate prisoners. Many never left."

"It's not used for anything today?"

"No, it's a National Park now. Sometimes a wayward sailor will hole up here to get away from a tropical storm."

We slowly idled around the east side of Bush Key, then circled the north side of the Fort and around to the west side, following the same channel that seventeenth-century mariners had used, gliding into the little harbor. The docks were all empty, not a soul in sight. Looked like we had the island to ourselves, at least for now.

As I pulled up to one of the docks, I said, "This is going to be a little tricky. Think you can handle the helm if we drift away from the dock before I can get a line on one of the davits?"

"I can try," Tina said. "Just tell me what to do."

"Sit here," I said. "You won't need to steer. If anything, I'll call up for you to shift either the right or left engine into forward or reverse."

"Sounds easy enough," she said. I checked again and we hadn't drifted, so I quickly climbed down the ladder and grabbed a fish gaff from the port side of the cockpit. I was able to hook one of the davits and, pulling the stern in close, I got a line on it. Hustling to the bow, I saw the boat had started to drift a little too far for me to reach the pier with the gaff, so I called up to Tina, "Put the right engine in forward and the left one in reverse. Hold that for two seconds and then shift both back to neutral."

She did as I instructed and the bow slowly swung toward the dock. Reaching out with the gaff, I hooked another davit and pulled the bow in and got a line on it. We were now secure.

"Okay," I said, "shut both engines off." It was suddenly very quiet, the only sound being the swish of the small waves breaking on the southern shore and an occasional gull, wheeling and crying overhead.

As I climbed back up to the bridge, Tina looked all around, then said, "Kind of spooky, but beautiful."

Looking at her, I said, "Yeah, I was thinking the exact same thing." She looked over at me and, realizing I was talking about her, she punched me on the shoulder again.

"Spooky?" she asked.

I laughed. Something I hadn't done a lot of in the last few months. "Yeah," I said. "You seem an open book, but there's still a mysteriousness I can't quite put a finger on."

"That'd be from my dad's side. He was French Creole, born and raised in southern Louisiana. His family had been there for many generations."

"And he left there for Nebraska?" I asked. "That's quite a change in scenery."

"His ancestors were fishermen, but he wanted to farm. He joined the Army, fought in Korea and when he got out, he never went back to Louisiana. Headed straight for the heartland and bought a farm. That's where he met Mom."

"A Cajun girl from Nebraska," I said. "Spooky."

She looked around again, then said, "Shall we go ashore?"

"Alright. I put together a little picnic lunch for later. But I have to catch the main course first. Let's go."

I climbed back down the ladder to the cockpit, then helped her down the last few steps, lifting her easily and setting her gently on the deck. I checked my phone and sure enough, no signal.

"Before we go ashore, I need to check something," I said. "Come inside and we'll get a cooler with some drinks while I do that."

In the salon, I got a small cooler and filled it with ice, several bottles of water and as an afterthought, the bottle of Beaujolais that Julie had opened the night before and two wine glasses. Then I opened my laptop on the settee and powered it up.

"There's no cell signal out here. You won't get the Internet," she said.

"I have a satellite link," I said. "I'm expecting an important message. If you'll take that cooler to the dock, I'll be right there."

I had one email, but it wasn't from Deuce. I opened it and saw that it was from the lawyer. He wrote that he was a probate attorney and needed my signature on some documents concerning Alex's estate. No idea what that was about, but it was going to have to wait.

I closed the laptop, plugged the headphone jack into the boat's stereo speaker system and picked up my fly rod case, heading out to where Tina waited on the dock. The sun was high now and it was warmer, already over eighty, as we walked to the small, sandy beach. "I'd like to get some sun," she said. "Do you mind?"

Do I mind watching a beautiful woman undress? Is she wearing a bathing suit under her clothes? These thoughts swirled through my mind, but all I could manage to say as she started unbuttoning her blouse was, "Um, no, go right ahead."

She shrugged off her blouse, folding it and putting it in an oversized handbag. She was wearing a bathing suit, thankfully. Not much of one, though. She unbuttoned her shorts and wiggled out of them, completely unaware of what her actions were doing to me. Folding the shorts and putting them in the bag also, she arched her back, spreading her arms wide and looking up so that the sun shone full on her face. *Maybe she was aware*, I thought as we walked along the sand.

"What's in the case?" she asked.

"This?" I said, lifting the fly rod case. "It's how we're going to catch lunch."

"Can you catch lobster with it?"

Laughing, I replied, "Lobster, she says. So, you want lobster, Miss La Mons?"

"You mean, you really can catch lobster with it?"

"Not with this," I replied, with a chuckle. "But, if the lady wants lobster, lobster it is. Let's carry this stuff over to the sandbar and I'll run back to the boat and get my mask and fins."

We walked along the sandy beach to the narrow sandbar that separates the fort from Bush Key. On the north side of the sandbar, we spread out a blanket and set the cooler in the sand next to it. There wasn't a breath of wind on the water. The small bay on the north side of the sandbar was flat and reflected the puffy white clouds in the distance, like a polished mirror.

"Hard to believe such a beautiful place exists so close to Key West and I never even heard of it," she said.

"Key West is close to a lot of small uninhabited islands like this," I said. "Several years ago, the state tried to sell a lot of the smaller ones, but not a lot of people were interested. That's when I bought mine."

"You own a whole island?" she asked incredulously.

"It's really tiny," I said. "A couple of acres at high tide. Make yourself at home and I'll be right back."

I ran back to the boat, hoping that I could make good on my promise. While lobsters were plentiful and currently in season, I'd never dived this harbor and had no idea what I'd find. Climbing back aboard the *Revenge*, I opened the hatch to the salon, raised the settee bench seat top and grabbed my mask, fins, heavy gloves, and a weight belt I use for skin diving. The water was only twelve to fifteen feet, so I didn't need anything more than that. I strapped a dive knife to the inside of the left calf, feeling lucky. I'd need it, if I caught a lobster.

I trotted back to the sandbar and Tina was lying on the small blanket, with a rolled-up towel under her head. I stopped short and looked her over more closely. Her skin was coppery brown. She apparently spent her days in the sun before work. The tiny bikini she had on was lime green, making her skin look all the more dark. Her flat belly and narrow waist gave her an athletic quality. I'm usually attracted to taller women, but, nonetheless, I was drawn to her. She turned her head then and noticed me staring.

"What's wrong?" she asked.

"Nothing," I said. Then I grinned and added, "Just admiring the beauty."

"Oh, come on, Jesse. Go get me a lobster!"

"Your wish is my command," I said as I pulled off my tee shirt and waded into the harbor. It wasn't ideal for skin diving, maybe seventy-three degrees. In waist-deep water, I put on my mask, fins, belt, and gloves, then disappeared below the surface. I followed the bottom, heading straight out away from shore. It dropped off quickly and, when I reached the turtle-grass-covered bottom, I turned to the left and followed the coral ledge. There were a lot of reef fish. Blennies, wrasses, even a couple of spotfin butterfly fish, swimming in a pair, as they usually do. Further ahead, I saw a large queen angelfish and right next to it, sticking out of an undercut part of the coral, was what I was looking for. Two long, spiny antennae poked out from under the ledge.

Normally, I can hold my breath for about a minute and a half. Two minutes with good preparation. I'd been down nearly a minute when I found the lobster. Approaching his hiding place from the side, I quickly thrust my hand in and under it. It never had a chance, but tried desperately to grab my hand and push me off its belly. Once I had a firm grip around the base of its tail, I could tell it was a big one, probably five or six pounds. More than enough for the two of us. Pushing away from the reef with my left hand, I pulled the lobster out from its lair and headed back up along the ledge, angling to the left.

I surfaced pretty much where I had gone down and Tina was sitting up, with her knees drawn up to her chest and her arms wrapped around them. "I thought you were in trouble, you were underwater a long time. Did you see anything?"

"Lots of pretty reef fish," I said. Then, lifting the big lobster out of the water, I added, "And lunch."

She jumped to her feet, her mouth falling open. "You actually caught one!"

"And he's big enough for both of us," I said. Wading out of the water, I tossed my gear and the bug up onto the sand, where it flipped its tail crazily for a minute before resigning itself to its fate. Tina ran down the little beach and leaped into my arms, knocking us both backwards into the water. For such a tiny woman, she was surprisingly strong. We rolled in the shallow water, until she had me on my back, with her legs wrapped tightly around my waist.

That's when she kissed me. A very passionate first kiss, her lips devouring mine, her tongue exploring my teeth and inside my mouth. She sat up, straddling me. Her hair was wet and dripping, as I reached up and pulled her back down. Her breasts pressed firmly against my chest and I kissed her again. Slower, but just as passionately.

We broke apart from our embrace and she said, "I've been wanting to do that since you walked into Blue Heaven the first time."

"We'd better get out of the water," I said. "Might get all the little fish excited." She laughed, then got up, and we walked to the blanket, holding hands.

"Can you show me how you do that?" she asked.

"Sure," I said and spun her around into my arms, wrapping my arms around her and kissing her again. She kissed me back, pressing her body tightly into mine.

Then she stepped back and slugged me in the chest, saying, "That's not what I meant."

"Can you swim?" I asked, as we knelt down on the blanket and shared the towel to dry our faces.

"Yes," she said. "I was on the swim team in college."

"Really?" I said. "Where'd you go to college?"

"I'm a Cornhusker," she said proudly. "Bachelor of Arts in Theater. Played on the tennis team, too."

"Wow," I said. "When I was looking at you lying here a few minutes ago, I thought you looked like an athlete."

"Where'd you go to college?" she asked.

"USMC, School of Hard Knocks," I replied, laughing. It felt good to laugh. "Seriously, though, I took a few classes in community college, but the Corps moved me around too much to finish anything."

She looked at the recent scar on my chest, then the scars on my side and left thigh. She reached out and traced each one, sending shivers down my spine. "Is that where you got those?" she asked.

"Yeah," I lied. Then changing the subject, I said, "If you want to learn to skin-dive, that's easy. Scuba diving's a little harder, but for an athlete, it's a cakewalk."

"I'd like to learn. Can you teach me?"

"Sure," I said. Then remembering why I was in Key West in the first place, I added, "I'll be busy during the week, but I might have next weekend free. I better get that lobster cleaned, before the crabs carry it off." I got up from the blanket and picked up the lobster, who started slapping its tail again, but with less enthusiasm.

"There's wine in the cooler," I said. "Why don't you pour us a glass, to get the salt taste out of our mouth? I'll be back in a sec."

I walked over toward the sea grapes on Bush Key, until I found a suitable limestone rock and knelt down. Placing the lobster on the rock, I unsheathed my dive knife and quickly removed the tail. Spiny lobster have spindly little legs and no claws. There's very little edible meat in the body and the tail is really the only part that's worth the effort. I tossed the carcass into the sea grapes, where I was sure a few lucky gulls and crabs would make short work of it.

When I got back to the blanket, Tina handed me a glass of wine as I put the big lobster tail in the cooler. "Beaujolais," she said. "My favorite, whenever I can get it. You don't like to talk about your time in the service, do you? My dad was the same way."

"I was in Recon," I said. "We went a lot of places and did a lot of things that aren't talked about in polite company."

She thought about it for a while and said, "Okay, I won't bring it up anymore."

We talked for an hour, then I suggested we head back to the boat for lunch. She gathered up the blanket and towel as I grabbed the cooler and fly rod case and we walked back to the boat. I rinsed my dive gear and put it away, while she set things up in the salon. I have a small charcoal grill that mounts into one of the rod holders on the gunwale in the cockpit, and I took it out and set it up, lighting the charcoal.

Tina came out and I told her she could grab a shower if she wanted while I grilled the lobster tail. I showed her the head, then went back out to split and butter the tail. A few minutes later, she came back out, dressed in a short white skirt and black tank top. I'd added two ears of corn to the coals and everything was about ready.

We enjoyed a great lunch and finished off the bottle of wine. The woman had a hearty appetite. We were sitting in the cockpit, watching a pair of sailboats on a broad reach, heading east about a mile south.

She got up and came over to me, sitting on my lap and resting her head on my shoulder. She kissed my neck then and whispered in my ear, "Are you going to show me your bedroom?"

I turned my face toward her and looked long into her dark, smoky eyes. "No," I said. "Not yet. It wouldn't be right. I want to, but it's too soon. I hope you understand."

There wasn't a trace of hurt on her face as she smiled and said, "Part of me hoped you'd pick me up and carry me in there. But, another part of me hoped you'd say just what you said. I'm not usually like this, especially with a man I just met. Key West isn't the best place in the world for dating decent guys. I'll be around when you are ready."

"A large part of me wanted to pick you up and carry you in there," I said. "You're not angry? We can be friends?"

"Friends with benefits," she said and gave me a deep soulful kiss. "I'm not going anywhere, Jesse."

Just then a Klaxon horn sounded over the exterior speakers, causing her to jump suddenly and land with a thud on the deck.

"What the hell was that?" she said.

Laughing, I reached down, took her hand and helped her to her feet, saying, "I've got mail. Why don't you grab a few beers from the galley and take them up to the bridge? We'll have to leave soon. I'll be right back."

We went into the salon and I helped her load the cooler with ice and beer. After she headed up to the bridg

I opened the laptop and saw there was an email from Deuce. I opened it and read:

Director says go. Make nice with Santiago. Try to get him to like you. I know that'll be difficult. Pretend to be someone he wants moving his product. Call or email when you can.

I clicked the reply button and wrote one word, *Roger*, and clicked send. I closed the laptop and unplugged the speaker jack, then went out to the cockpit.

"We have to go," I said to Tina up on the bridge. "Will you start the engines for me while I cast off?"

She started both engines as I stepped up to the dock and untied first the bowline, then the stern. Shoving the *Revenge* out away from the dock, I stepped aboard and climbed up to the bridge. Tina was sitting in the second seat and I had her slide over behind the helm.

"Stand up," I said. "Put your back against the wheel and your hands on the throttles."

She did as I said and I told her to use her left hand and put the starboard engine in reverse. The *Revenge* started backwards, pulling the bow away from the dock, and I told her to do the same with her right hand, putting the port engine in reverse. We slowly started backing straight away then and I told her to put the starboard engine in forward and use her back to nudge the wheel to her right. Slowly, the *Revenge* began spinning, pointing her bow toward open water.

"Nice maneuvering," I said. "Now have a seat and take us home."

She sat down at the helm and asked, "Was it an important message?"

"No," I lied. "Just confirmation of what time I have to leave in the morning. Now, in a narrow channel like this, you have to go nice and slow. Use the engines and the wheel to steer. You ever drive a tracked vehicle, like a bulldozer, back on the farm?"

"Yeah," she said. "As a matter of fact, I have."

"Same principle. Use the throttles like you would the track controls on a dozer."

I saw her face light up as it came to her. "The propellers are like the tracks. Stop one and the other will drive forward and turn."

"Beautiful and intelligent," I said with a laugh. "I think I'm in trouble."

She took the *Revenge* through the narrow channels, going clockwise around the two islands, using only the throttles, like she was born to it. Then, pointing the bow due south, she nudged both throttles just a little and the big boat responded. Once we cleared the outer channel marker, I turned on the radar, sonar, VHF and GPS, then punched in the saved destination for the marina.

"Always check the radar and sonar before lifting the boat up on plane," I said. "Remember, we're as tall as a house and speed is deceiving. You want to make sure you have at least ten feet of water under the keel and nothing out in front of you for a ways."

She looked over the digital display and said, "It says we only have two feet of water under us."

"The sonar reads in fathoms," I said. "One fathom is six feet, so we have plenty of depth."

"Oh geez," she said. "Port, starboard, helm, fathom. Why do you have to speak a foreign language?"

I opened a beer and nearly doubled over, laughing so hard. When I got control, I said, "It'll all come to you. In time."

"What's that red thing on the radar?" she asked.

"It's big, so it's probably a container ship. Looks to be heading toward the Mississippi River and it's about ten miles away."

"So, we're good to go?"

"Saturday night, rock and roll," I said.

"Well, it's Sunday afternoon," she said, smiling. "But I'm guessing that's more Marine talk and it means something like 'hammer down'?"

"Hammer down, babe!"

She shoved the throttles about halfway and the *Revenge* dropped down at the stern, the big props displacing the water under the hull as the bow rose and the bridge tilted back. Then, as she gathered speed, the bow came back down and she lifted up on plane.

"Holy shit!" she said. "Can I do that again?"

"Sure, why not," I replied. "Just ease the throttles back. You don't want to come down off plane too fast, or the wake will swamp the cockpit."

She eased the throttles back and the boat settled back into the water. Then she pushed them forward again, lifting the eighteen-ton boat back up on plane.

"That's such a cool feeling," she said, with an ear-to-ear grin on her face.

She looked over at me and I said, "I do believe the worm has turned."

She piloted the *Revenge* all the way back to the marina, but asked me to 'park it' when we got to the docks.

"I don't want to hit anything," she said.

I backed the boat into the slip and had her sit at the helm, in case it needed a slight move, while I climbed down and made her fast. She shut down the engines and I joined her on the bridge to watch the sun go down. We talked for nearly an hour, as the moon started to peek above the horizon to the east. I'd really enjoyed her company and I felt she had enjoyed being with me, too.

As if reading my mind, she said, "I'm glad you asked me out today. All this time, I never realized what I was missing out there. I can't wait until next weekend."

She left a little while later, kissing me deeply on the dock before getting on her bike and riding away toward town. I went into the salon to call Doc. I had a feeling he wasn't going to like playing pirate. And I was right.

CHAPTER NINE:

Pirates on the Bay

As usual, I was up before dawn, the sound of the coffeemaker and the fresh smell of Colombia's finest product filling the salon just beyond the stateroom hatch. I turned on the light in the salon and poured a cup. I took it up to the bridge and sat down, watching the stars.

Last night, I'd called Doc and given him the news that we were going to join Santiago in smuggling pot into Key West. At first, he thought I'd lost my mind and wanted no part of it. I explained that the problem went far beyond Trent and his crew. Santiago had his claws in dozens of people all over town. I said that rather than get Trent off the hook, I was planning to get Santiago out of everyone's hair. When he asked how I planned to do that, I just said he'd have to trust me.

Doc had said that they planned to get underway about 0900, to make it out to New Ground Reef by midafternoon. That would allow the crew to get some sleep before starting the trawl just after dark. He gave me the name of the boat and I told him that I'd arrive there about 0830. I reminded him that he should act pissed because Trent was late, then concerned when I told him about his 'accident'. After I finished talking to him, I called Lawrence and asked if he could pick me up at 0800 at the marina. That gave me two hours.

My phone chirped, sitting inside the small storage cabinet next to the helm. I looked at it, but didn't recognize the number. I usually don't, but I answered it anyway, saying, "McDermitt."

"You're sitting on the bridge in your skivvies," I heard a woman's voice say. Then I realized it was Tina.

"Hi, Tina," I said, looking out toward the gate. "You're up early."

"I like to run early in the mornings after a night off," she said. "I just wanted to call and thank you again for letting me drive your boat."

"Pilot," I said, grinning. "You drive a car, you pilot a boat. And you're welcome. I had a good time, too."

"I'll never get the lingo down," she said laughing.

"You will if you hang around boat bums a lot," I said.

"I think I'd like that a lot," she said.

"Where do you run?" I asked. "I can't run much, living on a tiny island, but I try to swim at least two miles every other day."

"That's a long swim. I run through Old Town, a long loop that takes me to the south side of the island, along the water. About four or five miles."

"Do you always have Sundays off?" I asked.

"Sundays and Mondays," she said. "Sometimes I change shifts with one of the other bartenders, to get a weekend night off."

"Think you could do that and have Friday off?"

"Probably," she replied. "What did you have in mind?"

"I have to make a run to the Content Keys Friday evening, to take some groceries to a friend. You're welcome to come along. Should be back by noon on Saturday."

"Hmmm," she said, teasing me.

"My boat has two staterooms," I said.

"Okay, if you're sure."

"Yeah, I want you to meet my dog." *Not my smoothest line*, I thought. But she laughed.

"Be careful out there today," she said.

"I'll see you in a few days," I said and ended the call.

I went below and filled a thermos, then put on a pair of work jeans and a long-sleeve denim shirt. I grabbed my sea bag, with the fly rod case strapped to it and my thermos, then headed out to the gate after locking the hatch.

I didn't have long to wait. Lawrence pulled up and, checking my Submariner watch, I saw he was right on time. I liked people that were punctual. It says something about a person.

He popped the release on the trunk before he even stopped, and the lid flew up. He was out the driver's door and around the back of the cab before I'd even taken a step.

"Mornin sar," he said.

"Lawrence, calling me sir is like a fishing pole with no hook. It don't work. Would you please just call me Jesse?"

He grinned and said, "Ya mon, Mister Jesse, sar."

Oh well, I thought. *Some people you just can't change.* "You know where *Miss Charlie*'s docked?" I asked.

"Cap'n Trent's boat? Ya mon, I tek him der most mornins. He usually der ver early, bout six."

We got in and Lawrence pulled away from the marina, heading west on US-1, over the bridge and into Key West. He turned onto Palm and crossed over the causeway to Old Town, then made a series of quick lefts and rights and stopped at the north end of Front Street, again popping the trunk before coming to a complete stop.

Lawrence was at the back of the car and lifted my heavy sea bag and handed it to me. I gave him a twenty and asked if Santiago was still on the island.

"Ya mon," he said. "He was at di Blue Parrot till ver late. A fren took he an two gulls to his hotel."

"Thanks, Lawrence," I said. "I'll see you in a few days."

"Be careful, Cap'n."

I threw the sea bag over my shoulder and walked the half block to the dock. A motorcycle roared by and I noticed it was Nikki, Doc's girlfriend, driving it. Nice-looking bike, I thought.

Several shrimp boats were active with men working, loading food, drinks, and ice aboard. I found the *Charlie* and saw Doc on the deck, directing the crew and seeming to be in a foul mood. A slight, dark-haired man was leaning against a pier post not far away. I caught Doc's eye as I reached the foot of the gangway.

"Permission to board?" I called up.

"Who the hell are you?" he yelled, causing the crew to stop what they were doing and look down.

"Captain McDermitt," I said. "Captain Trent sent me. He's had an accident."

FALLEN HUNTER

The man leaning against the post turned suddenly from looking down to the end of the street and looked at me. Doc came down the gangway and I handed him my Master's papers, which he looked over.

Looking up, he said loud enough for the man at the post to hear, "What happened to the Captain?"

"His wife called me late last night," I replied. "He was scuba diving and suffered an embolism yesterday. He's in the hyperbaric chamber in Key Largo. She said that he asked her to call me and see if I could fill in, so you guys don't have to miss any trawling time."

"Is he okay?" Doc asked. "I'm Bob Talbot, First Mate."

He handed my papers back and we shook hands. "Name's Jesse," I said. "Jesse McDermitt. I run a fishing charter in Marathon and my boat's being refitted. Guess that's why Carl had Charlie call me."

"Welcome aboard, Captain," he said. "We should be ready to be underway in half an hour. We're going out to New Ground."

"No, we're not," I said, surprising Doc. "We'll go on out to Rebecca Shoals, before bedding down."

Doc looked up at the crew, who were all standing at the rail watching us. One crewman looked over at the man by the post, then back at me. *Gotcha*, I thought.

"You're the Captain," Doc said, then headed up the gangplank.

The man by the post started forward and said, "Excuse me, Captain."

I turned to look at him. He was a small man, with dark hair and eyes. His face was pocked with old acne scars and his front teeth were crooked.

"Yes?" I asked.

"Did Captain Trent tell you that I would be here?" he asked. "I work for Carlos Santiago."

"No," I said and started to turn. He placed a hand on my shoulder and I stopped. I half turned and looked down at his hand, then into his eyes. "You have something against that hand?" I asked. "Cause if it ain't off my shoulder in half a heartbeat, I'll feed it to the sharks."

The man yanked his hand back like he'd touched a hot stove. "I work for Señor Santiago. As does Captain Trent. I'm here to give him the GPS coordinates for the pickup he, and now you, are to make."

"Pick up what?" I asked.

"Trent picks up a small package every week for Señor Santiago. Since you are *el capitán* this week, the responsibility for this week's pickup is now yours."

"You're talking about drugs, aren't you?"

"*Sí*," he replied openly. "You will have to make Trent's pickup this week. If you do not, bad things might happen."

I slowly set my sea bag on the dock at my feet. Then in a fast, fluid motion, I straightened, grabbed the man by the collar and lifted him up so that his feet were dangling. I growled into his face, "How much?"

"Is only five hundred pounds, señor," he whined. "Please, put me down."

"No!" I snarled. "*Cuanto dinero, idiota.*"

"Please, señor, I am only the carrier. When you bring the package in on Friday, I will be waiting and give you five thousand dollars, for you and the crew."

"I take all the risk?" I asked. "For only one percent of street value? Not likely, amigo. Call your boss and tell him if he wants this *capitán* to be his gopher, the price is tripled."

Then I shoved him backwards, picked up my sea bag and went aboard. Every set of eyes was on me. At the top of the gangplank, I turned to the man, now sitting on the dock, and said, "We leave in thirty minutes, *cabrón*!"

I turned to Doc and said, "I'll be on the bridge, getting familiar with the boat. Where's my bunk?"

"Main deck, Captain," he replied. "Aft the wheelhouse. We'll be ready to be underway shortly, sir."

I left Doc and the crew standing there and went along the starboard side and through the wheelhouse to Trent's quarters. It was a tiny room by any standards, but functional and accessed only through the wheelhouse, I noticed. I dropped my sea bag on the bunk and went back into the wheelhouse, to familiarize myself with it. Trent had given me a pretty good run down on how the boat operated and where everything was, so this was mostly for show.

A few minutes later, Doc stuck his head in and said, "Are you sure, you're not a pirate? Drug runner, maybe?"

"How'd the crew react?" I asked.

"Mixed feelings," he said. "Two are like me, they want nothing to do with drugs. The other four are excited that they might get a bigger cut with you on board. Odds are split on whether or not Santiago kills you."

"Who was the bag man on the dock?" I asked.

"Goes by the name of Raphael. Don't know if that's his first or last name. He's a scary dude. Word on the street is, he's done some wet work for Santiago. You sure had him pissing his pants, though."

"Think the word on the streets is accurate?"

"Some," he said. "Probably pumped up a bit."

I considered the possibility that I'd made a dangerous enemy, then discarded it. I'd made dangerous enemies before.

Changing the subject, I asked, "Was that Nikki I saw leaving on a motorcycle?"

"Yeah," he replied. "It's an '03 Indian Chief."

"I thought they went out of business before I was born," I said.

"They did," he said. "They reopened a few years ago and went bankrupt almost immediately. I got one of the few hundred-cubic-inch Chiefs built. I've been hearing rumors they're going to start production back up soon."

He turned at the sound of commotion on the dock, then said, "Oh, shit. Santiago's already here and he don't look happy."

"Go on out there," I said. "Yell when he wants to talk to me."

Doc went back to the work deck and a minute later I heard him yell, "Captain! Someone wants to see you."

I went to the cabin, retrieved my Sig from the sea bag and put it down the back of my pants, pulling my shirt over it. Then I walked out of the pilothouse and menacingly moved across the port side, toward Santiago.

"Talbot!" I said authoritatively. "Did you give this *visitor* permission to board my vessel?"

Doc turned to me, bewildered. "Um, no sir."

"Mister," I said as I strode across the deck toward Santiago. "I don't know who the hell you think you are, but boarding a vessel without the Captain's permission could get you turned into shark chum."

"My name is Carlos Santiago," he said with the arrogant air of someone used to people cringing at the mere mention of his name. "And this is not your boat to be giving anyone permission to board."

"Santiago, huh," I said. "I was hired to skipper this vessel. That makes everything on it, and in it, mine until I relinquish command back to the owner." Then I lowered my voice and hissed, "Are you the weasel that's been paying shit wages to Trent to smuggle dope?"

He looked up at me, first perplexed, then angry. He looked over at Doc and started to reach into his jacket pocket, probably for a handkerchief or maybe a smoke, but I moved faster. I reached back, pulled the Sig and had it under his chin in a flash.

"I asked you a question, señor," I hissed. "*Es usted el jefe, o no?*"

"I'm the man that can make you rich," he said defiantly. "Or arrange to have your wife disappear," he added, noting the ring still on my finger.

"*Es demasiado tarde*, señor," I growled. "Some other punk murdered her four months ago. So, here's the deal. You got nothing to threaten me with. I got no family. I don't know, nor do I give one rat's ass about, a single man aboard this boat and if you have me killed, you'd be doing me a favor. Now, since I'm the one holding a nine millimeter under your chin at the moment, maybe you'd like to talk about that first option. Making me rich."

Little beads of sweat were starting to form on his brow from the sudden knowledge that he had no sway over a man holding a gun on him.

"*Podemos hablar en privado, capitán?*"

"After you," I said, motioning toward the wheelhouse.

I had to credit the man, he recovered quickly. He walked straight and tall along the port rail to the wheelhouse, as I followed. Only when we were inside did I put the Sig back into my waistband.

"I know two hundred and twenty-five kilos of grass has a street value of about half a million bucks, Santiago," I said. "You've been paying Trent only five grand. That ain't enough. You want me to haul it, it's gonna cost you four times that. That's twenty grand. Paid on delivery. Not negotiable."

"Raphael said three times as much," he said.

I smiled, knowing that I already had him backpedaling. "That was before you boarded my vessel without permission and tried to undermine my authority in front of my crew. Take it or leave it. Either way, you're off this boat, most riki tik."

"I like you, *Capitán* McDermitt," he said. "I think we might have a future together."

"Yes or no?"

"Yes, I will pay you the twenty thousand. When your job for *Capitán* Trent is finished, perhaps you might consider working for me? I can use a man that can't be threatened."

His eyes were slightly red, no doubt from the night's partying at the Blue Parrot. His clothes were a little rumpled, probably from having to come down here in a hurry. Still, I could tell they were top of the line. He had a thin scar on the side of his face, just below the hairline. Hardly noticeable, except when he smiled. He was smiling now.

"I'll consider it," I said. "But, I ain't cheap."

"I can make it worth your while, *Capitán*. Do you know Miami?"

"I hate Miami," I said. "I know my way around well enough, though. Why?"

"*Conoces la Habana?* Have you ever been across the Straits?"

"A few times. Again, why?"

"I usually travel with a bodyguard," he said. "He got himself killed in Little Havana just last week. *Asesinado*, for the money in his pocket. I need someone of your, let's say, stature and demeanor to take his place. I travel to Cuba once a month."

"Have a number in mind when I get back," I said, with as menacing a grin as I could muster. "We'll talk."

"Sí, Capitán. *Ten un bien viaje.*" He handed me a piece of paper and added, "The time and coordinates for your pickup. The boat will be *El Cazador* and he will come alongside to barter beer for your bycatch."

As he turned to walk out of the wheelhouse, I looked at the paper and said, "This looks to be east of where I plan to fish, Santiago. Tell your pickup man he can find me on Rebecca Shoals, same day and time."

"That's a lot further west, isn't it?" he asked.

"Yeah," I replied. "Fewer people around." He nodded and left the pilothouse.

I waited until I was sure he was off the boat, then went out on deck. Two crewmen were lowering the hatch over the hold and Doc turned and said, "Ready to get underway, Captain."

"Get the crew together in the galley," I said as I turned and went down the ladder well. I took a seat at the far end of the large dining table as the crew filed in. I waited until they were all inside and stopped fidgeting, while I measured each one with a hard eye. I'd been a Gunnery Sergeant in the Corps, in charge of a whole company of Infantry, at one time. I knew how to measure men. I easily picked out the two that Doc had said were against hauling pot for Santiago by their body language.

I stood up and said, "My name's Captain Jesse McDermitt. Captain Trent was in a diving accident yesterday and he hired me to run the boat in his stead. I just renegotiated Trent's take on his little side business with Santiago, tripling it. That's a guarantee of sixteen hundred dollars to each of you, two thousand to Mister Talbot and five thousand to Captain Trent, on top of our week's catch. Be warned, I don't condone drug use on board. I catch anyone lighting up a spliff, you'll swim back to Key West. Also, I demand instant obedience to any and all orders. I won't be trifled with. Do I make myself clear?"

Each man nodded, including the two on Doc's side. Then I pointed to the man on the far left, who was the one in Santiago's pocket, and said, "Sound off with your name and primary job."

"John Lupori, deckhand," said Santiago's man.

"Paul Laudenslager, cook," said the second man.

"Phil McWhorter, deckhand."

"David Williams, engineer."

"Jan Sims, navigator."

"Bob Talbot, First Mate."

"Okay," I said. "Let's get underway. Any questions?"

"Yes sir," McWhorter said. "I overheard you tell Bob we were going straight to Rebecca Shoals. We always start at New Ground. Just wondering why."

"Because, McWhorter, that's where every other boat in the Key West fleet starts. We're going further west and working our way back. Now, if there's no more questions, let's rock and roll." The men all filed out, except for Doc, Williams and Sims.

"Captain," Williams said. "We're not comfortable with running drugs." I looked at Doc and got an almost imperceptible nod, meaning he vouched for these two men.

"Close the hatch, Doc," I said. When he'd closed it, I continued. "Everything that just happened in this last half hour was for Lupori. I'm not comfortable with it either, and am aware that he's also working for Santiago. I'm here to get Santiago off your back. With any luck, maybe off the backs of everyone in Key West. Doc vouches for you two and if he trusts you, I do too."

"I thought I recognized that tattoo," Williams said, noting that I'd called the First Mate Doc. "My kid's in the Corps. Afghanistan. My eldest recently left the Corps."

"I have a daughter in the Guard," said Sims.

"Can I count on you guys to help us out?" I asked. "All I can tell you is we're not alone. I can't tell you who's going to be helping us, but they cast a big shadow."

Just then, Laudenslager knocked on the hatch and opened it. "Skipper," he said. "There's a lady at the dock wants to see you."

"I'll be right there," I said and he closed the hatch. "Well?" I said.

"I'm in, Skipper," said Sims.

"Me too," said Williams.

"Okay, then," I said. "Let's get this boat moving. Mister Williams, how's the engine?"

"All set, Skipper," he said. "Ran a complete diagnostics early this morning. Anytime you're ready, you can fire her up."

"Good, I'll be right back." I went through the hatch, expecting to see Tina on the dock, but was surprised to see it was Julie. I looked around the docks and on the street to see if Santiago or Raphael were still in the area and didn't see either of them.

Julie was holding a briefcase and was dressed like some kind of secretary, in black slacks and a dark blue blouse. I walked down the gangplank. "What are you doing here, Jules?"

"The office sent me, Captain. I have some papers for you to look over." Then under her breath she added, "That'd be Russell. Take this case. There's a satellite phone inside."

I took the briefcase and said, "Anything else?"

"That's it," she said louder, obviously enjoying the secret agent game. "Just look those papers over and get back to the board members when you can." Then she turned and walked away. I watched her all the way to the corner of Simonton Street, where she got in Alex's yellow Jeep and drove away.

I walked back up the gangplank and went to my cabin, behind the pilothouse. I left the briefcase with my sea bag and went forward, into the pilothouse. Trent's boat was a sixty-six-foot custom trawler, built by St. Augustine Marine Center in 1978. Trent had taken good care of her, it looked like. I turned the key and the engine immediately fired up.

Doc came in through the hatch and said, "We're all set, Jesse."

"Tell the crew to cast off," I said. This was going to be my first test. Depending on how I maneuvered out of port, the crew would either accept me as the skipper, or not.

Doc gave the orders over the loudspeaker and the crew wrestled the large hawsers aboard. When we were free of the pier, Doc nodded his head and I checked the wheel to ensure the rudder was amidships and put the *Charlie* in forward. I nudged the throttle to start the big boat moving, then brought it back to idle.

It had been a while since I'd piloted a boat this big, but I guess it's like riding a bike. We cleared the docks and I managed to get her around the pier and into Key West Bight, heading west, without incident or running over anything.

"Radar's clear, Captain," Doc said. "No cruise ships in the channel. We're clear to enter."

"Thanks, Doc," I said. "Maneuvering with twin engines is a lot easier."

"You made it look pretty easy, Jesse," he said. Then he gave me a lopsided grin and added, "Now, just stay between the big green and red markers."

I maneuvered the big boat around and into the channel, heading southwest between Tank Island and the cruise ship docks. When we were off the southwest tip of Key West, I started a slow turn to the north and entered Northwest Channel. As soon as we were through the narrows, I bumped the throttle up to 1800 rpm and the big boat slowly accelerated to ten knots. Being already familiar with it, I knew the big Cat engine would get its best fuel economy at 1600 rpm, but I wanted to get out ahead of the other boats before we made New Ground.

There were two other shrimp boats ahead of us and another just coming out of the harbor. Doc reached up and turned on the VHF radio. Then he keyed the mic and spoke into it, "Gangway, fellas. *Miss Charlie's* coming into the channel with a new Skipper at the helm."

A voice came over the radio, "Morning, Bob. Where's Carl?"

"That's Charlie Hofbauer," Doc said. "He Skippers the *Morning Mist*, just ahead of us."

Keying the mic he said, "Morning, Charlie. Carl had a little scuba diving accident yesterday and will be in the chamber up in Key Largo for a day or so."

"Sorry to hear that," came the voice over the radio. "Who you got taking his place?"

"Captain McDermitt," Doc said. "He runs a fishing boat out of Marathon."

Another voice came over the radio, "Jesse, this is Al Fader on *Night Moves*. Thought I recognized you at the dock. Sorry to hear about Alex. Went out on the flats with her about two years ago. Nice lady."

I took the mic and said, "Thanks, Al. Haven't seen you around the *Anchor* in a while."

"Got married last year," he said. "The old lady won't let me out from under her thumb. Maybe we can get together out on New Ground and have a beer in the morning."

"We're going on out to Rebecca Shoal today," I said. "Should be back on New Ground by Wednesday. Save me a Carib."

"You got it, man," Al said.

We motored on northward, slowly gaining on, then passing the other two shrimp boats. I was playing a hunch. I know fish, but don't know much about shrimp, except that fish like to eat them. Certain fish in particular, like Spanish mackerel. The night before, I studied the fishing forecast, past years' fishing reports, weather forecast, and water conditions in the shrimping grounds north and west of Key West. From a fisherman's point of view, everything I read said that Spanish mackerel fishing would be good on Rebecca Shoals early this week. Since fish go where the food is, and Spanish mackerel feed primarily on shrimp, the past fishing reports pointed to an abundance of them, and therefore shrimp, further west.

Two hours later, we were passing New Ground and Doc came into the pilothouse. Turning to him, I gave him the paper Santiago had given me and said, "This is nearby, isn't it?"

Doc took the paper and looked at it, then said, "Yeah, on the western edge, though. Another two miles, but it's only about thirty feet of water. Is this where Santiago said to make the pickup?"

"Yeah," I replied. "But I told him Rebecca Shoals, same day and time. After the pickup, the boat making the delivery is going to disappear. Señor Santiago is going to need a new transporter. That's how I plan to get on the inside."

"How do you know it's going to disappear?" he asked. "Or is that a question I shouldn't ask."

I eyed Doc closely. My first instinct when I met him was that he was a good man. That hadn't diminished since then. If anything, I felt even stronger that my initial instinct was right.

"Doc," I said. "I work as a private contractor for DHS. Santiago has come up on their radar and that's part of the reason I'm here. Once the exchange is made, a go-fast boat will intercept the carrier and take them into custody." I hoped I was right, at least. I still needed to contact Deuce and arrange for it to happen.

"You're a fed?" he asked incredulously.

"More of a merc than a fed," I said, grinning. "I don't carry a badge, or anything. They just pay me to do odd jobs. Write the GPS numbers for Rebecca Shoals on the back, then take the wheel, I need to make a phone call."

I took the piece of paper back from him as he took the wheel and he said, "You won't get a signal out here. Nobody does."

I went into the cabin and opened the briefcase Julie had given me. Inside it were several file folders and a satellite phone. The new kind, with a big screen you can see pictures on. Maybe even do a video call with. I set it aside and looked at the file folders. The top one was a dossier on Santiago. I set it aside also and looked at the others. They were complete workups on every man in the crew. I pulled the one out for Doc and opened it. I scanned through it but didn't see any red flags, which would have surprised me.

I picked up the phone and turned it on. It took a minute to familiarize myself with it, but I eventually found the contact list and Deuce's number. I hit send and Deuce answered after two rings.

"About time you called," he said.

"Hey, thanks for all the paperwork," I said. "Thought I was through with that crap when I left the Corps." He laughed and asked what he could do for me.

I read him the coordinates Doc had written and said, "I'm meeting another boat there tomorrow, to pick up five hundred pounds of marijuana. Think you can arrange to have the boat picked up after the drop is made?"

"Sure," he said. "No problem at all. How long do they need to be held?"

"At least a week," I said. "Santiago offered me a job as his bodyguard this morning. I think I can get him to offer me a better job if his delivery man disappears."

"You don't waste any time, do you?"

"You said to cozy up to the guy," I said.

"What's the end game? I'll have to run all this by Director Smith, you know." Deuce knew that I wasn't particularly fond of Jason Smith, his boss.

"Not sure just yet," I said. "I want to get inside his operation as far as possible. He likes me. Says a man with nothing to lose can be valuable to him. It may mean going into Cuba."

"Cuba!" he exclaimed. "I don't think Smith's gonna go for that, Jesse."

"So, don't tell him. Nothing's definite yet, anyway. One more thing. The *Revenge* is still at Oceanside. Can you get some things aboard for me?"

"What do you need?" he asked.

"High-tech electronics," I said. "Real high-tech, but easy enough for a Jarhead to use. Something that will impress Santiago and some kind of listening device that I can put in his case, or something."

"Well, you already have a lot of high-tech stuff aboard," he said. "I'll get with our IT person. She's top notch, used to be an analyst for the CIA. The bugs are easy enough. I'll have her send you a video message on whatever she comes up with. She loves this kind of freelancing stuff. Her name's Chyrel Koshinski."

"Just remember to tell her that the directions have to be at grunt level," I said. "I'll call the marina ahead of time and let them know someone will be dropping off a package and to let them aboard. There's a spare key to the salon under the seat at the helm." I ended the connection and went back into the pilothouse.

"It's all set," I said. "The boat will be detained for at least a week. You never mentioned you received a Purple Heart."

"What the hell!" he said. "Nobody knows that, not even Nikki. How the hell did you find out? Never mind, I don't want to know. Just keep it to yourself, okay."

"Why the big secret?" I said. "Because you were shot in the ass?"

"Alright, alright," he said laughing. "You made your point. Your friends 'cast a big shadow.'"

We were moving west, past New Ground now and Doc asked, "Why the rush to get to Rebecca Shoals? You have people looking at satellite imaging, following the shrimp?"

"No," I replied. "Just a hunch."

An hour later, we were near Rebecca Shoals and I had Doc get the crew to drop the hook. We anchored just off the shoals in about eighty feet of water and ate supper, then I told the crew to get some shuteye and we'd start our first trawl an hour after sunset.

CHAPTER TEN:
Shrimp Rodeo

I got a few hours of sleep, but was awakened an hour before sunset, by a chirping sound, like a cricket. It was the satellite phone in the briefcase. There was a video message. I opened it and saw a young woman in an office. She had short blond hair and wore glasses. In the video, she held up two listening devices and explained how to use them. One was a flat piece of clear plastic, with a black adhesive backing, that could be stuck to clothing, preferably under a jacket lapel, she explained. All I had to do was peel off the black backing and press it in place. The second one was a round, whitish blob that she said could be stuck under a table. It looked just like a bubble of excess urethane. It worked the same way: it would activate when the backing was peeled off. Both bugs would work for forty-eight hours, then become inactive and drop off. She said there would be six of each in a small case that resembled a sunglass case.

Then she held up what looked like a regular ballpoint pen and explained that when you twisted the top, it activated a small charge that would emit a thick, heavy smoke once it was dropped and impacted the ground. She went on to explain that it had originally been armed by simply twisting the top, but the impact feature was added because too many people were accidentally activating it in their pocket. She said there would be three of these, each marked with innocuous company names in a color that would match the smoke, white, black, and red. The white and black were for cover and the red, for emergency.

Then she held up a small black box, about the size and shape of a tackle box. Opening it, she took out a small object and pressed a button on its side. It unfolded itself into a small parabolic mirror with tripod legs. She pointed out where to plug in a cord and attach it to the small amplifier in the tackle box. She then lifted a pair of headphones and showed where they plugged in and explained that it could pick up a quiet conversation over two hundred yards away, even through glass. She said it took a little practice and patience to finely adjust the aim for best results. This was the 'show-off' piece.

The last thing she displayed to me was a laptop, similar to my own. "In fact," she said, "Mister Livingston had insisted it be this particular model, because, and I quote, 'It's the same kind the Jarhead has on his boat.'" She went on to explain that it was loaded with an encrypted program to video conference with the other team members. It also had real-time satellite imaging capability, but satellite time was expensive and I should get authorization before using it.

She ended the video saying, "I look forward to meeting you in person, Captain, when we come down to your little island." I had no idea what that was about. I powered the phone down and put it back in the briefcase, thinking everything sounded like a bunch of James Bond stuff, and headed to the galley to make some coffee.

When I got to the galley, I smelled coffee and bacon. The cook was already up and getting breakfast ready. It seemed strange having breakfast as the sun was setting, but this is the life shrimpers live and I'd have to adjust to it, at least for the week.

"Good morning, Captain," Paul Laudenslager said as he poured me a cup from the pot. "Sugar and cream are on the table."

"Thanks, Paul," I said. "Don't need either."

"I can bring your breakfast up to the pilothouse, if you like," he said.

The tide was falling and the boat was facing north. So I said, "Thanks, I'll eat out on the deck, though." I took my coffee out to the work deck. Sitting on the gunwale, leaning back on the cabin bulkhead, I looked out over the water to the west. The sea was calm, with only a slight rolling motion, as small waves rolled across the shoals. The sun had disappeared behind a bank of low, dark clouds to the west, painting them in a blaze of red and purple hues. Gulls and pelicans were coming down onto the steel frame of the lighthouse to roost for the night. They knew that throughout the night there would be a lot of food in the water around our boat and all they had to do was follow us.

Paul brought a metal plate full with eggs, bacon, grits and toast out to me, along with the coffeepot. When he handed me the plate, I suddenly realized I was hungry and dug right in as he poured me another cup. He stood there a minute and when I looked up, I could tell he wanted to ask me something.

"What is it, Paul?" I asked.

"Well, sir," he started. "The crew's been talking. About you having a gun aboard."

"I carry a gun wherever I go. Is that a problem?"

"Well, it's also what you said to Santiago. About not caring about anyone on board."

"I don't," I said. "I was hired to do a job. My job is to bring you guys out here and bring you back safe, then put some money in your pockets at the end of the week. After that, if we never see one another again, it's not going to bother me. I'm not your Skipper, Paul. I'm your Captain. You know the difference, right?"

"Yes sir," he said. "I surely do."

"I'll do everything and anything I have to do to ensure that every man on board gets home safe and sound. That's my job. Simple as that."

"Scuttlebutt says you lost your wife not long ago and that you're kind of a wild card since then."

I looked hard at the man then growled, "Is there a question in there?"

"No sir," he said. "I'll leave you to your breakfast."

He started to turn and I dumped the rest of the plate overboard and said, "I'm done."

I walked forward to the pilothouse and started the engine. Then I switched the PA system over to boatwide and keyed the mic. "Rise and shine! Get to the galley and get your bellies full. Be ready to drop nets in thirty minutes. Mister Talbot, report to the pilothouse."

Three minutes later Doc came in and I said, "Any discussion on this boat about my wife is to cease, most riki tik, Doc."

"Sorry, Jesse," he said. "That's my fault. One of the crew asked and I didn't see the harm. It won't happen again."

"Good," I said. "Because if it does, I'll reinstate the time-honored tradition of keelhauling." I calmed down and told Doc to go ahead on down to the galley and get some breakfast.

Twenty minutes later the crew was on deck, ready for a night's work. We hoisted anchor and lowered the nets. We trawled the grassy flats to the east and north of Rebecca Shoals and after an hour, Doc came into the pilothouse. "Looks like your hunch is paying off," he said. "We already have to haul the nets. Take a break and I'll take the helm while they bring 'em up."

I went down to the galley and got another mug of coffee. Paul had already cleaned up and had just come down to fill a thermos for the crew. "How'd you know the shrimp would be here, Captain?" he asked.

"Sometimes," I said, "I just think like a fish. I checked the last few years of fishing reports for the area and noticed that a lot of mackerel were being taken here during this week, every year. Mackerel love shrimp. Hey, Paul, I'm sorry I blew up at you earlier."

"No worries," he said. "Let's go up and see what we got."

We went up on deck as the first net was brought aboard. It was loaded. A lot of bycatch, too. It was something I'd always hated about the shrimping industry. The nets have a device mounted in them to protect sea turtles, called a turtle extruder device, or TED for short. It's like a cage, with a trap door at the bottom and diagonal bars that force a large turtle toward the door and out of the net. I always thought the bars should be tighter, to force fish out also.

The net was dumped onto the deck and the sorting began. There were starfish, crabs, finfish of all types, even small stingrays. And there were a lot of shrimp. A whole lot. The crew was whooping and yelling with excitement as they sorted all the edible fish from the inedible. Anything that couldn't be consumed was thrown overboard, most of them already dead. I noticed several large hogfish and pointed them out to Lupori.

"Keep those in a separate bucket, Lupori," I said. "Once the sorting's done, clean them and take them down to the galley."

"The boat's not licensed to keep finfish, Captain," he said. "We toss most everything overboard, except what the sports fishermen can use for chum or bait. They'll be along in the morning to trade for beer."

"Fortunately for us," I said, "I am a licensed commercial fin fisherman. We're having blackened hogfish for supper."

"Whatever you say, Captain," he replied.

The other three nets yielded pretty much the same results. The moon was coming up and it was nearly midnight when we put the nets back out for another trawl. If our luck kept up, we'd have the hold filled early, and the crew was already looking forward to an extended weekend. I let Doc keep the helm on the next trawl and joined the crew waiting for the nets to fill up again. The storm that had been forming earlier to the west was moving closer. It was still a good ten miles away, but we had to keep a close eye on it. The lightning inside the storm was almost constant, lighting up the thunderheads from within. The wind was starting to shift and had picked up a little.

I went forward and entered the pilothouse. Doc was looking out over the bow toward the storm. "Doesn't look real good, Jesse."

"Anything come over the radiofax?" I asked. A radiofax is like a regular fax machine, but the information comes via high frequency radio.

"Just got one from NOAA," he said, handing me the printout. I looked it over, noting that while the storm looked bad from where we were, it was forecast to move slightly north of us. Good news for us, bad news for the other shrimp boats on New Ground.

"Did you warn the others yet?" I asked. "Looks like it's going to go right over New Ground."

"No," he said. "It just came in."

I picked up the mic and spoke into it, "*Miss Charlie* to *Night Moves*. Al, do you copy?"

Almost immediately his voice came back over the static, "This is *Night Moves*. You guys having any luck over there?"

"Not too bad," I said. "How's it going there?"

"About the same, Jesse," he said.

"Did you get the radiofax on that storm to the west?" I asked

"Hang on," he said. "Yeah, just pulled it off the machine. Can't see it from here, how's it look?"

"Looks like Independence Day from here, almost constant lightning." I looked at the radar and noticed the four blips on the north side of New Ground. "Maybe you guys ought to move south of New Ground before it gets too close. Hell of a lot of electricity out there."

"Thanks, Jesse," he said. "We just might do that."

I hung up the mic and looked at Doc.

"They're not going to," he said. "Al's about the most stubborn man I ever met."

"Well, I'm not," I said. We were heading west on the northeast side of the shoals, about half a mile away. "Come southwest and make for the windward side of Isaac Shoal. We'll pull the nets when we pass Isaac and see what the storm looks like then."

Doc made a slow, sweeping turn that took half an hour. By the time we were headed southwest, we were nearly due east of Isaac Shoal and the nets were full again. We kept a close eye on the storm as the crew emptied the nets and sorted the catch. When we were ready to drop the nets again, the storm was only about five miles northwest of us.

"Head south at ten knots for twenty minutes," I said. "That should put us far enough away from any stray lightning. I'll go tell the guys to get lunch."

After lunch, we dropped the nets again and headed west, then north, as the storm passed by us. The third and fourth trawls of the night were only slightly less productive than the first two, but with less bycatch. As the sky to the east started getting the first hints of purpling, the dawn not far off, the crew dropped anchor. Williams came into the pilothouse with a big grin.

"Over nine hundred pounds, first night out," he said. "You just broke Captain Trent's best night ever, Skipper."

"Really?" I said. "How much can we carry?"

Doc looked at Williams, then me, and said, "Four thousand pounds, but that'd mean a really slow ride home. Captain Trent usually calls it a week at three thousand pounds."

I ran the math in my head and said, "That'd be what, ten thousand dollars? If the next few nights go as well as tonight, I'd say that'd be a pretty profitable four days."

"Yeah," Doc said. "Ten grand is Captain Trent's target. Some weeks its five days, some weeks it's seven days out."

We left the pilothouse and joined the rest of the crew in the galley. Paul was about to start supper and said, "Skipper, you mentioned blackened hogfish. We got plenty, but I don't know how to do that. Would regular fried be okay?"

"Plain old fried hogfish?" I said with a laugh. "Are you out of your mind? Show me your seasoning locker."

He opened a cabinet and pulled out a rack of seasonings. He had a good assortment. I grabbed thyme, onion powder, oregano, chili powder, paprika, white and black pepper, and salt.

"Where's your flour?" I asked.

He opened another cabinet and pulled out an economy-sized twenty-pound canister and set it on the counter. The rest of the crew were drinking beer and watching a movie on the VCR, as I measured out the right amounts for the fourteen big fillets and put it all in a huge freezer bag with the fish.

"Okay, heat up a couple of large skillets with a half stick of butter in each," I said. I showed him what to do and together we cooked up the fish while two pots steamed corn on the cob and rice.

By the time the sun was fully up, the crew was fat and happy, commenting on how good the fish was. Paul had written everything down on a notecard as I mixed the seasonings. He stored the card in a small file box on the counter.

"Thanks, Skipper," Paul said with a smile. "I always wanted to try that, but never had a recipe."

"Boat approaching," Sims said, looking out a porthole. "Big center console."

"Lupori, McWhorter," I said. "You're with me."

Together, we went out to the work deck as the boat approached. It was a beauty, with a deep vee and wide Carolina flairs. It looked to be a thirty footer, with a big center console, set far aft. I'd seen one like it before, built by a guy named Tim Winter, near Raleigh, North Carolina. There were two Hispanic guys aboard, but they didn't look like fishermen.

"Permission to come alongside, *Capitán*?" the man at the helm asked. He was a tall, skinny man, about thirty, with hair down to his shoulders.

"*Que quieres*?" I asked.

"Greetings from Señor Santiago, *mi amigo*," the second man said. He was shorter and younger, maybe twenty-five, with close-cropped hair and a muscular physique.

"Yeah, come alongside and tie off," I said. "You got something for me?"

"*Sí, señor*," the younger man said. He seemed to be in charge. He went to the bow of the sleek-looking boat and started pulling tightly wrapped canvas packages from the fish box in the forward deck area. He handed each of them up to Lupori, who handed them to McWhorter. He started to carry them into the cabin, but I stopped him.

"Stack 'em on the scale," I said. The younger Cuban stopped and looked up at me.

"You no trust me, señor?" he asked.

"I don't know you," I replied.

He continued to hand up the packages until they were all on the scale, twenty-five of them. The scale read four hundred and ninety pounds.

"I was told I'd be picking up five hundred pounds," I said.

The man at the helm said, "We were told to deliver twenty-five packages. We did. *Vaya con dios.*"

With that, the younger man threw off the lines and the older man put the boat in gear and pushed the throttle to the stops. The boat's inboard diesel engine roared and they were up on plane, moving away fast.

"Stow those wherever it is you usually do," I said. Noting the angle of the sun, now high in the morning sky, I added. "Then get to your bunks."

Doc was in the pilothouse when I went forward. I said, "Go get some rest, Doc. I'll take the first watch. Tell Sims I'll wake him in two hours, then he's to wake Williams and Williams will wake you. You wake me at sunset and with a little luck, we can make our goal in four days."

"Aye aye, Skipper," he said and left the pilothouse.

I was wrong. The second night of trawling was better than the first, adding another thousand pounds to the hold. By the end of the third night's trawling, we had just shy of three thousand pounds in the hold.

Once the sorting was done on the third day, I asked the crew if they wanted to rest up before heading in, or start back to Key West immediately. To a man, they voted to head in. So shortly after sunrise, we ate supper, hoisted anchor and started back.

I was in the pilothouse when Lupori walked by with a broom, headed to the bow. I asked Doc what he was up to. "The broom signifies that we swept up," he said.

Lupori tied the broom in place, with the business end high above the bow. I walked out of the pilothouse and said to Lupori, "Take that down until we pass New Ground, okay. Bad form to show off in front of the other boats, don't you think?"

"Yeah," he said. "I guess you're right. But that *Morning Mist* crew is always giving us a hard time because of our small hold."

"You can put it back up once we clear New Ground," I said.

I returned to the pilothouse and told Doc he could take a break and catch a nap, if he wanted. He said, "There was a chirping noise from your cabin a few minutes ago. Sounded like a cricket."

"Thanks," I said. "I'll check it out."

Doc left the pilothouse and I waited until he went below, then went back to the cabin. I retrieved the satellite phone and saw that I had a video message. When I played it, I saw immediately that it was from none other than Jason Smith, Deuce's boss. His title is Associate Deputy Director, Department of Homeland Security, Caribbean Counter-terrorism Command. He reports to the Deputy Director, who reports to the Secretary of Homeland Security. I guess the Secretary reports to the President.

In his video message he congratulated me, somewhat prematurely, for getting tight with Santiago. He also said that the two men in the boat that delivered the grass to us had been apprehended and ten pounds of marijuana confiscated, along with the boat itself. They would be held at least a week, with no contact from anyone on suspicion of terrorism. He also said that Deuce had told him about the barracks I'd built and wanted to know how soon he could have the team there for a meet and greet.

I closed the video and dialed Deuce's number. He picked up on the first ring. "We got the delivery boat with ten pounds on board. They're not going anywhere for a while. How'd you manage that?"

"Not even a hi?" I said. He laughed and I went on, "I didn't have anything to do with it. He just chose the wrong time to try to skim from his employer."

"Well, it worked out good," he said. "Cuban nationals in American waters. We're sitting on them for a while, but they won't see the outside for at least five years. Nobody knows where they are."

"Okay, so you guys can take Santiago down, when I deliver the other four hundred and ninety pounds, right?"

"We could," he said. "But with his money, lawyers, and who knows how many judges in his pocket, he'd be out in less than five hours."

"Then what the hell was all this for?" I asked.

"We need to get him on the gun-running charges, Jesse. That'll put him away for a long time. Maybe even Gitmo."

"Guns, huh," I said. "I think I might be able to make something happen. With his courier out of the picture, he's going to need a new boat. Maybe I can plant a seed in his mind that he needs someone more reliable. Can you let it leak that his guys were popped?"

"I thought you didn't want that known," he said.

"Santiago needs to know they were arrested with ten pounds," I said. "When I get back in, I'll let him know the guy skimmed it, but our original deal still goes. If I work it right, I might be his new courier for both the grass and the guns."

"You're reaching, Jesse," he said. "The Director will never go for it."

"So don't tell him," I said once more.

"Call me after you meet with him," Deuce said.

"I'll call you in the morning," I said. "I'm gonna rack out, once we get back in."

"Okay, Jesse," he said. "Be careful." I ended the call and put the phone back in the briefcase. An hour later, we were nearing New Ground and I could see the other shrimp boats at anchor in deep water north of the shoal. Just then, I heard Al Fader's voice over the radio.

"*Night Moves* to *Miss Charlie*," he said. "You at the helm, Jesse?"

"Morning, Al," I said into the mic.

"How'd you do out there? We had a bad blow here, thanks for the warning."

"We did alright, Al," I said. "Any damage?"

"No, we all did as you suggested and hid behind the shoal. Come alongside, I owe you a beer."

"Have to take a rain check, Al," I said. "We're going on back home."

"Did alright, huh?" he said. "Trent'll be pissed if you go back in without a full hold."

"He won't be pissed," I said. "Catch up with me Saturday night at Blue Heaven. You buy the beer, I'll buy supper."

"You got it, man," he said. "*Night Moves* out."

Three hours later, we were entering Northwest Channel. I switched over to PA, picked up the mic and said, "All hands on deck, we're twenty minutes from the dock. Time to unload and see what we made."

The sun was sinking toward the horizon when the crew finally got the shrimp unloaded and weighed in. We had three-thousand and eighty pounds of shrimp and they were big. The wholesaler had to be called to come out, not expecting any of the boats back on Wednesday. He calculated the size to be 15/20 count and offered me $2.85 a pound. I looked over at Doc, who barely shook his head, his arms across his chest. He slightly moved three fingers on his left hand.

"I'm thinking more like three twenty a pound," I said. "A lot of this landing is bigger than fifteen-twenty."

He countered with an offer of $3.10 a pound and I agreed, shaking his hand. He counted out $9550 cash and handed it to me. Doc and I went back to the boat to pay the crew. We still had to wait around to offload our other cargo. A few minutes later, a garbage truck backed up to the dock, followed by a Chevy sedan. The sedan parked a couple spots away from the garbage truck.

"Lupori has already put the cargo in a pair of drums," Doc said. "The garbage truck will bring empty trash barrels aboard and take them, along with the boat's garbage."

"Tell Lupori and McWhorter to meet me in the galley," I said. "And don't let the garbage man board until I tell you."

Santiago got out of the Chevy and walked past the garbage collector toward the gangplank. He stopped short of it, looked up at me and said, "You're back early, *Capitán*. Permission to board?"

"Come aboard," I said. "We need to talk. In private." I led him to the galley, where the two crewmen waited nervously.

"*Pensé que dijiste en privado, Capitán*," he said.

"Yeah, just the four of us," I said. "Your deliveryman shorted us. When I told him I was hired to pick up five hundred pounds, he said he was hired to deliver twenty-five packages. They totaled four hundred and ninety pounds, as both these men witnessed. Our scales are accurate."

"I apologize, *Capitán*," he said. "Yes, they ripped me off. However, they were apprehended at sea and charged with possession of ten pounds, with intent."

The three of us looked at Santiago in surprise, Lupori and McWhorter because they didn't know. I nodded at the two crewmen and they left the galley.

"That doesn't change our agreement, *señor*," I said. "It's still twenty grand. You eat the loss for hiring disreputable people to work for you. If it were me, the charges would be the least of their worries."

He thought it over for a minute then said, "*Sí*. It is good business to deal reputably with reputable people." He handed me a large envelope, which I opened to find two bundles of $100 bills, each banded with a bank band marked $10,000. I closed the envelope and stuck it in my back pocket.

"You're not going to count it?" he asked.

"It's good business to deal reputably with reputable people," I parroted with a grin. "Besides, we both know what could happen if one of us screwed the other over."

"I understand you have a large, fast boat," he said. "I seem to be in need of a courier all of a sudden," he said.

How did he know about the *Revenge*? Or did he? "I have a small fishing boat," I lied. "With an oversized outboard."

"I'm talking about your Rampage, *señor*," he said.

"Just how do you know about this?" I asked.

"I have people that tell me things," he replied. "Would you be interested in a job?"

"You offered a security job, if I remember right," I said. "Not sure if I want to risk a delivery job."

"The security position has been filled. I'll pay you twice what you just put in your pocket, for a single run every month," he said. "I don't want to risk losing any more product to derelicts like Manny and Jose. From now on, I will personally make the pickups. I just need a man with a fast boat to pick me up with the cargo."

"You'll have to let me think that over, Santiago," I said. "Let me have your number and I'll call you in a day or two."

He handed me a business card and said, "Don't wait long, *Capitán*. My offer has an expiration date, two days from now."

"You'll have to give me more information," I said. "Like where do I pick you up and where do I take you?"

"If you accept, you'll pick me up across the Straits in a small bay on the western tip of Cuba. Then bring me here to Cayo Hueso. It is about five hundred and twenty miles round trip. How long will that take in your boat?"

"Cuba?" I said. "No deal. My boat's fast, but the Cuban patrol boats have cannons."

"There isn't a patrol boat for eighty miles of this bay," he said. "It's a simple fishing village."

"I'll think it over," I said. "But, to answer your question, that trip would take thirteen hours, not counting the stop time."

"That fast?" he said. "That will be good. I expect your call before this time on Friday. *Adiós, Capitán*."

He left then and I waited until he was off the boat, then stepped out of the galley and nodded at Doc. He motioned the garbage man to come aboard. The crew helped swap out the garbage cans and then assembled in the galley. I'd removed the bands from the two bundles and pocketed five grand for my own trouble. Smith said his team could keep anything they came across of value when on a mission, and I was part of the team. Sort of.

When all the crew was assembled, I set the cash from the wholesaler and Santiago on the table in two separate stacks and said, "We were paid ninety-five hundred and fifty for the shrimp and fifteen thousand for the other cargo. I'll let Mister Talbot settle up the shrimp pay, since I don't even know what your agreement is with Captain Trent."

As Doc split the smaller stack into several smaller stacks based on each man's take, I did the same with the larger stack, based on what I'd told them the day we left. Each crewman left the galley with over $2000 in his pocket. Doc, Williams, and Sims stayed behind until the men were walking down the gangplank, ready to blow their money in town.

"I think I may have gotten Trent off the hook with Santiago," I began. "His deliveryman shorted us ten pounds and just happened to get busted with it. Santiago has offered me the job of picking him and his cargo up, since he's going to ride it personally from now on, and bring him back here. If I accept, it will be with the stipulation that he never lures a shrimper into his business again."

"You don't really think he'll just keep his word on that, do you?" Sims asked.

"No, I don't," I said. "But I intend to make sure that he does."

After the other two men left, I told Doc to hang out for a few minutes while I gathered up my gear and called a taxi.

"No need for that, Jesse. Nikki will be here in a minute and we'll give you a ride to the marina."

"Thanks," I said. "I'd appreciate that. Give me a minute to grab my gear and call Trent."

Since my gear was already packed, I just had to grab it from the cabin. I called Trent and told him that we were back already and how the trip went.

"You filled the hold in just three days?" he asked.

"We got lucky," I said. I then told him about my plan to get Santiago off their backs. I said I'd be up there in the morning and asked if they needed anything. He put Charlie on the phone and I wrote down a list of a few items they could use, then ended the call.

I then called the Blue Heaven and asked to speak to Tina. I got her on the phone and told her we were back early and asked if she would be able to go up to the Content Keys a couple days early. She said she'd ask a co-worker and said to drop by if I could. I smiled at the thought of seeing her again and even though I'd been up for over twenty-four hours, was really looking forward to it.

I went back out to the work deck to find Doc and Nikki loading his gear into the back of their Dodge pickup. I walked down the gangplank and Nikki smiled and said, "Thanks for getting my man home early and in one piece, Gunny."

"I appreciate y'all giving me a lift."

"Bob doesn't need much of an excuse to go look at a nice boat," she said. "He was telling me about yours."

We climbed in the cab of the pickup and left the marina. Ten minutes later, we pulled up at the private dock at Oceanside Marina and I invited them aboard for a beer. It was fully dark as we boarded the *Revenge* and Orion was already rising in the night sky. I showed them the salon and grabbed a six-pack of Red Stripe from the galley, noting the three boxes sitting on the counter. We climbed up to the bridge and I put three of the beers in the small refrigerator up there and passed one to each of them.

"This is a very cool boat, Jesse."

"I'll say," Nikki added. "Do you live on it?"

"No, I have a house on a little island north of Big Pine."

"Gunny," Nikki said, "Bob told me about your plan to get him and the crew out of the problem they're in. I just want to thank you. You're taking quite a chance, aren't you?"

"Chance favors the prepared mind," I said. It was a quote often used by my old friend, Russ, when he was my Platoon Sergeant in Okinawa and later during the invasion of Grenada. "I'll be fine."

We finished our beer and Doc must have yawned a dozen times. "I better get Bob home," Nikki said. "We're probably keeping you up."

"Don't worry about me," I said. "I'm going to get a shower and head into town for a late supper at the Blue Heaven."

Nikki asked, "And to see a certain Cajun girl?"

My surprise must have been evident on my face. "It's a small island, Gunny," she said. "I sometimes pick up bartender shifts at different places, to help friends out. She called just before I got to the dock to pick you two up. I'm taking her shift tomorrow."

I walked them to the gate and said goodnight, then went back aboard to shower and shave.

CHAPTER ELEVEN:
Romance of the Sea

It was nearly 2230 when I called Lawrence for a ride. He said he was nearby and could be at Oceanside Marina in a few minutes. I dressed, locked up the *Revenge* and headed down the dock just as Lawrence pulled into the parking lot.

As I climbed in the front seat, he said, "Blue Hebin, sar?"

"Yeah," I replied. "How've you been, Lawrence?"

As he wheeled out of the parking he said, "Doin well, Cap'n. I heah yuh had a good landin."

"We did pretty good," I said.

"I heah Santiago is branchin out, mon," Lawrence said. "Some seh him runnin guns now."

"I'm hearing the same thing," I said. "What else did you hear?"

"He was in me taxi cab. Him seh he have a buyer from di Middle East."

"Now that I hadn't heard. How is it you hear all these things?"

"Most peepa tink Jamaicans ehr dumb, mon. But, I unnastand di Spahnish. Dey tot I not unnastand. Mistah Santiago seh ta his new worka, he tradin guns fa ganja, mon. Gwon mek a run ness week."

"That's good, Lawrence," I said. "Just the kind of intel I'm needing."

A few minutes later, we pulled up to the Blue Heaven. As I started to get out, I handed Lawrence a twenty. He protested that it was too much but I stopped him by saying, "It's not just for the ride, Lawrence."

He smiled and said, "Tell Miss Tina hi fo me, Cap'n. Yuh have a good night."

I stood on the curb for a minute, debating on calling Deuce this late. Finally, I opened my phone and sent a text message saying that Santiago was taking weapons to Cuba next week and I'd call him in the morning with more details.

A cold front had passed through in the early evening and by Key West standards it was downright cold, maybe even below sixty degrees. I walked through the arch to the outdoor area and it was empty, save for one couple at the end of the bar and Tina behind it.

She smiled when she saw me and came out from behind the bar to give me a hug. "You must be exhausted," she said. "I figured you'd be fast asleep by now. I want you to meet someone." She took my hand and led me to the couple sitting at the end of the bar.

"Jesse, this is Justin and Laura. Guys, this is Captain Jesse McDermitt." Then turning to me, she said, "Laura and I went to college together, they're down here doing research for Mote."

"Marine biologists?" I asked.

"Yes," Justin replied. "We've been doing research on shark migration along the Florida coast."

"Tina told us you own a fishing charter boat," Laura said.

"Yes," Tina said, "It's a beautiful boat. We're going out in it tomorrow."

"We're just going up to my house," I said.

"Do you catch many sharks," Justin asked.

"Not intentionally," I said. "Most of my clients are after mahi, marlin, grouper and other game fish. Sometimes a shark will get their catch, though."

"Makos, most likely," Laura said.

"Yeah," I said. "A lot of short-fin makos. They're common around here all year and plenty fast enough to catch a hooked marlin. Just about any shark can catch a grouper, or anything else we hook while bottom fishing."

Tina went behind the bar and got a cold Red Stripe out of the cooler and set it before me. "Are you going to eat?" she asked. "Frankie's already gone home, but the sous chef, Tim, is still here and he's going to close the kitchen soon."

"Yeah," I said. "Ask him if he can make me a fish sandwich. Anything's fine, he can surprise me."

She went to the little window and talked through it. I'd met Tim Hinson a couple of times. He'd been working under Frankie for years. He was good enough to be head chef anywhere else, but liked working here.

When she came back she said, "Tim said he's got some cobia. What time did you want to leave tomorrow?"

"As early as you want," I said.

"Skivvies time?"

I laughed and said, "Why don't you ride your bike over and we'll go for a run together before we head out."

"That sounds great," she said. "I don't usually get to run with anyone."

"We have to leave, Tina," Laura said. "We'll be here through Sunday. Call me when you get back."

I stood and shook hands with them. "It was nice meeting you both," I said.

We exchanged pleasantries and the couple left. A bell rang at the window and Tina brought my sandwich and set another cold beer in front of me.

"Looks like I'll be closing early," she said. "You have plans?"

"Well," I said, "I've been up for over twenty-four hours. What do you have in mind?"

"A lot of things," she said coyly. "But, you need your sleep. How about you take me out for a nightcap?"

"Deal," I said. I'd finished my sandwich when Tim came out from the kitchen.

"How's the sandwich, Jesse?" he asked.

"You two know each other?" Tina asked.

"Been a year or so, but yeah," I replied. Then to Tim I said, "It's really good. Tina said it was cobia. Did you bake it?"

"Yeah," he said. "With a parmesan crust and lemon juice. I gotta run, Tina. Good to see you again, Jesse."

"Why don't you go inside and I'll close up here."

I left a twenty on the bar and went inside. A band was playing a catchy song about a hollow man. I listened while I drank my beer between yawns. Tina walked up in the middle of a particularly long yawn.

"Long day, huh," she said.

"Too long," I said. "Especially at my age."

She was dressed in tight white jeans and a red tank top under a white sweater. She looked really good, especially since I knew that she'd probably been on her feet, slinging drinks, for the last six or seven hours. I stood and offered her a seat.

"Can we go somewhere quieter?" she asked.

"Sure," I said and followed her to the door.

The streets were nearly deserted as we walked north on Thomas, then a block east on Southard, and went into the Green Parrot, on Whitehead. There weren't a lot of people in the bar so we had no problem finding a quiet corner table not far from the stage. A small band was just setting up without much enthusiasm as the waitress came and took our drink order. I'm a beer man, but on occasion I like a good rum. I ordered a double Myers's, chilled, and Tina ordered a white wine.

The band started before our drinks came, a smooth jazz number by Coltrane. The sax player was very good, hitting the inflections just like Trane did. The only thing missing was a blue, smoky halo around the lights. We talked about her last couple of days at work and how I did on the shrimp trawler for a few minutes. I was really tired and I guess it showed.

"I need to get you to bed," she said. Then realizing how it sounded, she tried to correct herself.

I stopped her. "Don't worry about it. The idea has crossed my mind a time or two."

We left the bar and she took my arm as we walked east on Southard a few blocks, then took Elizabeth over to Angela, winding our way through Old Town.

As we passed the old graveyard, I asked her if she'd ever visited it. "Visit a graveyard?" she asked. "Why on earth would anyone do that, unless they knew someone buried there? Which I don't."

"I'm sure you've noticed some of the odd sort of people that live on this little rock. It's been that way for centuries. One of my favorite markers is a guy named Pearl Roberts. His epitaph reads, 'I told you I was sick.'"

She laughed and said, "You're making that up."

"No, really," I said. "Another one is a lady named Gloria something. Hers reads, 'I'm just resting my eyes.'"

We were passing the entrance to the cemetery and I said, "Come on, I want to show you something."

"In the cemetery?" she said hesitantly.

"It's just inside the gate," I said. "Don't worry, most of the ghosts are over on the far side."

She laughed nervously as we turned and walked through the gate. We came to an area that was fenced in with a short cast iron fence. I stopped at the gate and peered in. There was a short sidewalk which led to a statue at the center, with graves on either side of the walkway.

"He's called the Lone Oarsman," I said, pointing at the tall statue, with the American flag flying behind it. "That's the *USS Maine* memorial."

"I'm afraid I've never heard of it," she said.

"In early 1898 the *Maine* was sent out from Key West to Havana, Cuba," I said. "Three weeks later, while resting at anchor in Havana Harbor, there was a huge explosion and the *Maine* sank within minutes, taking two hundred and fifty-eight men to a watery grave. This was toward the end of the Cuban War of Independence from Spain. Shortly after that, America entered the fray and it became known as the Spanish-American War. 'Remember the *Maine*' was the battle cry of the day."

"So much history on this little island," she said. Then looking toward the statue she said, "You're a kindred spirit to him, you know."

"I am?"

"Yes, you are," she replied. "I can feel it."

"Ah," I said, "the Marie Laveau coming out?"

She jabbed me in the ribs with her elbow as we turned to walk back out of the cemetery. "Scoff if you must," she said. "But I really do get vibes about people. My dad said I had the gift."

We walked on up Angela Street for another block and I suddenly recognized her little house. "Hard to believe you live a stone's throw from the cemetery and never visited it," I said.

"Want to come inside and call Lawrence?" she asked. "I promise I won't bite."

"Yeah, but I might," I said with a laugh. "It's only a mile or so to Duval and I need to sort some things out in my head anyway. See you about zero-seven-hundred?"

"If that means seven o'clock, that'll be great. Do I need to bring anything?"

"Just a couple of days of clothes," I replied. Then, realizing for some women that could be six or seven outfits, I added, "Nothing fancy, just shorts, jeans and tee shirts."

"No evening gown?" she asked.

My face must have registered my reaction. She punched me in the shoulder and said, "I'm only kidding. I don't even own an evening gown."

Then she came into my arms, standing on her toes and kissed me. A long, passionate kiss. When she stepped back, she smiled and said, "I'm looking forward to it. You gonna let me drive, I mean pilot, again?"

"Absolutely," I said. I hugged her again and she turned and walked up the steps to her porch. I had to admit, she looked good in those tight jeans. She turned her head suddenly, flipping her long dark hair over her shoulder, and caught me looking. She winked and went inside.

As tired as I was, I wanted nothing more than to get to bed. Instead of walking, I called Lawrence. He said he was dropping a fare off in Old Town and I told him I'd be walking down Frances Street toward Eaton.

"Dot's neah weh Miss Tina lives, mon," he said.

I could hear his big, toothy grin over the phone and said, "Yeah, I think she lives somewhere around here."

"Ya mon," he said. "Be dere in a jiffy."

I walked slowly west on Frances, enjoying the cooler air. I knew it wouldn't last long, though. By tomorrow afternoon it would be back in the low seventies. As I walked, I thought about the past three days. Skippering the *Miss Charlie* was a challenge, but I'd thoroughly enjoyed it. I couldn't decide if it was the challenge itself, or just being in command. I thought back on my days in the Corps with sorrow sometimes.

Before I'd retired, I'd looked forward to leaving it behind. Then a little over two years later, the Towers came down. I went the next day to a prior service recruiter who told me, "Leave this one to the younger guys, Gunny." Many times I'd thought that I should have stayed for the full thirty-year ride. Being in command of a group of hard-charging warriors was very satisfying. The crew of the *Charlie* weren't highly trained Marines, but the feeling of satisfaction was still there.

A car turned the corner behind me and came to a stop alongside. It was Lawrence. I climbed in the front seat and said, "Thanks, Lawrence. Slow night?"

He started forward and said, "Ya mon, pretty slow. Dis cold weddah keeps folks inside. I heah Santiago got hisself a new mon. Fah security."

"Yeah," I said. "I heard his last bodyguard was killed a couple days ago."

"Also heah he got a new Cap'n," he said, looking over at me.

I didn't say anything. Something told me that Lawrence knew a lot more that he wasn't saying. A few minutes later we pulled up at the gated dock at Oceanside Marina. I looked over at him and asked, "You know anything about his new bodyguard?"

"He ride wit Santiago in my taxi cab, mon. Big mon, neah as big as yuh. Cuban, wid a bald head."

I handed him a twenty and got out. My legs were stiff as I made my way down the dock. I think I fell asleep halfway through the salon, long before my head hit the pillow.

At least I remembered to turn on the coffeemaker. The fresh aroma of the almighty Colombian bean roused me. It felt like I'd only been asleep for a few minutes. I got up, opened a drawer and pulled out my favorite running shorts and tee shirt, got dressed and put on my running shoes. I wasn't going to let Tina catch me in my skivvies today. I poured a cup of coffee and grabbed a banana out of the galley and went up to the bridge. The early morning air was cool and crisp, with a low fog blanketing the little bay. It would burn off shortly after sunrise, though.

A few minutes later I heard Tina's bike coming across the parking lot and walked down to open the gate.

"Good morning," she said. "Did you sleep alright?"

"I don't think I moved a muscle all night. Pulling an all-nighter was easy a couple decades ago. I must have gotten old and didn't notice."

"Old?" she said. "You can't be any more than thirty-eight or forty, right?"

I looked down at her as we walked along the dock to the *Revenge* and said, "Thanks, but that channel marker is well astern."

She looked up at me and studied my face in the dim glow of the dock lights and asked, "How old are you, then?"

"Turned forty-four last summer," I replied. "I'm guessing you're about thirty?"

She laughed and said, "Yes, as a matter of fact, that's exactly how old I am. With four years of experience, too."

I took her bag and set it inside the hatch to the salon, noting it was pretty light. That was a good indicator, in my book. "So, how far do you want to run?" I asked.

"Up to you," she said. "I can run quite a ways without tiring. Did a half marathon last spring."

"Well, we'll keep it shorter than that," I said. "How's five miles sound? Then we can shower and shove off after this fog burns off."

"Hmm," she said thinking. "We could do the loop around northern Stock Island, past the Naval Station and back. That's about five miles. I got a good warm up on the ride over."

"Then let's go," I said.

"You don't need to stretch, or warm up?"

"Never have before," I said and started down the dock, toward the gate.

I started off at a slow pace. She was a good foot shorter than me, but she had long legs for her size and a good running form. When we reached the end of MacDonald Avenue, we ran against the traffic, what little there was, on A-1-A. Then we turned north on College Road passing the botanical garden. The smell of night jasmine filled the air.

"How tall are you?" she asked.

"I'm a hair under six three," I replied. "Why?"

"Is this your normal pace?"

"No," I said. "I usually run faster."

"Don't think that just because I'm only five two you need to hold back," she said as she lengthened her stride and increased her rhythm.

I caught up and held her pace, looking over occasionally. I was wrong, she had a very good form. I'd obviously misjudged her. We held a six-minute-mile pace all the way around the loop and she was still breathing comfortably. When we crossed back over A-1-A and started down Second Street to MacDonald again, she even picked up the pace and we did the last mile in under five minutes.

As we jogged into the parking lot and slowed down I said, "I'm really impressed. That was a good run. How often do you do it?"

We slowed to a walk as we neared the dock, letting our bodies cool down. "I'd like to run every day, but at least every other day. I usually run the eight-mile loop around Roosevelt, along the beach."

"Eight miles every other day?" I said. "Very impressive."

We climbed aboard the *Revenge* and I showed her to the head. I told her to shower first, I needed to check my email. Once I heard the water running, I opened my laptop and saw that I had only one email. From the lawyer. He wrote that he really needed to meet with me, as soon as possible. He'd be in Marathon until Saturday, but then had to fly back to Oregon. He also said it would be very beneficial to me to meet him as soon as I could.

I still had no idea what this was all about, but I wrote back a quick note that I would be in Marathon Friday afternoon and he should meet me at the *Rusty Anchor* at noon.

Then I called Deuce. When he picked up, before he could say anything, I said, "I only have a minute. Santiago offered me the job of hauling his grass. I have to confirm that I'll do it by tomorrow."

"We leaked the information that his guys were arrested by DEA, like you said."

"It worked perfect. Now he doesn't want to trust anyone. He's going to personally ride each shipment from now on. If I take the job, he'll let me know when to pick him up. But, it's in a little fishing village on the western tip of Cuba."

"The ADD isn't going to go for that," he said. "I've already told you that."

"Yeah," I said, "and like I said before, just don't tell him. Look, your intel says he's moving guns to Hezbollah and my intel says he's trading guns for grass. If he's smuggling guns into Cuba, it can't be to Fidel's forces—he was adamant that the place wasn't patrolled by gunboats. He hasn't mentioned guns, though. I'll know more tonight. Gotta run."

"Jesse, wait—" He started to say something more, but I'd already turned the phone off as I heard the shower stop in the head.

Tina came into the salon, with a large towel wrapped around her and another one wrapped around her head. "I forgot my bag," she said.

The towel wrapped around her body barely touched her thighs. I just stood there with my mouth open. She reached past me and picked her bag up off the settee and I said, "Oh, yeah, um, your bag. Sorry."

She smiled and said, "The bathroom, I mean, the head is all yours. Where can I get dressed?"

Collecting my wits I said, "The guest bunk is across from the head." I brushed past her and stepped down into the companionway and opened the door to what used to be Jimmy's bunk. "Make yourself at home," I said. Then I went into the forward stateroom, grabbed a pair of cargo shorts and a tee shirt from my hanging locker and went into the head. I was glad to see her door was closed tight.

I was in and out of the shower in seven minutes. Another habit from the Corps. Her door was still closed, so I went into the galley and poured us both a cup of coffee. When she came into the salon, I was in the galley frying bacon and mixing up some eggs. She was wearing cutoff jeans and a Blue Heaven half tee shirt.

"Bacon-and-egg omelet okay?" I asked trying not to stare.

"Perfect," she said. "What can I do to help?"

"There's some chives, onions, and tomatoes in the fridge. Chop up whatever you'd like to put in it."

"Anything you don't like in an omelet?" she asked.

"I'll eat anything on this boat," I said. "Otherwise, it wouldn't be here."

"Anything?" she asked with a wicked smile.

I almost dropped the mixing bowl.

"Sorry," she said, with a chuckle. "I couldn't resist myself."

"You're making it damn hard for me," I said.

Then, realizing what I'd just said, we both laughed. "Just get to chopping, woman," I said.

We ate quickly and Tina volunteered to clean up while I got ready to make way. I went up to the bridge and started the engines as the sun was just starting to peek over the horizon. I switched on all the electronics, then climbed down and untied the mooring lines. By the time I stepped back aboard, Tina was just coming out of the salon.

"Everything's put away in the kitchen," she said.

"Galley," I corrected her.

She rolled her eyes and said, "Is there a book I can buy that has all these terms in it?" Then she handed me my thermos and two mugs of coffee and added, "I figured you'd like more."

"You figured right," I said. "We're all set, go ahead on up and I'll hand these up to you."

I tried not to look as she climbed the ladder, but it was hopeless. By this time, I was certain she was purposely enticing me. She got to the top, turned around and bent over the rail for the coffee, her breasts nearly spilling out of her shirt. I handed the thermos and mugs up to her, then climbed up myself. She took the second seat and poured us both a cup, setting mine in the cup holder by the helm.

I put the boat in gear and idled forward to the end of the piers, then reversed the starboard engine to make the tight turn. Minutes later, we were in the channel heading out of Stock Island. As we cleared the last markers I turned west and said, "When do you have to be back?"

"Nikki is filling in for me tonight," she said. "My shift tomorrow night starts at seven o'clock. Or should that be seventeen-hundred?"

"Nineteen-hundred," I said. "You add twelve, for a twenty-four hour clock. I have some business to see to at noon tomorrow in Marathon. Should be able to get back to Key West by eighteen-hundred easy."

I looked over and could see she was thinking. Then she said, "Six o'clock!"

I reached my arm around her and hugged her close. "I'll make a swab out of you yet."

"Is that good?" she asked.

"Well, it's a step up from Galley Wench."

"I know I'm not a boat person," she said. "But shouldn't we be going the other way?"

"Oh, dang," I said. She looked at me concerned and I laughed. "The water from the Atlantic up to my house is shallow, with lots of cuts and channels," I said. "We'll run the Gulf side to Harbor Key Bank and come down through Harbor Channel. Longer, but much faster. There's a chart in that cabinet to your right."

She opened it and I pointed out the one on top. "Number eleven-four-forty-two."

She pulled it out and unrolled it. Pointing out the different features I said, "Here's Harbor Key Bank. See the channel going south, then southwest? That's Harbor Channel. And that little dot, where the channel turns south, that's my island."

Throttling up, the *Revenge* raised her bow momentarily, then came up on plane. I synched the engines at sixteen-hundred rpm, its most economical speed. Thirty minutes later, we were through Northwest Channel and turning northeast at Smith Shoal. I had the sonar searching forward to keep us off the many obstructions in the area.

Once we were clear and running in deep water I said, "You want to take the helm?"

"I thought you'd never ask," she said and stood up to change seats.

I slid over as she squeezed between me and the helm, straddling my legs. She finally settled in at the helm and took the wheel. I'd already punched in the light at Harbor Key Bank on the GPS. "See the line on the chart plotter?" I asked. She nodded and I said, "Just follow that line. In about thirty minutes you should be able to see the light. It flashes every four seconds."

She looked out over the bow and I could tell she was looking for just the right cloud to follow, glancing at the GPS now and then. She looked right at home there, with her hair pulled back in a loose ponytail, and a big grin on her face. I was thinking it'd be nice to spend more time with her.

"You know," she said, as if reading my mind, "I could call Nikki and she'd probably take my Friday night shift, too."

She looked over at me, smiled and added, "Unless you have somewhere else to be."

"No," I said. "All I have is some business in Marathon at noon tomorrow and a phone call to make about some other business tomorrow afternoon. Can't think of anything else on my day planner."

Suddenly, my cell phone rang. I hadn't heard it in so long I didn't recognize it at first. Then it took a couple more rings for me to find it in the console. By the time I opened it up to see who it was, they'd hung up.

"Anything important?" Tina asked.

"An old friend," I said. "Rusty and I served together back in the early eighties. He owns the *Rusty Anchor Bar and Grill* in Marathon."

I hit redial and he picked up before the first ring ended. "Where the hell you been, bro?" he asked.

"Out past the Marquesas," I said. "Been piloting Trent's shrimp boat the last few days. What's up?"

"You gonna come around anytime soon?"

"Yeah," I said. "In fact, I'm meeting that lawyer at the *Anchor* at noon tomorrow."

"Perfect," he said. "Guess who's back in town?"

"Who?"

"Dan Sullivan," he said. "He's agreed to play here Friday, Saturday, and Sunday afternoon on the deck, for the next month."

Dan and I have been friends for a few years. He's a guitar player and used to make a decent living at it, up and down the Keys. We met at Dockside, just after I bought the *Revenge*. I learned he was into Tae Kwon Do and we started working out and sparring together. He left over a year ago, sailing across the Caribbean, spreading his laid-back island-style music. Last I heard he was on Tortola in the British Virgin Islands.

"Deck? What deck?"

"You need to come around more often," he said. "I built a nice deck out back with a stage last month. Dan's playing two sets on Saturday and Sunday afternoons, partial exchange for dock space."

I cupped the phone and said to Tina, "Go ahead and call Nikki. We're gonna be on Marathon until Saturday afternoon." She smiled.

"Who you talking to?" Rusty asked.

"Just a lady friend, piloting the *Revenge* for me," I said. "I'll introduce you tomorrow. Should be there by 1100 or so."

"Okay, bro," he said. "See ya then."

I ended the call, closed the phone and put it in my shirt pocket. Tina looked at me and said, "Didn't mean to eavesdrop, but he talks loud. An old friend in town, I gather?"

"Yeah, you'll like his music. He's playing and staying at the *Anchor*. We'll spend tonight at the house and go down there in the morning and stay at the docks."

"Where's Carl staying?" she asked.

"They're in the guest cottage on the back of the island," I said. "Their kids, too."

"Oh," she said. "I think I better go down and change before we get there."

"You look good to me," I said leering at her.

"That was the idea," she said with a sultry smile. "But, maybe something a little more conservative around the kids? Take the helm."

"Aye aye, Admiral," I said. She went down to the salon and was back up on the bridge in less than five minutes, wearing blue jeans and a long-sleeve green blouse.

"I didn't bring a whole lot of clothes," she said.

"Don't worry about it," I said. "I'll take you shopping Saturday morning." She seemed to like that idea, based on the huge smile and kiss she gave me.

The light for Harbor Key Bank was visible about a mile ahead. I slowed the big boat to barely above planing speed and started a slow turn to the south.

"There's a narrow natural channel coming up," I said. "See those red crab trap floats up ahead?"

"Yeah, they look pretty close together," she said.

"That they are," I said as I brought the *Revenge* down off plane. I switched the sonar to forward scan and idled toward the crab floats. "I call this Narrow Cut. It doesn't have a name on any chart. Actually, it's not even on a lot of charts." We eased between the floats, barely five feet on either side, then wound slowly toward Harbor Channel. I was on my feet for a better view and used the engines as much as the helm to maneuver through it.

Once clear of Narrow Cut, I turned southwest and followed Harbor Channel for about a mile. "Is that it?" Tina asked, pointing to my dock and the roof of my house showing above the mangroves and buttonwoods.

"Yep," I said. "That's home." I could see Trent's two kids running out onto the dock, with Pescador trotting along happily behind them. I suddenly realized I really missed the big shaggy mutt.

I started to turn south, following the channel, then reversed the port engine and revved it until the big boat spun around. I dropped it to idle and reversed the starboard engine and slowly backed up the little channel. I pressed the button on the key fob and the big doors on the west side of the house slowly opened.

Tina looked around and said, "You have electricity? I don't see any power lines."

"The doors open by springs," I said. "There's a solar panel and wind turbine that charge big batteries to run the place. The motor to close the doors and everything else on the island is twelve volt."

Trent came down the steps to the dock as I backed under the house, gently bumping the fenders hanging on the rear and side dock at about the same time. He took a line, lashed the stern cleats and looked up at us. "Welcome home, McDermitt."

"Good to see ya, Trent," I said. "Have any trouble?"

"Had a great time," he said. "Charlie really loves it here. The kids, too. Hi, Tina, what are you doing here?"

Just then, Pescador came running down the steps and leaped into the cockpit. He sat down and his tail was almost wagging him, as he looked up at us on the bridge. I shut off the engines and started to climb down.

"I shanghaied her," I said. "Tina, this is my best buddy, Pescador." I stepped over onto the deck, knelt down and scratched him behind the ears. In a rare display of affection, he licked my face. I turned as Tina came down the ladder and lifted her off the last step. She turned around and Pescador looked at her, then at me.

"Pescador, this is my friend, Tina." I said. He looked at her again, wagged his tail and barked once. Turning to her I said, "He likes you."

"How can you tell?" she asked.

Trent answered for me, "If he didn't, there'd be no question about it. Jesse, that's about the smartest dog I've ever seen in my life. He killed a little spinner yesterday. It almost bit Patty. Snatched it up out of the water and just slung it back and forth till it was dead."

Tina reached out and seeing what I did, she scratched Pescador behind the ear. "What's a spinner?" she asked.

"A shark," I said. "There's lots of them around here. Mostly little, like Trent said."

Charlie came down the steps and said, "I thought I heard your voice, Tina. How've you been?"

"Fine," she said. "You look good."

"It's this island," she said with a smile. "I can't remember a time I've been so relaxed. Y'all come on out back, after you drop your gear in the house. I have lunch almost ready."

"Hope you don't mind, Jesse," Trent said. "There's a lot of lumber back there, so I built a big outdoor table."

"That's what it was for," I said. "I need about four of them."

I went into the salon and picked up both our bags and carried them as we walked up the steps to where the kids were waiting at the top. They said hi and took off down the back steps. Pescador looked up at me and I nodded. He was off running after the kids.

"Y'all go ahead," I said. "We'll be just a second." I opened the door to the house for Tina and we walked in. She went first to the kitchen side of the main room, as I carried both our bags into the bedroom. When I came out, she was standing in the middle of the room, noting that I'd put both our bags in the bedroom.

"You have two rooms back there?" she asked.

I shook my head.

"Just one room with two beds?" she asked.

I shook my head.

"One bed and a hammock? One bed and a couch?"

"Just one big bed," I said.

She walked past me and looked inside. Then she slowly turned back toward me, her dark eyes smoldering.

"Are you sure about this, Jesse?"

"Yes," I said. "Let's go eat, then I'll have Pescador catch us something for supper."

"This I've got to see," she said and took my hand as we walked toward the back steps. Before we got to the steps, my phone rang again. "Popular guy today," she said.

I opened the phone and saw it was Deuce. I told her to go ahead, that I needed to take the call and didn't get a signal off the deck. I opened the phone and said, "Not a good time, Deuce."

"Never is," he said. "I had to tell the ADD about Cuba and Santiago trading guns for marijuana."

"You need to lighten up a little, buddy," I said. "Grass, pot, or weed."

"Whatever," he said. "The Director wants to catch him in the act of delivering arms. We're pretty sure the people he's trading *weed* for guns is a Hezbollah cell, working out of western Cuba."

"Hezbollah controlled most of Lebanon when I was there in eighty-two. A pretty unfriendly group of people."

"That's an understatement," Deuce said. "Here's the deal, Jesse. Mister Smith is arriving here in about an hour and wants to meet with you."

"When?" I asked. "I'm at home right now."

"Perfect," he said. "We can be there by fifteen-hundred."

"No good," I said. "I have guests here."

"Trent?" he asked. "That's good. The Director wants me to debrief him. See if he can give us any more to work with."

"Trent, his wife, his kids, and a friend of mine," I said irritably.

"This is important, Jesse. Who's the friend?"

"A lady I met in Key West, if you gotta know."

"Trent needs to know who you are working with, so clue him in. But your friend is out of the loop."

"Hey, Deuce," I said sternly. "This is my island, remember. On my boat and on my island, I call the shots. That's not debatable."

"Like I said, Jesse, this is *muy importante*. Think you can make something up, so that the four of us can sit down together for half an hour?"

"You flying in a DHS chopper would make that difficult," I said.

"It'll be a civilian chopper. Tell your friend and Mrs. Trent that we want to see your island about a base for a fishing expedition or something."

"Okay," I said reluctantly. "But remind Smith that I'm not his lapdog or errand boy."

Smith's voice came over the phone and I realized Deuce had me on speaker, "I'd never considered you anything of the kind, Gunny."

"See you at fifteen-hundred," I said irritably. "And don't be late."

I walked down the steps and joined the others for lunch. After we'd eaten, I invited Trent to walk out onto the north dock, while Charlie and Tina cleaned up. Once we were at the end of the long dock I said, "I have to tell you something, Trent."

"If you're gonna brag about your landing, save it," he said. "But, I might call you from time to time to check those fishing reports."

"I work for Homeland Security," I said. I let that sink in while he pulled a cigarette out of a pack and lit it. "When I came down to Key West last week, it was only to help a friend's dad out of a jam. Then it turned out that Santiago has been on DHS's radar for some time."

"You're a damn fed?" he asked. "So, why you telling me this now? Can't you just bust him for the pickup you made?"

"It's complicated, Carl," I said. "He's involved in arms smuggling, too. He's trading weapons for grass to a terrorist organization in Cuba. If he got picked up for trafficking drugs, he would barely see the inside of the booking office and be right back on the streets. If we get him on terrorism, he goes to Gitmo, no lawyer, no right to remain silent, nothing. He's just gone."

"Okay, I follow that. But why are you telling me? I'm just a shrimper."

"The Deputy Director and one of his team leaders will be here in a few hours. The team leader is a good friend of mine. The Director wants to talk to both of us. I'm really just kind of a subcontractor. I move men and equipment on the *Revenge*, disguised as anglers."

"They're coming here?"

"Yeah," I said. "We can tell the women they're a prospective charter."

"I don't like that, Jesse. Charlie and I have an honest relationship. I learned from lying to a woman I was involved with, with my first wife. I don't hide anything from Char."

I looked back up the dock toward shore. I could see Tina between the two shacks, throwing a stick for Pescador. Suddenly, I felt very cheap. I didn't want to lie to her, any more than Trent wanted to lie to his wife.

"You don't like it either, do you?" he said. "I know about you, Jesse. You're a straight shooter. That gal is, too, from what I seen. If you screw things up in the beginning, she'll bolt. I can guarantee that."

"So," I said. "The other option is to tell them."

"That'd be my choice," he said.

"Let's go," I said as I started walking back up the dock. Tina saw us coming and smiled. She ran out to meet us at the end of the dock.

"Your dog's too cool," she said. "He'll do almost anything I tell him. It's like he understands what I'm saying."

"Really?" I said. "He's never paid attention to any woman."

"It's true," said Trent. "He totally ignores Charlie."

"We need to talk, Tina," I said. "All four of us."

We walked over to the table Trent had built and I complimented him on his craftsmanship. "Think you could build three more just like it," I asked.

"Why do you need four tables?" Tina asked as the four of us sat down. "Or for that matter, two guest houses, that have twelve beds each?"

"That's kinda what I wanted to talk to you about," I said. I went on to tell her and Charlie the whole story. How I worked as a part-time contractor for the government.

How Santiago was dealing arms to terrorists and how we were going to stop him and end his threats against everyone in the Keys. How, in less than two hours, a chopper was going to land in the middle of the clearing and a big shot DHS agent was going to talk to all four of us. When I was done, I just sat there.

"So, all this time, you've been working for the government?" Tina asked. "When you took me out to Fort Jefferson, what were you doing? Scouting?"

"No," Trent said. "He came to Key West to help us, Tina. It wasn't until later that he found out that Santiago was running guns."

She looked from Trent to me and said, "Is that true? Why are you telling us?"

Charlie hadn't said anything since we sat down. She leaned forward and smiled at me. Then she smiled at her husband and turned to Tina. "Carl and I don't hide anything from one another. I suspect that little pow wow out on the dock was to make up some kind of lie about what those men arriving in the chopper were coming here for. A good relationship must be built on honesty from the start, or it'll never grow."

"I swear, Jesse," Trent said, "That woman can read my mind. It'd just be a waste of time to try to pull anything over on her."

"So, you were going to lie to me?" Tina said.

Trent looked at her and said, "I could see that it was tearing him up to do it, Tina. These islands are small and people that have never met know about everyone else. Before I ever met Jesse, I knew him to be an honorable man."

"Well, aren't you gonna say anything?" she asked.

"I told you now," I said, "because I don't want to hide anything from you. Why that's important to me, I don't fully understand because I've only known you a few days. I'm sorry I couldn't tell you anything before. But, now it seems important to me to tell you."

"Okay," she said. "So who are these two guys?"

"Smith is the Associate Deputy Director of the Department of Homeland Security's Caribbean Counter-terrorism Command. Deuce is the son of my old Platoon Sergeant, back when I first started in Marine Recon. He's a former Lieutenant Commander in the Navy SEALs and has become a very good friend. Now, he's the team leader of the counter-terrorism interdiction team. I've only met five others on his team, only two by name. The whole team consists of about thirty people, half of which are hardcore door kickers, like I used to be. My job, as a part-time contractor, is to move members of the team and their equipment to where they're needed in the Caribbean Basin. I built those two bunkhouses for them to come here and train. That's also why I need three more tables."

"I've seen you in action, Jesse," Tina said, smiling. "You're still a 'hardcore door kicker' yourself."

"That seems to bring us full circle," Trent said. "Who wants a beer?" He got up from the table and went into the western bunkhouse and came back out with a cooler. Opening it, he passed around four icy Bahamian Kaliks.

"Doesn't anyone on these islands drink Budweiser?" Tina asked, laughing. "I can always tell a local by the beer he orders."

We talked a little more about what was coming up, then I showed Tina around the rest of the island. We were out on the dock when she turned and said, "Charlie told me you built all this yourself, even the channel. Is that true?"

"Not everything," I said. "I had this dock built in Flamingo and barged down, along with the lumber for the bunkhouses."

"I think you missed your true calling," she said.

"No," I said. "I enjoy building things. Probably wouldn't enjoy it half as much if it was how I earned a living."

We were on the end of the dock and I was leaning against the railing. She stepped toward me and I took her in my arms and held her close. It was hard not to mentally compare her to my late wife. They didn't have much of anything in common. Where Tina was petite and curvy, Alex had been slim, and nearly a foot taller. Alex had been blonde, with clear, pale blue eyes that showed her every emotion. Tina's hair was as dark as the deepest ocean trench and her eyes so dark they were nearly black and sultry with promise. Alex was outgoing, where Tina was somewhat demure. Both were athletic, as I'd learned that morning. I suddenly realized that if things had been reversed, I would have wanted Alex to move on, enjoy life and find someone to enjoy it with. I looked down at Tina. Her lips parted and we kissed slowly, clinging to one another as if lost at sea. She melted further into my arms and kissed me passionately.

That's when I heard the far-off thumping of a chopper slowing down. Looking off to the northeast I mumbled, "Great timing, Deuce. C'mon, we better get to the clearing."

We ran down the pier and found Trent and Charlie still sitting at the table, the kids playing in the middle of the clearing with Pescador. I whistled sharply and Pescador came running. I turned to Trent and said, "Chopper's incoming. Be here in three or four minutes."

Charlie got up and called to the kids. She told them to stand over by the bunkhouse because a helicopter was about to land in the clearing. I looked up at the flagpole and noted that the wind was coming out of the south. The pilot would fly over and see the flag then turn and come back in from over the house. The beating of the blades got louder, the pitch changing as he pulled the nose up to bleed off speed. It roared over from the north, about two hundred feet up. It continued in a sweeping turn away to the southwest.

"He's not landing?" asked Tina.

"Just turning around to make his approach into the wind," I said as the bird banked around the house, coming in slower. I stepped away from the group and spread my arms wide, then moved my forearms up and back out to the side, signaling him forward. When he was nearly over the center, I stopped, keeping both arms fully extended to the sides, and he came to a hover. I then moved my arms downward and he began descending. When he made contact with the ground, I brought my arms all the way down and crossed them, signaling him to cut the engine.

As the engine shut down and the rotors began to slow, the front right door and both back doors opened. Smith and Deuce climbed out, along with a woman I recognized from the video she'd sent me. It was the tech guru, Chyrel Koshinski, and she was carrying a case of some kind. The three of them bent over and trotted over to where we were standing.

Pescador was standing next to me on full alert, the scraggly hair on his neck and back standing up, and I said, "They're friends, Pescador."

Smith reached out his hand and said, "Captain McDermitt, I assume?"

I took his hand and said, "Can it, Smith." Turning to those behind me I said, "This is Associate Deputy Director Jason Smith. The big guy is my friend Deuce Livingston and the young lady is DHS technician Chyrel Koshinski."

Turning back to Smith I said, "These are my friends, Carl and Charlie Trent and Monroe County Deputy Christina La Mons. Welcome to my island, Smith. Good to see you again, Deuce. Pleased to finally meet you, Ms. Koshinski. Let's sit down."

We sat down at the new table, the four of us on one side and the three of them on the other. Charlie told the kids to go inside and play a game.

Smith didn't look very happy. I grinned at him and said, "Like I said, my boat, my island, and my rules. I don't lie to people that are important to me. I was told by a very wise man that was the best rule."

Smith looked over at Deuce, who nodded openly. Then Smith said, "Captain, it's most unprofessional to divulge national security information to civilians."

"I'm a civilian, Smith," I said. "Have been for nearly seven years. On the boat, it's Captain, or just Skipper. Ashore, I'm Jesse, or just McDermitt. For twenty years before, I survived because I'm a damn good judge of people. These are my friends, they're to be trusted. They're up to speed on everything I know. Which, I might add, is more than you know. Now, what's on your mind?"

"Very well, McDermitt," he said. "Ms. Koshinski has a few things to show you while I talk with Mr. and Mrs. Trent."

He stood up and said, "Mr. Trent, I'd like you to tell me everything you know about Carlos Santiago while your friends talk about some technical stuff."

The three of them walked over to the western bunkhouse and went inside. I could see them sit down at the desk inside.

"Are you out of your mind, Jesse?" Deuce said. "He's the third most powerful man at Homeland. He has the ear of the President, for crying out loud."

"I don't like him," I said. "And I don't care if he's got the President's balls, Deuce."

"Geez, man, you're such an asshole sometimes," he said. Then he smiled and added, "No wonder my old man liked you."

"Jesse, please just call me Chyrel." She reached across and shook hands with Tina and said, "Pleased to meet you, Deputy."

"Just Tina," she said.

"I'm sorry Deuce, but ever since I saw that guy on my boat without permission, I couldn't stand his smarmy ass. Probably never gonna change."

"Yeah, I warned him about that when he asked," Deuce said. Then he reached across and took Tina's hand and said, "Any friend of Jesse's is someone I'd take a bullet for. Real nice to meet you, Tina."

Chyrel opened the case, took out a file and opened it, laying three pictures on the table. They were overhead shots of a small camp on a bay. "These were taken at one-month intervals, the most recent at noon today," she said. "This is the village of La Fe."

"Faith," I said. "Probably an old Spanish mission."

"Yes," she said. "It's on Guadiana Bay, on the western tip of Cuba. It's only a little further from Cancun, Mexico, than it is from Havana. As you can see, there's a small camp that's been set up recently just outside the village to the south. CIA intelligence assets tell us it's a Hezbollah training camp, there with Castro's blessings."

"Damn," I said. "How's Santiago tied to Castro? Any connection?"

"None that our assets have found," she said. "Santiago's a midlevel player, son of a Marielista. His father was convicted of several torture murders, before Castro put him on one of the boats during the boat lift in nineteen-eighty. Santiago's mother was a Havana prostitute. Both are dead. Santiago's suspected of rape, torture, and murder in several fishing villages in western Cuba. But he's still allowed to come and go with impunity because he bribes the local magistrates."

"He's a real dangerous man, Jesse," Deuce said. "See this boat, anchored just off the beach, near the camp? It's that Winter you had us pick up. Assets in the area confirmed it, by both the name on the stern, *El Cazador*, and the description of the two men on it, which matches the guys we have in custody."

"*The Hunter*," I said. "Fitting name."

"We want to infiltrate this area," he said, pointing to a spot about a mile south of the camp. "A two-man team, to get more intel on the weaponry they have and what's coming in. Tony and Art volunteered. We need you to take them on a *fishing trip* to Cancun, then drop them two miles offshore on the return. Can you do it?"

I thought it over and said, "Yeah, I'll have to take at least a hundred extra gallons of fuel. That's four hundred and seventy-five miles. My range is three fifty."

"How about a heavy-duty collapsible bladder, like they use in the desert? You could put it in one of the fish boxes."

"Each fish box can hold a hundred and fifty gallons. Make it two bladders," I said. "That three-hundred-and-fifty-mile range is at cruising speed. If I have to do any fast running, I'll need the extra fuel. When do you want to do this?"

Deuce grinned and said, "The two bladders are already requisitioned. Tony and Art can be ready on a moment's notice."

"Let's shoot for Monday," I said. "I need to talk to Santiago about his job offer."

"Job offer?" Tina said.

"He wants to hire me to run his dope into Key West," I said. "I told him I'd think it over and get back to him by tomorrow evening. We're hoping that he'll also offer me the job of moving the guns down there."

"Is it dangerous?" she asked.

Deuce grinned and said, "For Santiago, maybe." Then to me he said, "Tony and Art will be self-sustainable for five days, so we'll have to pick them up either before you make the first dope run or during the first run."

"That won't work," I said. "Santiago wants to sit on his shipment all the way back from Cuba and I'm betting he has someone ride down with me to pick it up."

"Damn," Deuce said. "I was afraid of that. We'll have to exfiltrate them once they get the intel and before that dope run."

"Why not drop them on the way to Cancun and pick them up on the way back?" I asked.

"Santiago might have eyes on you," he said. "The ruse of them being charter fishermen only works if they go fishing in and around Cancun. A single man going down there invites scrutiny."

"Why not a different ruse, then?" I said. "Two couples spending a few days diving in sunny Cozumel?"

Deuce grinned again. "Yeah, I like that. Tony and Art could stay below decks and drop over the side after dark. An overnight trip down there and an overnight trip back."

We both looked at Tina. "Think Nikki would cover your shift for a few days next week?" I asked.

"Me?" she said. "Go to Cozumel? No way. I can't afford to take that much time off work."

"It's a paid gig, Tina," Deuce said. "Jesse gets ten thousand dollars. Up to him how he wants to split it. We can contact the Sheriff and have you temporarily assigned to DHS, undercover."

"Holy crap," she said. "You can do that? You want to pay me to go to Cozumel with a tall, handsome boat Captain and the two of you?"

"No, not me," Chyrel said laughing. "The team would fall apart without me on my computers. And yes, I can have the temporary assignment done in less than an hour. What are your primary duties with the Sheriff's Office?"

"Mostly vice," she said. "Who's the other woman going?"

"I have a certain bar wench in mind," Deuce said.

"Tina's in law enforcement," I said. "You think it's wise to bring Julie?"

"Yeah," Deuce said. "She was really torn up after what happened. Guess she must have felt somewhat responsible. Plus, she wanted to be closer to what I do, so she joined the Coast Guard Reserves. She just graduated basic last week. Chyrel will have her TAD with us, too."

"Really? Julie a Coastie?"

"Yeah," he said. "Surprised the hell out of me too. She didn't want to tell you until she finished her MOS training. Get this, she's going to Camp Lejeune for Maritime Enforcement training."

Julie in the Coast Guard? That took me aback a little. Not that she couldn't handle the training. She was every bit as tough as her old man, maybe more so. But she'd never been very fond of the Coast Guard and had been pretty vocal about it on more than one occasion.

"Maritime Enforcement?" I asked. "I know they had a port security training facility there. It'd just opened before I retired."

"It's been upgraded and enlarged for their new unit. She'll report there in April and once she graduates, she'll be tapped for duty with us. Two of our team came from Coast Guard port security and they'll go up for further training with her."

Tina looked from Deuce to me, puzzled. "You'll meet Julie tomorrow," I said.

She didn't have to think about it long. "Okay," she said, "I'm in. I'm sure Nikki will take my shifts. I'll call her tomorrow."

"Do you have a passport?" I asked.

"Yeah," she replied. "I went to Australia five years ago to watch the Olympics. I had friends on the swim team."

"I'll have Tony come down here tomorrow," Deuce said. "He'll install the bladders and put the underwater scooters aboard."

"We'll be at the *Anchor* by noon," I said. "Any time after that, until Sunday morning, will work fine."

Smith and the Trents came out of the bunkhouse and walked over to where we were sitting. Deuce said, "The insertion's a go, Director. With a few minor changes. I'm going along, with Deputy La Mons here and Julie. We'll drop our men on the way down to Cozumel and pick them up three days later on the way back."

"Very good," Smith said. "The Trents provided a few insights and cleared up some details. I suspect if McDermitt makes the right negotiations with Santiago, they'll be off the hook with him by tomorrow?"

"That'll be my stipulation," I said. "I can be a greedy bastard sometimes. I'll tell him I'll run his drugs, but only if I get the whole contract. No more drug boats meeting with the shrimpers."

"And you think he'll accept those terms?"

"I do," I said. "It's just good business."

"Very well," he said. "May I have a word with you in private?"

I got up and followed Smith out to the pier. Once we were out of earshot, he turned and said, "I don't appreciate your freelancing, nor divulging my identity."

"Tough shit," I said. "I don't appreciate your boarding my boat and coming here without an invitation."

He gave me a hard look and said, "You need to learn your place, McDermitt."

"I'm in my place, Smith," I growled. "You came to me, remember? I'd be just as happy, belay that, I'd be a hell of a lot more happy, if I'd never met you."

He softened a little, knowing that it was because of him and Deuce trying to recruit me that Alex got killed. "You have a point," he said. "But, in the future, please clear it with me before we bring any more outsiders in. Understood?"

He started to walk away, but I put a hand on his shoulder. "Speaking of which," I said. "I want you to do a more in-depth look at someone. My First Mate has found another job and I'd like to hire someone that will fit both our needs."

"Who would that be?" he asked.

"Robert Talbot, Trent's First Mate on the shrimp boat. He's a former FMF Navy Corpsman, served with One Nine in Afghanistan and Iraq. You did a short run up on him already."

"Yes, I remember looking it over," he said. "You were right. You are a good judge of talent. I was thinking the same thing when I saw his full jacket."

"I don't fish much. But when I do, I need someone I can count on. That means he'd have to quit working for Trent and be available at any time. He'd need a monthly stipend to be on call. I was thinking three thousand a month."

"I was thinking four thousand. You talk to him and if he agrees, let Mister Livingston know and I'll set it up."

We walked back to the table and Smith started past the group toward the chopper, spinning his hand in the air to tell the pilot to power up. Deuce stopped him and said, "I'd like to stay behind, sir. To make arrangements with Julie. I'll ride back with Tony tomorrow afternoon."

"Take the weekend, Mister Livingston," Smith said. "Jacobs and Newman, too. Have them both come down tomorrow and bring their gear." Then turning to Chyrel, he said, "Perhaps you'd like to stay also, Ms. Koshinski? I'll have Mister Jacobs bring the rest of your electronics to put aboard the boat."

"Yes sir," she said. Smith bent over and trotted toward the chopper, its blades already spinning. Turning to me, Chyrel asked, "Is there a motel nearby?"

The chopper was already lifting off the ground when I said, "Yeah, welcome to McDermitt Manor." Turning to Deuce, I said, "Keys to the skiff are hanging in the box at the bottom of the steps. Just try to keep it off the reef, Squid."

Chyrel and Deuce walked over to the middle of the clearing, where Smith had dropped two small duffle bags. "Now I know why you insist we carry these," she said. "Where will I be staying?"

"The eastern bunkhouse is empty," I said. "But you'd probably be a lot more comfortable aboard the *Revenge*. Your packages are still aboard. I haven't even opened them yet. After dinner, maybe you can show me in more detail how all that stuff works."

"Speaking of dinner," Tina said. "I doubt there's ever been this many people on this island since the dawn of time. What's on the menu?"

At the same time, Deuce and I said, "Fish."

Trent said, "Or lobster and stone crab claws. I've been busy the last few days. The refrigerator in the house is full."

"I'm going to head on out," Deuce said. "Nice meeting you, Mr. and Mrs. Trent. See you tomorrow, Jesse."

"Hang on a minute, Deuce. Tina, would you mind getting Chyrel settled aboard and show her how to work the head?" I said. "I need to talk to Carl and Charlie."

"Sure," she said. "Follow me, Chyrel."

"And put on your bathing suit," I said. "We're going for a swim." She looked back over her shoulder at me and smiled as they walked away.

I turned to Trent and said, "The deal I'm going to make with Santiago will be for the whole importation. No more shrimpers hauling drugs, or being threatened. Just to be on the safe side you and your family should stay here until Sunday." Then I reached into my pocket and took out the money I got from Santiago, the owner's cut of the shrimp landing and the extra money I'd skimmed and handed it to him. Altogether, it was a little over twelve thousand dollars. "Just in case this takes longer than that, you can pay your crew to stay in port."

"I can't take your money, Jesse," he said.

"It's not my money," I said. "I upped the take with Santiago. The rest is your cut from the landing. But, I have some bad news."

"What's that?" he asked.

"I want to hire Bob away from you," I said. "You and I both know he's not cut out for shrimping. He misses the jazz, I could sense it."

"Yeah," Charlie said, "You're right. I have no idea what jazz means, but if it means he misses the action when he was in the Navy, I got that sense, too."

"So, where do I find a good First Mate?" Trent asked. "Bob's the most reliable man in the whole Key West fleet."

"My old First Mate is looking for steady work," I said. "He's never done any trawling, but he knows boats, knows the water and has never let me down."

"Jimmy?" he asked. "I don't know, man."

"Your daughter is straightening him up," I said. "Besides, he doesn't touch the stuff when he's working. You got my word."

"Okay," Charlie said, "We'll talk to him."

"Walk with me, Deuce," I said and headed over to the little cove on the western side of the island. When we got through the trees and were standing on the little sandbar, I reached into my pocket and pulled out a Spanish gold doubloon, mounted on a gold chain, and handed it to him. He looked down at it in his palm, then back up to me.

Pointing across the water I said, "You see that little island just to the north of the larger one?"

He looked out across the shallows and said, "Yeah, the one with the coconut palms on it?"

"Yeah, that's it," I said. "That's where I found Lester. He was nearly dead from dehydration. I left him there." Deuce stared at the little island about two miles distant. Lester was the man that had murdered his father and stolen the doubloon, along with a few other pieces of treasure. He was also part of the group of men that had raped and murdered my wife.

"No loose ends," he said. I noticed a single tear at the corner of his eye. "Thanks, brother." He turned and walked back through the trees and across the clearing. I returned to the table as Tina was coming back across the clearing, wearing a red one-piece and carrying two towels. It covered a whole lot more than the bikini she wore last weekend, but was very flattering.

"We'll be back in about an hour," I said to Carl and Charlie as I pulled off my shirt and emptied my pockets on the table. Then Tina and I walked out to the end of the dock together.

Pointing to the northeast I said, "See that little island out there? That's Upper Harbor Key. The water here is five feet deep. Harbor Channel, which we came through in the boat, has an eddy channel running north around that island and back to Harbor Channel. Staying in the channel the water's ten to twenty feet deep. It's a mile and a half there and back. Think you can handle that?"

"Just a mile and a half? No problem," she said with a confident grin.

"Open ocean swimming isn't like a pool," I said. "The tide's falling. We'll be swimming against the current going out. So a three-quarter-mile swim is like a mile and a half. The water's only a couple feet deep just outside the channel. If you get tired, just swim out of the channel."

She turned and looked at the island, then tossed her dark hair over her shoulder as she turned her head and said, "Just try to keep up." Then she dove in the water. She surfaced immediately and let out a shriek.

"Oh," I said, "I forgot to tell you. The water coming in from the Gulf is about seventy-three degrees."

She splashed water at me, then turned and started swimming toward the island. I dove in, went to the bottom and made four long strokes before surfacing, thinking I'd come up right beside her.

I was wrong. She was ten yards ahead. I struck out, swimming hard to catch up. Too hard. By the time I was alongside her, I was having to breathe with every other stroke. I was on her right, breathing with every stroke of my left arm so I could watch her. She was swimming effortlessly, taking a breath with every third stroke, alternating left and right.

I had to admit, for a woman her size she was fast. She had flawless form as she cut through the water. Soon, I had my breathing back under control, taking a breath with every fourth stroke. By the time we were halfway to Upper Harbor Key, I could feel the burn in my shoulders and legs. Every other breath I could catch a quick glimpse of her and could hear her when she took a breath.

She maintained the same third-stroke breathing all the way to the eddy channel, where I started to crowd her to make her turn. She took the hint and followed the dropoff, staying close to the inside edge of the channel. We rounded the island and started south to the main channel in what I figured was close to my best time.

The swim back was much faster and easier, with the following current. By the clock in my head, I figured we made it back to the pier in about thirty minutes, which I confirmed by checking my dive watch when I stood up a few feet from the end of the pier.

Treading water she said, "That was exhilarating! Did you see that turtle?"

"Yeah," I said, "It was a green turtle. They feed on the turtle grass."

"It didn't look green to me," she said.

I laughed as she swam over and came into my arms, wrapping her strong legs around my waist. "The meat's green," I said. "From eating the grass."

She leaned her head back, arching herself until her face went underwater. Then levering herself upward using me as a fulcrum, she lifted her face from the water so her hair was pulled straight back. Then she climbed higher and kissed me deeply. "I could get used to this," she said. "I kept seeing bright-colored fish darting around the rocks. Even the rocks were colorful."

"Coral," I said. "Not rocks. Coral is a bunch of tiny animals grouped together. Tomorrow, when we go shopping, we'll get you a wetsuit and do some snorkeling on my favorite reef."

I helped her up onto the pier, then sunk down into the water to push myself up onto it with her. We toweled off and wrapped the big towels around our shoulders for warmth and walked back to the house. Pescador came running to greet us halfway across the clearing.

"Where's the Trents, boy?" I said. He looked over to the west side of the island and I could see the four of them wading through the shallows, carrying buckets. "Looks like we'll have some clams, along with the fish, lobster, and crab claws."

"Sounds delicious," she said. "Everything you need is right here, isn't it?"

"Pretty much," I said. "I cleared this patch to grow a garden, but the soil's not good enough."

"Ever hear of aquaculture?" she said.

"Aquaculture? No."

"You grow plants, floating in trays, in a large tank," she said. "And you raise fish in another large tank. The plants get their nutrients from the fish waste, filtering the water."

"That could work," I said smiling. "Plenty of fish around here."

We went up the steps to the house and I told her to go ahead and shower inside, I'd use the outdoor shower around back. I have a cistern that collects rainwater since there's no freshwater source in the Keys, except a small spring in Key West and No Name Key. All the water in the Keys comes from a pipeline down from Miami. My cistern has a gauge that shows the water level. It's nothing more than a clear tube connected to the top and bottom of the two-thousand-gallon tank. I checked it and was pleasantly surprised to see that the water level was still above fifteen hundred gallons. With four people on the island, I was worried it'd be lower. The Trents must have been conservative. I have a desalinization unit aboard the *Revenge* that I can use to add water to the cistern if need be.

I showered quickly in my shorts, dried off and went inside to change. Tina was still in the head, so I quickly changed in the bedroom, then went down to the *Revenge* and started bringing up the supplies I'd bought before leaving Key West. It took three trips, with a box under each arm, but it was more than enough to last for a couple of weeks.

Tina was just coming out of the head when I brought in the last of the groceries and helped me put them away. She was wearing a lime green tank top and khaki cargo shorts. "This is the last of my clean clothes," she said. "What do you do when you need to do laundry? I didn't see a machine anywhere."

"There's a small washer and dryer on the boat," I said. "But living alone on an island, I really don't have a lot of laundry."

We put together a large salad and wrapped a dozen ears of corn and a dozen small potatoes in foil. I loaded an empty box with them, adding several snapper fillets, lobster tails, and a big bowl full of stone crab claws from the fridge. We carried everything down to the table in the clearing. I noticed that Trent, probably with Pescador's help, had gathered a large pile of driftwood behind the eastern bunkhouse. I carried an armload and with some dried palm fronds, soon had a good fire going in the large grill.

Tina was looking into the fire and said, "I've never seen such colorful flames."

"It's the driftwood," I said. "Salt and minerals from the water soak into the wood and remain after the wood dries. You should see a bonfire."

The Trents came through the trees, all of them carrying buckets. "We got some clams," Trent said. "We'll go up and get cleaned up. Be back in a few minutes."

Tina and I started preparing the lobster tails for the grill by splitting them with my heavy dive knife. The kids' squealing caught my attention and when I glanced up to the house, I realized why there was still so much water left. Trent, Charlie and both kids were showering together under the cistern, washing their clothes at the same time. They soon returned and went into the western bunkhouse to change. When they came out, they were wearing dry clothes and Charlie had their wet things in a plastic tub. She carried them over to a line I hadn't noticed and hung them to dry.

"You guys don't have to use the cold shower," I said. "The propane tank is full and will last for months."

Trent grinned and said, "The kids love it and to tell the truth, it's a lot of fun. Especially after the kids go to bed."

That evening, we had a great seafood feast. I kept thinking about Tina's idea of growing vegetables using aquaculture and my mind was already devising how big the tanks would have to be. Fresh water from the *Revenge* wouldn't be a problem. It can produce two hundred gallons a day. The freshwater fish would be the hard part. I'd have to buy them. There was a tilapia and catfish farm up in Homestead I could probably get them from.

"This is delicious," Chyrel said. "I've never eaten stone crab or clams and the only lobster I've ever had were Maine lobster."

"You don't live in south Florida?" Charlie asked.

"No," she replied. "I live in Georgetown, just outside of DC."

"Tina," I said. "I've been thinking about what you said earlier. How much do you know about that aquaculture you mentioned?"

"Not a lot, just something I read," she replied.

"I know a guy in Central America doing it," Trent said. "Raises freshwater shrimp in one tank and grows pineapple in another. You thinking of doing something like that here?"

"Yeah," I said. "I cleared this area to try to grow food, but the soil's all wrong and the groundwater is salty. Tina mentioned aquaculture."

"I saw his operation once," Trent said. "Seems simple enough. Kinda like cleaner shrimp and big groupers. They help one another. What ya call a symbiotic relationship. Your biggest problem here would be electricity to run the pumps. You can only go so far with the setup you have. You could do a standalone battery-power system, with a big old voltage-regulated generator, like's on the *Charlie*. Kicks on automatically when the voltage in the batteries gets too low and shuts off when they're fully charged."

"I'll have to look into that more," I said. "It'd be great to be more self-sufficient out here."

When we were finished eating, Trent and Charlie took the kids into the bunkhouse to get ready for bed. Our plates were banana leaves from one of the dozens of trees on the island and everything was finger food. Since there were no dishes to clean up, we just tossed the leaves in the fire and the lobster and clam shells in the water.

"If you like, Jesse," Chyrel said, "I can go over the electronics with you. I had a late night and would like to go to sleep soon, myself."

"Then let's do it in the morning," I said, "while we're heading down to Marathon."

"You're a multitasker, huh?" she said. "Drive a boat and learn sophisticated electronic devices at the same time?"

"Pilot a boat," Tina said, grinning. "You can go over it while I pilot, right?"

"It's like you were reading my mind," I said.

"Okay," said Chyrel as she stood up. "I'll see you in the morning, then."

She headed across the clearing, leaving Tina and I alone as the sun dipped below the trees. "Come on," I said. "I want to show you something."

"I've been hoping you'd say that all day," she said, getting to her feet.

"Later," I said. "What I want you to see is out on the pier."

We started between the bunkhouses and Pescador ran ahead. He and I sat on the pier at sunset every day, so he knew where we were going. We reached the end of the pier and he was already lying in his favorite spot, looking at the sun falling toward the horizon. We sat down on the pier next to him, with our feet dangling just above the gin-clear water.

As the lower part of the sun reached the horizon, the water seemed to reach up and grab it, flaring out the bottom edge of the big orange ball. Tina let out a little gasp, while holding my hand. "Watch for a green flash, just as the last of the sun disappears," I said.

Slowly, the sun sank into the ocean, flattening out as it got lower. High clouds above the horizon darkened from pink, to red, to purple. As the last part of the sun, almost flat and red now, got close to the horizon, a small section seemed to separate itself from it. Then the orb of the sun disappeared and the small separated part flashed to green for an instant and disappeared.

Tina's eyes were wide with wonder. "I've lived here for almost two years," she said. "I don't think I've ever completely watched this. Does it always do that? The green flash? What causes it?"

"You can't see it every time," I said. "Pretty rare, actually. Over the years, I've learned when it's more likely to happen, but counting this evening, I probably wouldn't have to use my toes to add up the number of times I've seen it. No idea what causes it, I just like that it does."

"It was absolutely amazing. Thanks for sharing it with me." She leaned her head on my shoulder and we watched as the last light quickly bled itself from the sky. Through the gray light, I could see Trent and Charlie sitting on a little sandbar, on the northwest corner of the island. I envied him.

Tina shivered a little and I said, "Are you cold? Want to go inside?"

She looked up into my eyes and sighed, "Yes."

We passed Trent and Charlie as we walked back to the house. She was holding his arm and leaning on his shoulder, much the same as Tina was doing. We only nodded to one another as we passed. Halfway across the clearing Tina said, "They seem to be very much in love."

"I think you're right," I said as we reached the bottom of the steps.

She stopped there and took both my hands in hers, turning toward me. "Are you completely sure, Jesse?"

"I've never been more sure about anything in my life," I said. We walked up the steps with Pescador ahead of us. I opened the door and he trotted straight over to his old poncho liner and, after a couple of turns, laid down on it.

I closed and locked the door as Tina said, "I'll be just a minute," and disappeared into the head. I went into the bedroom, which had an adjoining door to the head, and turned down the bed. A cold front was starting to push down and it was cooler inside, so I lit two hurricane lamps and turned them down low. I'd found they provided enough heat on most nights.

I pulled off my shirt and shorts and had just gotten under the covers when the door to the head opened and the light inside turned off. Tina came over to the bed wearing nothing but a long white tee shirt, her voluptuous body outlined under it by the lamp on the dresser. She lifted the covers and climbed in beside me, shivering. Squirming over next to me, I smelled jasmine and coconut, a very intoxicating scent, as I wrapped my arms around her and drew her in.

CHAPTER TWELVE:
Homeward Bound

I woke to the smell of coffee. At first, I thought I was on the boat. I don't have an automatic coffeemaker in the house. Just a copper-bottomed percolator. Then I realized Tina wasn't in the bed and I smiled. I got up and pulled on my skivvies and walked into the main room, quietly. She was at the counter, pouring coffee into two mugs. As I started to walk toward her she said, "About time you got up."

I stopped and looked over at Pescador, and he just lifted his head with a puzzled look, like he couldn't explain it either.

"I was a Recon Marine," I said. "There's no way you heard me."

"You must have lost your touch," she said.

I looked at Pescador and he just laid his head back down on the poncho liner, like he'd already discussed it with her. Then she turned around and handed me a cup of coffee and laughed. "Actually, I said the same thing every thirty seconds since I got up."

"Good to know I hadn't lost my touch," I said.

"Oh, you haven't lost your touch," she said. "That was you last night, wasn't it? Both times?"

I walked over to the door, opened it and looked back at Pescador as I sipped my coffee.

"I don't think he wants to go out," she said. "I already tried."

I nodded my head at him and he bolted out the door. I turned to Tina and said, "We have a morning ritual. Be right back."

Pescador ran down the steps and hiked his leg on the banyan tree by the bottom and I pissed over the back rail. Then I went back inside, while he went exploring for ghost crabs on the small beach.

Inside, I took Tina in my arms and held her tightly to my chest, stroking her long dark hair. "Let's get dressed," I said. "Sunrise is in an hour and it's nearly as spectacular as sunset."

"I don't know how that could ever be topped," she said and went into the bedroom. I followed her, set my coffee on the dresser, then grabbed her and fell into bed. We made love again, slow and easy.

Afterwards, I filled a thermos with coffee and we went out to the pier. Pescador was lying in his usual spot. Trent, Charlie and the kids were sitting next to him, all facing east, as if waiting for the curtain to rise. We sat down next to them, without saying a word. I saw that their coffee mugs were empty, so I took the lid off the thermos and held it out to Trent. He took it and poured for him and his wife and handed it back.

The seven of us looked toward the east and the sky slowly began to turn purple. Within minutes the top portion of the sun peeked up over the horizon and turned the high, wispy clouds pink. Suddenly, we heard a voice calling from the middle of the clearing, "Hello! Where is everyone?"

I laughed and called out, "On the pier, Chyrel."

She came out from between the bunkhouses, dressed pretty much the same as yesterday, like she was going into a business office. She walked out onto the pier and I noticed she was barefoot. She saw me looking at her feet and said, "This is as *island chic* as I can get. My go bag is packed with business clothes."

We all laughed as she sat down in her business slacks on the pier and watched the sun come up with us. When it was fully risen, Charlie turned to Chyrel and said, "We're about the same size. Would you like to borrow some shorts and a tank top? It's supposed to be near eighty today."

"Oh, could I?" she said. "I feel like such an outcast here."

The two of them disappeared down the dock and into the bunkhouse. Little Patty looked up at Trent and said, "That was pretty, Daddy. Can you do it again?"

We laughed and Trent said, "Tomorrow, sweetie. We don't want to burn it out." Then he turned to me and said, "What time are y'all heading down to Marathon?"

"In a couple of hours," I said. "Anyone not like pancakes?"

The kids both clapped and I said, "Y'all come on up to the deck in twenty minutes."

Tina and I got up and walked, hand in hand, back to the house. "You're really going to make breakfast for everyone?"

"No," I said. "We are."

An hour later, we were all full of blueberry pancakes and the dishes were all cleaned up and put away. I told Trent they didn't need to stay in the bunkhouse, they were welcome to stay in the main house. He said that they did the first night, but the creaking of the boats tied to the docks below kept the kids awake and after the first night in the bunkhouse, they actually preferred it. Cooking on an open fire was a great treat for the kids and it reminded him of when he was young.

"In the seventies," he said, "we had a little conch house on Cudjoe Key, sitting on about five acres. No neighbors, mosquitoes as big as crows in the summer time, no electricity and a big cistern like you got. Momma cooked over an open fire and we showered together under the cistern before bed." He looked out over the clearing and added, "These past few days have brought us closer together than we've ever been before. Papa sold the land to the government in '78. Fat Albert lives there now."

I nodded, knowing the exact spot he was talking about on northern Cudjoe Key. "Fat Albert?" Tina asked. "Who's that?"

"Not a who," Trent said. "A what. There's two big blimps that are tethered there. They're radar blimps, used to track drug planes and boats. Don't work too good, though."

"This should all be over in a few days," I said. "A week at the most."

FALLEN HUNTER

"To tell you the truth," he said. "I ain't in no hurry. Been thinking about selling the boat, buying a little piece of land and going back to fishing. Shrimping ain't as good as it was a few years ago."

"Nothing ever is," I said as I got up. "Come on Tina, let's get ready to shove off."

We didn't have much to pack, her less than me. We took everything down to the *Revenge* and stowed it away. I told Tina to take Chyrel up to the bridge and start the engines while I cast off the lines. Trent and Charlie came down to see us off, along with Pescador. I could tell he wanted to go and said, "Not this time, buddy. You stay here and watch after those kids." He barked once and ran up the steps and I heard him go down the rear steps, looking for them. The girls said goodbye to the Trents as I climbed up to join them on the bridge.

We idled out the channel, into Harbor Channel and turned northeast. I continued past the narrow channel we came in through, crossed between Turtlecrawl Bank and Spanish Banks, and then pushed the throttles up to sixteen-hundred rpm. Coming up on plane, I turned due east toward the light on Bullfrog Banks, then south into Rocky Channel. I told Chyrel and Tina the names of the islands we passed as we headed south toward the Seven Mile Bridge.

"Did you grow up here?" Chyrel asked.

"No," I said. "I've only lived here about seven years. But I've been coming down here since I was little. My dad and his dad were both fishermen."

"So," Tina said, "what exactly are we going to Marathon for?"

"A party," I said with a grin. "Irish style. Why don't you take the helm and I'll go below and bring up our tech guru's gizmos."

"You sure?" Tina asked. "The open ocean is one thing, but we're in a channel."

"Look way out ahead. You'll see a green light flash every five seconds. Just head straight for it. I'll just be a minute. Or, I can set the auto pilot, if you want."

"Get up."

I went down to the salon to get the boxes and overheard Chyrel say, "Have you two been together a long time?"

"No," Tina replied. "We only met a little over a week ago."

"Really," Chyrel said. "You seem perfect for each other. I thought you were married."

"The ring?" Tina said. "He lost his wife some time ago. I don't know how to approach him about that."

I looked down at the ring still on my finger. It had only been five months ago, but suddenly it felt like another lifetime. I took the ring off my finger and looked at it. My friend Rusty had given us his and his late wife's wedding rings the day we got married. He'd hung on to them for twenty-three years. He should have them back. I went into the forward stateroom, opened the bottom drawer of the dresser and took out a small box. Opening it, I put the ring inside with the one that Alex had worn. Putting the little box away, I picked up the two containers in the salon and as an afterthought, I grabbed a cooler, put a few beers in it and some bottled water, before heading back up to the bridge.

"Did ya miss me?" I said as I sat down next to Chyrel, placing the boxes on the deck at my feet. Opening the cooler, I took out a cold Red Stripe. "Either of you two ladies want a beer?"

"Jesse," Tina said, "It's only eleven, I mean, eleven-hundred."

"Hey," I said. "It's five o'clock somewhere."

"Water for me, thanks," said Chyrel.

"Same for me," Tina added, then changed her mind and said, "Oh hell, why not?"

I handed her a beer and Chyrel a bottle of water. Tina's eyes lingered on my left hand as I handed her the bottle.

"Okay, Chyrel," I said. "Tell me about these gadgets you had smuggled aboard my vessel."

She put her water in a drink holder and opened the smaller of the two boxes and showed me the pen smoke bombs again, pointing out the way to arm them. Then she showed me the bugs and how easy the backing was to peel off with one finger while still in my pocket. She put those away and opened the larger black box. "This is a parabolic microphone," she said, holding it up. She pointed out the release catch on the side and it opened up into a little radar-looking device with three small legs. "You just set the microphone on a stable platform, point in the direction you want to listen, then control the fine adjustments with these two knobs. A full turn of either knob will move the dish up, down, left, or right only one degree." She showed me how to power up the amplifier and where to plug in the microphone and headphones. "To close it up, you just push the release button on the bottom and fold one of the legs up. The other two will move with it and the dish will fold itself in and down.

Your new laptop is exactly like your old one. I took the liberty of downloading all your software and files from the old one onto it. It has two new icons on the desktop that your old one didn't have. One says 'Soft Jazz.' That's the encrypted video phone. The other says 'Tide Charts.' That's the satellite imaging. Other than that, it's a hundred percent identical to your old one, only a whole lot faster."

"You really did your homework," I said.

"Thanks," she said.

I looked out ahead of us and saw that we were nearing the first light for Money Key Channel. Tina said, "I think you better take the helm."

"You're fine," I said. "See the red marker ahead and on the left? There's a green one just a little to the right of it and a little further away. Go between those two markers and turn left. Then you'll see two more green lights and another red marker. Keep the green on the right and the red on the left. Aim for a spot about a quarter mile out from the high span of the bridge. That's Moser Channel. We'll go under the bridge there, and follow the markers out about a mile before turning east again and heading to the channel into the *Rusty Anchor*."

"Geez," she said, laughing. "You want me to remember all that?"

"It takes a little getting used to," I said. "You didn't jump on the freeway your first time driving a car, did you?"

"Are you kidding?" she replied. "I never even drove on a paved road until I was eighteen."

Gathering up the two boxes, I carried them back down to the salon and stowed them in a cabinet under the TV. When I got back up to the bridge, Tina was passing between the two markers and slowly swinging eastward. "See there," I said. "Just like falling off a bike. Keep that green light up ahead on the right and you'll see a red marker, keep that on your left. I'll take the helm before we go under the bridge."

Five minutes later, she slid over and I took the helm. I pushed the throttles on up to twenty-four hundred rpm and the big boat leaped forward.

"Holy crap!" Chyrel said. "I thought we were going full speed this whole time."

Tina smiled and said, "We're still not." Then I watched as she looked at the knot meter, doing the math in her head, and said, "We're only going about forty-five miles per hour. She's got a little more to go." I put my arm around her and pulled her close, giving her a kiss on the forehead.

"See, you're learning," I said.

Twenty minutes later, just before noon, I pulled back the throttles and brought the *Revenge* down off of plane as we neared the mouth of the canal. It seemed like it had been a long time ago since I was last here. I idled up the canal and noticed quite a few differences. There were a number of boats docked along the left side of the canal. I recognized Dan's sloop among them. The others weren't familiar. Some had home ports from way up the coast, Boston, Chesapeake Bay and Kennebunkport. I eased into the turning basin and used the engines to spin the *Revenge* around. Rusty and Deuce were standing on Rusty's old barge, ready to tie us off.

Rusty had a big grin on his face as he said, "Welcome home, brother." I hadn't seen him since he came out to have a drink with me on the Marine Corps' birthday.

I climbed down from the bridge ahead of the girls and stepped onto the barge as he and Deuce finished tying us off. I embraced the big man and said, "It looks like you've lost some weight there, Jarhead. What are you down to, three fifty?"

I turned and took Deuce's hand as Julie crossed over the barge to greet us. Tina and Chyrel stepped across and I said, "Rusty, I'd like you to meet Tina La Mons. Tina, this big, hairy orangutan is my best friend, Rusty Thurman." Rusty stepped forward and brushed aside Tina's outstretched hand and lifted her off the deck in a bear hug.

"Damn nice to know ya, Tina," he said as he set her on her feet. "Any friend of this old barracuda is a friend of mine."

Deuce stepped forward and said, "Chyrel, this is my fiancée, Julie, and her dad. Chyrel and I work together." Julie beat Rusty to it and gave Chyrel a light hug, then the big man stepped in and lifted her off the deck, also.

"Fiancée?" I asked. "I have been away too long."

"Just happened last night," Deuce said.

"Well, congratulations to both of you," I said.

Rusty pulled me aside and said, "That lawyer fella is here. Inside. You can't miss him." Then to the others he said, "Come on in, y'all. Beers are on the house."

Tina took my hand as we walked with the others up to the bar. She whispered in my ear and said, "He's a friendly guy."

"Sorry about that," I whispered back with a grin. "Forgot to tell you he's a hugger."

As we entered the bar, I turned to Tina, "Go make friends, I have to talk to that guy over in the corner."

She looked over at a smallish man in a blue suit and said, "The business you mentioned? He looks like a lawyer."

"He is," I said. "I'll be along in a few minutes."

I walked over to the man, sat down across from him and said, "You're looking for me?"

"Are you Mister McDermitt?" he asked.

"Yeah, I am."

"May I see some identification?" he asked.

"No," I said. "Not until you tell me what this is about."

He pushed his glasses up on his nose and said, "My name is Greg Neff. As I said in the email, I'm here to get your signature on some documents. I represent the estate of your late wife, Alex McDermitt, nee Dubois."

I pulled out my wallet and showed him my driver license. "What do you mean, her estate?"

"You mean you didn't know?" he asked.

"Mister Neff, I'm not the kind of man that asks about things I already know."

"When your wife's parents died twelve years ago, she and her brother were named co-beneficiaries on their life insurance. When her brother died last summer, she was his beneficiary and she inherited his holdings in the estate. As her only legal next of kin, you will now inherit all of it."

"Wait a minute," I said. "I neither want nor need it. Isn't there a charity you can give it to? Seems like a lot of trouble, you coming all the way down here over a few thousand bucks. We could have done this over the phone a lot easier."

"Mister McDermitt, it's more than a few thousand dollars and you, of course, may do with it anything you wish. My job is to simply get your signature on the documents and arrange the transfer of funds."

He opened his briefcase and took out a file folder. Opening it, he turned it towards me and, pointing to a number at the bottom of the top sheet of paper, he said, "This is the total holdings of the estate."

I glanced down, then slowly looked back up at him. "You're kidding, right? Who put you up to this? Rusty?"

"No sir, I never joke about the estate of a deceased client. Once you sign these documents, I'll arrange the transfer of the liquid assets, totaling two point nine million dollars, to your bank. The rest of the holdings, totaling roughly another five point one million, are in stocks, bonds, and land holdings in Oregon. If you wish, my office can take care of liquidating those holdings and transfer them to your bank as well. It will be a total of eight million dollars, minus our fee of ten percent."

"I don't want it," I said forcefully.

"That's completely up to you," he said. "You're free to do with it what you will. However, want it or not, it's yours. Along with the responsibility that goes with it."

"What responsibility?"

"Have you ever heard of the Outward Bound School?"

"Yeah," I said. "They teach sailing to troubled teens."

"Your late wife created a school similar to it in Oregon, called Catching It. It's sort of a camp where at-risk inner-city kids from all over the northwest are sent. She and several full-time counselors teach them fly fishing, mountaineering, and survival."

I laughed hard. When I got it together I said, "Okay, now I know you're for real. I could totally see Alex doing that."

"It's become quite successful, Mister McDermitt. But now, if you'll allow me a metaphor familiar to you, the school is like a ship without a rudder."

"Whoa," I said. "Don't look at me to be that rudder, Neff. My own kids haven't seen or spoken to me in twelve years."

"There's no actual contact required," he said. "The counselors have been doing a very good job up there. Alex was looking to do the same thing down here. That's where you'd come in. You know the people here. From what I've gathered, they trust and respect you. A few introductions of the school's acting CEO to local fishing guides and her permanent appointment by you will ensure that the school not only continues, but grows and expands."

"Okay, I can do that," I said. "But I still don't want the money."

"Like I said, it's yours to do with what you will. You can set up a trust fund for your own kids or a college fund for kids of local fishermen, create a new wing at Fisherman's Hospital, anything you want. I'm only here to get your signature and arrange the transfer."

I thought about what he'd said. Julie brought me another beer and a coffee for Neff. "Everything alright, Jesse?" she asked.

"Yeah, Jules," I said. Then as she turned to go I said, "Hey, wait. Sit down a minute."

She sat down and I looked at her, then at Neff and back to her. "Jules, think about this a second, okay. Suppose you won the lottery and got a whole bunch of money. What would be some of the things you'd do?"

I'd known Julie almost all her life. She never had it easy, but never complained. She and Rusty made their way in these islands doing whatever they could. I knew that she had no aspirations beyond watching the next sunset and helping her friends.

"That's easy," she said. "If it was enough, I'd set up a college fund for the kids of local watermen. Why?"

"What if it was more than that?" I asked.

She looked at Neff, then at me and said, "Well, I suppose Dad could retire. I'd set up some kind of sharing fund, where fishermen and boaters could get repairs done, without getting ripped off by the boatyards up in Miami. Hey, what's this all about?"

"Thanks, Jules," I said. "I'll tell you all about it later, okay."

She got up and went back to the bar. I turned to Neff and said, "How do I go about doing the things like she just said?"

"I have no idea," he said. "I'm a probate attorney and have never been to Florida until this week. I'm sure our firm can recommend a local law firm for you. Now, about these documents."

"Okay," I said. "First thing, you got one there that appoints the acting CEO as permanent?"

"Right here on top, sir," he said. "I like the way you think." I signed it and initialed the parts he said.

"Next thing," I said. "Is it possible to transfer half of the non-liquid assets to the school?"

"Yes," he said. "That will take a week or so. My firm will draw up the documents and have them overnighted to a firm here in the Keys for you to sign."

"Do it," I said. "And arrange for the new CEO to come here. Alex would want her dream fulfilled, I think."

"She's already planning on it," Neff said. "She was only waiting for your invitation. Her name is Cindy Saturday. She actually took lessons from your late wife years ago and has become a prominent figure in the fly fishing community."

"I'd also like to set up exactly what Julie just said. Liquidate the other half of the non-liquid holdings and set up a college fund for kids of local fishermen and a boatyard to help out the locals. Plus one of my own, a college fund for kids of Florida's military men and women who are killed in action. Yeah, I think Alex would have liked that. Can you help me out with it?"

"I'll have the firm start researching local organizations that specialize in that sort of thing," he said. "If you'll sign these other documents transferring ownership of the estate to you, we can get started right away."

I signed all the documents he pulled out of his briefcase and there were a lot. "All that's left is the transfer of liquid funds. We'll need to go to your bank and sign these forms in front of the bank manager."

"It's a couple miles away," I said. "I don't have a car. Do you?"

He laughed and said, "Of course, Mister McDermitt. Perhaps you could get a car now."

"No," I said. "Alex always chided me about *The Beast*, that's my car. I think I'll get it fixed and keep it. Let's go."

I got up and went over to the bar where my friends were and said, "I gotta run out for a minute. Shouldn't be more than an hour."

"What's going on?" Rusty asked. "Who is that guy?"

"I'll explain it all when I get back," I said. Then turning to Tina I said, "Will you be okay waiting here with these deadbeats?"

"Your friends are nice, Jesse. Go take care of business and hurry back."

Neff and I left the bar, got in his car and drove to my bank. As we pulled in he said, "Perhaps you should open a new account at one of the larger banks."

"Not a chance, Neff," I said. "State Bank of the Florida Keys is a local bank, where they all know everyone."

We walked inside and just as I said the bank manager, Pam Lamarre, came out of her office. "Jesse, it's so good to see you. I missed you at the memorial service. I'm really sorry about Alex, she had become a good friend. What can we do for you today?"

"Pam, this is Mister Neff, from Oregon," I said. They shook hands and I continued, "Mister Neff is a probate attorney for Alex's estate. We need to make arrangements for the transfer of funds. Also, I was wondering if you could help me set up a college fund for the kids of some local watermen, and create some kind of board to oversee it."

"Wow, that's a lot. I assume we're talking about a lot of money?" she said.

"Substantial," Neff replied.

"Look," I said, "I don't want to get my hands in it. I really don't know much about finances. If you and some of the other local leaders can handle setting up the fund and who gets allocated what, it'd be a big help to me."

"A college fund for the underprivileged kids of local fishermen?" she said. "Yes, Alex would have liked that. Count me in. I'll talk to some of the other people in town and I'm sure we can put together a board of about six people. Is that what you want?"

"Perfect," I said. "Neff's firm is going to reach out to local legal people here, to handle the legal end of it."

We went into her office and Neff produced the last few necessary documents for me to sign and Pam to notarize. Then he handed her a cashier's check, for the liquid assets.

Pam sat back in her chair and stared at it. "Um, Jesse, maybe you should have Bank of America handle this. This is more than double the total assets of all of our customers combined."

"No," I said. "Keys Bank is in touch with people around here. Those megabanks aren't. Pam, you helped me out a lot when I bought my island and boat. I'm not going to trust anyone else."

"Okay," she said. "Would you like this in large bills or tens and twenties?"

Neff laughed for the first time. I said, "Just put it in my savings for now and transfer fifty thousand dollars to my checking. Once you get the board set up, we'll look at moving it into mutual funds or whatever you recommend. The bulk will probably take a while to liquidate. Neff here will arrange that transfer when it's ready."

"There's more?" she said.

"Yes ma'am," Neff said. "This is about one third of the total estate. Jesse has generously donated another third of the estate to a school that Miss DuBois, er, Mrs. McDermitt started in Oregon, to allow it to expand here. The final third he wishes to use in the creation of this charity and another to benefit the children of our fallen military people."

"I think Alex would have liked that too, Jesse," Pam said.

"That's another reason I came to you, Pam," I said as I got up. "Now, I just found out yesterday that Dan Sullivan is in town and playing over at the *Anchor*, so if you two will excuse me, I'll leave the rest of this in your hands. I'll walk back, Neff. Thanks for the lift."

I left the bank and walked back to the *Anchor*. I really didn't have any need for the money, but I was going to use some of it for some ideas I had. First was to set up an aquaculture system to grow fruits and vegetables on the island. Plus, a standalone electrical system to run both it and a reverse-osmosis water maker, bigger than the one on the *Revenge*. I wanted to talk to Deuce about moving his field operatives to the island on a more permanent basis once this was done. Although I'd come to grips personally with the loss of Alex, there were still a lot of bad people out there and other good people being hurt by them. Santiago was dead center in my crosshairs.

When I got back to the *Anchor*, I could hear Dan doing a sound check out back. I walked in the bar and it was empty except for Rufus, an old Jamaican man who was the cook. "Dey all out bock, Cap'n," he said. "Ahn welcome bock, brudda."

"Thanks, Rufus," I said. He passed me a cold Red Stripe as I walked by the bar toward the back door. The new deck was impressive. The smaller old deck had been completely torn down and the new one was four times the size, with umbrella-covered tables scattered around the edges and uncovered tables in the middle, maybe twenty in all. On the far side was an elevated stage. The tables were about half full as Dan warmed up on the stage. Another younger man was behind him on a small drum set. Rusty, Deuce, Tina, Chyrel and Julie were at a table close to the canal. I noticed Julie had her guitar case leaning against the railing behind her.

Dan saw me crossing the deck toward my friends and said into the microphone, "I'll get started in a second, y'all. First I have to say hi to someone." He stepped down off the stage and met me halfway.

"Jesse," he said grabbing me by the shoulders. Then in a thick Irish brogue, "Ow's your onions?"

"What's the craic, Dan?" I said back in my best best brogue.

"Been a long time, man," he said. "Rusty told me what happened, damn shame."

"Thanks, Dan," I said. "How was the islands?"

"Arseways at times, but a lot of fun, mostly. You gonna be around a while?"

"Here for the night," I said.

"Yeah, I saw that big Rampage when I woke up a little while ago. Hey, I gotta get to work, we'll talk later." He went back to his brogue and said, "Tear your hole off the haggart, boyo."

I went over to the table and sat down next to Tina. All eyes were on me as I took a long pull on my beer. "Well?" Rusty said.

"Well, what?"

"The lawyer, ya dim-witted ground pounder!" he said.

"He just needed my signature on some papers concerning Alex's estate," I said. "I gave most of it to charity."

"She would have liked that," Rusty said. "Buy some books for the school kids or something?"

"Yeah," I lied. "Something like that." Then I turned to Deuce and said, "I need to talk to you a minute." I leaned over and gave Tina a kiss and said, "Be right back."

"You better," she said. "Or I'll run off with Rusty."

Deuce and I walked over to the barge, out of earshot of everyone else as Dan launched into his first song, "She Only Loves Me."

"What's up?" Deuce asked.

"What would you think about moving your team, at least the field operatives, to the island?" I asked him point blank.

"Books for the kids, huh? Lawyers don't travel three thousand miles for a small estate."

"Wasn't a lie exactly," I said. "Alex started a kind of Outward Bound School to teach kids in Oregon survivalist skills and how to fly fish. She was planning to start one here. A third of her estate is going to that. Another third will be used to start the school here, set up college scholarships here for kids of local fishermen and fallen warriors."

"And the last third?" he asked.

"About two point seven million dollars," I said and watched his mouth fall open.

"You're kidding."

"No," I said. "I thought we could set the island up to be completely self-sustainable and use it as an operating base for training. What do you think?"

"That's really generous, Jesse. But, we have a state-of-the-art training facility at Homestead."

"Yeah," I said. "I was thinking something more basic, not high-tech training. Somewhere that nobody can see what's going on, next to a town full of gossips."

"You have a point," he said. "What do you mean by self-sustainable?"

I gave him a brief rundown on my idea to grow and catch our own food, make our own water and add to the accommodations. "Give me five men and a week and I can have things ready to house the whole team. Two months later and food won't be a problem."

"I like the concept," he said. "Especially just before a mission. Isolated training and planning. I'll talk to Smith, see what he thinks."

"Just Smith now?" I said sarcastically. "Not 'the ADD' or 'the Director'?"

"Your insubordinate ways must be rubbing off on me," he said with a grin.

"Want to go diving tomorrow?" I asked. "Me, you, Julie and Tina?"

"Just a fun dive?" he asked. "Nothing to blow up or people to kill?"

"Yeah, I was thinking of Conrad Reef," I said. It was where we'd taken Deuce's dad's ashes almost five months earlier.

"Sounds like fun," he said.

We went back to the group and I noticed there were a lot more people on the deck. More than forty, at least. Rusty looked happy.

After Dan finished his first song, he said, "I'd like to have a friend join me on this next number. Julie?"

Julie got up, took her guitar from the case and stepped up on the stage. "Miss Julie Thurmond, everyone," Dan said into the microphone, to an already cheering crowd of locals. "This is a new song I wrote and Julie's gonna back me up on guitar. It's called 'Stormfront.' Hope you like it."

Tina took my arm as we listened. I always liked Dan's style and Julie played a great accompaniment. The song itself was very visual, full of lightning, high wind, and waves, even on a bright, clear January day.

Tina said, "That song's more about you than the weather, I think. What were you and Deuce talking about?"

"Just future plans," I said. "We're going scuba diving tomorrow."

"Just the two of you?" she asked.

"The four of us," I said. "Remember, I promised to show you how."

We listened to Dan play for another half hour, then he took a break and came over to sit down. I introduced him to Tina and Deuce and we caught up on old times until he had to go back up on stage. It was a pretty good turnout. Just before sunset, I told Rusty and Deuce we had to run out for a bit and asked if I could borrow Rusty's pickup.

"Sure," he said. "Keys are in it."

As Tina and I walked out to the front of the bar I said, "I need to make a call to Santiago. Could you go inside and get us a couple of bottles of water?"

"Sure," she said and headed into the bar.

I pulled up Santiago's number and he picked up after two rings. "I thought you were going to back out, *Capitán*," he said.

"Had things to do. Offer still on the table?"

"Sí, but we need to meet in person," he replied.

"I'm not in Key West, but I can get down there tomorrow," I said.

"Nor am I, *señor*. Can you come up to Miami?"

"No," I said. "I don't have reliable wheels. Do you have a boat?"

He laughed and said, "*Sí*, I have a boat. Very cautious, eh? Where would you like to meet and what time?"

"I'll text you the GPS coordinates," I said. "It's offshore near Long Key, Alligator Reef. Early morning, about nine?"

"*Perfecto*," he said. "You'll be alone?"

"No," I said, "And I doubt you will be either. Nor will I be unarmed. There'll be three people with me. One man and two women. A dive charter."

"I will be with a young lady myself," he said.

"*Hasta mañana*," I said, ending the call just as Tina walked up to me.

We went out to the pickup and Tina asked, "Where are we going?"

"I told you I'd take you shopping," I said. "Not just for clothes, either."

"You don't have to do that, Jesse."

"I want to," I said with a grin. "Besides, you'll need a new wardrobe for Cozumel."

We got in Rusty's Chevy pickup and drove first to Hall's Dive Center. In about an hour of negotiating, we had a complete set of scuba gear and a wet suit for Tina. I also bought a new buoyancy compensator for myself, since my old one had a leaky air bladder. We put everything in the small seat in back and drove to Anthony's, a ladies' clothing store just across A-1-A from the *Anchor*.

I told Tina that she needed at least two new bathing suits, three outfits for the evening, three outfits for casual hanging out and whatever shoes, underwear, night clothes and accessories she'd need to go with them. "Jesse," she said, "The dive gear alone cost nearly a thousand dollars. There's no way I can afford to repay you for that, let alone this."

"You don't need to repay me," I said. "We need to look like a classy couple on vacation down there. Our next stop is a men's store. The money Smith is paying me was already in the bank before he even mentioned it. If you want, I can take it out of the five thousand dollars I was going to give you to go along."

"Is this for real?" she asked. "They're paying you ten thousand dollars to go to Cozumel for a few days and I get half?"

I got serious for a second and said, "This isn't just a fun trip, though we'll try to make it as fun as we can. We'll be going into Cuban waters, so there is some risk involved. That's why we're being compensated so well. If you don't want to do it, say so."

She thought about it for a few minutes then said, "I'll go." For the next hour, she tried on dozens of outfits, finally choosing six. She also bought a few things from the lingerie department that made me smile. We piled these boxes on top of the dive gear and headed down by the airport to Bayshore Clothing, where I bought the first suit I'd bought in many years. I was surprised they had a forty-six long to fit me. I also bought a few casual, but sturdy, pairs of pants and shirts. Shoes were a problem. They only had a few styles in a size thirteen and I didn't really like any of them, but settled on the least ugly.

Once we stowed these in the front seat, there was barely room for the two of us. We drove back to the *Anchor* and carried everything to the boat. Before we finished putting everything aboard, I heard a familiar voice from the yard.

"Permission to come aboard, Skipper?"

It was Tony Jacobs. He used to be one of Deuce's SEAL team operators and moved with him to DHS. "Tony," I said, "How the hell ya been?"

He reached out his hand and took mine saying, "Doing well, Jesse. How about you?"

"Better every day, brother," I said. "Tony, I'd like you to meet Deputy Christina La Mons. Tina, this is Tony Jacobs, part of Deuce's team."

The two shook hands and Tony said, "Looks like y'all been out shopping. I have a few more goodies in the SUV. Can you give me a hand?"

"Sure," I said and the three of us walked over to Tony's black Expedition. He'd backed it up close to the barge so we could unload it without being seen.

"I have a message for you from Smith," he said. "He says Ms. La Mons's temporary assignment has been approved by the local Sheriff."

"Please, Tony," Tina said, "Just call me Tina. Everyone else does."

"Look forward to working with you, Tina," he said. "But I'm kind of in the dark as to what a Sheriff's Deputy will add to our mission."

"Oh," she said, "I'm just arm candy."

"I guess Smith and Deuce didn't update you," I said. "We're going diving in Cozumel. We'll drop you and Art off on the way down, then the two of us, plus Deuce and Julie, will make a show of having a good time in the sun down there for a couple days and pick you guys up on the way back."

"He also said to tell you that he'd like Talbot to come up to Homestead for a day to meet the team. Then Deuce can schedule him for training."

"What do you think he'd say about bringing the whole team to the island?" I asked. "Hell, I've only met the three of you."

"I don't know, Gunny," he said. "He's a weird cat sometimes. I think he's got political ambitions. Came to us from the CIA, but was never a field operator."

"That's the exact same thing I thought when I met him," Tina said. "I gotta ask. Gunny? Is that another nautical term?"

Tony and I looked at one another and laughed. "No," I said. "That was my rank in the Marine Corps. Gunnery Sergeant."

"And you were in the Marines too, Tony?" she asked.

"No ma'am," he said between chuckles. "My head doesn't fit in a jar. I used to be in the Navy."

"Now you guys have lost me," she said. "Gunners, jars, port, and starboard. I really need to get a book or start taking detailed notes."

"Back to Smith," I said. "What kind of boss is he?"

"I really don't have a lot of interaction with him," Tony said. "From what I gathered, he seems to think he's on the way up, though. He micromanages too. Which is why I doubt he'd send the whole team down here. Putting about twenty people up in motel rooms would make steam come out of his ears."

"You guys don't talk much, do you?" I asked. "I built a pair of bunkhouses on the north side of the island. Bunks for twenty-four men."

"Maybe we can just do it and not even tell him," Tony said as he opened the hatch on the big SUV. "He gives Deuce pretty free rein, as far as training goes."

In the back of the car were two large crates and two smaller ones. He grabbed one of the smaller ones and I grabbed the other. We carried them across the barge to the *Revenge* and stacked them beside the gunwale on the dock. The two larger ones required us making two trips. They were the compact underwater scooters. Once we got them aboard, Tony said, "Y'all don't mind me. It'll take me about ten minutes to get these bladders set up in the fish boxes. Each one has its own battery-powered pump and fuel line. All we'll have to do is open the fish box, pull the line over to the fuel tank cap and turn it on."

I helped him wrestle the two scooter crates into the engine room below the salon. It was a tight fit, but stacked and lashed down, there was just enough room to get past them if needed.

"Come on in for a beer when you get it done," I said. "I need to make a couple calls."

Tina and I carried our new stuff inside and I showed her where to put the clothes while I stowed the dive gear. Then I sat down at the settee and sent a text message to Santiago with the GPS numbers for the meet. Next, I made the first call to Trent. He picked up and said, "Hey, Jesse. You wouldn't want to trade this island for a run-down old shrimp boat, would ya?"

"You still thinking about selling the boat?" I asked.

"I'd like to, but fishing and shrimping is the only thing I know. I doubt I could find much of a job doing anything else."

"I don't know," I said. "That table you built is damn sturdy. You could do something along that line."

"You haven't been to a construction site lately, have you?" he said. "Mostly Mexicans, getting paid cheap wages under the table. I did a little construction work once before. No way I could feed my family on what those guys are paid."

"That's kind of the reason I called," I said. "That island's going to get crowded soon, with both people and things. I was hoping that you were actually serious about selling the boat. I'd like to hire you and Charlie as full-time caretakers."

There was silence on the phone for a few seconds. "Are you still there?" I asked.

"Um, yeah," he said. "Are you offering me a job?"

"Yeah. Remember talking about aquaculture? Think you could build a system like your buddy has?"

"Well, yeah," he said. "It's not hard to build, but the cost is pretty steep for the equipment."

"Let me worry about that," I said. "Think you could build three more of those tables and a house for you and your family, over by that little cove on the western side? I noticed you and Charlie kind of favored that spot."

"Yeah," he said, "I can do all that. Why would you want to do all this?"

"I'll explain it all when I come up there in a couple of days," I said. "Two more questions. Would Charlie be willing to cook for a large group of people on occasion, maybe once a month or so? And lastly, what was the best landing you ever had in a single week?"

"I'm sure she could handle it," he said. "You're gonna start up a fishing camp, aren't you?"

"Something like that," I said.

"Hmmm, my best week ever was about a year ago. Brought in a full load in five days and sold them for just over twelve thousand dollars. If I remember right, I took home about two thousand after fuel."

"Talk it over with Charlie," I said. "If you're willing, I'll pay you fifty thousand a year, but you'll have to live on the island. Room, board, and a boat, too."

"I'll talk to Charlie," he said, "and get more details from you, but I like the idea."

"We'll talk more when I get back up there. I'm meeting Santiago tomorrow. I'll call you and let you know how that turns out. I'll be up there Monday." We said good-bye and I ended the call and pulled up Doc's number.

"Hi, Gunny. Nikki and I were just talking about you. How're things going? Will you be going out with us again next week?"

"The crew might have the week off with pay, Doc. Things with Santiago got complicated and now Trent's thinking about selling out."

"Selling the boat?" he asked. "Guess that's it, then. I've been thinking of going back in the Navy."

"Care to listen to an alternate idea?" I asked.

"Sure," he said, "But to be honest, I miss the action. Don't tell Nikki I said that, though."

"How would you like to come to work for me?"

"Work for you?" he asked. "Doing what?"

"First Mate on the *Revenge*," I said, then in a conspiratorial tone, I added, "Maybe a little work on the side, when it comes up."

"Merc work?" he asked.

"Come up to the *Rusty Anchor* in Marathon, Monday morning about zero eight-hundred. Know where it is?"

"Yeah," he said.

"I'll have someone pick you up there and bring you out to my island. Ask for the owner, Rusty. He'll point you in the right direction. I offered Trent and Charlie jobs working here and there'll be a few others here, too."

"What kind of money would I be looking at?" he asked. "I gotta think about the future, too."

"How's sixty thousand a year sound?" I asked.

Nothing but silence on the other end. Then he said, "Are you serious?"

"Yeah, it's already approved," I said. "Come up here and meet the team. Later, you'll have to go spend some time up in Homestead training with them. Nothing you can't handle, though. And bring Nikki. She should know everything, if you two are serious about a life together."

"We're getting married in the spring," he said.

"Congratulations," I said. "I gotta go."

Tina came up from the stateroom and said, "I didn't mean to listen in, but it's a small boat. Are you really hiring the Trents and Bob?"

"Sit down here," I said. "I need to tell you something."

She sat down with a concerned look on her face. "What is it," she asked.

"That lawyer that was at the *Anchor*? The paperwork he needed me to sign? I inherited quite a bit of money from my late wife and I'm going to use it for good. Most of it will go to charities that she'd have liked. But, a large chunk of it's going into my war chest."

"Is that why you weren't bothered about buying all that stuff today?" she asked.

"No, not really," I said. "The government pays me a pretty good retirement, plus what they pay me to be on call for jobs like Monday is way more than I need. We didn't even put a dent in that."

Just then Tony came in and said, "You're all set. The bladders fit the fish boxes perfectly."

"Thanks, Tony," I said as I got up and went across to the galley and got two cans of Carib lager. I looked at Tina and asked, "Beer or wine?"

"Do you have any white?" she asked.

"I have a Mondavi Moscato I think you'll like," I said. I handed the two Caribs to Tony and he sat down across from Tina while I got a bottle from the wine cooler and a corkscrew. I poured a glass, put the wine bottle back in the cooler and carried it over to the settee.

"Are you and Chyrel going back to Homestead tonight, or in the morning?" I asked Tony.

"In the morning," he said.

"Think she'd do some research for me and keep it on the down low?"

"Oh yeah," he said. "She's a team player. Hates Smith, probably about as much as you."

"I doubt that," I said as I took out a pen and the notepad that I'd jotted down the last GPS numbers Russ had saved on it and pulled the sheet off the spiral binding and wrote *CSS Lynx* under the numbers and handed it to him. "Ask her to research this Confederate blockade runner and see if there's any correlation with it and that location. Tell her to call me, or better yet, since she likes to show off her tech stuff, tell her to send me a video message if she finds anything."

"What's this all about?" he asked. "A hundred-and-forty-year-old wreck?"

"It's what Deuce's dad was trying to find when he died," I said. "He was looking for a dozen gold bars that were supposed to be on that ship. I think he found at least one of them and that's what got him killed."

"Whoa," said Tina. "Twelve gold bars? What do you think they'd be worth?"

"Gold bars are usually ten pounds," I said. "At today's rate maybe two million dollars. But that's just melt value. Intrinsic value could be twice that."

"I'll have her check it out," he said.

"You seen Deuce?" I asked.

"He and Julie went out for dinner," he said. "They should be back shortly."

"Where you staying tonight?" I asked.

"Same hotel that Chyrel is staying at," he said. "We're leaving early to go back to Homestead."

We talked a little while longer, then Tony said he had to leave so he could get some sleep. "See you Monday morning," he said as he left.

"I'm nervous about diving tomorrow," Tina said. "Are you sure I don't have to take a class or something?"

"We'll be shallow diving," I said. "No more than ten or twelve feet. You'll be fine. That shallow, there's really only two rules you need to remember."

"What're those," she asked.

"First one is to always breathe," I said. "The second one is, don't breathe the water." She reached across and punched my shoulder.

"Seriously," she said. "I'm a good swimmer and all, but I've never even used a snorkel."

"Look," I said, "I've made over three thousand dives and am a certified civilian dive master. In the Corps, I was a combat diver, too. Plus, Deuce was a Navy Diving School Instructor and a SEAL. Julie's made probably a thousand dives herself. You don't have a single thing to worry about. Now, why don't we take the rest of that bottle to the stateroom?"

CHAPTER THIRTEEN:
Underwater World

I woke to the sound of voices. I looked over and Tina wasn't there. I got up and put on a clean pair of shorts and walked up into the salon. Tina, Deuce, and Julie were sitting at the settee and Tina said, "You were sleeping so soundly, I didn't want to disturb you."

"Come on," I said. "I'm a light sleeper. It must have taken you a good ten minutes to get up quiet enough for me not to notice."

She poured me a cup of coffee and I sat down next to her against the bulkhead. "Deuce was just telling me about the place we're diving. Where you and he spread his dad's ashes."

"It's a beautiful little patch reef, not far from here," I said. "But we have to take sort of a roundabout way to get to it. I told Santiago I'd meet him off Alligator Reef at zero nine-hundred. He wants to discuss terms in person. I told him I had a dive charter near there."

"Jesse," Julie said. "I need to talk to you for a minute. Can we go outside?"

I went back into the stateroom and put on a tee shirt and the two of us took our coffee up to the bridge. I sat down at the helm and she sat on the bench seat on the port side. I could tell something was bothering her. At first I thought it might be Tina. It had only been five months since Alex died. But I was way off base.

"I joined the Coast Guard," she blurted out. "I know I've never been a fan, but after what happened and I saw how professional they were and well, I was impressed. I guess I wanted to do something to make a difference."

I looked at her and tried to act surprised. "So, hassling fishermen and divers is how you plan to make a difference?"

"No," she said. "My MOS will be Maritime Enforcement. At least it will be if I graduate the school. I'm the only woman to apply for it so far."

I pretended to think hard about it and finally smiled and said, "You'll set the bar for the male swabs to try to reach. I'm proud of you, Jules."

Her face lit up. "Really, Jesse? That means a lot to me. I've always thought of you as my second dad."

"What did your first dad have to say about it?" I asked.

"He wasn't very thrilled," she said. "I had to go all the way to New Jersey for basic training. That was scary. You know I've never been further north than Palm Beach. I never realized it could be so cold. He hasn't said so, but I think he's kind of proud of me for doing it."

"I know he is," I said. "So, tell me about Maritime Enforcement."

She talked excitedly about what the school was going to be like and how she'd train to board ships and boats from a small, fast-moving boat. I could tell it was something she was really excited about and knowing her as well as I did, there was no doubt in my mind that she'd do well. Finally, she proudly said, "I graduated as the honor recruit and was promoted to Seaman Apprentice."

"You'll be a Master Chief in no time, kiddo," I said and gave her a big hug. "Now, let's go blow some bubbles. Tina's sort of worried about this."

"She's nice," Julie said. "You kind of fit together in a yin yang sort of way."

I clicked on the intercom and said, "Y'all ready to get this show on the road? It's nearly an hour to Alligator Reef."

Tina joined us on the bridge as I started the engines and Deuce cast off the lines. He climbed back up to the bridge and joined Julie on the bench seat. I put the port engine in reverse and the starboard in forward, and the *Revenge* pushed her stern against the fender and swung her bow away from the barge. Then I shifted the port engine to forward and we idled down the long canal to open water. Once we were in deep water I pushed both throttles halfway and the bow rose up and the big 1015-horsepower engines brought her up on plane with ease.

Tina smiled and said, "I love when it does that. It's almost like taking off in a plane."

Julie looked at me and said, "Well, maybe not so yin and yang."

It was nearly zero eight-hundred and I wanted to be early, so once clear of the reef line, I pushed the throttles a little more and brought her up above cruising speed to thirty-five knots. The ocean was very flat and the sun was just above the horizon. The steady hum of the engines and swish of the bow wave continued as we enjoyed the morning, drinking coffee.

Forty minutes later we were about a half mile south of the Alligator Reef light and I brought the big boat down off plane, then turned into the wind, reversed the engines and brought her to a full stop. I dropped the anchor in about forty feet of water and reversed the engines, paying out about a hundred feet of anchor line before I felt the anchor grab.

"We might be here a while," I said as I switched on the radar. There were a few boats anchored on the reef line and a couple of freighters out in the straits. Then I noticed a boat moving pretty fast but still ten miles away. "Or maybe not," I said.

Deuce came over next to me and we watched the blip on the screen. It was moving at about thirty or thirty-five knots and was a mile off the reef. "You carrying?" I asked Deuce.

"Yeah," he said. "You expecting trouble?"

"No, but I like to be prepared."

"Be back in a minute," he said and climbed down the ladder.

"What do you want us to do?" Tina asked. "And before you ask, yes, I'm carrying, too."

"You are?" I asked. "Where?"

She opened her purse and took a small .38 service revolver partway out.

"Good for you," I said. "If you want to upgrade, I have an extra Sig in the cabin."

"This'll do fine," she said.

Deuce came back up on the bridge and we watched the blip on the radar screen getting closer, still holding at thirty-two knots now, about three miles away. I looked up from the screen and out over the port side toward the northeast. Opening the small cabinet below the helm, I took out my binoculars and scanned the horizon. Finally I saw it, a beautiful wooden boat. I handed the binoculars to Deuce and asked, "What do you make it to be?"

He looked through the binoculars as I studied the radar. The approaching boat's speed suddenly increased to forty-one knots as Deuce said, "Man, that's a lot of money heading this way. It's a thirty-three-foot Riva, I think."

"That's what I thought," I said. "Half a million bucks, easy. He just increased speed to forty-one knots."

"Who in their right mind would spend that kind of money on a boat?" Tina asked.

"A drug and arms smuggler," Deuce said.

"He'll probably speak only in Spanish," I said. "Pretend like you don't understand."

Minutes later the sleek boat came down off plane as it neared us. It was Santiago. In the cockpit with him was a beautiful Hispanic woman in sunglasses. Both of them were dressed like they were going out on the town, not out on the water.

"*Buenos dias*," Santiago said as he piloted the boat up close to the side of the *Revenge*.

I climbed down from the bridge and looked the boat over. It was a breathtaking piece of nautical art. Its elegant, flowing lines reflected its owner's taste for money. The decks were beautifully carved mahogany, inlaid with maple. The cockpit and dash were trimmed with real leather and the console looked state-of-the-art.

I whistled low in appreciation and in a low voice I said, "'I have a boat,' he says. That's not a boat, Santiago. This is a boat. That's a piece of art."

"*Gracias, Capitán,*" he said. "*Por favor venga a bordo.*"

"What'd he say, Skipper?" Deuce asked.

"*Que quieres?*" I asked Santiago somewhat louder.

"*Parecemos estar perdido,*" he said.

I looked up at Deuce. "They seem to be lost. I'll be right back." Then I stepped carefully across and down into the small cockpit of the Riva.

"Capitan McDermitt, this is Isabella Espinosa," Santiago said in a low voice. "Isabella, *este es Capitán* Jesse McDermitt."

"*Encantada,*" she said.

I looked at Santiago and said, "What did you want to talk about that couldn't be done over the phone? And make it fast, before my clients suspect something." Then I leaned over his console and pretended to be examining his GPS.

"The nature of your business with me," he said as he leaned over and also pretended to fuss with the equipment. "In one week, I'll have a shipment to move out of western Cuba, to Key West. On Sunday night. I will pay you as we agreed, forty thousand dollars. This will be the same every month, if you accept."

"I agree on one condition," I said. "I want to be your only carrier. If I find out you're using anyone else, I quit."

"Most agreeable," he said. "I've been hoping to consolidate. Using shrimp boats has been a problem. They don't always return on the day they say."

"What's the weight of the shipment?" I asked.

"One thousand kilos," he said. "It could be more, but I don't want to overload your boat."

"She can be adapted to move twice that," I said thinking it over. "But that would take some time. One thousand kilos she can do as is."

"Is your boat fast enough?" he asked.

"Faster than this one," I replied.

The smug look on his face said it all. "I doubt that, *señor*. You have no idea how fast this boat is."

"Cruising speed of about thirty-five knots and a top speed of forty-one," I said. "Watched you approach on radar, then speed up when you saw us."

The smug look left his face. "Your boat is faster?"

"Twin one-thousand-horsepower engines," I said. "Top speed is forty-five knots on calm seas."

I could see that he was impressed. "Perhaps I could use you and your boat for another enterprise," he said.

He'd taken the bait. Time to set the hook. "No gun running," I said.

Again, his face showed his thoughts. The man would make a poor poker player. He recovered quickly and said, "You've done your homework, *Capitán*. I can make it worth your while."

I pretended to think it over for a minute then said, "Maybe. Think it over and you can give me a number next Sunday when I come to Cuba. Do you still plan to ride back with me?"

"*Sí*," he said. "I will call you on Friday to give you the exact location. And I'll give you your number at that time also. Perhaps if you like the number, you can move things for me both ways."

"Better make it a good number," I said. "It'd be nice if I didn't have to lug divers and fishermen around on my boat. I'm taking these three to Cozumel from here." I leaned on the console and using my left hand, hidden from his view, I quickly pulled the tab off one of the little resin-drop-looking bugs and stuck it to the underside of the dash, as I pressed a few buttons on the GPS. "That should do it," I said loudly as I straightened up. Then turning to the woman I said, "*El placer es mio.*" Before he could say anything more, I stepped up on the leather-edged gunwale and back over to the *Revenge*. Then turning I said, "*Buena suerte, señor.*"

Santiago waved, then jammed the throttle, launching the sleek boat forward and turning east. I climbed back up to the bridge where I found Deuce smiling. "You're good," he said. "He was almost begging you to take a shipment of guns down. Too bad you couldn't have dropped one of those bugs while you were onboard."

I smiled and said, "I did."

He looked at me, surprised. "I was watching your every move," he said.

"Hopefully he didn't catch it either," I said.

"Every sound on board his boat is being recorded," he said. "We can call Chyrel later and see if anything good is picked up. We'll have to start making plans once we get the intel about the camp. It won't leave us much time, though. I'm betting he'll ride down with you too."

"No," I said, "If anything he'll have his new hired muscle ride down with me and the two of them ride back."

"It'd be better if he rode down with you," he said. "Then we could take him down at sea. On Cuban soil would bring all kinds of problems."

"You want the terrorists too, right?"

"That'd be a bonus," he said.

"Okay," I said, "Let's go diving."

I started the engines and engaged the windlass to pull up the anchor. Minutes later, we were up on plane heading west. Twenty minutes later, we were anchored a few yards off of Conrad and climbed down to suit up.

I'd removed the fighting chair from the cockpit and put a four-seat back-to-back bench in its place before leaving the island. Deuce and I brought four tanks up from the engine room, squeezing between the two stacked crates and the generator. I showed Tina how to attach her new buoyancy compensator and the first stage of her new regulator to one of the tanks, then attach the low-pressure hose to the BC. Wearing the new wetsuit, I figured she'd need at least five pounds on her weight belt, so I set that up, while she wriggled into her wetsuit. When she was all set, I had her sit on the bench and we adjusted the straps on the BC.

"Now, to stand up you'll have to lean forward, like you're wearing a really heavy backpack, centering your weight over your legs. It's a lot of weight and bulky, but once you're in the water you'll be weightless." I inflated the BC for her and showed her how to dump air from it so she could descend. "It's only fifteen feet here so getting neutrally buoyant will take a little practice." Explaining the Valsalva maneuver to equalize the air in her inner ear, I told her she'd probably only have to do it once or twice as she went down.

"You're sure I don't need to take a class?" she asked. "That's an awful lot to remember for just a shallow dive."

Julie was sitting behind her and said, "I've never taken a scuba class. Dad and Jesse taught me to dive when I was a kid. We'll be right with you the whole time. Just remember to breathe."

"And don't breathe the water?" Tina said.

Julie laughed. "Yeah, that's exactly what they said to me when I was ten."

"You did this at ten years old?" Tina asked.

"Yep," she replied. "Used a little tiny air tank that's normally used as a backup. What you're about to see is breathtaking, so remembering to breathe really is important."

Putting just a backpack rig on my tank, I attached my first stage to it. Then I put on my weight belt and fins and lifted the rig over my head, letting the tank slide down my back as my arms went through the straps. Grabbing my mask, I shuffled over to the transom door, opened it and stepped down onto the swim platform. "Shuffle your feet like that and take tiny steps."

"You're not wearing a wetsuit or one of these vest things?" she asked.

Deuce and I laughed and he said, "We'll stay down until the first person's air reaches eight hundred pounds. With a new diver, that's usually about fifteen minutes. He won't get cold that fast."

"I rarely use a BC," I added. "After a few dives, you'll know exactly how much weight to use and won't need one either."

Deuce stood up, ready to go and helped Julie up, then shuffled around and helped Tina to her feet. By then, Julie had stepped down onto the platform, put her mask on and said, "Watch how Deuce and I enter the water and do the same thing."

When Tina had made her way to the transom door, Julie took a long stride while holding one hand over her mask. Her head barely went under. Once she was clear of the platform Deuce did the same thing, but since he wasn't wearing a BC either he went under for a second.

"Okay," I said. "You see how they did that? It's called a giant stride entry. Step way out and keep your legs apart like you're trying to do a split. Once you're in the water, scissor your legs together. Keep one hand on your mask and regulator and the other extended out to the side. I'll be in the water before you know it. You ready?"

"As ready as I'll ever be, I guess," she said somewhat hesitantly.

"Good girl," I said. "Whenever you're ready." I pulled my mask on and put my regulator in my mouth and waited. First-timers are always hesitant, but she stepped right off, with Deuce on one side and Julie on the other. I fell backwards off the side of the platform, then kicked over and surfaced right in front of her as she came up.

Taking my regulator out I said, "Now just let a little air out of your BC, like I showed you, until you feel like you're starting to descend." She did so and we started down to the sandy bottom together.

At first she tried to use her fins like she was walking, pushing with the bottom of them. I stopped her and pointed two fingers at my eyes, then pointed to Julie and Deuce ahead of us, finning toward the reef. She watched them for a second, then nodded her head and started finning after them. She was a bit too heavy, so I came up beside her and pushed the auto-inflator on her BC, putting a small charge of air into it. The sudden sound startled her, but she came up off the bottom a little. I gave her the okay sign and she nodded.

Holding her hand, we finned toward the reef after Deuce and Julie. They had already reached the outer fringe and were looking back, waiting. Just ahead of us, a pair of porgies swam past, followed by a large French angelfish. The angels have always been my favorite. Reaching up to eighteen inches long, they were nearly as tall. The French angel is all black, except for the tips of their scales, which were yellow. I felt the excitement in the squeeze of Tina's hand.

As we approached the edge of the reef, more and more fish became visible against the multicolored reef. There were several blue-striped grunts and yellowtail snappers hanging above the reef. A queen angelfish swam out of a crevice and disappeared into another. As large as the French angel, the queen is more brightly colored, with yellow and blue scales and a pronounced blue ring on the forehead, resembling a crown. Dozens of tiny damselfish of several kinds darted in and out of holes and cracks and a pair of spotfin butterfly fish cruised along the sandy bottom at the edge of the reef. Spotfins get their name from a large black spot on the dorsal fin. Bright yellow and gray, they have a black vertical band across their black eyes. The band and spot confuse predators, who mistake the head for the tail. There are butterfly fish of different types all over the world's reefs. Each species may look different, but all have one thing in common. They're almost always in bonded pairs, staying with the same mate throughout their lives.

Looking at Tina, her eyes were wide behind her mask. A near constant stream of bubbles were coming out of her regulator. We followed Deuce and Julie as they finned around the right side of the reef. Conrad only covers a little over a quarter acre, but there's more life in that one quarter acre than about any reef I've ever seen. Deuce had a catch bag and was looking for lobster for lunch. This reef usually has quite a few, so I knew lunch was virtually in the bag. We came to a narrow cut in the reef and let Julie and Deuce go on ahead while we turned into the cut, staying close to the sandy bottom. Under one ledge we found a nurse shark about four feet long, just resting. Tina was startled at first, but followed my lead as we slowly approached the docile fish. Near its tail I reached out and gently stroked its skin, then pointed to Tina to do the same. She tentatively reached out and ran her fingertips over the coarse skin. A shark's skin is covered with tiny denticles, similar to teeth, giving it the feel of rough sandpaper.

We continued further into the cut to the end and then went up and over the top, where some beautiful staghorn coral was growing along with giant barrel sponges, brain coral, red gorgonian coral, and purple sea fans. The gorgonian and sea fans gently swayed in the light surge, performing a seductive and suggestive dance. A large barracuda hung motionless just off the edge of the reef as we finned back down to the bottom. Near the sand we spotted a juvenile French angelfish, silky black with bright vertical yellow stripes. In the same crevice were two rock beauties, bright orange and black, dancing in and out of the light filtering through a narrow gap in the surrounding coral.

Tapping Tina's shoulder, I pointed to her eyes with two fingers and then made a motion with my hand directing her to look closer. With her fins lightly touching the sandy bottom, she inched closer to where I was pointing, until her face was less than a foot away. Moving my finger closer to the clusters of translucent white tentacles of the coral polyps on the small gorgonian, one pulled instantly into its base, followed by another next to it. Tina looked at me with wide eyed wonder, reminding me of my own excitement, seeing the reef underwater for the first time as a young boy. It's only when looking very close does a person realize for the first time that a reef's not just a jumble of rocks, but a living, growing colony of millions of individuals.

Turning right, we met Deuce and Julie halfway around the reef as Deuce was putting a lobster in the catch bag. From the bulge, I could tell it wasn't alone. I held my pressure gauge up in front of Tina and she lifted hers up to look at it. I held up nine fingers, then jerked my thumb upward. Deuce motioned that they were going to continue around the rest of the reef with a circular motion of his fingers. I nodded and took Tina's hand as we slowly finned our way over the reef toward the boat. We'd only been down about fifteen minutes, but I was already getting a little cold.

When we broke the surface Tina pulled her mask down below her chin, looked at me and grinned. "Can we go back down again?" she asked.

"I only have four tanks," I said and saw her grin turn into a frown. "But I have a compressor to refill them," I added. "We'll start them filling while we have lunch.

Deuce should have enough to eat. Next dive, I'll show you how to catch lobster for tonight's dinner."

As we climbed back aboard the *Revenge* and started removing our dive gear, Tina began chattering, "I can't believe all those beautiful fish. I want to know what each one is. I've never seen or imagined anything like that before. And I touched a frigging shark! None of my friends are going to believe that. And the rock! It's not a rock at all is it?"

I wrapped a big towel around her and removed the two tanks from both our rigs. "No, coral reefs are large cities. This reef has about the same population as New York. I'll get the hoses ready to refill the tanks. Deuce and Julie will be up in about five minutes."

"Anything I can do to help?" she asked.

"I got this," I said, opening the hatch to the engine room. "Why don't you help them up, when they get to the platform?"

I went down to the engine room, unrolled the four air hoses and started the generator, which powers all the onboard electrical systems, including the small air compressor. When I got back out on deck, Deuce and Julie were handing their fins up to Tina and climbing aboard.

"A quarter of our limit down," Deuce said as he lifted his catch bag up to me.

"What's that mean?" Tina asked.

"Means he's already started on dinner," I said. "The bag limit is six per person."

I opened the bag and looked inside. "All nice size, too," I said.

Deuce helped me hang the tanks in the water to fill. Then I mounted the small portable grill in one of the rod holders so that it hung over the side of the boat. We had a lunch of grilled lobster tails, with steamed broccoli from the galley and sliced pineapple.

The sun was just past its peak, by the time we finished lunch. Our bodies warmed from the near perfect weather and the tanks full, we got ready for our second dive. I gave Tina a net and tickle stick and explained to her how to use the stick to coax the lobster out of a crevice and into the net.

When we got back in the water Tina was much more comfortable. We found lobster almost immediately and she managed to catch three with the net. I got another three by hand, while Deuce and Julie got another eight. We had sixteen to take back with us. We hoisted anchor and started back to Marathon with three hours of daylight left.

"I could stay out here all day," Tina said, leaning back in the second seat, the sun full in her face through the windshield. "I still can't believe all that beauty was just below the surface."

"Not to mention all that bounty," Deuce said.

"Bounty?" Tina asked.

"For over three centuries," Deuce explained. "Spanish treasure ships have followed the route out of Havana to Key West, then east following the Keys and the coastline all the way up to the middle of Florida, before turning east for Europe. Hundreds wrecked on these reefs."

Our plan was to bring Deuce and Julie to the island and they'd go back to Marathon, taking both the Grady and my skiff. With Rusty and his skiff, they'd be able to bring nine people to the island when Doc and Deuce's team arrived in the morning. Tony, Art, and Chyrel would come by helicopter, along with two other team members that were Tony and Art's backups.

An hour later, we were tied up under my house. Deuce and Julie wanted to get back to Marathon before dark, so we pulled the Grady and my skiff out and they left an hour before dark. "Don't eat all that lobster before we get back," he said as they pulled away from the dock.

"I put four traps in the deep part of Harbor Channel yesterday," I said. "Should be able to have a lobster lunch for the whole crew tomorrow. See you guys in the morning."

Tina and I walked up the steps to the deck as Trent and Pescador came up the rear steps. "I overheard you," he said. "Been catching a lot of fish with your dog's help. How many will there be tomorrow?"

"About two dozen," I said, "Counting your family."

"I have plenty enough, then," he said. "Put about forty fillets in the cooler the last couple of days."

"Good, we're gonna need it. You wanna go out with me early in the morning and pull the lobster traps?"

"Sure," he said. "I got those other three tables built you wanted. Had some lumber left over and made some stone crab traps and set them out."

"You're an industrious man, Trent," I said as I looked out over the trees to the southwest. "Sunset's in about an hour, have y'all eaten?"

"No, we were waiting for you to get back," he said. "Charlie has about a dozen stone crab claws already and is making blackened snapper."

We followed Trent down to the tables on the far side of the clearing. He had done an exceptional job on them and Charlie made a great meal. Tina and I cleaned up so they could get the two kids to bed and then we walked out to the dock. Pescador was in his usual spot waiting for the light show to begin.

"When are we going to leave tomorrow?" Tina asked.

"I'd like to be able to drop Tony and Art about midnight. We'll probably leave here just before sunset."

"How long will we be gone?"

"I'm thinking they should be able to get enough information in three days to be helpful. We'll be getting back here by Friday, at least. I don't suppose you have any vacation time coming, do you?"

"I can call the manager and request it," she said.

Carl and Charlie walked out onto the sandbar and sat down. They seemed to be having a discussion, Trent was pointing toward shore and motioning with his hands. I could see Charlie smile at him and nod her head, agreeing with what he was saying. Slowly the sun started to slip toward the far horizon. There was a bank of high cumulus clouds just to the north of it and the sun bathed them in a beautiful red glow. Tina leaned her head on my shoulder as we quietly watched the sun set. It almost seemed to sizzle as the water reached up and grabbed the lower edge of the orb. The air all around seemed to take on an orange glow, casting long shadows from the trees on the nearby islands.

Slowly, the sun sank into the sea and as it disappeared and the sky started to grow dark, Tina said, "No green flash tonight?"

"No," I said. "It's rare. We were lucky the other night."

We sat there a few more minutes and I noticed Trent and his wife got up from the sandbar and walked, hand in hand, to the little cabin. "We should go to bed," I said. "Tomorrow's going to be a long day."

We got up and walked to the house, with Pescador trotting ahead.

CHAPTER FOURTEEN:
Stars Over Cuba

I woke very early the next morning and was able to get out of bed without rousing Tina. I let Pescador out and started the coffeepot. Breakfast would have to wait a while. I wanted to get out to the lobster traps and be back before anyone arrived. Deuce had texted me to expect the chopper about zero nine-hundred and the rest of the team were meeting him at the *Anchor* a little earlier than that, so everyone should be here by midmorning.

Stepping out onto the deck, I heard, or rather felt, someone coming up the back steps. It was Trent, with Pescador leading the way.

"Figured you'd be up early," he said. "Gonna be a long day for you."

"Yeah," I said. "No rest for the wicked."

"Wanna go out and pull those traps?"

"Yeah. Coffee's about ready. Want a cup?" He nodded. "Wait here a minute," I said and went into the galley to find Tina already pouring three cups and filling a thermos.

"Thanks," I said. "But you didn't need to get up. It's barely zero four hundred."

She smiled and said, "I've always been an early riser."

"Farm life, huh? Trent's out on the deck. We're leaving in a minute to go pull those lobster traps. Want to come along."

"Y'all go ahead," she said. "Charlie and I are going to get things ready here. Have you thought about where everyone's going to stay?"

I thought about it a minute. There'd be Trent's family, Chyrel and a bunch of door kickers. I didn't know how many would be staying on after we left for Cozumel. I assumed Chyrel and the two standby operators would stay. "Chyrel can stay here," I said. "The Trents can stay where they are and anyone else that stays over can fill up the other cabin and sleep under the stars."

"You'd have your guests sleep outside?"

"They're not guests," I said. "Half of them will probably prefer it, anyway. From what Deuce told me, most of these guys came from elite military units. Snake eaters."

We carried our coffee outside. I handed a cup to Trent and we sat down at the table on the back of the deck. "What time are y'all shovin' off?" Trent asked.

"Before sunset," I replied. "That'll put us just off Cuba near midnight and in Cozumel by midmorning."

"If you'd like, I can have Williams run up here and check over the engines," he said. "No better mechanic anywhere around."

"Might not be a bad idea," I said. "It's an eighteen-hour run."

"I'll call him," he said as he was getting up. "He'll be here by the time we get back."

"He must have a fast boat," I said.

"Nope," he replied. "He's got an old de Havilland Beaver float plane."

"Really?" I asked.

"Oh yeah. He doesn't need much of an excuse to fly. And gas money."

"Call him," I said. "Tell him I'll pay him five hundred dollars to come up and look the engines over. It'd be worth that just to see one of those old planes."

Trent got his phone out and made the call. "We should be back in an hour," I told Tina. "When Williams gets here, would you show him to the boat?"

"Sure," she said.

I got up and walked to the front steps, kissing her on the cheek, then went down to the docks and opened the east door, before climbing aboard the Grady and starting the engine.

Trent came down the steps and as he was untying the lines he said, "Williams'll be here in twenty minutes. He was already at the airport planning to go for a ride anyway. I told him he could tie up to the end of the pier. He wasn't real happy when I told him I was putting *Miss Charlie* up for sale."

"If he's as good as you say, he won't have any trouble finding work," I said. "I could pay him to come out here once a week and spend a day or two going over the boats. Maybe three days, when we get the generator and aquaculture system going."

We idled out to Harbor Channel and turned northeast. It was about a mile to the first trap float, but we idled all the way, enjoying the early morning air and quiet for a half hour. Pulling up the trap, I could tell by the weight it was going to be a good lunch. It had nine legal-sized lobster in it and a few that we had to let go.

"How's Williams gonna land in the dark?" I asked.

"There's enough starlight for him," Trent replied. "Besides, he hasn't always been against drug smuggling." He rebaited the trap and tossed it back in the water. I shined the light in the direction of the next trap and finding it, pointed the boat toward it.

In the distance I heard the sound of an airplane with a radial engine. A minute later it flew over, banking sharply to the left. Two bright spotlights came on as it lined up for a water landing on the north side of the island. We quickly pulled, emptied, and rebaited the other three traps and started back to the island. Altogether, we had another thirty lobster to add to what was already in the refrigerator.

As we idled up the channel and under the house, Williams came down the steps carrying two large toolboxes. He set them on the dock next to the *Revenge* and said, "Hey, Skipper, how ya doing, Jesse?"

"Doing well enough," I said. "Thanks for coming up."

"Sorry if I cut your fun flight short," Trent said.

"Don't worry about it, Skipper," he said. "Happy to oblige."

Trent and I tied off the Grady and I showed Williams aboard the *Revenge*, while Trent carried the cooler full of lobster up the steps.

"This is a real beauty," Williams said. "I'm guessing you have the bigger 865-horse engines right?" he asked.

"Drop on down and take a look," I said. "There's a couple crates stored below, but you can squeeze past them easy enough."

He opened the hatch, squatted down and stepped into the engine room. He let out a low whistle, then stuck his head back up through the hatch. "Drug runner special, huh?" he said.

"Bought her at a Coast Guard auction," I said. "Some smuggler's loss was my gain."

"I've only seen one other Rampage with twin ten-fifteens," he said. "You've taken great care of this boat, Jesse. I could eat off this deck down here."

"Thanks," I said. "But the credit goes to my old First Mate, Jimmy Saunders."

"I know Jimmy," he said. "Good kid. I doubt there's any problems, but I'll run a full diagnostics on my laptop on both the main engines and the gen-set, check all the fluids and filters. Won't take but about an hour."

I headed back up the steps to the house. Tina wasn't inside so I went down the rear steps and crossed the clearing. It was starting to get light to the east and I had a pretty good idea where she was.

"Thought I'd find you out here," I said as I walked out to the end of the pier. She was sitting with Pescador under the wing of Williams's plane. I walked along the old bird, admiring the lines. The Beaver is used in a lot of remote places, especially up in Canada and Alaska. It was able to take off in a short distance, due to its large wings, and could carry six passengers and the pilot or over a ton of cargo.

Tina looked up and said, "It's a real pretty plane your friend has. I've seen it fly around Key West sometimes. Is it new?"

"New?" I said. "No, it was probably built before I was born." I sat down next to her on the pier and she took my hand in hers as we waited for the sun to rise. There were low clouds to the east blocking the sun, but the colors were still pretty spectacular. Living on an island you learn not only to live off the sea but to appreciate the beauty in everything around you.

Far in the distance, I heard the sound of a heavy helicopter. Sound carries over water and I knew it was probably still a few miles away. "Let's get back to the clearing," I said. "We're about to have company."

As we passed between the two bunkhouses, Trent and Charlie came out with the kids. The chopper passed slowly over our heads. It was a Bell UH-1, commonly called a Huey. Noting the flag, the LED lights mounted on top of the pole still on, the pilot continued over the island, turned a wide circle and approached from the southeast. I trotted to the upwind side and guided him into the center of the clearing. Tony, Art, and two other men jumped from the skids while the chopper was still a foot off the ground. They turned around and pulled several bags and cases from the two open doors as Chyrel climbed out of the right front of the aircraft.

I walked toward them and nodded in the direction of the tables by the bunkhouses as the chopper lifted off the ground and disappeared over the west side of the island.

"Good to see you again Art," I said, once the noise died down.

"Nice to see you again too, Jesse. These two guys are Donnie Hinkle and Glenn Mitchel. Both SEALs before coming over to DHS. Guys, this is former Recon Marine, Gunnery Sergeant Jesse McDermitt."

Reaching out my hand to the two men I said, "Haven't been that in a few years. Just call me Jesse."

"Pleasure, mate," said Hinkle with an Aussie accent.

"Heard about you, Jesse," Mitchel said, taking my hand after setting his bag on one of the tables. "One of my instructors at Camp Atterbury told us about an impossible shot some Jarhead made in the Mog in ninety-three."

Tina looked from Mitchel to me and I said, "Lucky was all. Donnie, Glenn, meet Deputy Christina La Mons. She'll be going with Deuce and me to drop Tony and Art off. And these are my caretakers for the island, Carl and Charlie Trent."

The two men shook hands with Tina and Charlie, then Trent stepped forward and shook hands with them, saying, "If there's anything you need, just yell. Since you're the first to arrive, I guess you get dibs on the bunks in the east bunkhouse over there."

Looking around the clearing, Hinkle topped on a small area under some hibiscus and jasmine. "Thanks, mate. But I think we'll pitch camp over yonder. Leave the bunks for the city boys."

Trent looked at the two men, then at me, and shrugged. I nodded to Hinkle and they picked up two of the four packs and walked towards the wood line. I made them to be a sniper team as soon as Mitchel mentioned Atterbury. The massive old base in Indiana is where SEAL snipers are trained.

Once they were out of earshot, Chyrel said, "Those two are kind of strange if you ask me."

"Not strange at all," I said. "In the spring, I string a hammock over there at night."

Tina looked up at me and said, "What was he talking about an impossible shot in the Mog? What's a Mog?"

"Mogadishu," I replied. Then changing the subject I said, "Deuce and the rest should be arriving in a few minutes. Let's get down to the docks."

Without waiting I turned and headed across the clearing. Tina ran to catch up and said, "You're a sniper?"

"I was. A long time ago," I said. "Now I'm a fisherman."

Walking up the steps to the house I could hear the approaching boats. Deuce was right on time. As I walked down the front steps, Williams was just coming up out of the engine room.

"Everything looks great, Jesse," he said. "You had a loose clamp on one of the air-to-airs, but I tightened it up. Also tweaked the injectors a little over the stock setting on the computer. You might get another knot at wide open throttle."

"Thanks Dave," I said. "Every little knot counts. Stick around for lunch? Got lots of fish, lobster, and stone crab claws."

"Don't mind if I do," he said, looking down the dock where the first of three boats was idling up. "Looks like you're having a party."

The first boat to tie up was Rusty, with Doc and Nikki aboard, along with two other men. Deuce pulled up behind him with four men aboard and Julie brought up the rear with two women and another man aboard. That surprised me. I thought all of Deuce's field team would be men. Deuce left the boat for his team members to tie up and unload, coming to where Williams and I were standing beside the *Revenge* just as Doc and Nikki walked up.

"Deuce," I said. "This is Dave Williams, mechanic extraordinaire, my new First Mate and former Navy Corpsman, Bob Talbot, and his fiancée, Nikki Godsey. Dave just squeezed another couple knots out of the *Revenge*'s engines. He also owns one beautiful de Havilland Beaver docked at the north pier."

"No kidding?" Deuce said. "You gonna be around a while? I'd love to see her." Knowing Deuce as well as I did, I knew this question was as much to me as it was to Williams. He was asking if Williams could be trusted.

"Yeah," I said. "He's gonna stay for lunch at least." I was telling Deuce that I trusted him and he should, too. Then I said, "I'm thinking of offering him a job as well." Williams looked at me, puzzled, and I added, "Trent's selling his shrimp boat and Williams is his engineer. With all these boats I seem to be collecting, plus the power plant and aquaculture system, I think I can keep him busy enough. Hell, he could work full time on *The Beast* and never run out of work. Besides, I'm hoping he'll let me have some seat time in his Beaver."

"You fly?" Williams asked.

"Not fixed-wing," I said. "Flew rotaries in the Corps from time to time."

"Nice to meet both of you," Deuce said. "Doc, I'd like to get a minute alone sometime today, if you don't mind?"

"Absolutely, sir," Doc said.

"We're a very informal team, Doc," Deuce said. "I prefer Deuce. It's short for Russell Livingston Junior. Dad served with Jesse, here." Then to me he said, "Speaking of your boat collection. You can add a Cigarette and a Winter to it. The Director said he doesn't want to pay for the dockage and to either sell them at auction or find somewhere to dock them for free."

"Beech's Cigarette?" I asked. Sonny Beech used to be a loan shark, drug smuggler, and terrorist sympathizer. He was the boss of the men who killed my wife and Deuce's dad. Right now, he was being held in Guantanamo Bay along with five terrorists he tried to smuggle into the country and the man that arranged it.

"Yeah," Deuce said. "They're both yours if you want them. Otherwise he's going to give them to the Coast Guard to auction off and you know what they'll do with them."

"Yeah, target practice," I said. "I'll take them and have Trent build a boathouse up by the bunkhouses for the smaller boats. The go fast and the Winter can go in here."

The others were starting to file down the dock, Rusty, Julie, and the two women in the front. They all stopped just in front of where we were standing and Deuce said, "Team, this is Captain Jesse McDermitt, our transporter, his engineer, Dave Williams and our newest team member, if he accepts, Bob Talbot, former Navy Corpsman and recipient of the Bronze Star. Jesse's a former Recon Marine Gunnery Sergeant and one of the best in the Corps with a long gun. Y'all head on up the ladder, cross the deck and down the other side. There's two bunkhouses on the far side. We'll assemble there and make introductions."

As the group headed up the steps Williams asked me, "Is that cistern your only water supply?"

"Yeah, why?"

"I noticed you have a water maker aboard," he said. "If you want, I'll run a hose up to the cistern and get it running."

"Thanks," I said. "But it only makes about ten gallons an hour. That tank up there holds two thousand gallons."

"Well," he said, "your water tanks on the boat are full. Might as well add what you can. Can I ask you a question?" I nodded. "Some of these guys are pretty rough-looking. There's nothing illegal going on here, is there?"

I laughed and said, "No, just the opposite. These folks work for the government. We have a mission tonight. That's why I wanted the boat checked out."

"If ya like, I can inspect your outboards too," he said. "I have programs on my laptop for just about every make and model."

"Thanks, Dave. When you finish let's talk about that job, okay?"

He nodded and headed across the rear dock to the smaller boats.

Doc, Nikki and I caught up with Tina, Deuce, and Julie. When we got to the tables, I saw that Trent had placed two huge coolers full of beer, soft drinks and water on one of them. "Where'd the coolers come from?" I asked him.

"I had Dave bring them up," he replied. "Thought these guys might be thirsty. He also brought a portable generator, in case Chyrel needs it."

"Everyone," Deuce said. "Just ground your gear over by the coolers for a minute. We're off duty for the next few hours, some of you for the next day or two. Jesse has provided us a great place to relax and unwind."

I said, "I've been looking forward to meeting all of you and look forward to working with you and getting to know you." I walked over to the Trents and said, "This is Captain Carl Trent and his wife Charlie, the caretakers on the island. If you need anything, just ask one of them. I gotta warn you, though. This isn't a resort. There's only one outdoor cold-water shower, fed by a rain cistern, and a hot-water shower powered by solar-charged batteries. Anyone who stays over, plan on bathing in the sea and rinsing under the cold water. There's fishing gear in the hanging lockers by the docks and a long pier over there between the bunkhouses. The bunkhouses themselves are rustic. No electricity or running water, but the bunks are new and comfortable. The boats you came in on are available if you want to catch lobster or look around the reefs. The Trent kids, Junior and Patty over there, can show you the best places to find clams." They'd been hiding behind Charlie's legs, but stepped out smiling when I said that. "We eat from the sea here, so any help replenishing the food stores would be much appreciated."

I walked over to Tina and said, "I assume you met Julie and Rusty at the *Anchor*. This is Monroe County Deputy Christina La Mons. She'll be on the insertion team tonight." Then turning to Deuce I said, "How about a quick introduction of your team?"

"You already met Donnie and Glenn," he began. "They usually tend to stay to themselves, as you probably understand." Nodding to the two women, one a tall, athletic-looking redhead, the other a shorter blonde with very short hair, he said, "Over here's Charity Styles and Sherri Fallon. They both came to us from Miami-Dade PD. Charity's a martial arts instructor and Sherri was an armorer for SWAT and now handles all our weapons."

Pointing to a dark-skinned man with shoulder-length hair and a full beard, he said, "This is Kumar Sayef. Kumar came from Delta Force and speaks most Arabic dialects fluently."

Next to Sayef stood two obvious Marines, both black guys with high and tight haircuts. "These two are fellow Recon Marines, Scott Grayson and Jeremiah Simpson," Deuce said. "They're our resident underwater experts. Both came from Recon dive school, where they were instructors."

Nodding toward the man next to the Marines, he said, "This is former Lieutenant Scott Bond. Scott came to us from SEAL Team Two, where he served as Dive Supervisor at the SEAL dive school and attended the Navy War College before that."

Pointing to the next man, an innocuous-looking man of average height, weight and features, he said, "This is Brent Shepherd. Brent came to us from the CIA and speaks a number of European languages. He's our go-to guy for disguises."

Standing with Julie were two broad-shouldered blond men, both wearing mustaches. Deuce said, "This is Andrew Bourke and Ralph Goodman, both from Coast Guard Port Protection. They'll be leaving us in a few weeks to go with Julie for further training in maritime enforcement, then come back to train the rest of the team in small boat tactics and force boarding."

"Jesse," he said, turning to me "All our team cross train one another in their own specialties. Every week, we get better and better at all our individual specialties by teaching them to each other. With the exception of the two loners over there," he said, nodding toward the tree line, where a small tent had been set up and the two shooters sat hunched over a small campfire. "As you know, their specialty isn't something that can be taught."

"Thanks for coming, y'all," I said. "Chyrel, you can set up in the main house. Dave, can you help her out and hook the generator directly to the batteries under the house? They're in a box in the far corner by the red skiff and are connected to an inverter in the house." I nodded to the two women and said, "If you two plan to stay the night, the three of you can bunk there. There's extra cots in the bunkhouse. The rest of you, there's twelve bunks in the east bunkhouse, make yourselves at home. Lunch will be at noon. Fish, lobster, stone crab claws, mango, papaya, banana and a tossed salad."

Dave and Chyrel headed to the house, carrying the two cases brought in on the chopper, and the other two women went to the bunkhouse to get a couple of cots. The men followed them, carrying their sea bags and cases, then broke up to explore the island. Deuce and Julie walked over to talk to the Trents, along with Doc and Nikki.

Grayson and Simpson came back and Grayson said, "Good to meet ya, Gunny. We're both from First Recon. I once had a Platoon Sergeant, Master Sergeant Blalock, who told us about a Staff Sergeant McDermitt he served with in Grenada."

"Bullet Bart Blalock?" I said. "Looks like a fire hydrant, short, wide and no neck? He made Master Sergeant?"

Both men laughed and Simpson said, "Yeah, that was him, alright."

"Was?" I asked.

"Killed in Fallujah last year," Grayson said. "Posthumous Silver Star."

"Damn," I said. "Good Marine. We can hoist a beer to him at lunch."

As the two men wandered off toward the pier, Tina said, "I feel really out of place here. Everyone seems to be the best of the best. All fighters and warriors."

"Don't worry about it," I said. "They're just people, like anyone else."

"You seem to fit in with them," she said. "Even though they never met you, most of them seem to have heard of you. I'm not sure I know you at all now."

"That was a different life, long time ago," I said. "I'm just a simple fisherman now."

"I don't think there's anything simple about you," she said. "Can you tell me more about what you did in the Marines?"

"Nothing much to tell," I lied. "I served from '79 to '99. After Vietnam and before the 9/11 attacks."

"But that one guy mentioned Mogadishu and just now those two mentioned Grenada. I'm guessing the first Gulf War, too?"

"Small skirmishes I was involved in," I said. "Ancient history." Then changing the subject I said, "Wanna go for a swim?"

She smiled. "Glutton for punishment?"

"Go change," I said. "I'll see if anyone else wants to come along."

"I'll ask the girls," she said.

Deuce, Julie, Tony, and Art walked up and, overhearing the end of our conversation, Deuce asked, "How far are you swimming?"

"A mile and a half," I said. "Against the current one way and with the current the other."

"I'm in," he said. "We can make it a competition. That is, if Tina doesn't mind."

I laughed, "Her? Hope you SEALs have a thick skin."

"Come on," Tony said. "Really fast swimmers are tall and lanky, like you."

"Don't say I didn't warn you," I said. "She stayed right with me and did it in close to my best ever time. And I don't think she was really trying that hard."

Deuce got up on one of the tables and yelled out, "All hands fall in for PT!"

Within seconds the team was gathered around the tables. All but the women, who probably couldn't hear Deuce through the dense lignum vitae wood walls. A second later, I saw Tina and the martial arts instructor, Charity Styles. They both were wearing one-piece suits, Tina in red and Charity in blue. I couldn't help but notice that Charity's physique was even more athletic than I first thought. They trotted across the clearing and Charity said, "What's going on Boss?"

Deuce looked around the group and said, "Jesse suggested a little motivational swim competition. What's the course and rules, Jesse?"

"From the north pier," I said. "There's a small island to the northeast about three quarters of a mile away. We swim due east to a red lobster trap float. That's Harbor Channel. Follow the channel northeast to the island and there's an eddy channel that goes completely around it that's about ten feet deep. Back into Harbor Channel to the red float, then due west back to the pier. Outside the channels, the water's only a few feet deep. Tide's rising, so we'll be going with the current out and against it coming back. Everybody to the pier."

They all charged between the bunkhouses, stripping off shirts as they went. A couple guys had to duck into the bunkhouse to change out of long pants. I turned to Tina and said, "Don't hold back like you did with me the other day, okay?"

"What makes you think I was holding back?" she asked with a grin.

"I could tell," I said. "I was, too."

"You're on, mister," she said.

Half the guys were gathered around Dave's Beaver at the end of the pier, not realizing it was there until now. I called out, "Line up along the pier and space out from the end about five feet apart."

We lined up and I was on the end closest to shore, with Tina and Charity next to me, Julie and Deuce beyond them, then Tony and Art and the rest of the group. Shouting toward the far end, I said, "Water's eight feet deep at the end and only about four at this end. Give us a three count, Deuce," I said.

"One, two, three!" he shouted and all fourteen of us dove into the water. Only Tina and I knew how cold it was going to be, so that gave us maybe a half a second advantage as the others immediately rose to the surface, gasping.

Tina lit out at a very fast pace, taking a breath every third stroke, just like she had before. I stayed right with her, then slowly pulled ahead a little. She increased speed, changing to every fourth stroke. I noticed someone just beyond her keeping pace. I rose slightly on my next breath and caught sight of the blue bathing suit and close cropped blond hair. It was Charity Styles. By the time we got to the float, three others had gained and passed the three of us. Two I knew were Grayson and Simpson. The third I guessed would be Bond, the SEAL dive supervisor, but I couldn't tell for sure.

The current picked them up in the channel and the three divers moved further ahead of us. When we got into the channel we moved further ahead of the rest of the pack. Knowing that the current would carry us faster, I struck out at a quicker pace. Tina and Charity sensed this and both did the same. Slowly Charity started to pull away from Tina and me and close on the three divers ahead of us.

As we rounded Upper Harbor Key I chanced a look behind us and saw that three swimmers had broken away from the pack and were closing. The rest of the way back was much harder as the current was flowing at its fullest, over a knot. I was pushing as hard as I could now, breathing every other stroke. Tina was back to every third stroke. The three divers ahead of us started to slow and soon we were alongside and pulling away. Halfway back, the three behind us were nearly on top of us. Tina and Charity must have seen or sensed them. Tina changed her breathing to every other stroke and soon caught and passed Charity, who started swimming harder and stayed right with her, both of them leaving me behind, like they had outboard engines.

That's how we finished. With the Trents, Nikki, Williams, and Rusty on the pier cheering, Tina and Charity pretty much arrived at a dead heat, with me a couple seconds behind. The three that were gaining turned out to be Deuce, Julie and one of the Coasties, Bourke. Behind them were Grayson, Simpson and the other Coastie, Goodman. The dive supervisor, Bond, was part of the larger group the whole time. I glanced at my dive watch and noticed that I'd just swam my best ever time by a good ten seconds, meaning the two women had just trounced the hell out of me.

Tina and Charity were high-fiving each other as I got to the pier. Together the three of us cheered on the rest of the group. As they arrived, I heard Tina say to Charity, "Now I remember why your name sounded familiar."

"Same here," Charity said. "You made the final cut, didn't you?"

"Yeah," Tina said, "And you won the bronze in the four hundred individual medley."

I looked at the two women and said, "What are y'all talking about?"

Tina turned to me and smiled. "We've been had, Jesse. Charity was on the 2000 Olympic swim team."

"And you're not a ringer?" Charity said. "Tina nearly made the team. She would have made it easily if she hadn't pulled a muscle in the finals. She was the NCAA freestyle champion in ninety-four, setting the U.S. record."

I looked from one to the other, surprised. Deuce and Julie had joined us on the pier and Deuce said, "Okay, so you got your ringer and I got mine." He slapped me on the back and added, "Call it a draw?"

The others were climbing out of the water and word spread that their ringer didn't crush us as expected. The men all gathered around, shook Tina's hand and slapped her on the shoulder. I could tell it meant a lot to her that these warriors seemed to accept her as one of their own. The best of the best.

I told everyone that lunch would be in an hour and reminded them to go easy on the fresh water. Everyone broke up into groups, some to grab a quick rinse under the cistern and others to explore the island. The two Marines asked Junior and Patty if they'd show them where the clams were. The two kids grinned, then ran off with buckets to the cove on the west side of the island with the two Marines following along.

"Want to grab a shower aboard?" I asked Tina.

"You wash my back and I'll wash yours?"

"Deal," I said.

We passed Williams as he was headed to his plane to put away his tools. "Outboards are all tuned up. Whoever rebuilt the carb on the one-fifty did a pretty good job."

"Thanks," I said.

"You did it?" he asked. "What the hell you need me around for?"

I laughed, clapped him on the shoulder and said, "Carbs I know, computers are a whole different thing. We're gonna grab a shower. Lunch will be in about an hour."

We went to the *Revenge* and I locked the salon hatch. We took a quick shower together, but it was more of a rinse, because of the cramped space. It was impossible to be in the shower without being in full contact with one another and my excitement was very evident.

"Do we have time?" Tina asked, seductively.

Thirty minutes later we were drying off in the stateroom and putting on clean clothes. We walked up to the house, went inside and it looked like Chyrel had turned the main room into a high tech communications center.

"Sorry for the mess," she said. "But all this is necessary. I'm just glad you have a south-facing window for my satellite link. Everything's all set. We'll have constant communication, both voice and video, from the boat and the insertion team. A satellite will be available if we need it for eyes in the sky."

"Did you get anything from the bug?" Deuce asked as he and Julie walked in.

"Sure did," Chyrel said. "He and the woman talked at length about getting you to carry an arms shipment down to Cuba next week. He mentioned he thought relying on one boat would be better than the three he was currently using. That means there's two other boats out there. He told her to seduce you, Jesse. Oh, and she speaks perfect English."

"Seduce you?" Tina asked.

"Not gonna happen," I said.

"Let's take a look at the transcript on the way over," Deuce said. "And email the recording to Jesse on the boat."

"The transcript will have to be emailed too," Chyrel said. "With all the background noise, they're still working on it up in DC. Those three things were clear enough, though."

"Then let's go get some lunch," Deuce said. "And afterwards maybe get a nap in. It's going to be a long night. Tina, have you ever piloted a boat? We can use the help on shifts tonight."

"Only Jesse's a few times," she said, "But only in daylight."

"You'll do fine," I said. "We'll be on autopilot almost all the way. Whoever's on duty will just be watching the radar and even that has an alarm."

We walked over to where the tables were. Trent had a hot fire going in the grill and was already steaming the clams and stone crab claws in a big pot. Charlie had the tables nearly set and most of the crew were already sitting, some drinking beer and some water. I noticed that Hinkle and Mitchel were tending their small fire and walked over to them. I squatted down next to Hinkle and gazed into the fire. Neither man said anything. I just stayed hunched like that staring into the flames.

Finally Hinkle said, "You'll burn out your retinas staring into the flame like that, mate."

I continued looking intently at the fire.

"He's right, you know," said Mitchel after another minute.

"Urban legend," I said, still looking into the fire. "Told to boots by old salts. Mostly to keep them from wanting to have a fire at night."

"Who you calling a boot?" Mitchel asked, somewhat pissed.

"You two," I said, still watching the flames dance.

Mitchel was the more volatile of the two. I'd already picked up on that much. He shifted slightly, turning a few degrees toward me.

"We were SEALs for eight years, man," Mitchel said. "Not exactly what—"

I cut him off midsentence saying, "Exactly. Two boots still wet behind the ears."

His right fist came around quickly as he pivoted further toward me, aiming straight for the side of my head.

I was not only ready, but expecting it. I caught his fist in my left hand, while still gazing into the fire. I slowly turned my head towards him and quietly growled, "Think long and hard about your next move, swab."

I could see the fire die in his eyes. I released his fist and said, "You distance yourself from your teammates and they start to think you're a little weird. Yeah, what we do is a whole lot different than the type of warfare they engage in and it takes a whole different mindset. But, if you can't turn it on and off at will, you're completely useless. The more distant you become, the less trust they have in you. They start to think you don't like them. A team like this without complete trust in each other, especially toward the guys with the long guns, is doomed to failure. Nobody trusts the guy they don't know."

I stood up and walked back over to the group. Trent was loading lobster onto a large tray and Williams was loading clams and crab claws onto it. A large platter of assorted fish fillets was warming beside the fire. Everything looked delicious.

I took a seat next to Tina and leaned over and kissed her. "What was that for?" she asked.

"No reason," I said. "I just feel happy."

Doc and Nikki sat down across from us and Doc said, "We both talked to Deuce, then I sat with him alone while he described in more detail what the team does. I shared what I could with Nikki and we both agree, I'm a good fit. I went back and told him I'm in."

"Knew you would be," I said. "When not training or on a mission, you'll be my First Mate, too. Pay will be twenty percent of what the boat brings in. That's usually about two hundred dollars a day to you, whenever I work, and that's not often. The government stipend will keep you from having to find full-time work so you can be available. Sound fair to you?"

"Sounds great," he said. "Even if it's only once a month, to get out on the blue."

"You're gonna have a lot of free time," I said.

"I'll keep him busy," Nikki said. "We made an offer on a house on Cudjoe Key yesterday. It's a real fixer-upper."

Charlie came out of the west bunkhouse with a big tray of sliced fruit and a bowl in the middle with a huge salad and placed it on the table. "Hey, Charlie," I said. "Where'd all these utensils come from?"

"Dave brought it out," she said. "He has a lot of stuff always on board the plane."

Just then Mitchel sat down next to me and Hinkle across from him, next to Doc. I looked from one to the other and Mitchel said, "I want to apologize, Gunny."

"Consider it done, brother," I said. "Grab a banana leaf and pass me one of those lobster tails, would ya?"

He passed one of the biggest tails to me, then took one for himself. Hinkle stood up and said, "Can I 'ave your attention, mates?"

Everyone stopped talking and looked at him. He raised his beer and said, "I ain't much of a speaker. So 'ere's an old Orstralian toast. Ere's to the US, the land of the push. Where a bird in the 'and's worth two in the bush. 'Ere's to Orstralia, me own native land. Where a push in the bush, is worth two in the 'and."

The whole table erupted in laughter and Hinkle raised his hands to get everyone to quiet down. Then he continued, "Seriously, mates, I just want to thank the Gunny 'ere, for his generous 'ospitality. And for yankin a coupla boots straight."

We all ate our fill and surprisingly there was nothing left over. I only had one beer, as did Deuce, Tony, and Art. The rest of the team had a few more, but none got drunk. Hinkle and Mitchel opened up a bit more. Hinkle made it look easy, but by midafternoon Mitchel was cracking jokes with the rest of the team.

I pulled Deuce aside. "I converted the crew quarters to a double berth. The four of us should get a little rest, maybe an hour or two."

"Yeah, it's going to be a long night. Everyone's staying over, to wait until Tony and Art are inserted at least. Odds are, they'll all be here when we get back in four days. Hey, what did you say to those two to get them out of their shells?"

"Just a little advice from someone that's been where they are," I said. "You're good with a long gun, but you're not a sniper. Those two are. Totally different mindset."

"Well, whatever it was, thanks."

He turned to the team and said, "It's time to get started. I want all six of us that are leaving to get a little rest. The rest of you try to hold it down to a dull roar, okay. Tony, you and Art bunk in the salon. You won't be pulling watch on the trip over. I want you completely rested when we arrive at the insertion point."

Williams stood up and said, "Would it be alright if I hang out here tonight? I got a hammock strung up in the Beaver."

"Us too?" asked Doc.

"Sure," I said. "Make yourself at home. Don't know where you'll be able to bunk, Doc."

"More than enough room in the bunkhouse," Trent said. "They've spent the night with us plenty of times before tonight."

The six of us walked to the *Revenge* and tried to get some rest. It wasn't easy. I never was one that could force myself to sleep. I dozed off for about an hour, then got up and went into the galley and started the coffeemaker. Tony and Art must not have had my problem. Both men were snoring away on the settee and couch in the salon. When the coffee was done, I poured a cup, then heard the latch on the crew quarters' hatch softly close and reached into the cupboard for another cup. I poured coffee for Deuce and we took it up to the bridge and sat down. I used the key fob and released the catch on the big door, which slowly started opening on its big tension springs.

"You think we'll have any problems?" Deuce asked.

"No," I said. "Not on the trip over. I just hope those two guys don't run into any trouble."

"I picked them because they're the absolute best at infiltration, concealment and intelligence gathering," he said. "Hell, Tony could sneak right into their camp and post himself in the rafters of one of their huts."

We sat and looked through the windshield out over the water. In a few minutes, Tina joined us with a cup of coffee and a thermos. She silently refilled our cups and sat down in the second seat.

"I'm nervous," she said. "We didn't train for anything like this at the academy."

"It's a cakewalk," I said. "We're just going diving."

A moment later Julie was climbing the ladder. She sat down next to Deuce on the bench seat and held out an empty cup. "The pot's empty," she said. "I put on another brew."

Tina poured her cup and set the thermos in the small cabinet by the helm. We each sat silently and drank coffee, watching the pelicans dive on bait fish in the channel.

At fifteen-hundred, I reached down and started the engines. Within a few minutes the rest of the team was gathered on the dock, Hinkle and Mitchel untying the lines. Tony and Art came out into the cockpit and shook hands with everyone. Words of good luck were said by everyone to the two men. They'd probably have no trouble, as remote as the village is, but still, it was communist Cuba. I put the engines in gear and slowly idled out into Harbor Channel.

I stepped the throttles up to thirteen-hundred rpm, just enough to get the *Revenge* up on plane, as I turned northeast and followed the channel to the cut north of Upper Harbor Key. Tina turned on the radar and sonar and said, "Nothing on the radar all the way to Key West, Jesse."

I smiled and said, "I just might promote you from Galley Wench to swab before this is over."

Tony and Art came up and joined us on the bridge. Art sat down next to Julie and Tony leaned against my seat. Once we passed through the cut Tina leaned over, checked the sonar and said, "Ten fathoms under the keel, Captain."

"Now you're bucking for Vice Admiral," I said as I pushed the throttles on up to sixteen-hundred rpm and the big boat rushed forward to its cruising speed of twenty-six knots.

"You two should get back below," Deuce said. "Just in case. And try to get some rest."

"Aye aye, Commander," they both said in unison before climbing back down the ladder and disappearing into the salon.

"You're going to have a hard time choosing between those two, aren't you?" Julie said to Deuce.

"What do you mean?" he asked.

"To be your best man," she said with a smile.

"You two are getting married?" Tina asked.

"Yeah," Julie said. "In late May, when I get back from training."

"Congratulations," Tina said smiling.

"No," Deuce said. "I've already made up my mind."

"Which one?" I asked.

"You," he said. "It would have been Dad. Would you take his place?"

I looked at Deuce and said, "I could never take Russ's place in any way. However, I'd be damn proud to stand in for him."

We cruised west for almost an hour, then began a long, slow turn into Northwest Channel. Another half hour later and we were past Key West and into the Florida Straits. I set the GPS with a destination for Cozumel and a waypoint about fifteen miles off the western tip of Cuba, turned on the autopilot and let the computer take over. The waters were very calm and there were only small, puffy clouds to the west. It was going to be a nice smooth passage.

"Let's go see if Chyrel has emailed the transcripts," Deuce said.

"Tina, you have the helm," I said as I stood up. She slid over into the first seat and sipped her coffee while checking the radar.

Deuce and I climbed down the ladder and found Tony and Art asleep once again in the salon. I used to be able to do that, but find it harder to just flip the switch these days. Getting my laptop out, I powered it up and plugged in a set of earbuds, offering one to Deuce. Opening the email with the transcript first, then the audio file, we were able to follow the sound using the written transcript. The audio file was only eighteen minutes long, then we heard the engine shut off and Santiago and the woman leave the boat. The transcript stated that the audio continued with occasional words from passersby for another forty-two minutes before the bug powered down, having depleted its battery life.

We played it back again and reread the transcript. There really wasn't much more to it than what Chyrel had already told us. Santiago telling the woman how much he wanted to get me to haul the arms shipment, how he thought I'd be more dependable than the broken-down old shrimp boats he'd been using and the three Cuban crews that were ferrying for him now and him telling the woman to seduce me. The only part that Chyrel hadn't mentioned was her response, "*Será un placer, estoy segura,*" she'd said. "That will be a pleasure, I'm sure."

"Maybe we can use that," Deuce whispered to keep from waking the two men.

"Your new lady friend seems like the type that would go ballistic," Tony said without opening his eyes.

"Not a lady I'd want pissed at me," Art added, his eyes closed also.

"I'm not going to sleep with the woman," I said.

"Who said anything about sleeping?" Deuce said and the other two men started to chuckle.

"Y'all are Neanderthals," I said.

"And Jarheads are Cro-Magnons," Tony said.

"You two get some rest," Deuce said. Then to me he said, "Let's split the watch into two-hour shifts, starting at 1900. All hands on deck at midnight, when we'll be off Guadiana Bay, turn and make a fast run into the bay to a spot about two miles off the point of land between Guadiana Bay and La Fe. They can use the scooters to make it to the point on scuba and stash the scooters and scuba gear. It's about two and a half clicks across the point on foot and then less than a click across the smaller bay underwater using rebreathers. They should have no trouble getting on station half a mile from the camp well before sunrise."

"Just to be safe," I said, "we'll stay at least fifteen miles off the coast until we're almost past the bay. The wind's usually out of the west in that area and with calm seas, we can make about forty-five knots when we turn back toward the bay. We can be well inside it in twenty minutes and I'll turn completely around before they go feet wet. Shouldn't take more than two minutes to get them in the water and start back out to the twelve-mile limit, maybe another fifteen minutes to make that. Less than forty minutes of course deviation and there's no radar near the bay itself. The nearest military facility is the air base at San Julian, twenty miles inland from where we'll drop the guys. Their radar won't pick us up and just after midnight, we'll be in and out before anyone could even think of mounting a response, should anyone hear us and think to call it in. Once we're sure that we're in and out undetected, we can go back to two-hour watches until 0600, when we'll be getting close to Coz."

Deuce and I went back up to the bridge and I took over the helm. I checked the radar and noticed that a freighter was ahead about fifteen miles. I checked the GPS and saw that Tina had already plotted a course correction to take us aft of the freighter.

"I'm a quick learner," she said when I looked at her and smiled.

"Yeah," I said. "You sure are."

Once we cleared the freighter I entered the waypoint where we were going to make our turn into the bay to drop Tony and Art off. I planned to make the high-speed run completely blacked out, using only sonar and my night vision goggles. I didn't want to risk using active radar in case it might be picked up at the air base or by one of the mobile missile launchers the Cubans were known to have along the coast. I doubted there would be any on the far western tip of the island country, but I always preferred to minimize risk whenever possible.

An hour later the sun was slowly slipping toward the horizon. There wasn't a single cloud in the western sky and just some high, wispy clouds above us. "This sunset is going to surprise you," I told Tina.

"After that green flash the other night, I don't know how another sunset could be more surprising."

Deuce and Julie smiled, knowing what I meant. In the open ocean there is almost no twilight. As the sun sets you go from daylight to total darkness in a matter of minutes. We watched the sun, just off the starboard bow, as it fell lower and lower. At a point just above the horizon, the water seemed to leap up and grab it, startling Tina once again. The conditions were right, it was cool and perfectly clear. There was a good chance of another green flash. The clouds over our head streaked with hues of pink, orange, red and purple as the sun slowly started to flatten out and disappear below the far horizon. I reached up and turned on the running lights as well as the powerful spotlight. In these waters it wasn't uncommon to see floating debris, or even Cuban rafters.

Just as the last of the sun started to disappear, it happened. A small part of it seemed to separate from the main orb and lift up out of the water. Then the orb disappeared, the small separation flashed green and then it too disappeared, bringing a squeal from Tina. A few minutes later, we were enveloped in total darkness.

Tina felt around and found my hand, squeezing it and said, "What happened? Why'd it get so dark?"

Julie giggled and said, "That's the surprise. There's no twilight on the open ocean."

I turned on the low-level red overhead lights, bathing us in a soft red glow. "Deuce, why don't you take the first watch?" I said. "Julie can come up and relieve you in a couple of hours, then I'll take the watch as we get near the Cuban coast. Right now, I want to take Tina to the foredeck and show her something."

"Sure," said Deuce with a knowing smile.

Tina and I left the bridge and swung over to the wide side decks. "Watch your step," I said. "Keep a hand on the handrails." She made her way slowly forward in the near pitch darkness, with only the filtered red light from the bridge. Once we were clear of the salon bulkhead I said, "Take a couple of steps to your right, sit down on the deck and lean back against the forward bulkhead."

Once she was settled, I sat down beside her and she said, "What is it I'm supposed to see in this pitch darkness?"

As she felt around for my hand, I waited a few seconds then heard her gasp. "Oh my."

Our eyes had become adjusted to the near darkness. At sea, it doesn't get completely dark. The moon was just a sliver, following the sun far to the west. But the stars provided quite a bit of light. On the open ocean, you can see more stars in one small part of the sky than you can see all across the whole sky when on shore.

"It's so beautiful," she said. "I never imagined there were so many stars. Why has nobody ever shown me this before?"

"Landlubbers never see it," I said. "Even if you go far out in the desert, or high up in the mountains, you can't see what you can out here on the blue. Right now we're about halfway between Key West and Cuba, forty miles from any light source that would dilute the sky."

We sat there for about twenty minutes and I pointed out the stars and constellations that I knew. "We'd better get some rest," I said. "I'll have the short watch from twenty-three-hundred to midnight and during the insertion. You won't need to take watch until we're sure we got in and out undetected."

"Are you worried about going into Cuban waters tonight?" she asked.

"Not really," I said. "That part of Cuba is mostly just tiny fishing villages. Most don't even have electricity.

And most of the patrol boats don't have enough fuel to even put out to sea."

We got up and made our way back to the cockpit, then through the salon, where Tony and Art were snoring away. We went forward to the stateroom, took off our shoes and climbed into bed with our clothes on. That didn't last long. We made love quietly, to the slow rocking of the boat. Finally we fell to sleep, exhausted. But not before getting fully dressed again.

A single light tap on the hatch awakened me. I glanced at my watch and saw that it was twenty-three-hundred. We should be skirting the coast of Cuba about twenty miles offshore about now, with a good thirty miles to go to the waypoint. I slipped on my Topsiders and opened the hatch. Deuce was just going out the salon hatch. I joined him on the bridge and checked our position on the GPS. We were almost exactly where I thought we'd be, but a little further from the coast. About thirty miles north of the long barrier reef, off Cayo de Buenavista, another fifty miles before we turned southeast into the bay.

I looked at Deuce. He just shrugged and said, "I felt thirty miles would be less obvious, in case we're being watched." I noticed he had brought his satellite phone up with him. "Probably a good thing, too. I just talked to Chyrel. She's picking up active radar from a mobile launch site near Santa Lucia, about fifty miles back. They just shut it down a few minutes ago. She checked the satellite using infrared and nothing's coming out of the port."

"Smart thinking," I said. "We still have plenty of time."

"I'm going to go down and uncrate the scooters and get their gear together," he said. "I want them to get as much rest as they can."

"My tool chest is under the ladder to port, in the engine room," I said. "There's a cordless drill there, too. Battery's on the charger on the opposite side of the generator."

He climbed down and disappeared through the engine room hatch. There were four tanks already set up for doubles on Tony and Art's personal BC and regulator. That would be more than enough air for the scooter ride in and back out. All they'd have to do would be put on their wetsuits, slip into the rigs, put on their masks and fins and get in the water. Deuce would have both scooters waiting on the swim platform, lashed in place with a strap I'd already put there.

Thirty minutes later, Deuce joined me again on the bridge. "Everything's all set," he said. He leaned over and checked the GPS. We were still fifteen miles from the turn, maybe another thirty minutes.

"Let's get everyone up," I said. "While they're gearing up, the girls can slice up some fruit and let them get a bite to eat before they get in the water."

Deuce nodded and I reached over and switched the stereo over to boatwide. I'd already put a CD into the stereo and Wagner's *Ride of the Valkyries* began to fill the cabin and bridge with the powerful music. The same song from the movie, Apocalypse Now, when the choppers come in over the beach.

Deuce looked over at me and said, "A bit overly dramatic, maybe?"

"No," I said. "Not at all. Overly dramatic would be if I also sent it out over the VHF to those waiting and watching on the island. Like this." Then I flipped another switch and did just that.

Deuce laughed and said, "You are a piece of work."

Deuce climbed down and went into the salon to tell the girls what to do, as Tony and Art came out into the cockpit. They already had their wetsuits on. Tony looked up at me and tapped his watch. I shouted down, "One five to turn, three zero to feet wet."

He gave me a thumbs up and started going over his gear, probably for the fourth time. Deuce came out with a long black case, opened it and helped the men check their weapons and communication equipment.

A few minutes later, Julie and Tina came out with several bowls full of sliced fruit. Tina brought one up to the bridge, set it on the console in front of the second seat and said, "I'll take over so you can get a bite to eat, too."

I slid over to the second seat and let her have the helm while I ate the fruit. We were now five miles from the turn, so I hurried. Tina took the bowl when I was finished and went back down below. She gathered up the rest and disappeared into the salon as Julie came up to the bridge. She sat down on the bench seat and said, "How far?"

"Coming up on the turn in about five minutes," I said.

Julie looked down at the three men checking and rechecking every piece of gear. "They're good at what they do," she said.

"Maybe the best in the world."

"I know Deuce wishes he was going, but I'm glad he's not," she said.

I looked over at her, looking down to the cockpit, under the dim red light. "There will be times when he does, Jules. Times when he might not even be able to tell you. Ya have to be ready for those times. It's a tougher job you'll have than he has."

Tina came back up to the bridge and took the second seat. Switching the radio so it would broadcast both PA and VHF, I picked up the mic and said, "Going dark." Then I switched off the running lights, interior lights, gauge lights, even the overhead red lights and put on my Pulsar Edge night vision optics, switching them on. I looked over at Julie, then over at Tina. Both looked scared in a grainy green haze.

Chyrel's voice came over the speakers, "Roger Alpha Team, God speed."

"Don't worry," I said to Julie and Tina. "Your eyes will adjust in a minute."

I looked down into the cockpit and saw that Deuce already had his night vision on, anticipating the lights out. Deuce looked up and I gave him the OK sign, which he returned. Tony and Art were sitting on the port side of the bench seat with their gear strapped on, waiting for my signal.

I checked the GPS and we were less than a tenth of a mile from the waypoint for the turn. I picked up the mic and said, "Hold on. Turning in five, four, three, two, one." Then I spun the wheel hard to port and pushed both throttles to the stops. The big boat responded instantly, heeling sharply and leaping forward. Checking the GPS, I saw that in seconds we were going forty-six knots. The tail wind must have been stronger than I figured. Then I remembered Williams saying he'd tweaked the injectors to get a couple more knots out of the engines. Glancing down again after straightening the wheel on a heading of one-hundred and ten degrees, the GPS read forty-eight knots at 2400 rpm, wide open throttle.

I picked up the mic and said, "Forty-eight knots, full stop in twenty minutes."

Chyrel had installed an encryption system on the VHF, so I wasn't worried about anyone listening in. We rode on in silence. I occasionally looked down into the cockpit. Deuce had filled a rinse bucket and placed it on the deck between the two men. They were busy rinsing their masks and doing a last-minute check of equipment by feel. The moon was long set. In the cockpit there was very little starlight and the two divers didn't have night vision. They relied on years of experience and training, plus a fine officer watching out for them.

I kept my eyes on the sonar screen through the night vision goggles, glancing occasionally at the GPS and ahead through the windshield. We were inside the bay, streaking toward shore, with thirty feet of water under us and ten miles away from the point. Even with the aid of the night vision goggles, I didn't see a single light anywhere along the coast. We were well inside Cuban territorial waters.

I picked up the mic and said, "Eight minutes."

Time seemed to move slowly. It felt like forever before we reached the spot three miles from shore, where I needed to start slowing down. I pulled back slowly on the throttles. I didn't want our stern wave to overtake us and swamp the cockpit, since Deuce already had the transom door open. Once we were off plane and idling, I spun the wheel and reversed the port engine, gunning it to twelve-hundred rpm, spinning the *Revenge*. Then I brought it back to forward idle for a second, checked the GPS and saw that we were very close to the spot I wanted to be, with the bow now pointed away from shore at a reverse course of two-hundred and ninety degrees.

I brought both engines to neutral, picked up the mic and said, "All stop, depth is twenty feet. Go!"

Deuce already had the divers on their feet and had stepped out onto the dive platform and unstrapped the scooters. He shoved one into the water and slapped one of the divers on the shoulder as he stepped onto the platform. When he surfaced, Deuce said, "To your ten o'clock, three meters." The diver struck out and grabbed the scooter in seconds while Deuce shoved the second one in and slapped the second diver on the shoulder. When he surfaced Deuce said, "At your one o'clock, arm's length."

The diver reached out and grabbed it and I heard Tony's voice over the speaker. "Clear. Submerging."

As soon as Deuce stepped back up into the cockpit, I jammed both throttles to the stops, knowing that Deuce would be expecting it. Seconds later we were up on plane and Deuce was climbing the ladder. Both men had full face masks with communications, but we'd agreed to keep talk to a minimum. Still, Deuce reached for the mic and said, "Com check."

"Alpha Two," came Tony's voice.

"Alpha Three," said Art. "All systems good."

"Check in from shore," Deuce said. "Be careful. Alpha One out."

I saw Deuce look at Julie and could tell she was still scared. He took her hand and said, "We'll be safe in just a few minutes." He looked at me and I gave him a thumbs up. "I'm going back down and fill the tanks from the bladders. We must be low on fuel."

"Yeah," I said. "About a quarter tank."

Five minutes later, he was back on the bridge.

We rode in silence. I kept an eye on the GPS and finally, twenty minutes later, I pulled back on the throttles to seventeen-hundred rpm and the big boat slowed to twenty-six knots. I turned to a heading of two-hundred and twenty-five degrees, straight for Cozumel, and engaged the autopilot.

Removing my night vision goggles, I reached up and turned the lights back on as well as the radar. Checking it, I saw nothing in front of us. More importantly, I saw nothing behind us. "We're clear, no pursuit," I said into the mic.

Deuce removed his night vision goggles as we heard Chyrel's voice over the radio. "Good job, Alpha Team. I have twenty people in your living room breathing again."

I keyed the mic and said, "Tell Dave thanks. Forty-eight knots."

Williams's voice came over the radio, saying, "Give me three days and a few thousand bucks and I can get that up to fifty-five."

"Might take you up on that," I said. "Alpha One out."

Tina grabbed my hand and said, "That was scary. How did you ever do that for a living?"

"What living?" Deuce and I said at the same time. That broke the tension and I added, "At least the money's better now."

"Speak for yourself," Deuce said. "I'm a lowly GS-11. You just made what it'll take me two months to earn."

"Once this is over," I said. "I might have something you can help me with to supplement that government income."

"What do you mean?" he asked.

"Remember that first night in Key West when I asked you about that French name?"

"Yeah," he said. "But it wasn't a name."

"Your dad was looking for the wreck of a Confederate blockade runner called the *Lynx*," I said. "I think that's what got him killed. He found it. Or at least part of it."

"You're telling me—" he started to say.

"Yeah," I interrupted. "He found one of a dozen gold bars. Lester was diving with him, took advantage of the find and killed him. The GPS coordinates are still on his GPS, saved on the day he drowned. I found that the same time I found his doubloon."

"If it's still there, how much do you think each bar would weigh?" he asked.

"I did a little research," I said. "Or actually Chyrel did it for me. It seems that on September twenty-fifth, 1864, the *Lynx* was sunk outside of Riviera Beach Inlet. A VIP passenger was aboard, a man by the name of Lieutenant Colonel Abner McCormick of the Second Florida Cavalry. The *Lynx* came under fire from three Union vessels and sank. Colonel McCormick drowned, but the rest of the crew made it to shore. That's all in the history books and is what Chyrel found out for me. What wasn't known, except by McCormick himself, was that he was carrying twelve gold bars, each weighing ten pounds. Probably why he drowned and the others didn't. It was supposed to be going to a Colonel Harrison, with the First Florida Battalion, to fund the Confederate cause. At the time, it was worth sixteen dollars an ounce, or about thirty-one thousand for the hundred and twenty pounds. At today's rate, it would be worth two point five million."

"Wait," he said. "How do you know, or how did my dad know, that the gold was on board?"

"Colonel McCormick wrote to his wife and family before they sailed," I said, "saying that he had a Frenchman aboard by the name of Douzaine Lingots Dior. Your dad found one of McCormick's descendants, who had his great-grandfather's letters to his wife and the guy let him read them. Your dad spoke French and immediately figured out that it wasn't a Frenchman, but twelve gold bars. Apparently the Colonel and his wife spoke French but never taught any of their children. The mystery of who the Frenchman was always eluded them."

"And you know where the gold is?" Julie asked.

"I know where Russ last dived," I replied. "When I went through his things up in Fort Pierce, both of his metal detectors were missing, along with those pieces of treasure you had mentioned. When I found Lester, I also found his GPS and journal. It's there. We just have to go find it."

"Who is this Lester?" Tina asked.

Before I could say anything, Deuce said, "He was the man that killed my father."

"Julie, is Rusty's salvage license still good?" I asked.

"Yeah," she replied. "He always keeps it current."

"We have the license," I said. "And the manpower and location. Once this is done, I think a few of us should go treasure hunting."

"I'm in," Deuce said. Julie smiled and he added, "But I won't be quitting my day job."

We rode on for another twenty minutes, the silence finally broken by the sound of Tony's voice over the radio speaker, "Alpha One?"

Deuce grabbed the mic and said, "Go ahead."

"First objective secured," Tony said. "Moving overland. Will call when feet dry."

"Roger," Deuce said. "Alpha One out."

A second later Chyrel's voice came over the speaker, "Alpha Base has eyes, clear ahead."

"Roger, Base," Tony said. "Alpha Two out."

"How long will it take them to get where they're going now?" Tina asked.

"Maybe forty minutes over land," Deuce said. "Then another half hour under water and a slow thirty-minute crawl to cover the last hundred yards to their objective." Checking his watch, he said, "Probably won't hear from them again until zero three-hundred."

We rode on in silence for another ten minutes, then Tina said, "You guys go get some rest. I can keep watch for a while."

"I'll come up and relieve you in two hours," Julie said.

I gave Tina a kiss, then the three of us climbed down the ladder and into the salon. "I don't know if I'll be able to sleep," Deuce said.

"At least lay down and rest," I said. "Julie, wake me at zero five-hundred or earlier, if you need to."

I went forward and crawled into the bunk and was soon fast asleep.

CHAPTER FIFTEEN:
Diving With Mayans

I felt Tina crawl into bed beside me, but didn't hear her. I rolled over and said, "Everything okay?"

"Sorry," she said. "I tried not to wake you. Everything's fine. Julie's at the helm and the guys are, and I quote, 'hunkered down.'"

I kissed her and went back to sleep. It felt like ten minutes later when I heard a light tapping on the hatch. I quietly got out of bed and opened the door. I nodded at Julie, who turned and slipped quietly into the crew quarters as I slipped on my Topsiders. There was coffee in the pot and the timer was set for ten minutes ago. My guess is that Tina set it before coming to bed. I poured a cup, filled a thermos, set it up to brew another pot and then went up to the bridge. I checked the GPS and saw that we were only sixty miles from Cozumel. I opened the cabinet and pulled out a book on Mexican ports of entry. I'd already gathered everyone's passports. I found the listing for the main commercial port docks on the west side of the island. I'd had Chyrel call there to let them know of our arrival. I entered the precise coordinates for the dock into the GPS and returned it to autopilot. Mexican Immigration and Customs was at the end of the cruise ship pier and I knew from past experience that I could be there a while.

Just before sunrise, Tina joined me on the bridge. The clouds to the east were starting to be colored by the sun in pastel pink hues. They spanned the horizon, north to south in an unbroken line. She stretched her legs out in front of her and arched her back. Then leaning forward, she checked the GPS, which showed we were twenty-five miles from the Mexican island.

"I thought we would be there by seven o'clock," she said. "Have you heard anything more from Tony and Art?"

"They're probably still asleep," I said. "Doubt we'll hear from them for a while. The GPS displays our time. Cozumel is an hour different from Florida. It's zero six-hundred local time."

An hour later, with our quarantine and courtesy flags flying, we tied off at the commercial dock, next to the immigration and customs building. I took the boat's paperwork and all four of our passports into the building, hoping that since there wasn't a cruise ship currently at the dock I might get lucky and be in and out quickly. It wasn't record pace, but faster than usual. The customs officer walked with me back to the dock. Deuce and Julie had joined Tina on the bridge. We stepped aboard and I noticed that someone, probably Deuce, had dutifully opened all the fish boxes, hatches and drawers in the cockpit.

The customs officer made a cursory inspection of the cockpit, then dropped down into the engine room. He was back out in a minute and we proceeded into the salon.

"What is the nature of your visit, Captain?" he asked as he looked slowly around.

"*Buceo sus arrecifes hermosos, como de costumbre, señor,*" I responded.

"They are quite beautiful, *sí,*" he said. "Our records show you are a frequent visitor here. Your friends know not to touch the reefs?"

"My charter," I said. "I never even allow divers to wear gloves. Makes them less apt to do any damage."

"It is just the four of you?" he asked, looking toward the cabins.

"Yes," I said. "Feel free to look around. I'll be topside tending to my charter. Those three are a handful."

I left the salon and called up to the bridge. "Can I get you some fresh fruit? Or perhaps a bagel?"

"We're fine, Captain," Deuce said. "When can we go ashore? I understand there are some fine shops and stores here in San Miguel. The ladies would like to do some shopping."

As if Deuce had rung the dinner bell, the customs officer stepped down from the salon and said, "Everything's in order, *Capitán.* Yours is a beautiful vessel. Here are your visas. We hope you and your guests will enjoy your stay on Isla Cozumel."

"*Gracias, señor,*" I said, taking the visas and passports from him. Then I quietly added, "*Si estos esnobs ricos no volverme loco, lo haré.*"

He looked up at Deuce, Julie, and Tina on the bridge, smiled at them and said, "Enjoy your stay." Then quietly to me as he stepped toward the gunwale, he added, "*Si gastan un montón de dinero, ambos seremos felices, señor.*"

I climbed up to the bridge and Julie said, "Rich snobs, huh?"

"Nothing moves a customs officer quicker than the knowledge that someone is waiting to spend lots of money in his country," I said. "Let's go ashore and do just that. It's a safe bet that Santiago has someone here that's going to report back to him. I want it to look like you three are wealthy charter customers."

"I need to check in with Tony and Art before we do that," Deuce said.

We went down to the salon and I powered up the laptop. Deuce first checked in with Chyrel via video. She looked like she hadn't had a lot of sleep. "How much sleep did you get last night?" he asked her.

"I got a couple of power naps in," she said a little defensively. "Charity's been monitoring the com with me."

"Any word from our boys?" Deuce asked.

"They checked in at zero six-hundred," she said. "They're on a small knoll about two hundred meters from the Hezbollah camp, in a thick tangle of underbrush. Tony sent an audio file of a conversation they picked up with the parabolic mic. Nothing much on it, just a couple guards grumbling."

"Can you patch me through to him on video?" Deuce asked.

"Just a sec," Chyrel said. A few seconds later a smaller picture appeared in the corner. Tony's face was covered with flat green and tan markings obviously inside the hood of his ghillie suit. I could barely see that he had a headset with a boom mic on.

"Everything alright?" Deuce asked.

"Shoulda brought a stronger bug repellant," Tony whispered. "These Cuban mosquitoes are the size of crows. We have line of sight with the camp, but there's no way they can see us, even if they walked by right in front of us. Art's set up a little north of me, in a similar blind. We're west of the camp, so we'll get better visual in a couple of hours."

The sun's in their eyes, I thought. They were probably loading up on energy bars and napping until the sun got higher.

"Send any audio or video you pick up to Chyrel," Deuce said. "And keep your ass down."

"Roger that," Tony said and the screen went blank.

"Chyrel," he said. "Anything they send you, have it translated and send it to me in a text. Just the good stuff, you know what I want."

"Will do, boss," she said and the whole screen went blank.

Deuce turned to me and said, "I just don't feel right being down here while they're out in the bush."

"Hazard of command, brother," I said. "You're not a field operative anymore. Get used to it. I can see you in Smith's immaculate suit one day."

"Never gonna happen, man," he said.

We left the boat and strolled the streets of San Miguel, visiting the many shops. I gave Tina, Julie, and Deuce each a wad of cash. In two hours, we'd spent over a thousand dollars, including a stop at Aqua Safari Dive Shop, where I bought the latest dive computer.

We shopped some more and ate lunch at Señor Frog's across from the docks. After lunch we took a cab to El Cid Resort and booked two suites at three hundred dollars a night each and dock space. We carried our purchases to the suites and stopped in the Babieca Dive Shop on the premises and arranged to rent four tanks to be delivered to the *Revenge* at the commercial dock. I tipped the clerk generously and asked if he could have someone place them aboard, so we could do a dive before coming back to the hotel. He said that wouldn't be a problem and I told him the boat's name, where we were docked and to just strap them in place on the dive bench. We went to their private beach and relaxed a little and then we caught another cab back to the boat.

"We can do a shallow dive just a little ways north of here," I said. "There's a nice little patch reef across from the Coral Princess Hotel, where the wall is further out."

"Wall?" asked Tina.

"Most of the dive sites here are wall dives," Deuce said. "The bottom drops vertically to over two hundred feet in some places, very near shore."

"I can't go that deep," she said.

"Neither can we," I said. "Not without different equipment. We'll stick to shallow dives, until I think you're ready. Then we can drop over the wall a little deeper."

We cast off and headed north along the shoreline about two miles. While the girls were down below getting their swimsuits on, Deuce said, "Did you see her?"

"See who?" I asked.

"The woman from Santiago's boat," he said. "She was across the street at an outdoor café when we came out of the motel."

"No," I said. "I must be slipping."

"Guess he thought you could use some female company," he said with a grin.

"Well, I don't," I said. "I think you're enjoying this maybe a little too much. Maybe she's just here to keep tabs on me."

"You heard the recording," he said. "Guess you could play it like Tina seduced you on the trip down. She'll probably check the front desk to see how many rooms we booked and what kind. But it's a pretty safe bet that she's going to make a play at some point while we're here."

Julie and Tina came back up to the bridge just as I dropped the anchor in the gin-clear water. I'd dropped it about ten feet off a large reef in twelve feet of water and powered back until the anchor caught hold in the sand.

"Y'all take your time getting ready," I said. "I'm going to dive down and make sure the anchor's good and solid."

While they were gearing up, I grabbed a pair of goggles and a tag line, walked to the bow and dove in. I tied the tag line to the anchor line at water level and threw the coil and float out to the port side as far as I could. The water was warm, about eighty degrees. Taking a deep breath, I went hand over hand along the anchor line to the chain, then swam across the bottom to the anchor. It was jammed deep into the sand, no way would it come out. I swam back up at an angle and reached the surface about twenty feet from the bow then swam to the stern, checking the tag line to make sure that it had drifted to the stern on the port side, and climbed onto the swim platform..

"The water's great," I said.

We geared up and got ready to get in the water. Tina insisted on wearing her wetsuit, worried she'd get cold. "There's a line floating behind the boat," I said. "Once we're in the water, grab it and pull yourself to the anchor line, up at the bow. When we're all there, we'll follow the anchor line to the bottom and fin over to the reef."

"Is there a current?" Tina asked.

"Yeah, but not much of one," I said. "The tag line is more to save air. No sense going down here and finning to the reef. There's nothing to see under us but sand."

We entered the water one at a time and this time Tina was able to hold her head above water on entry. We swam and pulled ourselves to the anchor line. "It's about twenty feet at the anchor," I said. "You'll probably have to clear your ears a few times going down. Just don't be in a hurry about doing it. If it hurts come back up the anchor line a bit and try again. A lot of people have trouble doing this and have to be in an upright position, so try it that way by dumping almost all your air and hanging on the anchor line."

Tina nodded her head and said, "I'm ready."

We slowly descended down the line. Tina hung on it while the three of us slowly finned into the current, staying all around her. She didn't have any trouble clearing her ears, but I noticed she was having to hold on to the line tighter. I realized I hadn't told her about the effect water pressure would have on the air in her BC. I stopped her, pointed to the air bladders in her BC and made a constricting motion with my hands, then pointed down. She must have understood, because she immediately added just a little air to her BC until she was neutrally buoyant.

We continued to the bottom with no more problems and Tina actually controlled her buoyancy using her BC without any further instruction. We finned over to the little reef, where I motioned her to stop. I pointed to the reef, then to her hands, and shook my head. She gave me the OK sign and I pointed to the reef, then at her gauge cluster, and shook my head again. She understood and put her gauge cluster in the pocket of her BC.

We continued to the reef and the first thing we saw was a spotted moray, tucked into a crevice with only his head sticking out, opening and closing his mouth. This time I remembered to bring a small slate and pencil, so I could write the names of the fish down for her. I did so and showed it to her. We continued along the edge of the reef and saw a number of young angelfish and butterfly fish. Each time Tina would point and wait for me to identify it. At one point we saw a splendid toadfish, very rare in shallow water, which I also wrote. By the end of the dive, I'd filled the front and back and was having to erase names. We saw several kinds of parrotfish, angels and butterflies all over the reef. All very young. It seemed the reef was a nursery for hundreds of species. By the end of the dive, Tina was pointing at certain fish, then pointing to its corresponding name on my slate.

The dive lasted about twenty minutes. Tina was doing that much better at controlling her breathing. Deuce and I both still had over a thousand pounds of air when we started for the surface, though. We were halfway up when a large eagle ray swam by, probably eight feet across. Tina saw it first and grabbed my hand, pointing. It circled around us, Tina spinning on the anchor line to watch it, then swam off toward the wall.

When her head broke the surface, she spat out her regulator, pulled her mask down around her neck and said, "What was that?"

"An eagle ray," Julie said.

"Are they dangerous?" Tina asked. "It was beautiful."

"No," I said. "Unless they jump out of the water and land on you. That one was huge."

"There's so many baby fish here," Tina said. "It's beautiful."

We followed the tag line back to the stern of the boat and climbed aboard, Deuce and I first, then Tina and Julie. We sat down on the bench and took off our dive gear, grabbed our big towels and climbed up to the bridge. I engaged the windlass to hoist the anchor and started the engines, then turned and headed out to deeper water, heading south toward the hotel.

"Do we have enough time for another dive?" Tina asked.

Julie smiled and said, "The worm has turned."

We laughed and I said, "Let's wait until tomorrow. You catch on fast. We'll go over a few things this evening and I think you'll be ready for a wall dive in the morning."

"Why is wall diving so special?" she asked.

"That eagle ray we saw," Julie said. "It's a deep water fish. All the colorful tropical fish we saw are reef fish. That splendid toadfish is a deep water reef fish. We were lucky to see all those on a shallow reef. On a wall it's normal. You have the reef fish close to the wall, ocean-dwelling fish, sometimes even dolphins, sharks, sea turtles, even whales, just a few feet away and deep water fish just below you. Next to drift diving, wall diving is my favorite."

"Reef diving, wall diving and drift diving?" Tina said. "I'm going to have to get a book for this too?"

"We won't be doing any drift diving," Deuce said. "That involves someone staying on the boat and following the divers as they drift with the current."

"We could do a drift if y'all want," I said. "There's plenty of independent six-pack operators around here. I'm sure the concierge could find one for us."

"Six-pack?" Tina asked. "I'm going to guess that's a small boat."

"Small or big," Deuce said. "But limited to six passengers."

"Let's do that," I said. "Probably be cheaper than running two 1015-horse engines, anyway. Plus you get a better feel for the local islanders."

We arrived at the hotel's private dock and two staff members helped tie the boat off. The older one asked, "You have tanks empty, señor? Jose take to fill?"

"*Sí, cuatro, amigo*," I said. "*Podrías ponerlos de vuelta en el barco cuando estén llenos?*"

"*Sí, señor.*" He said smiling. "*Ahora mismo.*"

I reached into my pocket and handed him a one-hundred-peso bill and said, "*Gracias, no hay prisa.*"

We walked up the dock to the hotel and Tina said, "I know living in Key West, I should know Spanish, but I didn't understand any of that, except 'boat'."

"He asked if we had any empty tanks to refill," I said. "I asked him to put them aboard when they were full."

We took a cab to the Mayan ruins in the center of the island and spent the rest of the afternoon playing tourist. This time, I did notice the Cuban woman. She was sitting in the lobby of the hotel as we left, pretending to read a magazine. I held Tina's hand as we walked through the lobby, making sure that the Cuban woman saw.

Deuce was reading several text messages during the ride to the ruins, completely absorbed in them. When we got out of the cab outside the gates to the ruins he said, "Art picked up one side of a phone call from one of the terrorists. He was talking to Santiago, wanting to know when the next shipment was coming. From the conversation, he didn't sound very happy with the response, but finally said he'd wait a week, but wanted a reduced price. Tony sent a message saying he was able to get a count of people in the camp. Looked to be ten or eleven men and he thinks all the arms are stored in one tent. They're going to sleep this afternoon and sneak into the camp about midnight to get an inventory of what arms they have on hand."

"They can do that?" Julie asked.

Deuce chuckled and said, "Art's okay, but Tony could sneak into Jesse's bunk and count his pubic hairs, then sneak out again."

"No, he can't," I said. "I shave 'em."

Tina and Julie both slugged me on the shoulder. We went through the gates and hired a local guide. Tina was impressed with the ruins, asking all kinds of questions of our private guide. His name was Felipe and he spoke very good English. Julie asked him how he'd learned English so well and he said he'd once worked on a freighter for four years. The crew was from all over the world, but the Captain insisted they all learn and speak English, though he was Norwegian himself. "I also speak some German and French," he said.

Before sunset, we were about worn out, so we went back to the hotel. We decided to get cleaned up and meet for supper at La Chopa, right here at the resort. Within minutes of being seated, I spotted the Cuban woman at the bar. We had a really great meal of prime rib and I laughed and made sure the Cuban woman saw that Tina and I were a couple. No doubt she could have gotten the desk clerk to give her the information that we had two rooms and two to a room. I don't know why I thought it was important to make the woman see us as a couple, but I did. When we left to go back to our suites, I had my arm around Tina and let it slide down to her ass as we walked past the Cuban woman.

Our suites were right next to each other. When we got off the elevator I told Deuce, "I brought the laptop up. Let's check in before we call it a night."

"You saved me a walk," he said. "I was going to go down to the boat."

We went into our room and I powered up the laptop while Tina made drinks from the bar. Charity's face appeared on the video feed. "Hi, Deuce," she said. "Hey, Jesse. The team just started moving an hour ago. We're looking down from the satellite, but only for a few minutes at a time for right now. For the first half hour, they moved pretty fast. Covered just over a hundred meters. In the last half hour, they've only moved twenty-five meters. Tony reported in about ten minutes ago and expects he can be inside in another two hours. Art will stand by twenty meters outside. They have good cover until the last eight or ten meters."

"Roger that," Deuce said. "Glad to see Chyrel is getting some sleep."

"I had to force her, Deuce," Charity said. "She's a very stubborn woman."

"Call Jesse and me both, just before they go in," he said.

"Roger that, Alpha Base out." The screen went blank.

"An hour to go a hundred and twenty-five meters?" Tina asked.

"In our business that's a sprint," Deuce said. "To stay invisible a man in a ghillie suit has to look like a clump of grass. If someone looks at him and he's moved more than a few inches from the last time that person looked at him, he'll be discovered. Tony and Art are the best at avoiding that. Tony was a cover and concealment instructor in the SEALs, but his primary job was demolitions. I have a twenty-minute video of him crawling toward the camera and you never see him until he stands up."

"Let's get some sleep," I said. "If we're going to be up half the night and still be able to dive tomorrow, we'll need the rest."

Deuce and Julie left for their room and Tina said she was exhausted and wanted to go to bed. I was restless or I would have joined her. Instead, I told her I wanted to check the boat and would be back in a few minutes. I took the elevator to the lobby and went outside and over to the private docks. I saw the Cuban woman walking toward me from the dock. I kept walking, but stopped when I was just a few feet away from her.

"I know you," I said. "Señorita Espinosa?"

"Sí," she said. "You are *Capitán* McDermitt, yes? I thought I recognized that boat. I walked out to see the name."

She looked even more beautiful in the light of the setting moon. She was wearing tailored black jeans with a high waist and a long-sleeved black sweater that looked like, and probably was, cashmere. With her raven hair it gave her a very seductive and sexy look. It also made her nearly invisible in the darkness. Had she been aboard the *Revenge*?

"What are you doing in Cozumel?" I asked, smiling.

"I have a villa here," she said. "A, how do you say? A cold front was coming to Miami. So, I flew down here. I do not like the cold so much. You brought a charter down here?"

"A villa, of course," I said. "I assumed you lived in Miami. Yeah, I'm here with a charter, but it's become a little more than that."

"I have a home in Miami also," she said. Then she took a step closer so that she had to tilt her head up to look at me and said, "Will you be on the island for long? Perhaps we can have dinner together?"

"Only for another day or two," I said. "I'm sorry, I assumed you and Señor Santiago were a couple."

"Sí, but he is always so busy," she said as she reached out and stroked her long fingernails along my arm and the fragrance of her jasmine scented perfume filled my nostrils. "*Una mujer tiene necesidades*. Please, call me Isabella."

She'd taken the bait, though. "Most women do, señorita. But, I work for Señor Santiago now. Like him, I put a high price on loyalty." As I stepped around her, I turned and said, "*Buenas noches*, Señorita Espinosa."

I continued to the boat and vaulted aboard. I made a show of checking the tanks strapped to the bench and pulled a pressure gauge from a cabinet to check each one. As I connected the second one she walked up to the side of the cockpit and said, "I trust that you will not say anything about this to Carlos?"

"What and who you do is your business, señorita," I said. "But, if he should ask, I won't lie. You might want to keep that in mind, should you try to take another of his employees into your bed."

She wheeled around and stomped off toward shore. Halfway there I heard her say, "*Diviértete con tu puta, culo!*" I laughed loud enough for her to hear and watched as she strode across the beach.

I climbed up to the bridge and looked around. I was certain she'd been aboard, because I could faintly smell her perfume up here. The thing about bugs, as I'd recently learned, is that if you have enough money they can be very innocuous. This wasn't good. If she'd bugged my boat, we might never find it. I went back down to the cockpit, got a flashlight from one of the drawers and examined the hatch to the salon. I didn't see anything that would indicate the lock had been picked. Even a good burglar will leave minute scratch marks on the face of a polished brass lock. Maybe I surprised her before she could finish.

I stepped over to the dock and walked back over to the hotel. When I was on the elevator, I pulled my cell phone out and called Deuce. He picked up on the third ring, meaning I was probably interrupting him. "This better be important, Jesse," he said.

"She was on my boat," I said.

"Who? Wait, the Cuban woman?"

"Come to my room," I said. "We have a problem."

"Oh, great," he said. "Please tell me you didn't kill her, man."

"Just come to my room," I said as I stepped off the elevator. I swiped the card in the door and opened it. There were candles lit in the bedroom and when I walked in, Tina was sitting up seductively in the bed, wearing the sheer white nightie she'd bought in Marathon.

"Get dressed," I said. "I appreciate it, but Deuce and Julie will be here in a second."

She jumped out of the bed and pulled on her jeans, which were folded and sitting on a chair. "What's wrong?" she said.

"Just get dressed," I said. "I'll tell you when Deuce and Julie get here." Just then there was a knock on the door. I closed the bedroom door and went to let Deuce and Julie in.

"Did you kill her?" Deuce asked. "Because if you did, we're in a real jam here."

Tina came out of the bedroom and we all walked into the living room. "I'm pretty sure she bugged the boat," I said.

"Who?" Tina asked.

"Remember the woman on Santiago's boat?" I said. "She's here on Cozumel. I just met her out on the dock."

"The woman that was going to seduce you?" she asked with a pissed look on her face.

"Yeah," I said. "And she tried, just now. I blew her off, but when I went aboard I could smell her perfume on the bridge. I know she's been aboard."

"Just on the bridge?" Deuce asked.

"I think so," I said. "I didn't see anything to indicate she'd tried to pick the lock on the salon hatch. She probably saw me coming while she was on the bridge."

"That's good," he said. "If it's bugged, I can find it."

"How?" Julie asked.

"I have an RF detector in my bag, on board," Deuce said. "We can find it and either destroy it, or use it."

"Use it?" I asked.

"Misinformation," Tina said with a smile.

"She's good," Deuce said. "I wonder what Santiago would do if he thought I was his competition and was trying to hire you."

I grinned and said, "Yeah, I like that. Let's sweep it in the morning while we're heading to the first dive."

"Get your laptop," Deuce said. "We need to let the others know, so that they won't call us at a bad time."

I powered up the laptop and opened the video communications program. Chyrel turned toward the screen and said, "Hey, Jesse. What's up, Boss?"

Deuce sat down next to me and said, "The boat's been bugged. We plan to use it and pass some misinformation. Until further notice, if you have to reach us, call only Jesse. The rest of us are his charter clients."

"Roger, Boss," she said. "Tony and Art are in position. Tony will be going in, in just a few minutes. I was about to call you."

"Give me a satellite feed," he said. Within seconds, the screen switched to an infrared image from space, with a small screen at the top corner with Chyrel in it. She tapped a few keys and words appeared, identifying Tony, Art, two guards and the camp. Both Tony and Art barely showed up, as their ghillie suits provided insulation, making their heat signature harder to see with the infrared camera. Both men were inside the camp perimeter, with the guards between them and the bay. Art was stationary, but Tony was moving slightly, inching his way toward a structure that was labeled 'Arms Shack'. He appeared to be less than twenty feet from it, with Art another ten feet behind and to his north.

Art's voice came over the com in a whisper, "Tangos are looking away."

Tony got up from his prone position and walked quickly to the structure and disappeared inside. "I'm inside," he said.

"Negative reaction from the tangos," Art said.

Another box opened in the opposite corner from Chyrel. It was a video feed from Tony. "You getting this?" Tony asked.

"Roger," Chyrel said as the infrared camera scanned the inside of what looked to be an Army surplus tent. There were boxes of many shapes and sizes stacked along two sides. Tony moved toward the first stack and the lettering came into focus, Mk777.

"Quantity?" Deuce said.

Tony's camera panned down, counting three crates, then right, counting three stacks. Nine crates of Mk777 antitank grenade launchers.

"What else?" Deuce asked.

The camera panned quickly to the opposite side, where a lot more smaller crates were stacked. He zoomed in on one until the letters came into focus, OG-7V. He panned down counting five crates and then panned left to another stack of five with the same lettering. Panning further left was a third stack of the same, then two stacks of five crates with the lettering PG-7VR.

"Okay," Deuce said. "Get out of there."

"Wait one," Tony whispered.

The camera panned quickly to the door. There was a clipboard hanging on it, with a list of nine entries handwritten in Arabic.

"Freeze that," Deuce said. "Get it translated."

"Roger," said Chyrel.

"Get out, now," Deuce said.

"Wait one," said Art. Then he said, "Clear."

Tony's screen went blank and disappeared. We could see him leave the tent and move quickly toward Art. After twenty-five feet he went prone and became still. Slowly, he started moving parallel to Art, who was motionless. We watched for ten minutes until they both started moving toward a group of trees ten yards or so away. It took them another twenty minutes to reach the trees, then they stopped.

"Beef jerky time," said Tony, impersonating a movie character.

We heard several people laugh from my living room and then Deuce said, "Okay, when you finish your supper, get back to where you were while Sayef translates that list."

"Already got it," came Sayef's voice over the laptop speakers. "It's a list of shipments, with descriptions, quantities and dates. The first three are for the MKs and the next four are the ammo."

"I saw nine entries," Deuce said.

"A shipment of twenty-five AK-47s and twenty-five AK-74s is scheduled for tomorrow," Sayef said. "Another shipment of thirty-five thousand rounds of ammo for each is scheduled for next weekend. It was originally scheduled for Wednesday, but that was scratched out and Saturday's date penciled in."

"Roger," Deuce said. "Alpha One out."

I closed the laptop and looked at Deuce. He ran his fingers through his hair and let out a low whistle. "This is bad," I said.

"Yeah," he agreed.

"What were those boxes?" Tina asked.

"I recognized the larger ones," Julie said. "RPG launchers, right?"

"Yeah," I said. "The smaller ones are the grenades for the launchers. Fifteen cases of antipersonnel fragmentation and ten cases of armor piercing antitank rounds. It's the frags that scare me most. Terrorists having those means only one thing."

"Soft targets," Deuce said. "Civilian targets, malls, sports stadiums. Sayef said the next shipment is tomorrow and the last one was scheduled for Wednesday, but changed to Saturday. That fits with the conversation they picked up earlier and is probably the one he wants you to make. Seventy thousand rounds would weigh just over a ton and the rifles would be just under four hundred pounds. His other gunrunner must have a smaller boat."

"Yeah," I said. "The launchers are bulky, but light and the grenades are small, but heavy. The other boat would have to be big enough to carry nine large, lightweight crates, but a weight limit of less than a thousand pounds. That Winter fit the bill easy enough and could probably do the ton of ammo. Since he doesn't have that anymore, he's using something smaller, maybe a twenty-five footer, but needs the *Revenge* to fill the last part of the order. I doubt he's using that Riva, though."

"That's some good intel," Deuce said. "We're looking at a force armed with fifty automatic rifles and nine rocket launchers. At least sixty men. Get Chyrel back."

I powered up the laptop and got her back on video. Deuce said, "Chyrel, were you able to get an idea on how many people are in that camp?"

"Hard to be precise, Boss," she said. "The infrared doesn't pick up the heat signature as well when they're inside. My best guess, confirmed by analysts up in Quantico, is there are more than ten, but less than fifteen."

"Thanks, standby."

"The main force isn't there," I said. "Either they're coming, or already in the States. My bet is that they're coming. If they were already in the States, they wouldn't be shipping the arms to Cuba. Once the main body arrives there and the last shipment arrives, they'll undergo a couple of weeks of training, then load everything onto a cargo ship. They're planning an attack on a large group of civilians for early to mid-March, somewhere in south Florida."

"Carnaval Miami," Tina said. "First week of March, on Calle Ocho. The biggest Hispanic celebration in the country. There'll be hundreds of thousands of people there. In eighty-eight they set the record for the longest conga line, almost a hundred and twenty thousand people."

"I thought Carnival was in November," I said.

"That's Carnival, with an *i*," she said. "Carnaval, with an *a*, is in March."

Deuce looked at her and said, "If terrorists attack a large crowd of Hispanic civilians and the government's unable to protect them, there'll be a huge uprising in the Hispanic community."

"Checking terrorist chatter on Carnaval," Chyrel said. "Yes, increased chatter in the last two months, with Hezbollah."

"That's it then," Deuce said. "Get some rest, Chyrel. Remember starting tomorrow, any communication goes through Jesse, on normal channels and in code. Improvise."

"Roger, Alpha Base out."

"Holy shit," Julie said. "You guys are amazing."

"We, babe," Deuce said. "You're one of us now. Let's turn in, it's late. Chyrel will call if anything comes up."

The two of them left the room then. I leered at Tina and said, "You want to slip into something more comfortable?" She smiled and disappeared into the bedroom.

I was up before sunrise the next morning. Rigorous exercise, long nights and little sleep used to have little effect on me. However, I was tired. *I must be getting old*, I thought. There was an automatic coffeemaker with a timer in the kitchen and I'd set it last night before going down to the boat. The fresh aroma of Colombia's best filled my nostrils. I poured two cups when I heard Tina padding barefoot across the tile floor. "Good morning," I said.

"Good night, too," she said with a lecherous grin.

There was a knock on the door and I said, "That'll be Deuce and Julie. I saw him look at the coffeemaker before they left."

"I'll let them in," she said. I heard them exchange greetings as they came down the hall.

"Coffee?" I asked pouring a cup for Deuce.

"None for me," Julie said as Deuce took the cup.

"Are we going to dive the wall today?" Tina asked.

"Yeah," I said. "Nothing too deep, though. Palancar Gardens is thirty to eighty feet. We'll stay above fifty. There's some cool towers, caves, and swim throughs there."

"If you're comfortable with the Gardens, we could do Yucab for a second dive after lunch," Julie said. "It's fifty to sixty feet deep."

"Yeah," Deuce said. "Turtles."

"Yucab it is, then," I said. "We'll start the Gardens at thirty feet and slowly move down to fifty. The current's pretty strong there, so we'll anchor on the up current side and pay out a couple of hundred feet of anchor rode. That way when we surface, we can drift back to the boat."

An hour later, having had a nice breakfast in the hotel restaurant and not seeing Señorita Espinosa, we boarded the *Revenge*. Deuce studied the lock on the salon hatch closely. He even pulled a small magnifying glass from his bag. He looked at me and shook his head, letting me know it hadn't been tampered with. Then he pointed to himself and up to the bridge and pointed at me and made a talking motion with his hand.

I understood immediately. Most RF bugs are sound activated to conserve battery power. I started talking to Julie and Tina about the two reefs we were going to dive, while Deuce climbed up to the bridge. It only took him a few minutes, before he climbed back down. "Under the first seat," he whispered. Then in a louder voice he said, "Are we ready to get underway, Captain?"

"Yes sir, Mister Smith." I climbed up to the bridge and started the engines. Once both evened out to a quiet burble, I muttered under my breath, "Damned smug drugglers."

Deuce and I planned the charade during breakfast, using his generic name, Jason Smith. It was also his boss's name, but I was pretty sure not his real name. The three of them went up to the bridge while I cast off the lines. Tina and Julie were to play the subservient wife and sister.

As we motored away from the dock Deuce said, "Would you ladies excuse us? Maybe go powder your noses or whatever you do?"

"Of course, dear," Julie said, rolling her eyes.

Once they were below in the salon Deuce said, "Have you given any thought to my proposal from last night, Jesse? I want to land on both feet in West Palm when I move down there. My boss up in New York said that with that Beech character out of the way, there would be room to operate freely."

"It's a generous offer, Mister Smith," I said. "But, like I told you, I just agreed to work for someone else out of Miami. Wouldn't look right jumping ship the first week."

"What'd he offer you?"

"Fifty large," I said, intentionally exaggerating Santiago's offer. "Once a month, open ended."

"I'll match it," he said. "Same arrangement, once a month, three thousand pounds out of Freeport. That's a seventy-mile run versus a four-hundred-mile run, for the same money."

"You'll have to give me some time to think that over," I said. "Can I call you next week, after I see how the first run with my new boss goes?"

"Of course," he said. "It'll be at least two weeks before I move down there. My sister's taken quite a shine to you. Maybe she'll want to leave New York, too."

"Why don't you go below and get ready," I said. "We'll be on the reef in fifteen minutes." Deuce gave me a thumbs up and I pushed the throttles forward, bringing the *Revenge* up on plane.

Deuce went below, on the off chance that Isabella Espinoza was watching and listening. Twenty minutes later, we were anchored above the deeper end of Palancar Gardens, our dive flag flying, with two hundred feet of anchor rode out, set in the sandy, shallow bottom. We'd agreed over breakfast that after the misinformation session on the bridge, all talk would be about diving and anything else would be written on our slates.

Once we got in the water, we descended along the anchor line to the sandy bottom at thirty feet and drifted back through the Gardens. Some of the rock spires and cliffs are twenty feet tall here and covered with colorful gorgonian, sea fans, sponges and corals, with a few places you can actually swim through towering arches. There weren't a lot of tropical fish, but plenty of grouper, parrotfish, and one really large green moray eel. After one swim through, we saw a large male loggerhead sea turtle swimming along the wall and we drifted along with it until it dove deeper.

Tina wasn't having any trouble keeping her ears clear now, and I could tell by her bubbles she was getting better at managing her air supply.

We leveled off at fifty feet and drifted along the wall, turning into the current now and then to examine some of the more interesting features. After twenty minutes,

Tina swam next to me and showed me her air gauge. She was down to a thousand pounds, so I reached behind me and plucked at the steel ball attached to a rubber hose wrapped around my tank. The ringing sound it makes can be heard easily for quite a distance.

Deuce and Julie were swimming ahead of us and turned at the sound. I motioned them that it was time to go up. We slowly started up toward the surface. The boat was still down current from us and we angled toward the anchor line, then followed it to the surface.

Tina squealed and excitedly said, "Did you see that big turtle?"

"He was something, alright," I said.

"I could do this every day and never get bored," she said. "I've never seen so much color. How deep were we?"

"The anchor's at thirty feet and we passed below the fifty-foot mark for a minute or so, near the end."

We got back aboard the *Revenge*, with everyone talking at once. Deuce quickly dried and went into the salon, to check on Tony and Art's status. Seconds later, he opened the hatch and motioned me inside. The laptop was powered up and showed a view of the terrorists' camp from the hilltop the men were hiding out on. Sayef was in a smaller screen. Either Tony or Art was operating a parabolic microphone to listen in on the conversation in the camp and the Delta Force operator was translating the conversation in real time.

"Apparently, the Hezbollah leader is on the phone with Santiago," Deuce said.

Over the laptop speaker Sayef said, "It sounds like Santiago is on his way to the camp. Yes, he just asked how far out he is."

"Go to satellite imagery and zoom out," Deuce said. "See if you can pick him up."

The image on the screen switched to an overhead shot of the camp, then zoomed way out. Too much, in fact, as half of Florida and the Yucatan were visible.

"Sorry," Sayef said. "Miss Koshinski is sleeping. She was up all night monitoring the team's retreat."

The picture zoomed in slowly, until only the western third of Cuba was visible. The image tracked north slightly, then zoomed in a little more. The wake of a boat became visible, then the image tightened on it and zoomed in further.

"It may be him," Sayef said. "It's ten clicks out from the bay and closing."

The lines of the boat were easily recognizable for me, with its beamy bow, twin outboards and wood deck and trim in the cockpit. "It's him," I said. "That's a twenty-seven-foot Winter cuddy cabin. Matches the requirements perfectly."

"So," Deuce said as Tina and Julie came into the salon. "Santiago is accompanying the rifle shipment."

"He did say he was going to be more hands on, because of the ten-pound pot theft," I said.

Turning back to the laptop he said, "One of you turn and put eyes on the bay. I want to know for certain if Santiago is arriving on that boat and who, if anyone, is with him."

"Wait one," came Art's voice. A minute later a third video feed appeared, looking past the makeshift dock and out into the bay.

"Sayef, can you go split screen?" Deuce asked.

"I think so, sir," he said. The second feed went full screen for a second, then both feeds filled a half of the screen each. In the distance, a boat could be seen out on the bay. On the other feed activity increased around the arms tent as two men went inside and a third one waited outside. Three other men walked past the tent and went down a trail leading away from the camp.

"Stay on those three leaving," Deuce said. The first feed panned to the right and picked up the three men leaving the camp.

As the boat in the bay drew closer, the camera zoomed in. There were two men in the cockpit, the taller of the two piloting. After a few minutes, I could tell for sure. "That's Santiago, alright." The taller man was also broader, maybe 210 pounds and muscled. I remembered Lawrence saying Santiago's new bodyguard was close to my size. "I think the other man is his new bodyguard."

The three men from the camp arrived at the dock about the same time as the boat and tied it off. Within minutes they started to unload crates as Santiago left the dock and walked toward the camp.

"Try to get sound when Santiago gets there," Deuce said. "Maybe we'll get lucky and get a name. Keep the camera on him, too."

The sound of footsteps on stone and grass started coming from the speaker, fading in and out. I guessed that whoever was on the mic was trying to stay on Santiago by listening to his footsteps.

Another man came into the screen, walking toward Santiago. He was wearing camo fatigues and had a gray beard. For an instant I thought it might be Castro himself, but he wasn't nearly old enough, plus he was wearing a white pagri, a style of turban worn mostly in Pakistan.

"He's Pakistani," Deuce said.

Over the speaker we heard the man say, "Welcome back, Señor Santiago. Your accommodations are ready."

Even clearer was Santiago's response, "My apologies for the delay, Mister al Fayyad. It is unavoidable, due to the weight. I have found another boat that will handle it and as we agreed earlier, you may keep it after delivery is made."

"Keep the *Revenge*?" I said.

"Sounds like you're being double-crossed," Deuce said to me. Then into the mic he said, "Get a freeze frame and try to get a full name through facial recognition."

"No need," said Sayef. "I thought he looked familiar. It's Syed Qazi al Fayyad. He's a Shia cleric from the Punjab province. Suspected mastermind in at least a dozen mass killings all over the world. Mostly through the use of intersecting rifle and RPG attacks on civilian targets."

The image of the camp wobbled, then went blank. Over the speaker came a muffled, "Ummph." Shouting could be heard in the background.

"Sayef, go to satellite," Deuce said. It took him a few seconds, but when the overhead image zoomed in, we could see three men with guns surrounding what looked like a bush. Then the bush stood up.

"Tony and Art, report," Deuce said.

"Whoa guys, wait a minute," Tony said. "This isn't Jamaica?"

"Alpha Three," said Art.

"Base, kill Tony's receiver, but leave the transmitter active," Deuce said. "We'll get you out, Tony."

"What the hell's going on?" I asked.

"Looks like Tony's been discovered," Deuce said. Then into the mic he said, "Art, we have eyes on you, you're in the clear. Any way you can get an image on Tony's pos?"

"Wait one," came the whispered reply. Slowly, the image that had been on Santiago and Fayyad moved northward. Finally, it focused on three men escorting Tony, now stripped of his ghillie suit, toward the camp. "Engage?" Art asked eagerly.

"No," Deuce said. "Stand down. Tony knows we'll get him out. We need you to provide intel until then. Sayef, get Chyrel up now!"

CHAPTER SIXTEEN:
Have Faith

"I'll pull the hook," I said. "We can be there in three and a half hours."

"Hold on, Jesse," Deuce said.

"What the hell do you mean, hold on?" I said. "They've got Al.... I mean Tony."

All three of them stared at me. Finally Deuce said, "There's nothing we can do right now, bro. Let me get a status report from Chyrel. Besides, if we take off now it'll be midafternoon when we get there."

Dejected, I sat down. It wasn't in my nature to be patient. Chyrel came on the screen and said, "Sayef brought me up to speed, Boss. What do you need?"

Deuce turned back to the computer screen and said, "I need to know who all is still there on the island, what assets we have there and how fast we can get anyone back there."

Chyrel looked puzzled for a second and then said, "Well, everyone's here, Boss. Bourke and Goodman left early this morning by chopper, but came back with the two boats we had up in Miami."

"You mean the Cigarette's there?" Deuce asked.

She smiled as if reading his mind and said, "Yeah. They brought extra gas in the other boat, too. Twelve twenty-gallon tanks. All full."

Deuce thought for a minute, calculating the numbers in his head and then said, "That's a range of about six hundred miles in the Cigarette, with the added fuel. But neither it, nor Jesse's boat, is what you could call stealthy."

Rusty's face leaned into the picture, with a big grin on his face. "Would a ten-man Zodiac help?" he asked.

"Rusty!" I said. "You still have it?"

"With a brand new forty-horse muffled Merc mounted on her," he said.

I looked at Deuce and could see a plan starting to form in his mind. "How do we get it here?" he asked me. "Five men, with equipment and twelve fuel tanks, is about all that Cigarette can carry."

Just then Williams leaned in on the other side of Chyrel, also grinning. "Anything I can do to help?" he asked.

"Might be, Mister Williams," Deuce said. "Ever made a water landing in the open ocean?"

"Does a monkey have a climbing gear?" he said.

Deuce thought about it for a minute, then switched off the mic on the laptop and turned to me. "How well do you know Williams?" he asked.

"Well enough," I said. "He raised two Marines. One's in Afghanistan right now, and Doc vouches for him."

Deuce ran his fingers through his hair and said, "If the Cigarette leaves there at nineteen-hundred and we leave here at sixteen-hundred, we could rendezvous twenty miles offshore about twenty-two-hundred. Williams in his Beaver could be there in two hours with the Zodiac."

Turning back to the laptop, he switched the mic back on and said, "Mister Williams, what's your cruising range?"

"About five hundred miles at a hundred and fifty miles per hour," he replied.

"Not enough," Deuce said. "It's a six-hundred-mile round trip."

"Who says I gotta make a round trip?" Williams said. "I was thinkin' of doing some bone fishin' down in Cancun."

Deuce smiled and said, "Chyrel, let Doc know he's on the clock. Tell him, Grayson, Simpson, Bourke and Hinkle to leave there at nineteen-hundred in the Cigarette. We'll send them the rendezvous coordinates when they're underway. Rusty, get that Zodiac up there. You and Williams bring the Zodiac, with enough scuba tanks to inflate it, and rendezvous with us at twenty-two-hundred. I'll get you the coordinates."

Several more faces crowded around Chyrel. Shepherd said, "What about the rest of us?"

"Stand by there," Deuce said. "Any more weight aboard Mister Williams's plane and he might not make it to Cancun to refuel. Art, you need to make yourself really small, understand? Once we get you and Tony out, the two of you will fly back with Doc." Nobody needed to be told what the last statements meant. Tony would be tortured for information.

"So," Julie said, "What are we supposed to do for the next four hours?"

"Sounds like Santiago plans to spend the night," Deuce said. "We have to assume he's got someone listening in on the bridge and will pass any information to him that's out of the ordinary. The bug the Cuban woman planted has a battery life of only thirty-six hours. It'll be dead about the time we get back to Cuba. Until then he'll be aware of what we're doing. Jesse, how are you fixed on weapons? The guys will bring everything they need, but you and I will need a little more than our two sidearms."

"Got it covered," I said.

"Wait," Tina said to me, "You're going in too?"

"Yes," I said.

"Both of you?" Julie asked.

"Both of us," Deuce replied. "And no, you two aren't going."

"That's why you're having Dad come on the plane?" Julie asked.

"We need him here on the *Revenge*," I said. "And you on the Cigarette. Once we shove off in the Zodiac, take both boats at least thirty miles offshore until we need you to pick us up. Tina's okay piloting the *Revenge*, but not if a patrol boat shows up and y'all have to take some evasive action."

"What about evasive action in the Cigarette?" Julie said. "I've never piloted one of those."

"Evasive action in a Cigarette only involves pushing the throttles forward," Deuce said. "Damn thing has a top speed of almost a hundred knots."

"I'm not real crazy about you going," Tina said.

I looked at her for just a minute, then disappeared into the stateroom. Lifting the bedsheets, I punched the code into the keypad and pulled the release handle.

The bunk slowly raised up. Spinning the combination, I unlocked the large chest inside, removing two boxes, one large and one small. I closed the chest, locked it and pushed the button to lower the bunk back in place. Setting the two boxes on the bunk, I opened the larger one and removed two MTAR-21 assault rifles, manufactured by Israel Weapon Industries, and six thirty-round magazines. Each rifle was fitted with a suppressor. Opening the smaller box, I took out two boxes of 9mm ammo and started loading the mags.

Tina came into the stateroom and quietly watched as my hands moved methodically, loading each magazine. "Your wife was kidnapped and killed by terrorists?" she quietly asked.

"Yes," I said, loading the next magazine. "Gang raped and beaten to death."

She quietly turned and left the stateroom. When I had the mags loaded, I picked up the two rifles and the magazines and went back into the salon. I handed one of the rifles and three mags to Deuce. Julie and Tina were sitting on the couch and neither looked very happy. "Saturday night," I said.

"Rock and roll," added Deuce. "Let's head back to the hotel, turn in the tanks, refuel and check out. Remember, no talking on the bridge."

An hour later, we climbed back aboard the *Revenge* and were underway. Our plan was to rendezvous with the rest of the landing team twenty miles out from Guadiana Bay, then land in La Fe in the Zodiac at twenty-three-hundred. There hadn't been much talk on the bridge, but not because of the bug. Both women were upset that Deuce and I would be leading the extraction. Julie knew better. I guess I should have cut Tina some slack, but the truth is, I was suddenly feeling more alive than I had in several months. Along with that realization came another. Four months ago, hunting down Alex's killers had made me feel more alive than anything since I'd left the Corps. We called it 'the jazz,' that adrenaline rush that came with every new mission.

We were on autopilot and running at thirty knots. A little faster than optimum cruising speed, but barely noticeable. That is, unless you watched the fuel usage gauge. We were burning about seventy-five gallons of fuel every hour. With the addition of the two one-hundred-gallon fuel bladders, we'd barely have enough to get home.

Finally, I couldn't stand the silence any longer. I reached down, felt around and found the bug. I pulled it free and simply tossed it overboard. "Okay, let's have it," I said.

Both women saw me toss the bug and they both suddenly started venting about the upcoming mission, Tina more vocally than Julie. Deuce had missed seeing me toss the bug and his eyes went wide, pointing at the spot where it had been, under my seat.

"I tossed it, Deuce," I said. Julie and Tina both started in again, berating the both of us about the danger we were going to put ourselves through. After another minute of that, they both stopped. Neither Deuce nor I had said a word. I'd been through this before, having been married twice while I was in the Corps. Deuce must have just been following my lead. He'd come to me a few times about this very subject, how to both include and keep secret the different aspects of his life working for DHS.

"Look," I said to Tina. "I spent twenty years doing exactly what Deuce and I are going to do tonight." Then I looked at Julie and added, "And Deuce has spent nine years in probably a lot hairier places than I ever was. We are what we are and we're both damn good at it. We both know the danger. There isn't anything in writing about it, but all of us know that nothing will keep us from leaving a man behind. Tony needs us real bad right now. We won't let him down. If it were me sitting there where he is, I'd know that no matter what they did to me, help was on the way. That's exactly what's going through Tony's mind this very second. He knows we're coming and we're not going to let him down. The bad guys don't know we're coming. It's not in their mindset. Jules, you're a part of something way bigger than yourself now. With more training, these things will become a part of you too. Tina, you're a cop. What would the others on the force do, if it were one of their own?"

That was a lot more words than I normally say at one time. Finally Julie said, "What can we do to help?"

"I still don't like it," Tina said. "But, I'll help out any way I can."

"I thought you were a man of few words," Deuce said.

The three of them laughed at that, easing the tension we were all feeling. "There's about fifteen of them and seven of us. By my calculations, we have them outnumbered three to one." That brought on more laughter from all of us.

"Here's what you can do," Deuce said. I knew he hadn't just been sitting there quietly waiting. "Williams is going to come in barely above the waves to avoid the Cuban air defense systems. We're going to try to coordinate him and the Cigarette to meet us at the same time. Rusty will have the Zodiac ready to shove out of the plane and start inflating it right away. That'll only take him about five minutes. The Cigarette will tie off to the *Revenge* and four of the five men aboard will enter the water and swim to the plane. Rusty can finish inflating it and hanging the engine, while they move the extra fuel tanks to the Cigarette and hand them up to Bourke to refuel. Might be a good idea if Williams takes the empties with him to Cancun and brings back a little more fuel, just in case. Once Rusty has the Zodiac ready, he'll board the *Revenge* while Julie goes over to the Cigarette and the seven of us shove off in the Zodiac. Y'all will take the two boats ten miles due north and stand by, while Williams takes off for Cancun. Julie, you have the advantage of speed. The Cubans don't have anything as fast as that Cigarette and damn few patrol boats can match the *Revenge*. If it gets nasty, I'm sure Jesse has a little more under his bunk and I'm equally sure Rusty will know how to get to it and use it. At most, all of this shouldn't take more than ten minutes."

The three of us nodded and he continued, "Here's my plan. There's almost no chance of a muffled Zodiac being spotted, especially that late. We can make the twenty miles to where Tony and Art landed in about thirty minutes, gather their stashed gear and put it all on the Zodiac. We'll do the same as they did, go overland to the smaller bay and cross it underwater. All seven of us are perfectly capable of doing it alone with no problem. We'll regroup on shore and, using Chyrel with her satellite imaging, take out the guards at the dock first. I'll have Hinkle move to Arts position and Art can be his spotter to take out any sentries they have posted. I want Santiago and Fayyad alive. The six of us will go in, covered by Hinkle and the eye in the sky, find them and bring them and Tony back out. Tony, Art, and Doc go back in the plane. Bourke, Rusty, Hinkle, Julie, and Tina go back in the Cigarette and Grayson, Simpson, me and you, will take Fayyad and Santiago back on the *Revenge*. Well, at least halfway back. I'll have the Director arrange a Navy chopper to pick them up along the way and take them to Gitmo."

"Why do you want us to go back in the Cigarette?" Tina asked.

"You two and Rusty are non-combatants," I said. "The Cigarette will get you back faster and safer. Don't worry, we'll be back seven hours after you. Maybe sooner, if Williams brings enough fuel."

"Can you think of anything to add to my plan, Jesse?" Deuce asked.

"You know what your dad used to say about battle plans?" I asked him back.

"Yeah," he said. "The battle plan's always the first casualty of any battle."

"We have a big advantage," I said. "Even if they have night vision, we have an overhead view they can't hide from. I'd like to have Bond and Sayef both overseeing things. If Art is able to pick up any conversation, Sayef can translate on the fly and with Bond's tactical training, he can move us around like chess pieces."

Just then, Chyrel's voice came over the VHF. "McDermitt Charters calling the M/V *Gaspar's Revenge*. Do you copy?"

I picked up the mic and said, "We ditched the bug, Chyrel. What's up?"

"Suggest you go visual," she said.

"Give us a minute," I said. Then to Tina I asked, "Watch the helm?"

She slid over as I stood up and I opened the intercom to the salon and said, "You guys can listen in from here."

Deuce and I climbed down to the salon. I opened the laptop and Chyrel's face appeared. "I have a fix on where they're holding Tony," she said. "Putting it on screen."

"That's good. Did Rusty have any trouble getting the Zodiac up there?" Deuce asked.

"None," she replied, "They took off about an hour ago and Mister Williams rigged an inflating system to utilize multiple air tanks at once. Furthermore, Mister Thurman had four tanks filled with heliox. A ten-percent mix."

"Heliox?" I asked.

Deuce smiled. "Yeah, heliox is lighter than air. It'll make the Zodiac lighter. And faster."

"Mister Williams estimates a top speed of thirty-five knots," Chyrel said.

"Where's Tony being held?" I asked.

"Currently in a wooden structure," she said, "thirty meters southeast of the tent where the arms are stored. There are two others in there with him. I have it on satellite." An overhead view of the terrorist camp came on screen and zoomed in on a building, showing three faint heat signatures inside. Two appeared to be standing and one sitting.

"We're less than an hour from the rendezvous point," I said. "What's the status of the Cigarette?"

"They left about two hours ago," she said. "Hang on, I'll get a precise fix." A moment later she said, "At present speed all three of you should arrive at the coordinates you sent within minutes of one another."

"Thanks, Chyrel," Deuce said. "Anything else?"

"That's it for now," she replied.

"When we go in," Deuce said, "have Bond and Sayef on the coms. Let Bond know he'll be directing us tactically and Sayef will be listening and translating anything that Art picks up. Out."

Deuce closed the laptop and we quickly changed into our wetsuits. Then we went back up to the bridge. Forty minutes later, we were just four miles from the rendezvous and I picked up the Cigarette on radar. It was sixteen miles away and closing fast. The minutes seemed to tick slowly as we closed on the go-fast boat. When we were three miles from the rendezvous point, Williams and his Beaver suddenly appeared on the radar, about fifteen miles away and overtaking the Cigarette.

Deuce and I both put on our night vision goggles as I killed all the lights and said into the mic, "Going dark."

We watched the radar as the plane swung out from behind the Cigarette and slowed. It passed the fast-moving boat, then slowed even more. We were now only a mile from the Cigarette, so I pulled back the throttles and came down off of plane.

"I'll go down and tie them off when they get here," Deuce said as he started down the ladder. With the engines burbling now at a relatively quiet idle, I could easily hear the roar of the big radial engine. Hearing the engine's pitch change as it slowed and then a few seconds later, a loud swishing sound, I knew his pontoons had made contact with the water and he was down. Now I could see the plane as it settled onto the water and the engine quieted.

"We're down," came Williams's voice over the radio.

"Roger," I said into the mic, "Good job. Switching to personal com."

I turned on my earwig and could hear Deuce guiding the Cigarette alongside. Once he had it tied off, I put the *Revenge* in gear and slowly idled toward the airplane. I could see Rusty at the cargo door, already lowering the Zodiac into the water. When we were thirty feet away, I put the engines in neutral for a second and then shut them down. It became eerily quiet.

I stood up and said to Tina, "Take the helm until Rusty gets up here."

Julie and I went down to the cockpit, then she climbed over onto the Cigarette. Her job for the next few minutes was to become familiar with the controls of the fast boat as quickly as she could. Four of the men aboard were already in the water, swimming toward the plane, and Bourke was explaining the controls to her while he waited for the swimmers to return with the fuel. Deuce and I grabbed our dive gear, stepped over into the Cigarette and placed it with the others, ready to transfer to the Zodiac.

The first of the swimmers was approaching the starboard side, so I opened the fuel tank cover and removed the cap. When he got alongside, I reached down and lifted the twenty-gallon plastic gas can and handed it to Deuce, then grabbed one set of dive gear and handed it down to the swimmer to take to the Zodiac as Deuce started pouring the gas into the boat's fuel tank. We did this quickly six more times, filling the tank on the starved Cigarette. Within minutes the Zodiac was inflated and the engine mounted. Rusty brought it quietly alongside the Cigarette and we quickly transferred the rest of the gas, as he went up to the helm of the *Revenge*. Two swimmers carried the last of the gas cans back to the Beaver and then hurried back to the Zodiac.

With no reason to stay, Williams cranked the big Pratt and Whitney radial engine and idled away, turning into the wind. Once he was well clear, we all heard the big engine roar and watched the plane bounce a few times in the chop as the pontoons lifted it onto plane, then lift off the water and continue east out of sight. I heard one of the men, maybe Simpson, say, "Too cool."

Tina climbed down from the bridge, leaned across the gunwale and kissed me. "Be careful," she said and then went forward to untie the Cigarette. I cast off the stern line, then scrambled over the starboard side and into the Zodiac. I saw Deuce and Julie embrace in the back of the big go-fast boat, then he joined me. As we shoved away from the two boats, they both fired their engines and turned due north. Within seconds they were both up on plane and out of sight.

Bourke was at the tiller and the rest of us took up positions, three on each side, hunkered down as low in the little boat as we could get, each man with his weapon tucked neatly alongside him. Deuce and I were in front, across from one another. With both of us watching through the night vision goggles, the little boat quickly accelerated. Being so low to the water, it looked and felt like we were going a whole lot faster than thirty-five knots.

All seven of us were wearing night vision of one kind or another, except Hinkle. Bourke had taken a general heading, then chose a star to follow, but once underway, he was watching Deuce and me more than anything else. A log, turtle or just about anything on the surface could easily wreck the tiny boat, so he was watching us for hand signals to avoid anything in the water ahead.

In less than twenty minutes of bouncing along the surface of the ocean, we entered Guadiana Bay, where the water was as flat as glass. The engine barely made a whisper and the only noise was the slight wave being kicked up at the stern of the light boat.

The tide was with us. Tony and Art had stashed their equipment up a small creek that wound its way inland almost a hundred yards. Chyrel's voice came over my earwig, saying, "The creek mouth is ahead two hundred meters and just south of your heading."

Bourke adjusted course to the right slightly and I heard her say, "Dead ahead now. One hundred meters."

We didn't slow until we were into the mouth of the small creek. Bourke expertly navigated up the creek, branches hanging low enough to scrape our backs in places.

"Slow down," Chyrel said. "Twenty meters ahead on the right. Ten meters. Turn in now."

Bourke killed the engine and turned the boat to starboard, easing to a stop on a small sandy beach. We scrambled out of the boat, Simpson and Grayson moving toward the spot they knew to be where Tony and Art had stashed their gear as the other men fanned out and set up a quick defensive perimeter. Seconds later, the two Marines returned with the gear and put it aboard the boat. We could have left it there, but once we got Tony and Art out, we didn't want to leave any sign that we'd been in Cuba.

Each man had studied the satellite image of this peninsula carefully, in case we got separated. We gathered our scuba gear and set out. There were two small lakes between us and the opposite shoreline and we had to take a zigzag course through the lowland swamp. It wasn't easy going and we were in a hurry.

It took us an hour to cross the mile-and-a-half-wide peninsula to another, smaller creek that emptied into the small inland bay, just a mile across from the newly constructed pier at the terrorist camp. When we reached the creek, we quickly got our dive gear on and slipped into the water. All of us wore full face masks, so once we submerged we could talk without being heard. Not that a lot of talk was needed. We all knew where to go and what we would do when we got there. Simpson and Grayson broke away from the rest of us, angling toward the pier, slightly south of the camp. Both men were armed with ISR-300s. Basically it's an M-4 rifle with an integral suppressor, manufactured by Daniel Defense.

Hinkle soon broke away to the northeast, to enter a creek and come ashore just twenty yards from where Art was. The rest of us, Deuce, Bourke, Doc and I, continued due east, each following his own compass as the water was too murky to see much of anything. Our plan was for everyone to switch on a tiny infrared light mounted on our night vision goggles that flashed at two second intervals, once we made it to the shoreline. This would allow the four of us to regroup and also keep us from accidentally shooting one another.

It took us almost thirty minutes to cross the small bay. Fortunately, it was very shallow and nobody used even close to half their air supply. I surfaced near a tangle of mangrove roots. I looked to the left and saw two others surfacing. To my right, just a few feet away Doc surfaced. Deuce and Bourke quietly made their way to where Doc and I were, having noted the cover the mangroves gave us. We took off our dive gear and stashed it near the mangroves, with an infrared marker that could only be seen from the water's edge, the idea being to make a quick retreat to the water and locate the dive gear.

Bourke, Doc and I moved inland and quickly established a small perimeter to allow Deuce to contact the other three members of the team. Over my com I heard him say, "Com check."

Art's voice was heard first saying, "Hinkle's with me. There's two guards on the pier and I can see Simpson and Grayson directly below them."

Two clicks were followed by two more, a signal from the two Marines that they heard, but couldn't talk. The pier was only thirty yards south of where we were and when I looked that way I saw two simultaneous muzzle flashes from below the pier and the two men above collapsed without a sound. Then Grayson's voice came over the com, saying, "Two tangoes down."

"Tell us what you see, Base," Deuce said.

Bond's voice came back, saying, "Tony's still in the same building, about fifty meters at sixty degrees from your pos. There's two tangoes inside with him. Another structure right next to it, to the south, appears to be sleeping quarters. Five tangoes there in horizontal positions. The arms tent's next and has one guard at the front and another at the back. Next to it is another wood structure. Two tangoes inside that appear to be eating."

"That's Santiago and his bodyguard," Art said. "I watched them go in."

"One more tango in the wooden structure next to Santiago's," Bond said. "A single guard outside it."

"That's Fayyad," Art said.

"Recommendations?" Deuce asked.

"Looks like they have, or had, five guards on duty and five sleeping, probably working in four-hour shifts. Hinkle has a clear shot on the guard outside Fayyad's hut," Art said.

"Suggest a pincer movement from the pier," Bond said. "To take out the guards at the arms tent at the same time Hinkle takes his shot. That'll eliminate all the guards on duty. Then Simpson and Grayson can move on and blow the arms tent once the rest come out with their targets."

"After that, any plan we have will be out the window," Deuce said. "Jesse, you and Doc make your way to Fayyad. Bourke and I will get Tony. Simpson and Grayson will take down Santiago and the bodyguard. Art, can Hinkle cover the sleeping guards?"

"Affirmative," came Art's reply.

"I want Fayyad, Santiago and the bodyguard alive," Deuce said. "Let's get into position. Simpson, you two have the furthest to go, with the least cover. Take your time. We have good cover, but it'll be slow going. When each of us gets into position, point your infrared light toward the sky. When Bond sees that everyone's in position, he'll give the order."

We started moving then. Sticking to the mangroves for cover, we moved slowly and quietly through the swampy undergrowth. When we were twenty yards from the camp, we split into twos. Doc and I moved slowly toward the hut that Fayyad was in. When we were in position, I shined my beacon directly up.

Bond's voice came over the com. "Gunny and Doc are in position."

A few minutes later he said, "Deuce and Bourke are ready."

We had to wait a few more minutes until Simpson and Grayson made their way up from the pier. Then Bond said, "Everyone's in position. Wait for Hinkle's shot."

I watched the guard outside Fayyad's hut. He seemed restless, constantly shifting his weight from one leg to the other. Suddenly, he just crumpled where he stood, with barely a sound. Doc and I moved then. I glanced left as we moved forward and saw the guard in front of the arms tent drop and knew without seeing that the one in the back was falling at the same time. All five guards were down now.

As we neared the hut, either Simpson or Grayson moved past in front of us, heading toward Santiago's hut. Doc put a boot to the door of the hut and it splintered instantly. Both of us followed the remnants of the door inside, having switched to sidearms. Fayyad was kneeling on a prayer rug, his back to us.

We took him totally by surprise. While Doc held one hand over his mouth and pointed his Glock at the man's temple, I wrenched his arms back and used a pair of flexi-cuffs to quickly bind his hands, then put a ball gag into his mouth and tightened it behind his head. Together we yanked him to his feet and went back out. Seconds later, Grayson and Simpson came out of the next hut with Santiago and his bodyguard. Through the light of the night vision goggles, I thought he looked familiar.

Doc went straight past them to the tent where Tony was being held. Deuce and Bourke were just exiting, with Tony between them, holding him up by the shoulders. Doc took Deuce's place as Deuce disappeared into the arms tent. A second later I heard him whisper, "I'm going to set the charge for five minutes. Head to the beach."

I shoved Fayyad forward, down the path toward the pier, with the others following behind me. Once we were far enough away I asked, "How's Tony?"

"He'll make it," Doc said.

Then I heard Tony in the background say, "Y'all have a nice time down in Cozumel?"

It was hard not to laugh. I knew that he'd probably been beaten at least, but he was still cracking jokes. I reached a cutoff and shoved Fayyad down the path that ran along the edge of the mangrove swamp to the water. Art and Hinkle were already there, as they were only a few yards away to start with. Art had his and Tony's rebreathers and the rest of their dive gear.

"How are we going to get the prisoners across?" Art asked. I pulled an inflatable horse collar from my pocket, secured it around Fayyad's neck and inflated it.

A minute later, Doc and Bourke arrived with Tony. One of his eyes was swollen shut and his lips were busted and bleeding. But he didn't seem to be in too bad a shape. "Any injuries other than the obvious?" I asked.

Tony held up his right hand and I saw that his index and middle finger were missing. They appeared to be burnt where they had been severed. "Good thing SEALs are trained to shoot offhand," he said.

"Get him suited up, Doc," I said. "Get started across as quick as you can. Bourke, drag this piece of shit across. I'll wait for Deuce. All hell's about to break loose here."

The four men started wading out into the water when I heard gunshots coming from the camp. I turned to Doc and Bourke and said, "Get going! I'll get Deuce." Then I turned and started running back up the trail. Halfway to the camp I found Deuce stumbling down the trail. Just as I reached him, the charge he'd set went off with a deafening roar.

I put his arm over my shoulder and half-carried him back down the trail. The arms in the tent were going off like crazy and suddenly a rocket flew past and exploded just twenty feet ahead of us. The bright explosion blinded me for a second, as I was still wearing the night vision goggles. We both dropped to our knees. "Are you okay?" I asked.

"Took a round in the lower leg," Deuce said. "I think the bone's broke."

"Let's get the hell out of here," I said. "I can drag you across the bay if I have to."

We got back to our feet and struggled down the trail, our vision slowly returning. I suddenly felt something tug at my side and then felt my wetsuit becoming warm and wet, just above my hip. We got to the water and alternated return fire while we suited up and got into the water. Deuce wasn't going to be able to swim very well and I was losing blood. Once we were in waist-deep water we went under. I took him by the collar and said, "Kick with your good leg, if you can."

"What's wrong?" I heard Doc say.

"We're both hit," I said. "But we're underwater and moving."

"Y'all keep going," Deuce said. "That's an order."

A minute later, I saw something come at us out of the murky water. My heart skipped a beat, thinking that the blood I was leaking out had attracted a shark. Then I realized it was one of the others.

Art said, "We're not in the Navy anymore, screw your orders." He grabbed Deuce by the other side and we swam hard toward where we'd entered the water on the opposite shore. It took us thirty-five minutes to get there. I was fading fast and could taste blood in my mouth.

I collapsed as we crawled out of the water at the mouth of the little creek. Doc came over to us and he and Art helped us to shore. Deuce and I collapsed on the ground and Doc looked over us both. In seconds he had Deuce's wet suit slit up to his knee, put a coagulant on his wound and splinted his leg. Then he came over to me and cut open my wetsuit. The coagulant burned like all hell and he rolled me over a little. "No exit wound, Gunny. I'll have to wait until later to get that bullet out, though. I don't think we're out of the woods yet."

Deuce had struggled to his feet and said, "Open the valves on the tanks," he said. "Strap the weight belts to them and ditch everything in the deep part of the creek over there. We have to get across this spit to the Zodiac."

"He's not gonna be able to make it," Doc said.

"Hinkle, cut two of those bamboo trees about eight feet long. Bourke, get out of that wetsuit and use it to make a litter."

"Just get me to my feet," I said.

"Stay where you are, Gunny," Doc said. "You lost a shit-load of blood. We'll get you out of here."

A couple of minutes later Doc and Bourke lifted me onto the makeshift litter and we started across the peninsula. I could hear Deuce struggling, while Simpson and Grayson half-carried him. I started to say something, then everything went black.

When I woke up, it seemed like a minute later, we were bouncing across the ocean in the Zodiac. I could hear Chyrel asking, "How bad is he?"

Deuce said, "He took one in the back. Doc says he's got a collapsed lung and he lost a lot of blood. We're changing our exfiltration plan. Tony and Jesse will go back with Doc in the plane. My leg's okay enough. Art, Julie, and Tina will go back with Bourke in the Cigarette. Rusty, I'm pressing you into service to pilot the *Revenge* and bring the rest of us home."

I faded out again. Once more it only felt like a minute or two, but the next thing I heard was Doc saying, "Roger rescue, his pulse is weak and thready. BP is one ten over sixty. Our ETA to NAS Key West is ten minutes."

Then I heard Williams say, "NAS Key West tower, this is Beaver November one three eight five. I'm declaring a medical emergency. Requesting priority approach."

Over the speaker I heard, "Roger, Beaver November one three eight five, this is NAS Key West. We just received a dispatch from DHS clearing you with priority. Wind's out of the east at one zero knots. Ceiling is fifteen thousand and broken. You're clear for a straight-in approach to runway seven. Emergency personnel will meet you on the runway."

I moaned and felt a strong hand on my shoulder. Tony leaned over me and said, "You're too damn mean to give up, Devil Dog. Hang in there, we'll be down in just a few minutes."

CHAPTER SEVENTEEN:
Touch and Go

I faded out again. When I woke up, I was in a hammock on my island, wearing only a faded pair of cut-off jeans. I looked out over the sparkling, clear, blue-green water at the puffy white clouds slowly drifting across a clear azure sky. I could see Little Raccoon Key off in the distance, the palm trees gently swaying in the soft breeze. I smelled frangipani and jasmine, mixed with the salty scent of the sea. That scent had always made me feel comfortable and relaxed. I could hear the gentle lapping of the small waves on the shoreline just a few feet away and the soft rustle of the fronds of the coconut tree my hammock was tied to. My dog was lying on the ground to my right, next to the hammock. When I raised my head, he looked at me and barked once.

"It's not time yet, Captain Dreamy," Alex said. I looked to my left and she was standing right beside my hammock, smiling down at me. Why hadn't I seen her when I woke up? She looked absolutely, stunningly, beautiful.

Her golden hair was highlighted by the sun behind her shoulder. She was dressed in designer jeans and a long-sleeved white blouse with a ruffled neckline. The wind blew a strand of hair across her face and she tossed it over her shoulder with her left hand. She was wearing the wedding band that Rusty had given us as a wedding gift.

"Go back, now," she said. "I'll be waiting for you."

I reached out my hand for her and moaned, "Alex," as I drifted into darkness.

The next time I woke up, I knew that I'd been dreaming. My joints felt stiff and my mouth was dry. I could hear a gentle beeping noise. I knew what that meant. I was in a damned hospital again. It was dark when I opened my eyes, but I could see the room easily enough. A curtain hung by the door, which was partially open. I could hear voices outside the door. The beeping was coming from a heart monitor to my left. Tubes ran from two bags of clear fluid hung on a post in front of it and disappeared under the sheet on my left.

I slowly turned my head to the right. There was a window that looked out into a dark sky filled with stars. I recognized Orion immediately, his belt being one of the most recognizable features in the night sky. He was near the distant horizon, which told me that it was very early in the morning. I stared at the fallen hunter and recalled the mythological story of his great battles and ultimate demise.

I sensed a stirring further to my right and craned my neck. Deuce was asleep in a very uncomfortable-looking chair next to me. I saw his eyes open and lock onto mine. He sprang from the chair.

"Welcome back, you old war horse," he said. He quickly picked up a cup and poured water into it and held it to my mouth. I took a couple of sips, then leaned my head back on the pillows.

"How long?" I croaked.

He reached over the side of the bed and pushed the call button repeatedly before answering, "You were put into a medically induced coma five days," he said. "That bullet you took when you came back for me ricocheted off a rib and tore a big hole in your left lung then became lodged very close to your spine."

"Where am I?" I asked.

"This is the Navy Hospital on Boca Chica," he said.

A nurse came in and walked straight to the opposite side of the bed. She looked at the monitor and then reached down and gently lifted my wrist, taking my pulse. She was very pretty, I noticed. Tall and slender, with long blond hair pulled back in a ponytail.

"How are you feeling?" she asked as she wrote something on a clipboard.

"Stiff," I said.

"Everywhere?" she asked, looking down at me with sparkling deep blue eyes.

"Not everywhere," I said. "Just in my joints."

She blushed a little and said, "I meant, do you feel stiff in your arms and legs?"

"Yeah," I said. "What's your name?"

"Nurse Meadows," she said. "Call me Becky. You were real touch and go when they brought you in. A collapsed lung and a bullet lodged in your spine, just millimeters from the spinal cord. You're very lucky, Mister McDermitt."

"Jesse," I said. "My friends call me Jesse."

"I'll get the doctor on call, Jesse. Doctor Burdick did the operation to remove the bullet and patch you up, but she won't be in for another couple of hours. I'll leave word for her to stop in as soon as she gets here."

"Thanks, Becky," I said as she turned to leave.

When I turned back to Deuce, I caught him staring at the nurse's retreating form. When he looked back at me, he shrugged and said, "Not my type, but nice, huh?"

Just then, Tony came into the room, followed by Julie. "Welcome back, Gunny," Tony said. "I'm gonna hold you to that promise to learn fly fishing."

I looked at him, puzzled, as Julie hurried around to where Deuce was standing and leaned over to hug me, then kissed me on the forehead.

"What the hell are you talking about, Tony?" I asked hoarsely.

"On the plane, coming back," he said. "I made you promise to show me how to fly cast left-handed." He held up his right hand, where the stumps of his fingers were still bandaged and everything flooded back.

"You okay?" I asked him, then turned to Deuce and asked, "Your leg? How is it?"

"We're both fine," Deuce said. "I'll be on crutches for another couple of weeks and Tony's milking his injuries, as usual. I think he's got the hots for Nurse Meadows."

"You really scared us," Julie said. Then she leaned in, hugged me again and said, "Thanks for bringing my man back. Doctor Burdick says she can't understand how someone who was hurt as bad as you were could do anything, let alone drag someone for a mile underwater."

"Art did most of the dragging," I said.

"That's not what he said," Tony said. "He told me you were swimming so hard he almost had to let go of Deuce to keep from slowing you down."

"Did the mission go okay?" I asked.

"After we got you on the plane, Rusty piloted the *Revenge* to a rendezvous with a Navy chopper. They picked up our prisoners and flew them to Gitmo. Santiago was really pissed when we came up behind the *Revenge* and he saw the name on the stern. You should have seen his eyes bug out."

"Where's Tina?" I asked. Deuce looked at Julie, who looked over at Tony, then back to Deuce, before she lowered her head. Slowly, she reached into her back pocket and took out an envelope.

"She said to give you this, the morning after we got back," Julie said.

With some effort, I reached up and took the envelope from her. It was sealed and my fingers wouldn't work right to open it. Julie took it back, shook it and ripped the end off of the envelope. Then she blew into it and pulled the paper out that was inside. It was neatly folded. She handed it to me and then the three of them retreated to look out the window as I opened it.

Dear Jesse,

I'm writing this from the Chapel in the hospital. I insisted on riding back with you in the airplane and held your hand the whole way. I was still holding your hand when they wheeled you over to the ambulance. For a sec-

ond you opened your eyes and looked at me, but it wasn't me you saw. It was Alex.

Jesse, I can't live this kind of life. The not knowing, the danger, always being afraid for you, not knowing where you will be or when you'll be back.

Julie and I talked while we waited, after you and Deuce went ashore with those other men. I'm nothing like her. The worry would drive me nuts. I'm not that strong. I fell hard for you and I love you, but I have to think of myself first. There's simply no way I could live the kind of life I'd have to live with you. And to deprive you of living a life that you're suited for would be selfish.

Please don't try to contact me. It would be too much for both of us to bear. I'm going back home to watch the spring melt the snow. I probably won't stay there. You've introduced me to some of the most wonderful things I've ever experienced. I love the ocean and will always think of you when I'm near it.

Tina

I read it again, with a single tear falling from my cheek onto the paper. Then I crumpled it up and said, "When can I get the fuck out of here?"

Julie came back and took my hand. "She handed me that when we got here," she said. "She was standing next to an old black man, with a big black taxi. When she handed it to me, she just got in the front seat and they drove away. I saw the old man the next day, when I went into town to get Deuce some clothes. I asked about her and he said that he'd taken her to her house and waited while she went inside. He said she came back out a few minutes later with a suitcase and he took her to the airport. When I said we were friends, he told me his name was Lawrence, and to let him know when you were better and he'd come and visit and tell you more."

Just then the door opened and the doctor came in. "Good morning, Mister McDermitt," he said. "I'm Doctor Asan. I'm glad to see you are awake. I know Doctor Burdick will be pleased as well. How are you feeling?"

I glowered at him as he approached the bed. He stopped short and I said, "I want to go home. Now."

"Perhaps in a few days," he said, looking at Deuce and the others. "Doctor Burdick will have the final say."

"Bullshit," I said. "I have the only say." I threw back the sheet and yanked the tube out of my arm. When I started to sit up was when I noticed that I was naked and had been catheterized. It's also when I noticed I wasn't feeling too well. As I slid back into blackness, I felt Tony and Deuce gently pushing me back down onto the bed.

"Hang in there, Gunny," Deuce said. "Wait for the doc to come and check you out."

As I started to slip back into oblivion, I saw that all three of them were smiling and I heard Tony say, "Yeah, wait until you check out the doc." Then everything went black.

When I woke again, light was streaming in through the window. I had no idea how long I'd been out this time. I looked around and the room was empty. My stomach rumbled. It'd been at least five days since I'd eaten anything, being fed by a damn tube. I still felt stiff, but I also felt stronger. I lifted the sheet and looked down. The catheter was gone and I noticed the IV hadn't been reconnected. Unfortunately, I was still naked. I heard laughter coming from outside the room. It was hard to tell if it was a man or a woman, but it was a strong laugh. It stopped and I heard a woman's voice say, "Well, we'll see who has the last say."

Then the door opened and Deuce, Julie, Nurse Meadows and another woman walked in. The other woman was remarkable looking. Tall and athletic, with wide shoulders like a professional swimmer. Even under the smock she wore, I could tell she was very well put together. But it was her face and hair that drew me. She had a head full of wild dark red hair, framing an exquisite face that looked like it'd been chiseled from fine porcelain. Her hair hung down from her shoulders like a lion's mane, reaching nearly to her belly. Her eyes danced and sparkled, like two emeralds caught in a bright spotlight.

"So, Mister McDermitt," she said. "You think you're better qualified than me to say when you're ready to leave here? I'm Commander Jackie Burdick, your doctor."

She was intimidating and so sure of herself that she left nothing to negotiate. She walked around to the right side of the bed and lifted the sheet. "Good," she said. "They removed it."

I felt myself blushing a little. She noticed and said, "Oh, now you're feeling shy, huh? Doctor Asan said you were a holy terror just a little while ago. Well, not those exact words, he's Hindu."

My three friends stood behind her, with huge grins on their faces. "What the hell are you guys grinning at?" I growled.

"They seem to find it amusing that a man like you could meet your match in a little ole Irish lass," she said. "You think you can sit up by yourself, or should I have Becky get a couple of orderlies to lift you up?"

It was a challenge and I knew it. This was a no-nonsense woman. I grabbed the bed rails and pulled myself into a sitting position. "When can I go home?" I asked.

"That's better," she said. "You'll go home when I damn well say you're ready." She checked the bandage on my back, which I just realized hurt like hell. "Any pain here?" she asked.

"A little," I said.

"How about the middle of your back? Between these huge shoulder blades?" she asked with a wicked grin.

"Don't feel anything there. Why?" I asked.

"That's where the bullet lodged," she said. "It took me two hours to remove it. Your friends told me what you did. With that bullet lodged where it was, I doubted their statements. Until I saw you on my table."

I blushed again. I'm not the kind of man that is uneasy around women and right now, I didn't want anything to do with any woman.

"I bet you a steak dinner you can't stand up," she said as she lowered the bed rail.

I looked sharply at her and felt my belly rumble again at the mere mention of food. Another challenge? I wasn't about to let it slide. I flung the sheet off, swung my legs toward her and slowly stood up to my full height of six foot three. I stood in front of her, completely naked, and said, "I like my meat rare."

She looked me up and down, lingering on the other bullet scar on my shoulder, the knife scar on my chest, and the shrapnel scars on my hip. "I like mine rare, too. Good thing that shrapnel wasn't three inches to the left."

My three friends burst out laughing. I turned my head and glowered at them. Then my knees started to tremble and just as I started to collapse, the doctor caught me and eased me back down into the bed. "You're every bit as rugged as you look, Jesse," she said with a smile. "But, you're not going home today. If you don't mind a wheelchair, the Runway Grill serves a great New York strip. Pick you up at nineteen-hundred?"

She didn't wait for an answer, she just tossed her lion's mane of red hair over her shoulder and said, "Get some rest. Becky will bring you some lunch in a few minutes. And the deal's off if you don't make it to the head by yourself and take a piss in the next two hours. I want three-hundred milliliters, minimum. Otherwise, I'll come back and make you ride that silver stallion again."

My friends whooped with laughter at that. I couldn't hold back a grin myself and said, "You'll need those two orderlies to hold me down before that happens."

As she left the room, without missing a beat she said, "Don't ask, don't tell, Jesse." Then she was gone and my friends were doubled over, they were laughing so hard.

"I told ya," Tony said. "'Wait till you check her out,' I said. Wasn't wrong, was I?"

Becky was still in the room and said, "She's only like that with the patients she likes."

"I'd hate to think what she's like with the real assholes," I said.

"Oh, you're a real asshole," Deuce said.

"Y'all get the hell outa here," I yelled. "The doctor said I gotta get some rest."

"Yeah," Tony said. "For tonight. She likes her meat rare." He started laughing even harder.

Lawrence knocked on the open door and stood there with his hat in his hand. "We'll be back later, Jesse," Deuce said and the three of them walked out of the room.

"Come on in, Lawrence," I said.

"Don mean ta bother yuh," he said. "How are yuh?"

"Seen better days," I said. "Have a seat."

He sat down in the chair next to the bed, leaning forward and turning his hat in his hand. I let him sit there and gather his thoughts.

"Miss Tina went to har home," he said. "Back up nort. She tole me wha happen down dere in Cuba. Bout you getting hurt. She was toe up, sar. I sit wit har at di airport. She cried and cried. Say she wunt strong nuff, sar."

I sat there in the bed, thinking about all that had gone on. Months ago, Deuce had asked me about his relationship with Julie. I told him about my first two wives and how Julie wasn't weak like them. She was strong like Alex, I'd told him. Tina was right. She wasn't strong enough to handle the worry and pain of what my life would do to her. I should have seen that early on.

"I'm sorry I put her through that," I told Lawrence. "She's right, though. She's a woman that wears her heart on her sleeve. My life would make a wreck of her that couldn't be put back together."

"She dat, awright," he said. "But dere's a place fer dem soft womens. It jest ain't with a man like yuh, sar. No disrespect, sar. But yuh are what the Lawd made yuh."

"Thanks, Lawrence," I said. "I wish I could have seen it coming, but I didn't." *I am what I am*, I thought. Now, more than ever, I realized that. While we were down there in Cuba I had an adrenaline rush like I hadn't had in years. The jazz.

"Ave nah seen Santiago round, lately," he said, grinning broadly. "Would yuh know any ting bout dat?"

"You won't be seeing him around anymore," I said.

"I tink yuh a good mon, Cap'n," he said. "Liked yuh from di staht. I got ta git back to work, now. Take care, Cap'n."

He stood up and I offered him my hand. He took it and smiled, then he left the room. I was tired, so I closed my eyes and was soon fast asleep.

I woke again several hours later to the sound of voices outside the room. The sun was pouring in through the window now. Heading towards sunset. Doc and Rusty walked in. "Hey, Rusty," Then to Doc I said, "Glad to see you, Doc. I didn't get a chance to thank you."

"Don't mention it, Skipper," he said. "Glad I was there."

Rusty sat down next to me and said, "How ya feelin'?"

"Like I just went four hours with a six-hundred-pound tuna," I replied.

"Yeah," he said. "Ya look like shit."

"Thanks, buddy," I said. "Good to know I can count on my friends for a little pick-me-up."

"Speaking of friends," he said. "Julie told me about that gal, Tina. She wasn't right for you, bro. Fun little package, I expect. But no stomach for the long haul."

FALLEN HUNTER

I looked over at him. Rusty and I had known each other all of our adult lives. We could get away with saying things to one another that we wouldn't tolerate from anyone else.

"You're right, bro," I said. "I should have seen it early on. Could have saved her the grief."

Rusty laughed and said, "Julie also told me you're a quick rebound."

We both laughed and Doc asked, "Am I missing something here?"

"Probably not," Rusty said. "Ole Jesse's got a date this evening. Why I timed this visit for right now. She oughta be along any minute."

"A date?" Doc asked. "You just came out of a coma and you have a date?"

"You know what they say about Jarheads in a Squid hospital," Rusty said.

"What's that?" Doctor Burdick asked as she came through the door. Rusty was quickly to his feet, snatching his fishing cap off. He just stood there for a second staring, with his cover in his hand.

"Doc," I said. "Meet a couple of friends of mine. The one with his mouth hanging open is Rusty and this tall skinny guy is Doc Talbot."

"So," she said, "you're the Corpsman that saved this man's life?"

"Just doing what I was trained for, ma'am," he said.

"You're not active duty, are you?" she asked.

"No ma'am," he replied.

"Too bad," she said. "I'd have you transferred here in half a heartbeat. And since you're not active anymore, knock off the ma'am, okay. Call me Jackie, all of you."

Rusty finally stopped gawking and said, "Pleased to meet you, Jackie."

"Hide the nurses?" she asked, looking at Rusty.

Rusty looked at her puzzled and she said, "What they say about Jarheads in a Squid hospital?"

"Oh, um, sorry," Rusty stammered. "That wasn't meant for delicate conversation."

"I'm far from delicate, Rusty," she said. "Now, if you two will excuse us, it's time for Jesse's sponge bath."

Rusty was gawking again. "She's kidding, bro," I said. "Close your mouth before you swallow a bug." Then to Jackie I said, "You are kidding, right?"

"Got the economy-sized sponge," she said with a wicked grin. "Made especially for Jarheads."

Rusty and Doc left in a hurry. "You have a wide assortment of friends, Jesse. I just had a very interesting telephone conversation with one of them just a few minutes ago."

"A friend of mine?" I asked. "Who was it?"

"Secretary Chertoff," she said. "The highest government official that's ever called me on the phone."

"Don't know him," I said. "Met one of his flunkies a couple of times and wasn't impressed."

"Well, he's certainly impressed with you," she said. "He wanted to know when you'd be back on your feet. He'd like to go fishing with you. He and a friend."

I gave her a puzzled look and she said, "He wouldn't say exactly who it was, but that he used to fish a lot on the Texas coast where he used to live. Now, let's get you dressed."

She helped me get out of the bed and I was able to get a tee shirt and a pair of cargo shorts on without too much trouble.

"Still stiff in the joints?" she asked.

"Yeah," I said. "But I've had worse days."

"Well, judging from the many scars," she said, "I'd not argue that point. However, you need to understand something. You were in a medically induced coma for five days, to allow the swelling around your spine to heal. You haven't moved a muscle in all that time and you probably have mild atrophy. What's your normal body weight?"

"It fluctuates between two twenty-five and two thirty," I replied.

"Step over here on the scale," she ordered.

"Aye aye, ma'am," I said jokingly.

I stepped on the scale and she leaned in and moved the little weights to get an accurate reading. I could smell a faint coconut scent coming from her hair and just a hint of jasmine, maybe. Not perfume, probably her shampoo.

"Well," she said, "You're down to two hundred and twelve pounds. You'll probably feel tired with mild exertion. I'm going to schedule you with our in-house physical therapist. Do you swim?"

"At least once a day," I said. "Usually a mile or two."

"A mile or two?" she asked. "Every day?"

"Well, sometimes I can't," I said. "But I try to. There's a little island not far from the one I live on. It's about a mile and a half to swim around it."

"We have a pool in therapy," she said. "But it's not a lap pool."

"Just let me go home, Doc," I said. "I'll get all the exercise I need and be back in shape in a couple of weeks."

"Let's wait and see how tonight's therapy session goes. If the therapist says you're good to go, I'll discharge you tomorrow. Right now, I think I want you to stay here one more night."

I sat on the chair for a few minutes while she went out in the hallway and got a wheelchair. Rusty and Doc followed her back in.

"I'm a woman of my word, Jesse," she said. "The steak house is just a couple of blocks away, and I have a car waiting at the entrance."

"If it's all the same to you," I said. "I haven't seen the sun set in almost a week. Can we walk?"

"I can walk," she said. "Your ass isn't getting out of this chair. If your friends would like to join us, maybe one of them can push."

"I can't," Rusty said. "Gotta get back to the bar."

"Bar?" she asked.

"I own the *Rusty Anchor*, up in Marathon," he said.

"What about you, Doc?" she asked. "My treat."

"Sure," he said. "Never been known to turn down a steak dinner."

After hitting the head, I got in the chair and Doc wheeled me out into the corridor. The four of us went down three floors in the elevator, and Rusty said his goodbyes at the door before climbing into his old Chevy pickup to head back to Marathon.

"How are you feeling?" Jackie asked.

I took a deep breath and slowly exhaled. I was just glad to get out of the stuffiness of the hospital room. The big red sun was nearly to the horizon and there wasn't a cloud in the sky. "I feel a lot better now," I said.

"Thought you might," she said. "Are you going to tell me how you ended up on my operating table?"

I grinned up at her and said, "I would, but then I'd have to kill you."

"I've encountered men like you before," she said. "All of you. I know a spook when I see one. I won't ask anything more."

When we got to the restaurant, Jackie made sure we got a table on the west side, to watch the last of the sun disappear. Doc parked my wheelchair next to the wall, facing the door, and took the chair next to me, forcing Jackie to take one of the two remaining, with her back to the door.

"Yep," she said. "Spooks."

We had a great supper. The steak was thick and perfectly prepared. Jackie turned out to be a very good conversationalist, once outside the hospital. I told her about my island home and making a living pulling fish from the sea. I told her a little about how Doc and I met while I was running Trent's boat out of Key West. She said she'd been in the Navy for twelve years and her dad had been a career Navy officer.

When we finished our meal, Doc wheeled me back to the hospital. Jackie said goodbye at the door to the hospital, adding that she had to get home.

"Worried husband?" I asked.

She laughed and said, "No. A worried dog."

"A worried dog, that maybe the boyfriend forgot to feed?" I asked with a grin.

"You're not one to beat around the bush, are you?" she said. Before I could answer she added, "I like that quality. No boyfriend, no husband, just a dog. I was married once years ago, but have been single for almost a decade. Why are you asking? You planning to ask me out to repay the dinner?"

"It crossed my mind," I said.

"Well," she said, "Don't wait too long. Now go get some rest. Your therapist will come and get you in two hours." Then she placed a hand on my shoulder and said, "I'll see you in the morning."

As she turned to walk away, Doc started to turn the wheelchair to wheel me through the door, but I reached down and set the brakes.

"Hang on," I said. "She's gonna look back."

Jackie strode across the entrance road to the parking lot, with her hair blowing in the light breeze. I waited. She got to a Jaguar sedan that was facing away from us, unlocked the door and tossed her purse inside. I waited. Finally, she looked back over her right shoulder toward us, the wind blowing her hair across her face, and she reached up and tossed it over her shoulder. I waited. Then she smiled and waved. I waved back, reached down and released the brakes.

CHAPTER EIGHTEEN:

Homecoming

I was released from the hospital the next day, early in the afternoon. I was disappointed that Jackie wasn't there to say goodbye. Deuce picked me up in Julie's yellow Jeep. As we left the base and headed north on US-1, Deuce brought me up to date on what had transpired over the last week.

"Santiago has been singing like the proverbial canary," he said. "He didn't last four days of interrogation. Those CIA guys down there are very good at extracting information from people. Fayyad, on the other hand, hasn't said anything yet. He will, though. Santiago said something you might be interested in."

I was looking out the window, staring at the ocean, as we crossed Big Coppitt and Saddlebunch Keys. I noticed without thinking that it was a falling tide, the current running toward the open ocean. "What's that?" I asked.

"The Cuban woman that was with him out on the boat?" he said. "The one that was supposed to seduce you? Her name's not Isabella Espinosa."

I turned toward him and said, "Who is she?"

"She's not even Cuban," Deuce said.

"Who the hell is she, Deuce?" I asked.

He glanced over, his face showing the seriousness of what he was thinking. "Her name's Afia Qazi, Jesse. She's al Fayyad's daughter and a trained assassin. She's fluent in English, Spanish and French. We just assumed she was Cuban."

"His daughter?" I asked. "What the hell kind of man trains his daughter to be an assassin?"

We rode on in silence for a little while, crossing Sugarloaf and Cudjoe Keys. I looked over at Deuce and asked, "Did they get any information from Beech about Lester?" We hadn't talked about this since the day my wife was murdered. Lester Antonio killed Russ, Deuce's dad, a few weeks before that. He worked for Elijah "Sonny" Beech. Two of Beech's men were responsible for killing Alex.

"I was wondering if you were ever going to ask about that," he said. "Beech broke down on his first interrogation session. Confessed everything, including several unsolved murders in the Palm Beach area. Lester came to him with a few doubloons, the gold bar and a gold cross with emeralds. Beech fenced them locally and paid Lester less than half what they were worth."

"You think your dad found one of the gold bars from the *Lynx*?" I asked.

"Beech said it had the letters CSA stamped on it," he said. "He didn't mention anything about there being more than just the one."

"Your dad found that wreck," I said. "And it got him killed. I'm certain it's the last waypoint on his GPS. Wanna take a few days off next month?"

"Yeah," he said. "We could do that. Fayyad's daughter is a loose end. The new ADD wants her found, if she's still in the country."

"New?" I asked.

"I didn't tell you," he said with a grin. "Smith's been transferred. The new Assistant Deputy Director is an Army Officer. A bird Colonel by the name of Stockwell. You'll like him. No bullshit, no political ambition."

"Where'd Smith get transferred to?" I asked. "Probably some senator's aide?"

Deuce laughed heartily and said, "No, nothing like that. He pissed someone off and got his ass transferred to Djibouti."

I laughed so hard, it made my back hurt where I'd been shot. "You're kidding. He must have really pissed someone off bad." We rode on for a while, crossing Big Pine Key then and starting up the Seven Mile Bridge. "Djibouti," I said again. "Armpit of Africa."

"I'm sorry about Tina," he said after a while.

"Don't be, man. There wasn't anything there," I lied.

"So, what about that Navy doc?" he asked.

"Now, that's a woman," I said. "But, I think I better steer clear of her. Probably jumped into deep water too quick."

A few minutes later, we pulled off the highway onto the crushed shell driveway to the *Rusty Anchor*. There were a handful of cars in the lot, most of which I recognized.

I got out of the car and Deuce and I walked toward the bar. It was late afternoon and it looked like it might rain.

I was only going to stop in and say hi, maybe have a beer and then go to my boat and get some rest.

Suddenly, Pescador came running around the building toward us. I dropped down to one knee. "Pescador! Good to see you, buddy." The dog nearly tackled me, his huge tail swinging his whole body. I didn't realize just how much I'd missed him until just then. I stood up and the three of us walked to the bar.

Deuce opened the door to the bar and held it as Pescador and I walked in. Suddenly there was a loud cheer from about thirty people inside. Deuce came through the door and seeing my surprised look he said, "Welcome home, man. This was Tony's idea."

I looked around the room and noticed that all my friends were there, old and new. Jimmy and Angie came over with Trent, Charlie, and the kids. Angie and Charlie both hugged me and Trent extended his hand and said, "I just want to thank you for everything, Jesse." I took his grip and he pulled me to him and, in an unusual display of emotion, he said, "You saved my family. I won't ever forget that."

Tony approached me and offered his left fist for a bump. He said, "The whole time I was there, I knew that big-ass Rampage was on its way. You don't ever buy a drink if I'm anywhere around, hermano."

Rusty and Julie walked me to the bar and I sat down with my back to it. A lot of the team was there and each stopped to shake my hand and to thank me for going back to get Deuce. "We ain't got him trained quite right, yet," Hinkle said. "Be a bloody shame to have to start over with a noob."

Across the bar, I caught a glimpse of a wild mane of dark red hair, then someone got in the way. Al Fader handed me a cold Red Stripe and said, "I heard through the Coconut Telegraph what happened. That snake Santiago was trying to force me to do the same as what Trent did. Glad you're alright."

"Thanks, Al," I said, while trying to look over his shoulder. I got up and said, "Excuse me." I walked across the bar to where Jackie was talking to Chyrel, Doc and Nikki.

"Welcome home, Gunny," Doc said.

Nikki hugged me and said, "We were just talking to Doctor Burdick here about how close it was for you."

"Hi, Doc," I said. "Surprised to see you here."

"I try to keep an eye on my patients," she said. "Especially the interesting cases."

Williams came by and winked at Doc. "Think he's ready for the surprise?" he asked.

"A surprise party isn't a surprise?" Jackie asked.

"Dave has something special out back," Doc said.

"Mind if I join you?" Jackie said.

"I have no idea what this is about," I said. "But knowing these guys it could be embarrassing."

"For you, maybe," she said.

"To the backyard!" Doc yelled. He and Williams led the way out the back door and I followed, with the whole bar following behind me.

In the middle of the backyard was my old International, *The Beast*. Alex had named her the day we met. She looked a little different, though. Then I realized she was sitting a little higher and had brand new off-road tires. I'd never put new tires on her, because I'd always figured the next mile would be the last.

Williams walked over to the open driver's window and reached inside to turn the key. The engine sprang to life, with the chugging sound of a big diesel. I walked over as he came around to the front and opened the hood.

"Deuce and Julie's idea," he said. "It's a brand new 6.7 liter Cummins with a supercharger. Behind it's a Ford five-speed automatic Torqshift transmission and a nine-inch Ford rear end. If you can find a trailer, you can tow the *Revenge* with this thing now."

I was amazed. I loved the old Travelall and it certainly needed a little work, but I'd never dreamed of doing this.

"Skeeter cleaned it up on the outside and shot it with clear-coat, so it won't get any rustier than it already is," Rusty said. "And Chyrel and Charity put new seat covers in it along with some new electronics."

I didn't know what to say. I just stood there with my mouth hanging open. "You sure have some wonderful friends," Jackie said as she stepped in front of me.

Just then, a shot rang out and Jackie fell forward into my arms. I felt something warm and sticky on my hand and lifted it up. Blood. I looked where the sound of the shot had come from and saw Santiago's Riva about a hundred yards down the dock. Afia Qazi was standing at the stern, with a rifle in her hands.

Doc took Jackie and gently laid her on the ground. I looked at Deuce and then back at Qazi, who was untying the expensive speedboat. I ran across the lawn and boarded the *Revenge*. Everything was just as I'd left it. My seabag was leaning against the bulkhead in the salon, with my fly rod case still strapped to it. I grabbed the case, opened it and took out my M40A3 rifle, inserted a magazine and jacked a round in the chamber. I stepped back down to the cockpit. The *Revenge* is a big boat and she was tied tightly to the concrete dock. I dropped down onto one knee and braced the big rifle on the transom.

Qazi had untied the speedboat and already turned around. Looking through the scope, I saw her mash the throttles and the boat surged forward. As I adjusted the elevation, my mind automatically felt the air on my face. It was still and heavy. I added another click of elevation, as the boat started gathering speed about three hundred yards down the canal. She was up on plane and moving fast now, nearing the end of the canal and open water. My index finger found the trigger. My mind sensed others gathering on the dock and I heard someone shush them. I put them out of my mind and took a long slow breath, then let it out slowly. I had Qazi square in my crosshairs. I couldn't miss.

The barrel dropped imperceptibly and a second after I squeezed the trigger, the expensive boat erupted in a fireball and veered to the right, crashing into the rocks at the end of the canal. I jacked the bolt back and caught the spent shell casing in my hand in a single fluid motion, then deposited it in my pocket.

Standing up, I removed the magazine and closed the bolt, dropping the mag into my pocket with the spent shell. I stood there on the deck, looking up at my team and my friends. Then I went into the salon, put the rifle in the case and took it forward into the stateroom. I punched in the code, raised the bunk and stored it away. I walked back through the salon, down to the cockpit and climbed up onto the dock.

Deuce, Julie, Rusty and the rest of the team stood there looking at me. Deuce finally said, "You must have accidentally hit the gas tank."

"Wasn't an accident," I said. "No loose ends."

THE END

ABOUT THE AUTHOR

Wayne Stinnett is an American novelist and a Veteran of the United States Marine Corps. Between those careers, he's also worked as a deckhand, commercial fisherman, dive master, taxi driver, construction manager, and long-haul truck driver. He currently lives in the foothills of the Blue Ridge Mountains, near Travelers Rest, SC, with his wife and their youngest daughter. They also have three grown children, four grandchildren, three dogs and a whole flock of parakeets. He grew up in Melbourne, FL and has also lived in the Florida Keys, the Bahamas, and Cozumel.

If you'd like to receive my newsletter,
please sign up on my website:

WWW.WAYNESTINNETT.COM

Every two weeks, I'll bring you insights into my private life and writing habits, with updates on what I'm working on, special deals I hear about, and new books by other authors that I'm reading.

The Charity Styles Caribbean Thriller Series

Merciless Charity
Ruthless Charity
Reckless Charity
Enduring Charity
Vigilant Charity

The Jesse McDermitt Caribbean Adventure Series

Fallen Out	*Fallen Angel*
Fallen Palm	*Fallen Hero*
Fallen Hunter	*Rising Storm*
Fallen Pride	*Rising Fury*
Fallen Mangrove	*Rising Force*
Fallen King	*Rising Charity*
Fallen Honor	*Rising Water*
Fallen Tide	

THE GASPAR'S REVENGE SHIP'S STORE IS OPEN.

There, you can purchase all kinds of swag related to my books. You can find it at:

WWW.GASPARS-REVENGE.COM

Made in United States
Troutdale, OR
08/08/2025